"Sex, lies, and serial killers. Alison Gaylin takes us on a wild ride."
　　　　　　　　　　　　　　　　　　　—Lisa Gardner

"[Gaylin's] novels are quirky, suspenseful, passionate, endearing. Label me a big fan."　　　—Harlan Coben

"The hectic pace and huge cast of extras keep the reader guessing right to the end."　　　—*Publishers Weekly*

"Tapping into her own experiences as a journalist for *In Touch* magazine, Gaylin has written an action-packed tale of suspense that will appeal to fans of Mary Jane Clark and Lisa Gardner."　　　—*Library Journal*

"A perfect blend of ice-cold suspense and warmhearted good humor. . . . I'm not sure how Gaylin does it, but believe me, she does it."　　　　　—Lee Child

"Creepy and suspenseful . . . *Trashed* could have been trashy, but instead Gaylin makes it a fun and juicy read."
　　　　　　　　　　　　　　　　—*Chicago Sun-Times*

"*Trashed* succeeds because Gaylin is a talented writer. Her dialogue and observations are caustically hilarious."
　　　　　　　　　　　　　　　　—*Plain Dealer*

"The book is at i_____zing celebrity culture_____poignant, [this] is w_____."
　　　　　　　　　　　　　　　　　　—*Times*

continued...

"Highly entertaining and satisfying . . . Gaylin impresses us with her deft use of metaphors, analogies, and witticisms, and she skillfully keeps the story moving."

—*The Tennessean*

"Everything shines in *Trashed*. The tightly woven plot never fails, the wide-ranging cast of characters is drawn in razor-sharp fashion, and Simone is a wonderfully entertaining heroine. . . . A winner in every way."

—MyShelf.com

"A fluid, tight story blends the glitz and glamour of Hollywood with the 'trashiness' of the tabloids and paparazzi."

—*News and Sentinel* (Parkersburg, WV)

"Snappy and suspenseful, this contemporary thriller keeps you guessing right up to the end."

—*Hudson Valley* magazine

"The plot is compelling and believable. . . . If Gaylin writes another novel, I will try it without hesitation—no matter what the setting." —*American Way* magazine

"It is both a thriller and a send-up of the genre, a giddy frolic through La-La Land with a cast of characters that leave the reader smiling at human folly and guessing at whodunit until the very end."

—*Chronogram* (Hudson Valley, NY)

"The story contains color and elegance galore. Her fun characters and surprising plot twists keep the reader turning pages." —*Romantic Times*

"[Gaylin] writes what she knows, having survived ten years of entertainment journalism with her wit . . . intact."

—*San francisco Chronicle*

"Pure fun from beginning to end."

—Poe's Deadly Daughters

Other Books by Alison Gaylin

Hide Your Eyes
You Kill Me

Coming Soon

Heartless

TRASHED

Alison Gaylin

AN ONYX BOOK

ONYX
Published by New American Library, a division of
Penguin Group (USA) Inc., 375 Hudson Street,
New York, New York 10014, USA
Penguin Group (Canada), 90 Eglinton Avenue East, Suite 700, Toronto,
Ontario M4P 2Y3, Canada (a division of Pearson Penguin Canada Inc.)
Penguin Books Ltd., 80 Strand, London WC2R 0RL, England
Penguin Ireland, 25 St. Stephen's Green, Dublin 2,
Ireland (a division of Penguin Books Ltd.)
Penguin Group (Australia), 250 Camberwell Road, Camberwell, Victoria 3124,
Australia (a division of Pearson Australia Group Pty. Ltd.)
Penguin Books India Pvt. Ltd., 11 Community Centre, Panchsheel Park,
New Delhi - 110 017, India
Penguin Group (NZ), 67 Apollo Drive, Rosedale, North Shore 0632,
New Zealand (a division of Pearson New Zealand Ltd.)
Penguin Books (South Africa) (Pty.) Ltd., 24 Sturdee Avenue,
Rosebank, Johannesburg 2196, South Africa

Penguin Books Ltd., Registered Offices:
80 Strand, London WC2R 0RL, England

Published by Onyx, an imprint of New American Library, a division of Penguin
Group (USA) Inc. Previously published in an Obsidian hardcover edition.

First Onyx Printing, August 2008
10 9 8 7 6 5 4 3 2 1

To Mike, with admiration, amusement, and love.
Not necessarily in that order.

Acknowledgments

First off, special thanks go out to Det. Mike Coffee, retired, formerly of the LAPD's North Hollywood Division. Anything I got right in this book is due to his remarkable ability to answer all my idiotic questions clearly and precisely. Anything wrong . . . well, that was just me.

I'd also like to thank my terrific agent, Deborah Schneider, as well as everyone at NAL—especially Kara Welsh, Kristen Weber, Molly Boyle, and Tina Anderson; the tirelessly accurate copyeditor, Bill Harris; and the greatest thing since sliced bread, my editor, Ellen Edwards, without whom there would be no book.

Much as I love to make stuff up, it took a village of smart friends to help me with the research for this book. Specifically: Margaret Black; Catherine Kimbrough and Kathleen McLaughlin, who gave me an insider's view of LA; Cameron Keys and Tinker Lindsay, who set me up with sources on everything from homicide to hard partying and took me to bars and made me dinner and drove me superfast down Mulholland Drive at midnight and I could go on and on; Jon Beatty and Thomas Beatty for their insight into Young Hollywood; plus Dan Wakeford and Martin Gould, who helped me with Nigel's Britishisms and allowed me to experience the unique taste of Marmite. Thanks, blokes!

As ever, dear friends and family deserve thanks for their support, including Sheldon Gaylin, Marilyn Gaylin, Beverly Sloane, Abigail Thomas, Jo Treggiari, James Conrad, Paul Leone, my fellow First Offenders Karen E. Olson, Lori Armstrong, and Jeff Shelby . . . and many, many others. My mind is a sieve, but you know who you are.

And in a special circle of gratitude, my family: husband, father and structure god, Mike Gaylin. And Marissa Anne Gaylin—best daughter ever. I love you guys.

PROLOGUE

*T*he right pair of shoes can change your life forever.

An overstatement, maybe, but that's what Nia
Lawson was thinking when she put on the silver
Jimmy Choo heels, stood in front of the full-length mir-
ror affixed to the inside of her closet door, and whispered,
"Thank you, Jesus, for these shoes."

Nia had read Baum's *Wizard of Oz*—and in the book,
the magical slippers were silver. Ruby may have looked
better in Technicolor, but silver was the original idea, so
Nia saw these silver slippers—these thousand-dollar
marvels of modern couture—as her own personal talis-
man. For the past nine years she'd been lost, but these
babies would take her back up that Yellow Brick Road,
the road to stardom. She just knew it.

Plus, they made her legs look awesome.

Nia stared at her reflection—checked it out, the same
way a man would, starting at the shoes, then climbing the
length of her smooth, tanned legs, across the red mini-
skirt clinging to the soft bow of her hips, then up, lingering on the black silk blouse, unbuttoned just enough to
show the generosity of nature.

Nia ran her fingers through her platinum hair and gave the mirror her most seductive look: the one with the half-closed eyes, the moist, parted lips, the throat, offered up like a creamy dessert. . . . "Oh, Mr. Big Shot," Nia said to the mirror in her *Some Like It Hot* voice. "You're making me blush *ever so*."

Ten years ago, one of those tabloids—the crazy ones with the headlines about alien abductions and Hitler's secret love child—one of them had run a story claiming "scientific proof" that Nia was the reincarnation of Marilyn Monroe.

That was back when she first hit—when she'd just left the teen drama *Life as I Know It* and was shooting her first movie, *The Taste of Saffron*, and *Vanity Fair* included Nia on its Hot Young Hollywood cover and no one could mention her name without saying "It Girl" first. That was when *Esquire* waxed philosophical about "the sweet rebellion" of Nia's natural curves and her publicist was suggesting she insure her ass for one million dollars, "so we can give something cute to *People*."

It was before she met Mack Calloway—California congressman, former pro basketball player, happily married father of two, with the house in Mission Viejo and the big fluffy golden retriever . . . The Next President of the United States. It was before she met Mack and slept with Mack and fell in love with Mack and talked to the wrong person about Mack . . . her stylist, Renee, whom she had considered a friend. It was before Renee told the whole story to a tabloid reporter and Mack said, "How *could* you, Nia?" and she became Marilyn for real. Home wrecker Marilyn. "Happy Birthday, Mr. President" Marilyn. Mack's marriage fell apart, along with his presidential bid. "You ruined my life," he said. And though she swore to him she hadn't spoken to the tabloids, he didn't believe her.

No one believed her.

The Taste of Saffron tanked. Nia's agent dropped her. Her publicist dropped her too. She accepted a $200,000 offer from *Playboy*—but outside of a stint on *The Surreal World*, that was the last high-profile job Nia ever got. Until now.

Well, she had yet to sign an actual contract—but that was only a matter of time, with Mr. Big Shot in her life. "You've still got it," Mr. Big Shot had told her. "If anything, you've got it even more."

Mr. Big Shot had given her the shoes. She'd found them in front of her door in a box with a big red bow on top. No note, but she knew they were from him. She turned around, admired the stiletto heels, delicate as wishbones. "You even knew my size. I'm ever so flattered."

Nia heard a knock on her apartment door. She dropped the pose and scurried up to it, thousand-dollar shoes clacking on the floorboards as if they couldn't believe they were stuck here, in this eight-hundred-dollar-a-month roach palace, so close to LAX that if you opened your window you could smell jet fuel.

She pressed her cheek up against the smooth door and peered through the peephole. Mr. Big Shot was wearing a dark T-shirt and jeans, and said, "Hello, Nia," as if he knew she was watching him. Even his voice was important. As she opened the door, her heart pounded so she could feel it in her throat, her cheeks.

Nia hadn't felt this way since Mack, and she wasn't sure what was causing it. Was it *him*, or was it the *idea* of him?

He said, "You look perfect."

"How did you know my shoe size?"

He smiled. His teeth were so white—a white more suitable for cameras than the real world. "Careful research," he said.

And Nia found herself smiling back. "You are good."

He walked into her apartment. Nia had spent the past five hours cleaning it. She'd mopped the floors with Murphy Oil Soap and scrubbed the bathroom fixtures until they gleamed. She'd vacuumed her throw rug and laundered the sheets that covered her futon and dusted the coffee table within an inch of its long and battered life. She'd Windexed the framed *Saffron* poster that hung over her stereo—the only evidence of success she'd been able to hold on to, the rest having gone to creditors years before. She'd bought fresh flowers—tiger lilies and orchids—and put them in a vase she'd soaped and rinsed for half an hour. She'd even cleaned out the inside of her toaster, yet still she felt compelled to say it: "Sorry about the mess."

"I don't see any mess, Nia." He was tall—easily a head taller than her—and by that virtue alone he seemed to overpower the one little room. But it was status that made him enormous. As she watched him moving around her apartment, clicking off a lamp, drawing the shades closed, bending down to examine her collection of CDs with such quiet authority, Nia felt him taking over. Soon it was as if her entire living space and everything in it belonged to him—her included. Had it always been this overpowering, dating VIPs? "Do you want to listen to some music?" she said.

He smiled, clicked on the radio, and found a station he liked. One of those easy-listening stations they played in doctors' offices, the whispering deejay promising "music to relax by." No doubt it had some form of "L-I-T-E" in the call letters. Nia hated this crap. She was partial to guitar rock—Nickelback, The Offspring—though at thirty she was trying to grow out of it. She'd bought herself some John Mayer, some Coldplay. But she would never like this stuff. Not ever. A pale, liquid song started to play—probably Kenny G or Yanni or someone else too wimpy to use his full name.

"Perfect." He turned the music up loud.

She forced a smile. "Yes." Well, taste in music wasn't everything.

He moved toward the futon and sat down on it, patted the space next to him. His hand was very large and smooth, like polished rock. As Nia walked, she realized her legs were shaking.

He said, "Don't be nervous."

She closed her eyes for a few seconds, focused on the Kenny G or whatever it was. *Compose*, she told herself. *Compose*. . . . And by the time she was finally ready to speak, she had found it, the *Some Like It Hot* voice. "I'm not nervous. I'm excited. And that is *ever so* different." She could barely hear herself over the music.

He leaned in close. She smelled the chemical mint of his breath. "Excited?"

"Yes."

"Why?"

"Why?"

"You're sweating." He touched the tip of his finger to her upper lip. "Right there. Do you always sweat there when you're . . . excited?"

She didn't like the way he was looking at her, didn't like the way he brought the finger to his mouth and licked off her sweat. It wasn't sexy. It made Nia feel like a science experiment, and that, combined with the song . . . she'd never heard anything so soulless in her life. It sounded like a cell phone. It occurred to her that he might not be very good in bed, but then she brushed the thought out of her mind. *Don't pull diva attitude. Beggars can't be choosers.*

She said, "Do you mind if I turn the music down, sweetie? I can't hear myself think."

"What?"

She spoke more loudly. "Do you—"

"I'm just shitting you," he said. But when she got up to change it, he grabbed her hand and pulled her back down. "Pwetty please? I really like this song."

Pwetty please? "Uh . . . sure, okay."

He touched her hair, brushed his lips against hers so softly that the softness lingered, made her crave more. She thought, *What's wrong with a little baby talk? Nobody's perfect.* . . .

She felt his hand on her waist and a warmth spread through her. "You really are so Marilyn," he said.

"Thank you."

"Thank you what, Marilyn?"

"Thank you *ever so.*"

He smiled, and the music began to sound okay—well, not heinous at least. For a moment she thought he might kiss her, but instead he said, "You want to know something interesting about Marilyn Monroe?"

"Sure."

"She never left a suicide note."

"I . . . I knew that."

"Of course you did." He stroked her cheek with the back of his hand. "Can I use your bathroom?"

"Yeah. It's right over there."

"Don't go away. I've got a surprise."

He went into the bathroom, and she thought, *Surprise?* And soon he was standing over her, both hands behind his back. "Pick one."

"Huh?"

He nodded at each of his shoulders. "Go on."

"You have a present for me?"

"Two. But you have to pick."

A smile played at Nia's lips. She imagined turquoise boxes from Tiffany, airline tickets for Rome, a movie script with the perfect part. . . . "Eenie, meenie, minie, mo . . ."

She pointed at the left hand, and around it came. It held a small plastic bottle of pills. *I don't do pills,* she started to say. But she didn't get past the word "don't" before she noticed the glove—pale blue latex, like the kind a dentist would wear. She looked at the label on the pills, Nembutal, and her pulse sped up. She knew what Nembutal was, knew Marilyn had killed herself with it. "Is this . . . some kind of joke?"

"Want to see what's in the other hand?"

"No."

He clicked his tongue. "Pwetty please, Mawilyn?"

Tears sprung into her eyes. *This isn't funny. It isn't funny to take someone's dream and just . . .* "I . . . I don't like this game."

"Aww. You don't wike it."

One of the tears slipped down her cheek. "Please stop."

"Crybaby."

"I want you to leave. Now."

He showed her all his white, white teeth. "I don't think so." The right hand came around. She saw the glove first, and for some reason it took a few seconds longer to register what was in it. The long, narrow blade . . . the ugly black hilt. He touched the point to the hollow of her throat. She felt a slight sting, and the anger disappeared, devoured by fear, raw fear. *This can't be happening. Please, please let this be a dream, please, please, please. I'll never do anything wrong again, I promise. . . .* He brought it away, but just long enough to show Nia the red drop, glistening on the metal. This wasn't a dream. There would be no more dreams.

Nia tried to scream, but he clamped that gloved hand over her mouth, held the knife to her throat, and then the scream died. *Why*, she wanted to ask, *why me?* But she couldn't say a word.

"Relax, Nia," he said. "You picked the pills."

As he dragged her into the bathroom, Nia found herself thinking for the first time in years of Mack Calloway's face. The sweetness of his smile.

ONE

"Quite frankly, you're making a tremendous mistake," Simone Glass's sister, Greta, said while watching her pack up her Jeep.

Simone could have said a lot of things in response. She could have mentioned that Greta had uttered this exact sentence at least five or six hundred times since Simone had announced her decision to move to Los Angeles, and, *quite frankly*, she was sick and tired of hearing it. She could have added that it would be nice—*tremendously* nice—if Greta would shut up, bend over, and help load these boxes before Simone's spine *quite frankly* split in two.

Instead, she said nothing. It was easier on the lungs.

Greta said, "On top of everything else, it will be Santa Ana season in a month."

Simone could feel a statistic coming. . . .

"Do you realize that during Santa Ana season, violent crime in LA increases by ninety-eight percent?"

Yep, there it is. Regular as sunrise. "Really, Greta? Ninety-eight percent? And all because of some warm winds." Simone shoved her last box of books in the back of the Wrangler and gave her older sister a long, steady glare. To the core of Greta's soul, she was a cable TV news anchor. She oozed hyperbole. "Good thing it doesn't snow in LA," said Simone. "Or else we'd be talking . . . what? Anarchy?"

"Look, I could understand it if you were going out there for a real job—"

"Excuse me, but the *LA Edge* happens to be one of the most respected weekly newspapers in the United—"

"I'm sure it's very nice."

Simone's jaw tightened. She felt her cheeks heat up. She was glad she'd been exerting herself so she could blame the red face on that, but still . . . "Twenty-five people from my class at Columbia tried for this job and . . ." She could hear the hurt in her voice. "Forget it."

"Listen, I don't mean to upset you. But I've been a journalist a lot longer than you, and LA is no place to start a career." She put a hand on Simone's shoulder, and her face went serious. "Did you hear about Nia Lawson?"

Simone squinted at her. "You mean that actress who had an affair with . . . the congressman . . . What was his name?"

"She killed herself." Greta's tone was hushed and pained, as if she were talking about a dear friend rather than a Trivial Pursuit answer.

For a moment, Simone thought her sister was going to start crying. "Did you know her or something?" she said.

"No, but we're doing a story on her."

"Ah. Well, I'm sorry for your loss."

"Nia Lawson took a dozen Nembutal so she could die just like her idol, Marilyn Monroe. And when she couldn't keep the pills down, she cut her own throat with some kind of . . . fish-gutting knife."

"Why are you telling me this?"

Greta gazed at her sister as if she had a red ON AIR sign blinking atop her head. "Dreams don't just get crushed in LA, Simone. They crush you."

Simone rolled her eyes. "Good night, Greta, and have

a pleasant tomorrow." She opened the Jeep's driver's-side door and got in.

Greta said, "You're leaving? Now?"

"Yes," said Simone. "And by the way, I think you do."

"Think I do what?"

"Mean to upset me."

She pulled away from the curb without saying good-bye. Throughout her five-day drive across the country, Simone received text messages from her sister. (*U need 2 grow up.* Honestly, how could anyone *not* see the irony in that?) And Simone ignored them, telling herself she didn't care what Greta thought about her new job; she was more of a journalist at birth than Greta had been in her whole teeth-bleaching, spray-on-tanning, nose-job-getting lifetime.

But then there was that one night in the Best Western, just outside of Carson City, Nevada. Unable to sleep, Simone turned on the TV to a rebroadcast of Greta's new criminal law show, *Legal Tender.* She was about to snap it right off, until Nia Lawson's picture flashed on-screen and Simone finally remembered the name of the congressman and her curiosity got the best of her.

Simone turned the sound up. ". . . most disturbing and poignant of all," Greta was saying in voice-over. "No one has found the other open-toed Jimmy Choo stiletto heel. Nia Lawson killed herself wearing one silver shoe." Greta's face—as somber as a headstone—replaced Nia Lawson's. She spoke slowly, carefully. "As if to tell the world that in Hollywood there is no such thing as a Simo—sorry, I mean to say no such thing as a *Cinderella* story." Simone gaped at the TV. "You did that on purpose!" she said. "You started to say my name *on purpose.*"

"Next up, Ms. Lawson's manager, Randi DuMonde."

Simone flipped off the TV and said, "Next up, *nothing.*" But as she closed her eyes and waited for sleep, she couldn't stop her mind from replaying the image of Greta's face on the afternoon she'd left, her chlorine blue contact lenses sparkling from indignation and New York City sunlight and something else . . . Was it concern?

Dreams don't just get crushed in LA, Simone. They crush you.

She realized she had no idea what she'd be doing a week from now, what her life would be like, whom she would know. And she whispered, so quietly she couldn't hear the words as they came out of her own mouth: "Please don't let Greta be right."

"Please let me get this job," Simone whispered as she steered into the parking lot of the sleek white building in Beverly Hills. She'd been living in LA for a month—easily the worst month in the twenty-six years she had spent on this planet. And she was applying for a job as a supermarket tabloid reporter.

Nothing had turned out the way she'd hoped, dreamed about, or even expected. Her North Hollywood apartment, on which she'd signed a yearlong lease sight unseen, was . . . well, it was in North Hollywood, which, as it turned out, was nowhere near West Hollywood (where the *LA Edge* was located), or Hollywood, for that matter. North Hollywood was in the San Fernando Valley, which looked like Wappingers Falls—the Poughkeepsie, New York, suburb where Simone had grown up, or like any suburb anywhere, only with spindly palm trees, way too much traffic, and such potent sunlight that Simone's pupils shrieked if she didn't wear sunglasses.

To get to West Hollywood, she had to drive up Coldwater Canyon, a winding mountain road where everyone drove quickly and bitterly—as if they'd *all* signed their leases unaware of this annoying commute. Always, there were headlights pressed up against the rear of Simone's poor Jeep as she drove up crumbling, twisted Coldwater, desperately trying not to re-create the last scene of *Thelma and Louise*.

But Simone was adaptable, and anything beat going back to New York and telling Greta, "You were right." So she would have gotten used to LA by now—probably would have even grown to appreciate its sprawling, treacherous beauty—if she hadn't lost her job at the *LA Edge* before it even started.

On her first day of work, Simone had been greeted by a typed piece of paper, taped to the locked office door, informing her that the *Edge* was "closed indefinitely." Unable to pay its staff and suppliers, the fifteen-year-old paper had folded during Simone's drive across the country.

She still hadn't gotten around to telling her family. Her pride wouldn't let her do that—though it would let her get down on her knees and beg for a job at the *Asteroid* if she had to. Because even though the *Asteroid* had recently been dubbed "the lowest form of sleaze" by the editor of the *National Enquirer*, it had advertised for reporters. And after a full month of sending out résumés that never got read and making calls that were never returned and scanning the classifieds with a lump in her throat that grew larger by the day, that ad read like a love song.

Dreams don't just get crushed in LA. . . .

Simone was ten minutes early for the interview—a good thing, because it meant she didn't have to run through the parking lot in this weather. Santa Ana season had just begun. And, though Greta may have exaggerated her statistics, Simone could easily see how the Santa Anas could raise the violent crime rate.

They were not just warm winds. They blew in from the mountains as hot as breath, so dry they sucked the moisture right out of you. They were winds that violated, air that may as well have been wearing a Hawaiian shirt and a Shriner's hat, pushing you up against your car and blowing heat on you, blowing and blowing until you felt like passing out, or screaming, or both.

When she walked into the building and that blast of air-conditioning slapped her in the face, Simone felt as if she were finally breaking the surface of a deep, churning sea. *I can breathe!* Of course, her breath left her as soon as she saw the *Asteroid's* lurid red logo on the directory listing.

What if they didn't want her? Tens of thousands of dollars of her parents' money spent on college and journalism school and she couldn't even get a job reporting on some *American Idol* winner's boob job? She heard her mother's voice in her head: *Don't worry, dear. I'm sure Greta could find you something at her network. Come to think of it, I heard her saying she needed an assistant!*

Stop it. She got into the elevator and pressed the button for floor eight, trying not to think of anything at all.

When Simone had called to set up the interview, it had been five thirty p.m.—after hours—and the phone had been answered by the bureau chief, a fast-talking British man named Nigel Bloom. Nigel said "right" instead of "hello," and "very good" instead of "good-bye," and in the middle of Simone's sentence he'd hung up on her.

Immediately, Simone had started to wonder about Nigel Bloom's staff. Was everyone at the *Asteroid* stuck on fast-forward? Had they learned to speak in abbreviations? Did they consider breathing between sentences to be a waste of time?

If the receptionist was any indication . . . no.

A balding, middle-aged guy with a soft, pleasant face, he was on the phone when she entered. "So you're saying it's alopecia? Okay. . . . And what proof do you have she wears a wig on the show? Interesting. . . ." His voice was mellow to the point of anesthesia. Just listening to him slowed Simone's pulse. "You know, my mother has that same problem. Poor thing can't even go outside, what with these winds. . . ."

Simone sat on the white leather couch and gazed up at the series of framed *Asteroid* covers: BRITNEY GOES BERSERK! BRANGELINA BABY SCARE! CELEBRITY CELLULITE HALL OF SHAME! It was like an exclamation point convention up there.

"You're a very kind person," the receptionist was saying. "I'm going to put you through to Kathy Kinney. She handles most of the female hair loss stories, but can you give me the number of that wig maker first? Wonderful. . . . Can I help you?"

It took Simone a few seconds to realize he was talking to her, not another caller, but he didn't repeat himself. He just waited for her to look up at him.

When she told the receptionist she was here to interview for the reporting job, he smiled—but Simone looked into his eyes and saw nothing but pity. "Don't let him scare you," he said.

Nigel Bloom was short and wiry, with a face full of angles and tense, darting eyes. He spoke even faster in person than he did on the phone, words rushing out of his mouth and bumping into each other as if they were trying to escape the danger in his head. Meeting Simone in the reception area, Nigel gave her a tic of a nod and yanked the résumé out of her hands before she was able to think of offering it to him.

"You'reapplyingforthereportersjobverygoodthenright thisway."

She followed him down a long hallway lined with older *Asteroid* covers (*CHER DUMPS BAGEL BOY! MADONNA AND SEAN'S SEXXX-RATED SECRET!*) past a large room, no doubt the reporters' room, where muffled phone conversations barely penetrated the closed door. Finally, they reached Nigel's office. She looked around at the blank white walls. The desk, too, was empty, save for the phone and computer. *Strange.* In the entire space, the only sign of life was the empty Red Bull cans, which filled the wastebasket to near overflow.

Simone tried looking into Nigel's eyes. She'd always been able to tell a lot about people this way—Greta used to call it her lie detector stare—but she couldn't get the bureau chief to meet her gaze. He kept looking her up and down in this strange, self-protective way. She half expected him to frisk her for wires.

"Faseet," said Nigel. It took her a few seconds to translate. *Have a seat.*

She sat in the hard-backed chair across from his desk as he scanned her résumé.

Nigel said, "You've never worked for the *Enquirer*, have you?"

"Uh, no."

"What about the *Interloper*?" He scowled at her. "I could swear I've seen the name Simone Glass on their masthead at one time or another."

Simone's skin jumped. "It wasn't me. Must have been another—"

"Relatives? Friends? You have a boyfriend, perhaps, with a connection to the *Interloper*, *Enquirer*, *Globe*, or one of the British newspapers? The *Sun*? *News of the World*?"

"No . . . I . . . I swear."

He closed his eyes for a long, uncomfortable moment—then returned to the résumé. "I suppose I'll have to believe you."

Simone exhaled heavily. "Thank you."

Nigel said, "You went to Columbia University's Graduate School of Journalism."

"Yes, I did. I really enjoyed the—"

"Graduated with high honors."

"Yes."

Nigel raised an eyebrow. "So, why in God's name do you want to work *here*?"

Simone had prepared an answer to this very question—an enthusiastic but humble speech about the challenge of celebrity journalism. About how, when it came to reporting jobs, hands-on experience trumped subject matter every time, and how a daring publication like the *Asteroid* would be the ideal venue for Simone's well-honed investigative skills. But hearing the question now, asked at a hundred miles per hour in this safe house of an office, with Nigel Bloom's flinty gaze boring into her near-nonexistent job history, Simone could only think of Greta and her parents and the PAY RENT OR QUIT notice on her apartment door.

"I'm desperate," she said.

"Right," said Nigel. "We'll try you out, then, at a day rate of one hundred thirty dollars."

"You will?!" Simone would have hugged Nigel Bloom, if she didn't think it would make him call security. When he told her to "bugger off for now" and come back at eleven thirty p.m., "in head-to-toe black," she had to blink back tears of gratitude.

It wasn't until she got back into her Jeep and started driving home that she wondered what the "head-to-toe black" was all about . . . and what type of reporting could be done half an hour before midnight.

Santa Ana season was no time to be wearing a black T-shirt and jeans. Though night had fallen hours ago, Simone still felt as if she were trapped in an evil blow-dryer. She was close to swooning as she walked through the *Asteroid's* parking lot with the other reporter, Elliot, but she tried not to show it. Elliot seemed fine with the whole head-to-toe black thing.

Simone didn't know whether Elliot had a last name, but he looked just like Ted Kaczynski after a bar fight—wild hair and beard, skin so pale it glowed a little, and an angry purple welt under his left eye that Simone had no desire to ask about.

Nigel had introduced him as "our domestic refuse expert." Simone couldn't place his age; he could've been anywhere from twenty-five to fifty under all that hair. But his age didn't matter. Elliot had that stillness, that steady, calm gaze that said *experience*. He came armed with two pairs of thick rubber gloves—one for Simone, one for himself.

God help me, thought Simone as she slid behind the wheel of the rented Chevy Malibu, the domestic refuse expert riding shotgun. *I'm about to steal someone's trash.*

Twin rivulets of sweat trickled down her ribs, settled somewhere in the waistband of her jeans. It was a cold sweat, like runoff from ice cubes, and it made her heart pound. She craved a beer.

"Isn't this illegal?" Simone said.

Elliot shrugged.

"That a yes or a no?"

He shrugged again.

She turned the ignition, flipped on the air conditioner, adjusted her seat, and cleared her throat—just to hear a noise that wasn't mechanical. *Does Elliot ever say anything? Was he born without a tongue?* Then she pulled out of the parking lot onto the road.

Simone knew the address. She'd looked it up on Map-Quest back at the office: 1020 Linda Vista, in the Hollywood Hills. With no traffic, MapQuest had said, the ride should take around twenty minutes. Twenty minutes and she'd be getting out of this car, putting on the gloves, and sifting through the trash can of Emerald Deegan—the youngest, skinniest housewife on the popular nighttime soap *Suburban Indiscretions.* They were supposed to be looking, Nigel had said, "for evidence of cocaine addiction and/or eating disorder."

Think of it as investigative reporting. A fact-finding mission. No one will mind. You're not hurting anyone. . . .

Elliot said, "You like Duran Duran?" and Simone jumped a little. His voice was higher than she'd expected, reedy.

"Ummm . . ."

Elliot slipped a CD into the player, and when the song started, he turned the volume up so high that Simone could feel the thumping bass in her kidneys, her intestine.

"Hungry Like the Wolf." A song nearly as old as Simone. *One minute you're a baby, the next you're three thousand miles from home, driving a rental car up Beverly Drive at midnight with a Unabomber look-alike, getting ready to pick through some soap star's used Kleenex. . . .*

She saw a row of green traffic lights in front of her, a path beckoning her all the way up Beverly. She looked down at the rubber gloves bunched up in her lap and tried to think of something to say.

Elliot was harmonizing pretty well. His voice had a sort of woodwind quality. *"Do, do, do, do, do, do, do . . ."* When Simone turned to look at him, though, he stopped. "Don't worry," he said.

"How did you know I was worried?"

"I'm guessing you've never driven a getaway car before."

"A getaway . . ."

"Sssshhh." He put a finger to his lips and pointed to the CD player. "My favorite part." Still watching Simone, he mouthed words about catching the scent of human prey and being lost, then found. . . .

Simone braked at Sunset—a four-way stop on a very busy street, with no traffic lights, just signs. LA had a lot of these, and Simone wondered why. Maybe it was some city planner's way to force people to pay attention to one another. *Stop talking on your cell phone and staring at your reflection and look at your fellow human beings, just for a moment. Take enough interest in them to determine whether they're stopping or going. It could mean your life.*

Whatever, it was annoying.

It seemed Simone always let five or six people cross the intersection before she worked up the guts to do it herself. And tonight, she was even more reticent about it than usual.

Elliot was singing about his mouth being alive with juices like wine. She didn't want to think about juices in Elliot's mouth. *Okay, deep breath. . . .*

Soon, she would take a right on Sunset, head toward Hollywood. She'd pass some of those mansions she'd seen on the Map of the Stars' Homes she'd bought on her first day here. Excited as only someone who'd never been to LA could be, Simone had sat in the front seat of her Jeep and skimmed through the color-coded name index on the inside flap: Ava Gardner, Shelley Winters, Sammy Davis Jr., Freddie Prinze. . . . *Unbelievable.* Every star on the map was dead.

Elliot stopped singing and said, "Hey, what's on your mind?"

"Dead celebrities."

"Cool." To their left was the Beverly Hills Hotel. Its garden lights illuminated Elliot's eyes. They were white blue, like a malamute's. They scared her a little.

Emerald Deegan lived somewhere behind a wrought-iron gate, out of which glinted the beady red eye of a surveillance camera. "Big Brother's watching," Elliot hissed when Simone climbed Linda Vista and pulled up to the curb, just in front of Emerald's garbage cans.

"Oh, shit. Sorry."

He opened the glove compartment and took out a map. "Pretend you're reading this, count to eight, then pull away from the curb and drive thirty more feet."

By no mistake did Linda Vista mean "pretty view" in Spanish. The street ran straight up a mountain, on a near ninety-degree angle. Thirty more feet, and Linda Vista ended in a cul-de-sac, easily a mile up in the air. This city was all heights and depths—a testing ground for emergency brakes. As Simone parked, she yawned to stop her ears from clicking.

Elliot said, "I think you're better off staying in the car."

"I'm not sleepy," said Simone. "Just getting used to the alt—"

"I know."

She looked at him. "So . . . I'm not good enough to steal garbage?"

"Not yet," he said. "Keep the car running."

At least he trusts you to drive the getaway car. Simone sighed, raked her fingers through her short, spiky hair.

Doing this, touching her own hair, felt as strange as anything else did tonight. Her whole life she'd worn it blunt-cut at the shoulders. Shiny, medium brown—wholesome, as her mother liked to say. But she'd lopped it off and poured henna all over it before driving across the country.

Back then, Simone thought the hairstyle added a few years to her face, made her less approachable. After she'd washed the dye out and fixed it a little, she'd looked at herself in her bathroom mirror and whispered, "Intimidating." She'd pictured a layout in the *New York Times Magazine*—Simone leaning against a brick wall, unsmiling in her favorite black tank top, THE NEW FACE OF INVESTIGATIVE REPORTING hovering over her head in a bold red font that brought out the maroon in her hair. That night, Greta had dropped by her apartment, taken one look at Simone, and said, "Well, it's a good thing you want to go into print."

Simone closed her eyes and felt the silence thickening. What was Elliot doing out there, anyway?

She turned around. At first she saw nothing but the olive green plastic garbage cans outside Emerald's gate. Then she noticed the lids were open. Finally, she saw Elliot—the black-clad shadow that was Elliot—replacing the lids and trotting up the steep sidewalk with a shocking grace. Swift despite the heat and the three overstuffed bags he'd slung over his narrow shoulders. *A trash ninja—that's what he is.* What an incredibly weird thing to be skilled at.

Simone popped the trunk as Elliot opened the back door. "No trunks, man," he said.

The smell of the garbage was overpowering. She gritted her teeth. "Are you kidding me?"

"I don't trust trunks. Gotta be able to see the take."

He slammed the trunk closed and leapt into the passenger's seat. *Gotta be able to see the take? What is that supposed to mean?* Simone winced and turned the air conditioner up full blast.

As she hung a U-turn she glanced at the three garbage bags, side by side in the backseat like fat, stinking schoolchildren.

"I forgot the recycling," said Elliot.

"Do you want me to—"

"Nah, screw it. Nothing newsworthy in the recycling bins. She's not in AA."

"I thought we were supposed to go through the bags there," she said. "You know, take out the important stuff and leave the . . . rest."

"We'd get arrested if we stuck around that long."

"So this *is* illegal."

"No, it's not. Once the trash hits the can, it's public property."

"Then what—"

"Trespassing, impersonating sanitation workers. . . . Emerald's people would trump something up, and with those fucking stalker laws, it'd probably stick." Elliot's hand shot in front of Simone's eyes, a small pot of goo clasped between his thumb and index finger. "Rose salve," he said. "Wipe a little under your nose."

Now the car smelled like sewage *and* roses.

"It's the great equalizer, you know," said Elliot.

"Rose salve?"

"Trash," he said. "You see what Emerald Deegan wore to the Emmys?"

She shook her head.

"Let's just say the earrings alone could keep me in hookers and Courvoisier for at least five years."

"Okay. . . ."

"But lo and behold, her trash stinks just as much as mine."

"You can say that again." Simone tried opening a window, but that only made it worse, the hot Santa Anas rushing into the car, sucking the sour, decaying smell out of the tightly closed bags and swirling it straight up Simone's nostrils.

"You know whose garbage really reeks? That chick who used to sleep with . . . George Clooney, I think. Or maybe Nic Cage. No, wait a minute, I think she was nailin' that guy from the reality show who ate the live

rats. . . ." Elliot kept talking, barely taking a breath between words. He went from zero to one hundred, this
guy. Quiet as a gravestone 'til he stole a few trash bags
and turned into Chatty Cathy. Simone could tell he was
on some kind of professional high, and that perplexed her
as much as anything else.

On the most practical level, she couldn't figure out
how he could even open his mouth, what with that stench.
Santa Anas or not, there was something else in there besides food scraps and . . . what was it they were supposed
to be looking for? Razors edged with white dust? Empty
boxes of Ex-Lax?

No, this was earthier, more clinging.

"Elizabeth Taylor," Elliot was saying now. "She'd put
a little jasmine oil in her Heftys, sometimes a clove pot-
pourri, just to make our job easier. Now that's a star.
They don't make 'em like that anymore. . . ."

"Elliot," Simone said, "do you have any idea what
that smell could be?"

"If I give you my professional opinion, you have to
promise you won't freak out."

"Try me."

Elliot aimed his eyes at Simone's tense profile. "It's
death."

TWO

"**D**o I just . . ."

"Dig in," said Elliot.

They were on the floor of the reporters' room with Nigel pacing behind them and Emerald Deegan's refuse in front of them, atop a spread-out tarp. They'd been planning on going through the garbage in the alleyway next to the building, but Nigel had called Elliot's cell with at least four Red Bulls coursing through his veins, shouting, "I cannot be expected to wait any longer!"

So they'd done as told, with Elliot hauling all three bags into the elevator and Simone holding three empties and the tarp, which Elliot had stashed in the rental car's trunk. The idea: Sort out the trash, place irrelevant items in the new bags, and bring them downstairs to the building's Dumpsters as quickly as possible, before the smell had time to sink in. Newsworthy garbage would be brought into Nigel's office.

The reporters' room's windows didn't open, and even though the air conditioner was turned up to its highest level, Simone knew that, no matter how fast they went, the stink would linger well into the following day. *The death stink*. It sickened her, yes, but it disturbed her more—and Elliot's sense of humor didn't help. Throughout the car ride back to the office he'd offered up speculations as to what could be rotting in the bags—from Emerald's movie career to the severed head of someone who tried to offer her a donut.

"If you find, uh, anything in there that used to be attached to her cheating boyfriend, don't show it to me, okay?" he was saying now. "Some things even *I* can't look at."

"That reminds me," said Nigel. "I've heard Emerald had her tubes tied, so used condoms are considered newsworthy."

Simone shuddered.

Elliot said, "Hey, that's why we've got the gloves."

Simone held her breath as she untied the knot.

Elliot had opened his bag long before. Quickly, efficiently, he was pulling out items and placing them in an empty bag, categorizing them in a quiet monotone: "One rotten bunch of carrots. Six plastic-wrapped Zone meals, uneaten. One twenty-three-hundred-dollar receipt from . . . a clothing store called . . . the People's Republic." He stopped for a moment, looked at Simone. "Don't think about what you're doing. Just do it."

Simone's eyes watered. She reached her hand into her bag, grateful for the gloves and even for the sticky rose salve under her nose, but wishing, deeply, for one of those white hazmat suits. *Don't think about the death stink. Don't think about the death stink. . . .*

Something soft and limblike brushed the back of her glove. "Oh. . . ." Her throat tightened. She pushed the bag away.

"What?" said Nigel.

Elliot came up behind her. "This what you're ohing about?" He pulled out a good-sized spoiled zucchini.

Simone said, "A little spooked, I guess. You know . . . the death smell."

"There's no ruddy death smell," said Nigel.

Elliot said, "Maybe it's just cat turds."

Investigative reporting, investigative reporting, in-

vestigative . . . Simone removed three rotting tomatoes, a wasted head of broccoli, a mangled butternut squash. "Emerald Deegan does not eat her vegetables."

"Next week's headline," Nigel snapped. "Keep working. We don't have all night."

Elliot was already on the third bag. "You know what's weird to me? Deegan is a PETA spokesperson."

"So?" said Simone.

"I always figured animal rights activists would have better-smelling trash."

Nigel said, "Anyone find a condom yet?"

Simone reached back into her bag, felt a slender, sharp object, and started to pluck it out. But when Elliot said, "Found something!" she dropped it.

Nigel said, "What have you found?"

"Four dead bodies."

"Oh, my God," Simone breathed. "Wait. How could there possibly be four . . ."

"Well, for one thing," he said, "they're not human."

They were birds. Four parakeets in various stages of decomposition, tossed into garbage bags without the benefit of a shoe box.

"Just this past week, Emerald told *People* she'd never eat anything with a face." Nigel looked at the ruined little bodies, laid out on a paper towel that he'd spread across his desk. "Eating these poor dears would have been far more kind."

Wearing Elliot's gloves, Nigel picked up the most intact between his thumb and forefinger. Around six inches in length, its feathers were a sort of glowing, caution-light yellow. He glanced at Elliot. "Unusual."

"I'm on it."

The bureau chief's thin lips barely contained a grin. He was thrilled, that was for sure, but Simone couldn't figure out why. "Can I ask a question?" she said.

Nigel peered at her, as if he'd only just become aware of her existence in the universe.

"I . . . I was just wondering about the birds." She shot a look at Elliot, who was sitting cross-legged on the office floor, frantically typing into a laptop. "I mean, it's horrible the way they were thrown out like that. But . . ."

"But what?" Nigel said.

"It doesn't seem like an *Asteroid* story. Emerald Deegan doesn't give a proper burial to her pet birds. It's not what you'd call . . . juicy."

"Oh, we're not going to *run* it," said Nigel. "We're going to *use* it."

"Bingo-fucking-roonie," said Elliot.

"Speak to me."

"I think you're best off seeing this yourself."

Elliot brought the laptop to Nigel's desk and set it down in front of him with a maitre d's flourish. "Dinner is served," he said.

One minute later, Nigel was shouting into his cell phone. "Muzzy! Muzzy Schindler?"

Simone looked at Elliot.

"Emerald's flack," he said.

"It's one thirty in the morning," said Simone.

"Scandal never sleeps."

"Muzzy," Nigel was saying, "I wouldn't hang up on me if I were you. . . . Why? For one thing, I have some very disturbing information about your girl Emerald. . . . Oh, but I *do*." He paused for several seconds, the grin spreading across his gaunt face like butter melting on a grill.

Elliot whispered, "Wait for it. . . . Here it comes. . . ."

"Do the words 'illegal poaching' mean anything to you?"

"Yesss!"

As Simone listened, the bureau chief explained to Muzzy that her prized client, PETA poster girl Emerald Deegan, had in her possession four rare golden parakeets, poached from the Brazilian rain forest. An endangered species, illegal to keep as pets, they'd

received the most horrific treatment after death.
And . . . well . . . Nigel wasn't absolutely certain, but
he'd be willing to wager that during their all-too-brief
lives, the birds had been undernourished. Possibly even
abused. "PETA Princess Pummels Puny Poached Parakeets!" He practically sang it. "You know, it's just as
shocking as it is alliterative. Care to confirm? Deny?
Comment at all?"

Simone watched Nigel say all of this, every word,
without interruption. He could take his time now. No one
was hanging up on him. Elliot winked at Simone, because he too was aware of Muzzy Schindler's sudden,
staggering respect for a man whom two minutes ago she'd
viewed as tabloid scum, an irritating noise on the other
end of the phone.

This was, Simone had to admit, deeply satisfying.

"Now . . . now . . . there's no need to get hysterical,"
said Nigel. "Listen . . . listen, love. Perhaps . . . *Listen to
me!* Perhaps we could work something out."

In the next three minutes, Nigel had Muzzy agreeing
to a sit-down interview between Emerald and the *Asteroid* reporter of his choice, the topic: the actress's secret
heartbreak over her cheating boyfriend, club impresario
Keith Furlong. Parakeets would not be mentioned. But
Keith's "chronic lap-dance addiction" and "a certain underaged beauty" were both fair game.

"It was a pleasure doing business with you, Muzzy,"
Nigel said. "Now get some sleep. You sound terrible."

Just after he hit END, Nigel glanced at Elliot. "Thanks
for the birds."

"That," said Simone, "really, that was—"

"Genius," Elliot said.

"Right, are we through with the bags, then?"

"I'm not done with mine," said Simone.

"Well then, stop bimbling and complete the job."

As Elliot threw the bags of unnewsworthy trash over
his shoulders and headed out to the elevators, Simone
put her gloves back on and knelt in front of hers. Nigel

started out of the room. "Shout if you find anything," he said from the hallway. "Cocaine paraphernalia, empty bottles of diet pills, Ritalin and/or horse tranquilizer. . . ."

Simone heard his office door close. She reached in, scooped out a pile of cold sticky rice, and dropped it in the discard bag, then a broken wineglass, an empty bottle of Yves St. Laurent moisturizer, a carton of milk that had gone bad weeks prior. Now that the source of the death stink had been revealed, sorting through the trash was nowhere near as excruciating. *I could get used to this*, Simone thought. And then her finger hit the slender, sharp object she'd felt earlier, just before Elliot had found the birds. She pulled it out.

It was a shoe. A silver open-toed dress shoe that had been stained with the sour milk and something else—something a dark rust color that had soaked the back of the upper, then run down the heel in a thick, ugly rivulet. It was blood, Simone knew—crusted blood on a silver stiletto heel with an open toe. *No one has found the other open-toed Jimmy Choo stiletto heel. Nia Lawson killed herself, wearing one silver shoe.* Simone checked the label. There was more blood spattered across the inside of the shoe, but when she looked at it closely she could make out the name: Jimmy Choo.

She placed the shoe on the tarp and stared at it, her breath shallow, her pulse beating up into her ears. "Found something," she said. Her voice was barely a whisper.

"Put it in the discard bag," said Nigel.

"You've got to be kidding," Simone said. "This is . . . this *has* to be Nia Lawson's other shoe."

"I don't care if it is," he said. "She knocked off more than a month ago, and she couldn't even move issues back then."

"But isn't it strange that Emerald Deegan would be throwing out the missing shoe?"

"Perhaps Lawson went to a party at Emerald's house and left the shoe behind. I don't rightly give a piss."

"There's *blood* on it!"

"That is *not* blood. That's . . . some sort of wine sauce."

"But, Nigel—"

"Look. We've an exclusive interview with Emerald Deegan. We need material to confront her with during that interview. And a shoe that might have been worn by a has-been slut who's been dead for two fortnights is *not the material I'm looking for.*" He took a breath and glared at her. "So unless you can prove to me that Emerald Deegan was snorting coke off of that shoe, or that her boyfriend was *fucking* that shoe, I would like you to throw it out. *Immediately!*"

Slowly, Simone dropped the shoe in the discard bag.

"Good. Now off with you. Go home and get some sleep. You've got an early call tomorrow morning, and they won't use you if you have dark circles under your eyes."

"Huh?" she started to say. But before she made it to the second *h*, Nigel had left the room.

Greta was standing over Simone's pullout bed in a white satin evening gown and heavy rubber gloves. "What are you doing here?" Simone asked.

Her sister said nothing—just gestured like a game show spokesmodel at the bottom of her gown. Simone sat up and followed the gesture with her gaze.

Greta was wearing one silver Jimmy Choo.

"Oh."

Greta whispered, "They crush you."

Simone started to reply, but Greta made a sound like a ringing telephone. Then she melted, from the feet on up, into a deep pool on the floor. A pool of blood.

Simone's eyes flipped open and she heard her own phone ringing. It was six a.m. When she answered, she heard Nigel's voice: "TellmeIdidnotwakeyouup."

It took her several seconds to escape unconsciousness, to separate his words enough to understand them. "Wha . . ."

"I *told* you, you have an *early call*. You should be on your way to work *now.*"

Simone managed to say, "Early call?" but Nigel had already hung up.

Within fifteen minutes, she had showered, thrown on a reasonably clean T-shirt and a pair of jeans, and raced out of her apartment. She jumped into her Jeep and sped all the way to work, taking Coldwater Canyon like an action hero. At one point she found herself tailgating a Ferrari.

When she arrived at the *Asteroid*'s offices, winded from stress and dangerous driving, the words "early call" looping through her brain until they made even less sense than they had in the first place, she found Nigel in the reporters' room with a slender, fortyish blonde who resembled a soccer mom from a Chevrolet ad. They were watching *Today* on a small TV plugged into the far wall, the blonde saying, "Didn't you always used to wish Matt and Katie were doing each other?"

Nigel said, "You're a strange woman, Kath."

"Seriously, he and Meredith don't have the same chemistry."

Simone cleared her throat.

"Right." Nigel flipped off the TV. "Simone, this is Kathy Kinney. Stick with her, you might learn something."

Kathy smiled, stuck out her hand. "Well, I've been at it long enough."

"Reporting?" said Simone.

Nigel leveled his eyes at her, and Kathy let out a short, sharp laugh. "Not quite," she said.

The correct term, according to Nigel, was "infiltrating." In her fifteen years at the *Asteroid*, Kathy Kinney had infiltrated close to one hundred funerals, three dozen A-list charity benefits, fifty-some-odd weddings, and Fred Savage's bar mitzvah. She'd clocked more time in Cedars-Sinai's waiting room than she cared to think about, owned several sets of surgical scrubs, and swore to Simone on a stack of Bibles that she'd assisted in the birth of Julia Roberts's twins.

According to Nigel, Kathy was "tabloid gold." You have a Kathy Kinney—an attractive woman with good sharp ears who can blend in anywhere—you don't need to pay sources. Kathy's your source. Kathy's your "insider," your "eyewitness," your "close pal."

The *Asteroid*, Nigel said, needed more on staff like Kathy—which was the main reason he'd decided to try out Simone, master's degree or not. "Do whatever this woman says," he told her. "It'll be the best journalistic education you ever had."

Today's assignment—the one with the early call—was to pose as extras, infiltrate the Malibu set of *Suburban Indiscretions*, and find whatever dirt they could on Emerald for use in the exclusive interview.

"Cake" was how Kathy described it once they left the office. "Cute girl like you could do it blindfolded." They were on their way to the set—a rented mansion—in Kathy's pearlescent Audi. "You're familiar with the cast of characters?" Kathy said.

"Kind of," said Simone. "I've watched the show a couple of times."

"So you know Emerald plays Cambria."

"Yes, with the bracelets."

"She wears 'em in real life too. And she's schtupping the gardener."

"In real life?"

"No, honey—on the show. Rico Valdez plays the gardener and he's gay as a spring frock. What we're looking for with Emerald is coke. We want to say her cheating boyfriend drove her to drugs."

"Who's the source on that?"

"Her bony ass is the source."

"What about eating disorders?"

"Nigel's spy told him the *Interloper* is running an 'Emerald is bulimic' story next week, so we want to steer clear of that. The thing is, though, drugs freak Legal out like you wouldn't believe, so we need good solid evidence to throw in Em's face during the interview."

"How do we . . ."

"If there's any way you can sneak into her trailer, do it. And check out the bathroom."

"But . . . that sounds impossible."

"Anything is possible," she said. "Make that your mantra."

"Okay."

"Far as the rest of the cast goes, there's Vanessa Cornwall. Plays Georgina."

"Cambria's mother."

"Major lush. We don't care about that. But if you see her drinking out of the same can of Sprite for a couple hours, you might want to sidle up, offer her a cigarette, and ask her about Emerald's coke habit."

"I don't smoke."

"Neither do I, but you should have a pack on you at all times. Marlboro Lights. Everyone wants to bum those." She gestured at the backseat, where she kept four full cartons of the brand. "Go ahead. Take a couple packs."

The back of Simone's neck was starting to sweat, the hollows of her elbows. She felt as if she should be taking notes—but what would those notes say? She now understood, *fully* understood, what being "in too deep" was supposed to mean. She had a near-visceral sense of water rushing into her mouth, her nostrils, her eyes.

"Then there's Gregory Gunn, who plays Emerald's husband, Shane. In real life, he's married to Rain Devine."

"Who?"

"Country singer. Born-again Christian?"

"Never heard of—"

"Gregory's a total trash dick. What you do with him is, you rub up against him in the craft services tent, tell him how much you admire his work."

"Kathy . . ."

"Then you casually mention Emerald's coke habit. But

while you do it, you look at him like you want to eat him for brunch, hold the hollandaise."

"Kathy," said Simone, "I can't do this."

Kathy turned and gazed at Simone. She had Disney princess eyes—deep, velvety blue, with thick, curving lashes.

Simone said, "It's not that I think I'm above it. It's just . . ." Her voice trailed off.

"Go on."

"I'm not ready. What if I say something idiotic and get us both thrown off the set?"

"So don't say anything. Mute works." Kathy flipped on her blinker and pulled off Pacific Coast Highway. "You can be my baby sister, visiting from Utah. You've never done extra work before and you've always dreamed of being on TV and you're intimidated speechless." She broke into a grin. "Seriously. That *works*."

"So . . . I can just stand there, let you do the talking. And the rubbing."

"Sure. But my feeling about you is, mute's not going to last too long—especially when you find out what a rush it is to pretend you're someone you're not. Ever take acting lessons?"

"No."

"Well, you should. You can write 'em off. I study under Lorelei Hoffman—she's awesome." Kathy took a narrow private drive up the back end of a cliff, and Simone gazed out the window at burnt-orange rocks dotted with odd, scrubby plants. At first she couldn't figure out why it all looked so familiar—until she recognized it as the terrain of countless inhospitable planets from the old science-fiction movies she and Greta used to watch, late at night, huddled together on the living room floor with their blankets pulled up to their chins.

Kathy drove through an open gate and up a long driveway that led to a Tudor mansion with a lawn so green it hurt Simone's eyes. As they parked next to dozens of other cars, Kathy looked at Simone and patted her hand. "No worries," she said.

"Maybe we should just leave," said Simone.

"No way," Kathy said. "I'll figure something out."

They were standing at the periphery of the lawn, watching twenty or so extras of varying age, race, and hair color—all of them dressed for a cocktail party at the White House. Silk shifts, linen suits, luxurious leather shoes, ties and purses adorned with discreet, expensive-looking initials.

"How can extras afford clothes like that?" said Simone.

Kathy shrugged her shoulders. That wasn't the point, which Simone knew. The point was that they were grievously underdressed and, no matter what Kathy figured out, they weren't going to last here another minute.

Simone glanced at her fellow infiltrator. Kathy's baby T-shirt bore an angry monkey with devil horns whose facial expression was marginally happier than her own. "Does anybody here know where the *fuck* the assistant director is?!" Kathy yelled.

Simone's eyes widened. *Where the hell did that come from?*

Kathy's reply seeped out the corner of her mouth: "Trust me."

One of the extras—a goateed man wearing chinos and a tie festooned with interlocking *G*s—gestured a little nervously at a skinny red-haired guy who was working a walkie-talkie near the bank of trailers. "Uh, the AD's name is Jeff," he said.

"Thank you." Without pause, Kathy took off toward the AD, shouting, "Jeff! Jeff!" in such a way that made the name sound like an obscenity. Simone followed because she had no other choice, but she could feel at least forty eyes aimed at her back and desperately wished she could melt into her shoes. At this point, she had no doubt—absolutely none—that Kathy Kinney was certifiable. She couldn't believe she'd actually gotten into a car and let this woman drive it.

"Jeff!"

"What?" Jeff glared at Kathy, and Simone noticed that a dozen or so extras were now standing in a half circle behind her, gawking at the scene as if it were spontaneous performance art.

Kathy said, "That's all you have to say to me? 'What?'"

"Do I know you?"

"Duh! I've only done six episodes with you!"

"Ummm . . ."

Kathy scrunched up her face and began rubbing her temples. Was she having a nervous breakdown? Simone contemplated running away without looking back. She could ask one of the gawkers for a ride to the nearest gas station, then call a cab from her cell phone—and while she was at it, an ambulance for Kathy . . .

. . . who was taking a breath, getting ready to speak again. Simone braced herself.

But when Kathy's voice did emerge, it was surprisingly subdued. "Look, Jeff. I'm sorry. . . . It's just . . . the casting agency told me casual and I drove all the way from Pasadena and, you know. That wouldn't bother me so much, but my little sister's here. And she . . ." Kathy's princess eyes glistened. "She's only out for a week, and her . . . her goal in life is to be on *Suburban Indiscretions,* and look at us, Jeff. Just look at us!" She swallowed so hard it was visible, her slender throat sliding up and down with a strange, sad grace.

The poor thing, Simone thought—even though she knew better. *The poor thing.*

"We're in *jeans,*" Kathy said.

Simone noticed more people standing behind the assistant director—actresses in robes and curlers, a thick, smirking cluster of Teamster types, one guy—leaner and more intellectual looking than the teamsters—with an air of authority that made her nervous. When she looked into his eyes, he stared back at her. His eyes were a searing blue, like gas flames. Quickly, she turned away.

They were drawing an actual *crowd*, and Kathy was playing it with everything she had. "Our mom is going to kill me, Jeff. She said to me, 'If you don't do anything else, make sure Brittany gets on *Suburban Indiscretions*! You know how much she loves that show.' "

Brittany?

Jeff looked at Simone. "Where are you visiting from?"

She heard herself say, "Utah."

He nodded. "I'm sorry," he said. "Casting meant business casual. Not, uh, casual casual."

"Oh, for god's sake," said one of the actresses. "Give the poor girls a break!" She wore a plain terry-cloth robe, her black hair pulled back into a loose ponytail. Her face was free of makeup, but Simone would have recognized the bracelets anywhere. Dozens of them on each arm—some silver, some gold, some studded with jewels, clanging against each other like a tambourine whenever she moved.

Emerald Deegan. In the jingling, jangling flesh.

Despite the baggy robe, the actress looked about twenty pounds lighter in person, which was truly saying something. She wasn't just skinny; she was Gandhi thin. Her eyes were huge and sat atop her cheekbones like a split geode on a shelf.

"You ladies come with me," Emerald said. "I've got tons of cocktail dresses in my trailer. I'll set you up."

As they followed Emerald to her trailer, Kathy gave Simone a discreet wink. *What the hell just happened there?* Simone thought. She started to say it, too, but she stopped fast when she noticed the man with the gas-flame eyes standing still in the midst of the dispersing group, watching her.

Emerald's trailer smelled like a room full of goths—the sweet wet scent of stage makeup mingled with cigarette smoke, hairspray, and a nearly overpowering aroma of patchouli oil.

"What size do you girls take?" Emerald said.

"I'm a four if I don't breathe too deeply," said Kathy. "My sister's about a two, right, Brit?"

Simone nodded, but her attention was elsewhere: Emerald had fashioned an elaborate shrine in the middle of her coffee table—a small alabaster statue of the Virgin Mary next to a jade Buddha, surrounded by bouquets of dried roses, flat stone dishes of herbs, and lighted candles in square glass containers with Hebrew letters on the sides.

It was an interfaith firetrap. Simone couldn't take her eyes off it.

"Those are Kabbalah candles," Emerald said. "That cream-colored one symbolizes certainty. Then there's true love, self-respect . . . I can't remember what the others are supposed to mean." She ducked into her closet. "Anyway, I think I have a few size twos and fours. They're a little big on me these days. . . ."

"I'd kill to look like you, Emerald," said Kathy. "How do you stay so slim?"

"Nerves," she said.

Kathy glanced at Simone, raised a discreet eyebrow.

Emerald emerged jingling from the closet, four or five cocktail dresses clutched in her frail, musical arms. "My assistant just left with a bunch of my old Cambria clothes. We're donating them to a PETA auction, but it's too bad because there were a lot more size fours in there, and—" She was interrupted by the theme from *Suburban Indiscretions* ringing out from the coffee table shrine. Simone was confused until she realized it was coming from a cell phone—as tiny and delicate as its owner—that had been placed behind the Buddha.

Emerald dropped the dresses on her couch, picked up the phone, and looked at her caller ID. Her eyes went hard. The cell phone was dotted with pink and green crystals. She threw it across the room, and it hit her closet and fell to the floor, some of the crystals flying off, the theme song still playing for several uncomfortable beats. Emerald stood there, stone quiet, her arms trembling.

"Telemarketer," she said, finally. "Try that Dolce and Gabbana, Brittany. I think it would be perfect on you."

The Dolce and Gabbana was a wisp of a slip dress in pale pink silk. It was not something you wanted to sweat in, even once, but it was amazing looking. Simone held it up to herself, admiring her reflection in Emerald's full-length mirror before it hit her that, a couple of feet away, the cell phone still lay sprawled open on the floor. She stole a glimpse at the screen:

One missed call. Keith.

Emerald said, "I've got some shoes that might work, too."

Simone swallowed hard.

"Great!" said Kathy. "Isn't that great, Brittany?"

"Yeah. I . . . I love shoes." Simone closed her eyes for a few seconds and tried to shake the image out of her brain. The delicate silver straps, the stiletto heel crusted with blood. Nia Lawson's blood. . . .

"Check these out," Emerald said.

When Simone opened her eyes, the actress was standing in front of her holding a pair of white size seven Prada mules that looked as if they'd never been worn. The question filled her head: *Why did you have Nia Lawson's shoe?* But she couldn't ask it. Not unless she wanted Emerald to know she'd been through her trash. Simone's mouth was dry. "My size," she managed to say.

"You okay?" said Emerald.

"Sorry," said Simone. "I'm just a little—"

"Starstruck." Kathy said the word like a well-intentioned slap across the face.

Per Kathy and Emerald's request, Simone slipped on the mules and walked the length of the trailer. The heels were practically two-dimensional, so she teetered a bit at first, but before long she had the hang of it. "You look like a model, sis," said Kathy.

Simone glanced at Emerald. She was holding the cell phone, staring at the screen. "Either of you girls married?" Emerald asked.

"Divorced," said Kathy. Her gaze dropped to the floor.

Emerald nodded. "How long ago?"

"Three years." Kathy's voice went quiet. "He left me because . . . I . . . Wow. I can't believe it's still so hard to say."

Emerald glanced at Simone, who tried her best to look as if she knew what Kathy was talking about.

"I used to have a coke problem," Kathy said.

Whoa. Simone stared at her fellow reporter as she looked back up at Emerald, eyes watering slightly. "I . . . I'm sorry."

"Nothing to be sorry for," said Emerald.

"You know what? You're right," Kathy said. "I learned in rehab to stop acting like I'd screwed up on purpose. They didn't even want me to call it a coke *problem*. Because it's not a problem. It's an *illness*. And you know what? It is really easy to catch. Cocaine . . . there's something so . . . seductive about it." She directed her soft, Disney princess gaze at Emerald's face. "You know what I'm saying?"

Damn, she is good.

But Emerald did not take the bait. "How about you, Brittany? You live alone or what?"

Simone nodded.

"Good for you," she said. "I intend to live alone until I'm at least thirty. You don't really know yourself until you're out of your twenties, and you sure as hell don't know who to fall in love with. . . ." She ran a hand over her eyes and turned away. "Sorry. I don't know how much longer I can socialize."

"That's okay," said Kathy. "Listen, do you mind if my sister uses your bathroom to try on the dress? She's a little shy."

"Not at all."

Simone said, "Why are you being so nice to us?"

"Because she's a nice person, Brittany."

Simone got it. The snap of the tone, the narrowed, cautionary eyes. Kathy was telling her to hurry up and snoop in the bathroom while she still had a chance. But there were times, times like this, when Simone's curiosity truly burned. When her need to know answers trumped every other need, every other thought. "There was a whole group out there, and nobody else cared whether or not we got put in a scene," she said. "You've obviously been having a crappy day."

"I've had worse."

"But you don't know us from a crack in the wall. We could be stalkers. We could be—"

"Brittany has a kick-ass imagination. Our mom thinks she should write romantic suspense."

"I helped you guys because I've got good intuition about people." Emerald glanced at her cell phone. "Usually."

Simone turned her gaze back to the shrine.

Emerald looked at Kathy. "You know what?" she said. "I also thought it was great the way you stood up for Brittany. I always wished I had a big sister like you."

"Are you an only child?" Kathy said.

"Sort of," said Emerald. "I . . . had a brother."

"Had?" Simone thought and said the word at the same time.

A deep pain crept into Emerald's huge, glittering eyes; she closed them, almost as if to savor it. "Oz," she said.

"Your brother's name was Oz?"

"Emerald and Oz. My dad believed in magic. He still does." When she opened her eyes, a tear had trickled down her cheek, but she didn't wipe it away. "You'd better try that dress on, Brittany."

Simone brought the dress into the bathroom. Through the door, she heard Emerald say, "I still wish I had a big sister."

"Why?" said Kathy.

"Protection."

It wasn't until she slipped the dress over her head that Simone remembered she was supposed to look for evidence of a coke addiction, but there were no stray razor blades, no origami-like paper bundles, no tiny mirrors blurred with traces of powder.

Protection, she thought. *From what—Keith's cheating? The tabloids? That pain in her eyes?*

"Come on out and show us the dress, Brittany," Emerald called.

"Coming!" Simone made for the door, but stopped short when she noticed the sink. It was gleaming white, except for a pool of dark red liquid, just in front of the stopper. Blood.

THREE

Once they'd left Emerald's trailer and were out of her earshot, Simone told Kathy about the blood in the sink. "Could be Santeria," Kathy replied.

"Um . . . what?"

"She's obviously into alternative religions," she said. "Maybe she sacrificed a mouse—bled it out, flushed the carcass down the toilet."

Simone stared at her. The very fact that Kathy could utter a sentence like that, and in the same tone of voice someone might use to speculate about Botox usage . . . well, if nothing else, it spoke volumes about the fifteen years she'd spent working for a supermarket tabloid. "You honestly think—"

"All I know is, it *doesn't* say she's doing coke, which means we've got to go hit up the set-siders." She spotted a group of Teamsters and batted her lush eyelashes.

"Wait, Kathy."

Reluctantly, she turned back to Simone.

"I don't know if this has anything to do with the blood . . . I don't know why it *would*, but . . ." She took a breath. "I found Nia Lawson's shoe in Emerald's trash."

Kathy raised her eyebrows. "The *other shoe*? The Cinderella slipper?"

"Yes. Silver Jimmy Choo. . . . It even had blood on it—of course, Nigel thought it was wine sauce."

"You showed it to Nigel?"

"Yeah, and he made me throw it out."

Kathy shook her head. "I'm not surprised."

"Why?"

"Let's just say Nigel is not much of a Nia Lawson fan."

Simone squinted at her. "What do you mean by that?"

"Never mind, it's not important." Kathy examined her face in her compact. "Word of advice, honey. When you're infiltrating, try not to ask direct questions. It's like . . . shooting off with no foreplay."

"Okay. But . . . wait. Are you leaving me?"

"We'll do better apart—attract less attention, come away with twice as much information."

"But I'm not ready."

"Sure you are," Kathy said. "Remember, you're young and cute. That's powerful stuff in this business, so feel it. Work it."

"Exactly what business do you mean?" said Simone.

She smiled. "See you later, hon. If you need me, call my cell."

As she watched her coworker gliding toward the grinning Teamsters in the strapless size four she'd borrowed from Emerald, Simone whispered the question again: "Exactly what business do you mean?"

She felt a tap on her shoulder, and when she turned around she saw him—the authority figure with the unsettling blue stare. *Oh, wonderful.*

"Can I talk to you in private?"

"Uh . . . okay." What else could she say? She followed him away from the trailers, over the long stretch of lawn to a large oak tree.

"How are you enjoying your experience as an extra?"

Avoiding the burning eyes, Simone examined the man. He wore a white oxford shirt and jeans. He was good-looking in an intense, sleepless kind of way and his dark hair was tousled—but not artfully so. Parts of it stood on end, as if he frequently dragged his hands through it in pure frustration. Director. That's what he had to be. Maybe one of the writers. A writer being friendly. Welcoming an out-of-towner to the set. That made sense. "I'm liking it a lot. I've never done extra work before."

"You want to act?" he said. "That why you're visiting from Utah?"

"I'm just spending time with my sister. And . . . you know. I'm a really big fan of the show."

He gave her a hard, withering look, and Simone remembered what Kathy had told Jeff: *Her goal in life is to be on* Suburban Indiscretions.

Damn. . . . "Actually, I've always . . . yes . . . yes, I do want to act. I was just shy to say it because *Suburban Indiscretions* is my all-time favorite show, and—"

"How would you like a speaking part? It's an extra hundred and seventy-five bucks, and it'll work toward getting your SAG card. It wouldn't happen 'til late, though. You have plans for this afternoon . . . early evening?"

You mean besides the Emerald Deegan interview? "Well, I—"

"I thought so."

"Excuse me?"

"I'm on to you."

"*Excuse* me?"

He smiled, but only with his mouth. "I know you work for a tabloid," he said quietly. "I know your friend does too. So you have two choices. You can either take your friend, leave now, and no one finds out, or I tell the executive producer what I know, and you both get thrown off set. In front of everybody."

He watched her face, waiting. But he didn't need to wait long. The choice was an easy one.

"What did you say the name of that guy was who threw

us out?" said Kathy. This was the third time in the past half hour she'd asked Simone this question; it had officially crossed the line from rhetorical to hostile.

"I never got his name, Kathy. I told you that."

"Sorry. I just found it so hard to believe I had to ask again."

They were sitting in the reporters' room. Now that she was actually working in here, Simone saw what a scary, Orwellian place it was, with six identical desks lined up two by two, identical spotless computers placed squarely on top of all of them. There was nothing on the walls, nothing else in the room other than the TV, because Nigel believed personal touches—family photos, keepsakes, even pictures of favorite celebrities—revealed reporters' weaknesses to potential spies. If Kathy were to display her autographed headshot of Justin Timberlake, for instance, and the night maid turned out to be an agent for the *Interloper*, she'd know exactly which front-row tickets might tempt Kathy Kinney into revealing the details of next week's cover story. Nigel had explained all of this to Simone, and with a straight face. Obviously, he'd been in this business about ten years too long.

"So," Kathy said, "just to be clear, you got us thrown off a TV set by someone whose name and credentials you never even bothered to get."

A male voice said, "Take it easy on her, Kathy. It's her first day."

Kathy broke into an idiotic grin. And when Simone turned toward the sound of the voice, she could see why. In the reporters' room doorway Nigel stood alongside the most breathtakingly gorgeous man Simone had ever seen. "Simone Glass, Matthew Varrick," Nigel said. "He does most of our on-record interviews, as he can talk the knickers off a nun."

"Hi, Simone," said Matthew.

She sat there, gaping at those full, sensuous lips, the powerful arms encased in that enviable black T-shirt, the golden curls and glittering green eyes, thinking, *Talk? He talks? Why would he ever need to talk?*

If Simone was going to work with Matthew Varrick on a daily basis, she'd need to treat him like the sun and not look at him directly.

"You've got to remember, Kath," Matthew said, "it takes a little while to get as savvy as you."

"Sorry, Simone," Kathy said.

"I understand," she replied, both women looking down at their hands like chastised children.

As Nigel headed into his office, Matthew said, "I heard you guys met Emerald today. What's she like?"

Kathy turned to Simone. "Matthew's going to be doing the interview."

"She's definitely mad at Keith," Simone said to her computer screen. "She had a brother who died a long time ago."

"You see any rolled-up bills lying around her trailer? She touch her nose a lot? Take a phone call from someone who could have been a dealer?"

"None of the above," said Kathy.

"Damn."

Simone kept watching her screen, and then an image entered her mind and hovered there: the dark red pool just in front of the stopper—still glistening, still fresh. "There was some blood in her sink."

"Really?" said Matthew. "A lot?"

"Enough. . . ." Simone thought about how confident Emerald had seemed when she first asked her and Kathy into her trailer. How *happy* . . . as if, for a short time, she'd relieved the pain that later brought those tears, that later made her say, *I don't know how much longer I can socialize.* Then, again, Simone pictured that circle of blood—wet and telling in the pristine sink. "I mean . . . now that I think about it, just before she asked us into her trailer she could have been . . ."

"Injecting," Matthew said.

"Yeah."

Simone felt his glittering gaze lingering on her profile. "You're just as sharp," he said, "as you are cute."

Her mouth twitched into a grin. *One pair of knickers, coming right up.*

"Jesus, you guys are right," said Kathy. "Those bracelets. . . . She could be covering—"

"Track marks," Simone said.

"I can't believe I thought Santeria. What is *wrong* with me?"

"Track marks—fantastic," said Matthew. "Now all I have to do with the questioning is find a way in."

"Honey, if anybody can find a way *in* . . ."

"You make me blush, Kath."

Simone recalled the shoe in Emerald's garbage bag, the stain on the heel. *So much blood around one small woman.* "Can you ask Emerald if she knew Nia Lawson?"

"Why?"

"Simone thinks she may have found the Cinderella slipper in Emerald's trash," Kathy said. "Nigel made her throw it out though."

Matthew nodded. "Nigel is not much of a Nia fan."

"I told her."

He looked at Simone. "For you," he said, "I will ask her."

Before Simone was able to respond, the receptionist's soothing voice piped up from the speaker phone: "Get ready, Matty!" and Nigel was back in the doorway, telling Kathy and Simone, "Please make yourselves scarce. Emerald Deegan and her PR are in reception."

Kathy and Simone stood in the small office supply room as Matthew, Muzzy, and Emerald passed. Simone heard Emerald say, "Keith told me a year ago he was over the whole stripper thing."

Matthew said, "If you don't mind my saying, I don't know why any guy who had you would ever even look at another—" Nigel's door closed. Kathy opened the office supply room door and they headed back into the reporters' room. "Matthew's cute, huh?" she said.

"He's okay, I guess," said Simone. "I mean . . . if you like that Greek-god-meets-Michelangelo's-*David*-only-better-looking type." As quietly as she could, she moved toward Nigel's closed door.

"You'll get used to Matthew," Kathy said. "It just takes a little . . . Hey, what are you doing?"

Simone brought a finger to her lips, pressed her ear against the door until she could make out voices . . . Matthew's first: "How do you cope with it? Your lover of two years, your best friend in the world, *cheating on you. . . .*"

Then Emerald's: "Keith Furlong is *not* my best friend."

"Don't let Nigel see you doing that," Kathy whispered. "He doesn't let anyone sit in on interviews. He'll think you're a spy."

Inside the office, Matthew's voice was soothing, seductive. "Do you mind if I ask you something kind of . . . off topic?"

Another woman's voice—a smoker's rasp. "Depends on what it is."

"Don't worry, Muzzy," Matthew said. "It has nothing to do with those poor, poor birds."

Silence. *Good one, Matthew.*

He said, "Emerald, you have such beautiful, graceful arms. Why do you cover them with all those bracelets?"

A long pause. Simone held her breath.

Finally, Emerald said, "I like the way they look."

"But . . . a woman with a body as hot and lithe as yours chooses to cover up a part of it, you can't help but think . . ." Matthew's voice trailed off, then came back again softly, almost pleading. "You can't help but think . . . *What is underneath? What is she hiding?*"

"I thought we were supposed to be talking about Keith."

"I just wanted—"

"I didn't agree to answer questions about . . . my personal choices."

"Choices?"

"*Wardrobe* choices."

"Obviously, that's all she has to say about the bracelets. Next question, *please.*"

Kathy gestured at her to move away from the door. *"Nigel,"* she said.

And Simone heard the accent resounding from reception. "What do you *mean* she wasn't there?!"

She moved into the reporters' room with Kathy as Elliot's voice replied, "I waited for an hour, then I checked the strip club, Pleasures, it's called. I even checked Furlong's bar and—"

"This is fucked," Nigel said. "This is fucked beyond all fucking fuckedness."

Nigel stormed into the reporters' room poking at the numbers on his cell phone as if he wanted to cause them injury. Elliot trailed behind him.

"What's his problem?" Kathy asked Elliot.

"Keith Furlong's favorite underaged stripper," he said.

"Shit," said Kathy. "I forgot about that. She's a no-show?"

"Yep, along with the eight grand Nigel paid her up front."

"Well, maybe she'll turn up. . . . Of course, I don't know how long Matthew can keep Emerald in there. It's been, what, like twenty minutes already."

"Destiny," Nigel hissed into his cell phone. "I realize I'm being recorded, so I will keep this as civilized as possible and remind you that you did sign a binding contract and if you do not come to our offices and/or contact us within five minutes of this call, our legal team will *grind you into a pulp so fine your own mother won't even recognize you!*"

He ended the call. "Why can't you ever trust a stripper?"

"They tend to have issues with male authority figures."

"Don't you dare get arsey with me, Elliot, or I will sack you this minute."

"But . . . I wasn't *trying* to be arsey."

Simone looked at Kathy. "A stripper was supposed to be here?"

She nodded. "It was going to be an ambush. Destiny was going to show up in the middle of the interview, tell Emerald all about this hot night she spent with Keith."

"A raw porterhouse steak was involved," Elliot said.

Kathy winced. "Right. And we were going to take pictures of the moment of discovery. You know, Emerald learns the truth about the man she loves. . . ."

I still wish I had a big sister.

Why?

Protection.

"That is *awful*," said Simone.

Nigel glowered at her. "It would have been *brilliant*."

"Honey, we'd be doing Emerald a favor," Kathy said. "If my boyfriend did that with some other woman and a piece of raw meat, I'd want to know about it."

Elliot shuddered. "I wouldn't."

"This entire conversation is a waste of time," Nigel said. "We officially have nothing—not even a sodding coke addiction."

"Hold up—we just might," said Kathy. "Simone saw some blood in Emerald's sink. Matthew's going to find out if she's injecting."

Nigel perked up a bit. "*Really?* Well . . . we would need her on the record, admitting—"

"She didn't," Simone said.

Nigel glared at her. "How do you know that?"

"Well, I mean . . . I wouldn't *think* she'd admit—"

A loud beep escaped from Simone's speaker phone, followed by the receptionist's soporific voice. "Nigel? Are you in there?"

"Let me guess, Carl. It's *not* Destiny."

"Sorry," he said. "It's New York."

"Fuck me." Nigel sat on Simone's desk, picked up the phone, and said, "Right, Willard."

Kathy whispered, "The editor in chief."

"No, no," Nigel said. "Destiny's not here yet, but we're expecting . . ."

Simone knew enough to get up from her desk, to back away from the bureau chief as he stammered, "But . . . but . . . but . . . but . . ." into the receiver, like a dying outboard motor.

Elliot and Kathy were looking out one of the room's two small windows at Beverly Drive below. Simone stood next to them, watching brightly colored cars parading down the wide street, the sun glinting off their polished hoods like a smirk.

The three of them listened to Nigel saying, "Willard," and "But," and "Listen," over and over and over again, until finally Kathy put voice to her thoughts. "We're doomed."

"Why?" said Simone.

"We can't afford to piss off New York. Willard's been making noises about shutting down our bureau—just using freelancers who'd report directly to the editors in the main office back East."

"You're kidding," she said. "Who ever heard of a Hollywood gossip paper without an LA bureau?"

"Nobody," said Elliot. "Best job I'll ever have in my life and they're going to kill it because of arbitrary bullshit . . . because of sales, for chrissakes! I feel like I'm going to cry."

"Don't cry," said Kathy. "I really don't think I can look at that."

Simone said, "How can sales be that bad?"

"It's those glossy celeb weeklies," said Elliot. "Lamest headlines ever: *Stars walk their dogs, too! Stars get parking tickets, too! Stars order takeout! Stars take a crap!* I mean . . . that's news?! But they're *murdering* us with it. I mean, on top of everything else it's unbelievably insulting."

"There's also the *Enquirer*, which we can't even touch," said Kathy. "The *Globe*, the *Interloper*—"

"Word of advice," Elliot said. "Don't mention the *Interloper* in front of Nigel unless you want to wear your ass for a hat."

"We are *doomed*."

Simone thought of her apartment, of the eleven months left on her lease, and she could hear Greta as if she were in the room. *Wow, Monie. Two lost jobs in a month. That's got to be a record. Not to worry, though. I'm looking for an assistant. . . .*

She remembered what her mother had said, just after she'd accepted the job offer at the *LA Edge*. *Your sister stayed in New York, and look where she is.*

Reading off a teleprompter?

Jealousy is unattractive, Simone.

I'm not jealous.

I understand the way you feel, dear, but to pick up your entire life like that, all for a newspaper no one has ever heard of . . .

You know, the LA Edge *has won a lot of awards and—*

Let her go, Elaine, Simone's father said. *She's twenty-six. She's old enough to make her own mistakes.*

It's not a mistake!

Simone looked at Elliot and Kathy. "We *can't* be doomed! I just got here!"

When Nigel finally hung up, he called Elliot over, handed him a stack of blurry color photographs that looked as if they'd been taken in the dark with a camera phone.

Elliot peered at one. "That's Destiny?"

"I want you to go into that office," said Nigel. "Show these photos to Emerald Deegan and tell her everything."

"Not everything, Nigel."

"You heard me."

"But . . . the raw steak. I'm not sure I'm going to be able to describe that *out loud* to a woman."

Nigel narrowed his eyes. "Everything."

Elliot strode into the hallway, as grim as a soldier with marching orders. As she watched him go, Simone turned to Nigel. "Tell me what I can do to help."

"You can find that fuckwit stripper," he said. "Or Furlong. Or both. Or you can locate Emerald's dealer and get him to go on record, or you can get video-fucking-tape of Emerald Deegan shooting up."

Nigel stood up and walked out of the room, leaving nothing behind but a thick, gloomy silence.

Kathy looked at Simone. "Emerald wouldn't admit injecting, huh?"

Simone shook her head.

"I didn't think so. Remember how she was in the trailer, when I told her about my quote-unquote cocaine problem? Cool as a fucking fruit smoothie."

Simone stared at her. "You're right." She remembered Emerald's voice in Nigel's office, the way it had pitched up and trembled when Matthew had asked what was under those bracelets. *I didn't agree to answer questions about . . . my personal choices.* Not cool at all. Terrified.

Again, Simone envisioned that blood—fresh red blood, spilled into a sink. But there had been no needle in sight.

Why get rid of the needle but not the blood?

There had been no spent needles in Emerald's garbage either. But there had been blood—thick, crusted blood on the heel of a silver Jimmy Choo.

You can't help but think . . . What is underneath? What is she hiding? Spent needles or not, track marks or not, coke addiction or not, there was one fact of which Simone was certain.

Emerald Deegan was hiding something.

FOUR

Back when her name was Sara Rose Rogers, Destiny had one goal in life, and that was to work at Disneyland. At age four she'd gone there with her mom and had her picture taken with Snow White, just outside the entrance to Fantasyland. It was the happiest moment of her life, no contest. Thirteen years later, she still remembered the cotton candy her mother bought for her and the perfume Snow White had worn, which smelled faintly of apples. She remembered Snow White's shiny yellow dress and her voice, like the tinkling of bells. *You look just like a princess. Your mommy must be so proud.*

Yes, I am. Sara is my princess.

Mom died six years ago, and Destiny didn't want to work at Disneyland anymore, but still she kept that picture in her wallet. Every night before she went to Pleasures, the club where she danced, she took it out, gazed at it for a few minutes, and whispered, "Welcome to Fantasyland." Weird, she knew. But it helped her get psyched for the job.

She wasn't due at work for hours, but today she had something else to get psyched for, something that would change her life forever. "Welcome to Tomorrowland," she said to the picture. And like a response, her doorbell rang.

"Yeah?" She wasn't expecting anybody, but that didn't matter. The men in Destiny's life had a way of just dropping by.

"It's me, baby."

Destiny recognized the voice. She placed the photo on the kitchen counter and hurried up to her front door. "Coming!"

When she opened it, he didn't say a word to her; he just slid his hand up her shirt and kissed her full on the mouth.

That was what success did for you—it subtracted hesitation. All the Big Deal People she knew, the ones who moved with That Crowd . . . they never hesitated about anything, whether it was putting their tongue in your mouth or buying a thousand-dollar dinner at L'Orangerie or taking a private plane to Cabo, just to get a natural tan.

Destiny longed to be one of Them, and she'd be a lot closer soon, when her story made her famous. Dancing was so much easier with that picture in her mind—her face on the cover of the *Asteroid*, a hot, glittering description underneath—*Beauty . . . Vixen . . . Secret Lover.* Sometimes she'd see beyond next week's issue and into the future—paid on-camera interviews, reality TV, maybe a guest stint on some really good show, like *CSI.* And later, movies.

Twenty minutes in a room with Emerald Deegan, and that golden ball would start rolling. It would be tough, yes. Destiny didn't like to hurt people. But if there was one thing she had learned in the past few years, it was that anything was bearable—anything at all—so long as it took twenty minutes or less.

"What are you doing here?" she asked him.

Instead of answering, he walked into her kitchen. After a long silence, she heard him say, "Is this you, with Snow White?"

"Yeah," she said. "My mom took that picture."

He chuckled.

"What's so funny?"

"Just wondering what your mom would think of you now."

"What do you mean?"

He flipped on her kitchen radio. She heard a jumble of music fragments, of deejays' voices and news reports, until he found the station that he always listened to. The one with the dentist-chair music.

He left the kitchen and moved behind her, pressing himself against the small of her back. Destiny glanced at the clock on the wall; she was due at the *Asteroid* in forty-five minutes.

"I don't have time," she said.

His lips moved against her ear. "Pwetty please?"

"Well . . ." She closed her eyes and felt his fingertips, light on her throat. "Maybe I have twenty minutes."

"Might take longer than that," he said. His other arm encircled her waist as the fingers stroked her neck, then the palm of his hand—a hand that felt strange, slick . . .

"What will they call it, Destiny?"

"Call what?"

"The story," he said. "In the *Asteroid*."

Her eyes snapped open.

"You thought I didn't know." His grip tightened on her throat. " 'Keith Furlong's Whore Tells All'? Is that what they're going to call it?"

She looked at the hand on her waist. He'd put on gloves. Latex gloves. *Oh, no, this can't be happening. . . .* For a moment, the only thing she could feel were the blunt tips of his fingers tightening on her neck until tiny white flecks danced inside her eyes. "I . . . ," she gasped. She couldn't get the rest of it out—not enough air. *I didn't think you would mind. I thought you would understand.* Destiny's muscles strained against her skin, and then they went limp, her body surrendering as the flecks spread out, turned to white mist. She was vaguely aware of the dentist-chair deejay's voice floating out of her kitchen: "Music to relax by." But the voice faded away, and she heard nothing but the swirl of blood in her ears, like static. *I didn't think . . .*

His grip loosened and he let go of her neck. Destiny's breath came back—a wet, retching gasp. She fell to her knees. She could hear him laughing.

He said, "Guess I took that too far."

"What?" Her voice was barely a whisper.

"I was just playing a joke."

"You were?"

"Uh-huh."

"You mean . . . you don't mind?" Her legs were weak. Her head felt woozy.

"Of course I don't mind." He held out his hand, and she took it, and he pulled her to her feet.

Oh, thank you, thank you, thank you. . . .

"You're going to be famous," he said, "aren't you, baby?"

Destiny nodded, her throat still aching.

"You'll be like . . . the next Nia Lawson."

Destiny coughed. She wondered if he had left marks, wondered if Emerald Deegan would notice. She wondered if, later that night, once she got to work, she'd have to hide them with cover-up. . . . It was okay, though. Marks on her neck were okay, because he was joking, just joking. He had always been a kidder, and this time he went a little too far, that's all. Didn't know his own strength. Those gloves—he really had her going with those damn latex gloves. They were the killer.

She wanted to say, *Okay, joke's over, you can take off the gloves now.*

But then she looked at his face, and she couldn't say a word.

He was smiling, but it wasn't *his* smile—not the one Destiny knew. There was no feeling behind it, just teeth. And his eyes . . . it was like looking into the face of a shark.

His grip pinched her wrist. Then he grabbed the other—her two small hands trapped in his one, like a claw, covered in latex, tightening. He said, "I want you to give me your autograph."

With his other hand, he pulled something out of the pocket of his jeans, something black—and when he pressed the side of it, the blade popped out—long, angry. "If you scream," he said, "if you make a noise, I will cut you." He touched the blade to the hollow of her neck. "Right there."

"No," she said. "Please."

He pulled her hands up over her head, close to his face. *This can't be happening, this can't be real.* . . . Her arm muscles ached. That music he liked wafted out of the kitchen, mechanical and sterile. He frowned at her hands—a frown of concentration, as if he were threading a needle. "You're a rightie, aren't you?" he said.

Then he sliced off the tip of her right index finger.

As a kid, Destiny had once grabbed a frayed electrical cord attached to a fan. The current had thrown her across the room, and that's what this was like—this forceful, mean pain shooting all the way up her arm, all the way down her back. Blood gushed out of her finger, and she bit her lip, closed her eyes. *Don't scream, don't scream or he'll kill you.* . . . She felt the tears pushing up against the backs of her eyeballs and she wanted to weep, to call for her mother. Her nose was running and her whole body was shaking, but she kept her mouth clamped shut.

"Good girl," he said. "Now I want your autograph. On that wall."

He let go of her hands, and her knees gave way. The floor rushed up at her and hit her in the side of the head and she lay there, her eyes closed, her whole arm throbbing into that bleeding finger. . . .

"Get up," he said.

His voice was calm, so calm . . . and Destiny knew. He would make her sign the wall with her blood, and

then he would take that knife and he would kill her.
There was no question.

"Get up. Now."

As she struggled onto her side, a tiny voice inside her
said, *Surprise him.* And Destiny's reflexes took over. She
balled her good hand into a fist.

"If you do not get up now, I will cut you open on the
floor like the pig you are."

In one motion, she pushed herself to her feet and
punched him, square in the throat.

A sound escaped from him—a kind of voiceless
groan, a rush of air. She could have sworn she heard a
heavy thud on the floor, but she wouldn't believe it. She
couldn't believe anything she heard or felt right now, in
the middle of this nightmare.

Welcome to Tomorrowland.

She thought of nothing but the door in front of
her—several feet away and then an arm's length and then
she could touch it. She turned the handle and threw it
open and ran out onto the street to where her car was
parked.

Destiny had nothing in her purse but thirty dollars and
a maxed-out credit card, but that was enough, more than
enough, as she turned the key with her good hand and
drove as fast as she could to a place where she knew she
could disappear.

Bedrock was the highest priced and cheesiest looking bar
Simone had ever been in, but Keith Furlong owned it, and
Destiny loved to hang out in it, so Simone had been
drinking here for hours. She was telling everyone she
met that her name was Brittany—a carryover from the
afternoon—and she had a costume to match: skimpy red
halter top, painted-on jeans, fuck-me-now heels, all borrowed from the fathomless closet of Kathy Kinney.

She felt like a complete idiot.

Simone had been hoping at least to make contact
with Furlong—to ask him flat-out why there would be a

pool of blood in Emerald's sink, because the image nagged at her now, along with that blood-crusted shoe. *So much blood around one small woman. . . .* But Furlong was nowhere in sight—and neither was his underage stripper lover, whom Simone had assured Nigel she would find.

Simone had easily spoken to half a dozen regulars, all male, who claimed to be on a first-name basis with Keith or Destiny or both. Each was happy to answer her questions, just so long as she let him buy her drinks with alcohol in them. She didn't quite understand all the attention she was getting. Bedrock was in West LA, after all, where everyone looked as if they'd been designed via blueprint, carved out of marble and dipped in bronze. She was easily six inches shorter and two cup sizes smaller than any of the other women in the bar. But the men here didn't seem to mind.

Maybe it was because she looked refreshingly different. Or approachable. Or drunk. That had to be it.

For the past fifteen minutes she'd been chatting up the manager, Cole, who claimed to be a "silent partner" in Bedrock, with "an indie film project in the works" and "a sweet BMW Seven Series that you'd look hot climbing out of."

Simone was trying to get him to talk about Destiny, but she was running out of steam. During every lull in the conversation—and there were many of them—she found her gaze wandering around the room, encountering new levels of absurdity in Bedrock's Stone Age decor.

The bar stools were made of ersatz dinosaur bones, and the walls gleamed with glow-in-the-dark cave paintings. A statue of a brontosaurus stood obtrusively in the middle of the dance floor. Everyone who worked here wore faux animal skins, and some even carried clubs.

It rubbed her the wrong way, all of it. On top of the dinosaur bones being a sort of fluorescent, acid green, and the cave paintings seeming as if they'd been rendered in spray paint, Bedrock—and this was by far the most irritating thing of all—had its eras mixed up. Everyone knew that cavemen and dinosaurs never coexisted. It reminded Simone of those animated movies in which cows had male voices. Accepted stupidity. She just *hated* that. Honestly, would it kill them to stick to post-Jurassic animals?

Maybe she'd been in this place too long, drinking without food, but . . . there was a T. rex head *mounted on the wall.* As if a caveman would have been capable of killing a dinosaur the size of a parking garage and sawing off its head, *when they'd never even shared the same breathing space to begin with!*

"Your eyes are really exotic," Cole was saying. "What do you call that color?"

"Huh?" said Simone. "Oh, sorry. Green."

Cole was not in costume, but he definitely had a Neanderthal, drag-you-by-the-hair look and he was dressed in the spirit—Bedrock T-shirt, a necklace made of fake sharks' teeth. Or maybe they were supposed to be T. rex teeth. *Concentrate.*

"So, is Destiny going to show tonight or what?" said Simone. "She told me to meet her here, like . . . a while ago."

He rubbed his thick jaw. "Haven't seen her all night," he said. "And that's weird, because after she finishes at Pleasures, she always comes here."

"Keith isn't here either."

"Nope."

"Hasn't been here all night."

"Uh-uh."

"You sure he wasn't here earlier and you missed him?"

"No way. I'm Keith's number two. He's not around, I run the show." He smiled at her. "Even when he is, if you know what I'm saying. You know that guy they call the president's brain?"

"Karl Rove?"

"That's me."

She looked at him. Yeah, he was being serious. "Wow," she said. "So . . . you think maybe Keith and Destiny ran away together?"

"You're sort of naïve, aren't you?" Cole said. "I like that. It's cute."

"Why? I mean . . . Keith's totally into Destiny. She told me—"

"Baby, if there's one thing you shouldn't believe, it's what chicks tell their chick friends about guys being into them." He looked her up and down. "No offense."

"Excuse me, miss," said the bartender. "Gentleman over there would like to buy you a drink."

The bartender's bare arm was festooned with tiger-striped fur sweatbands. Simone's eyes followed the bulky stretch of it to the opposite end of the bar, where she saw the same guy who had thrown her off the *Suburban Indiscretions* set. He was smiling.

Oh, now come on. "I'll be back in a minute, Cole."

Simone picked up her drink, walked the circumference of the bar to where he sat, and glared down at him. She wasn't avoiding him this time. If nothing else, three and a half chardonnays had eased all fear of confrontation. "I never got your name," she said.

He turned his face up to her—with that wiseass smile, those gas-flame eyes. "Neil Walker," he said.

"Well . . . *Walker.* You can't throw me out of here. It's a free country and I can drink wherever I want, no matter what I do for a living."

His smile grew broader. "I'm off duty," he said. "Really, Brittany. I just wanted to buy you a drink. And to tell you I'm sorry about this morning."

Simone blinked a few times. "You're sorry?"

"I know you were just doing your job. Unfortunately, doing my job meant I couldn't let you stay on set."

"I . . . I thought you were a director or something."

"Nah, I'm not that glamorous," he said. "I'm in security. Barry Savage—he's the executive producer—his office contracts my firm to guard the *SI* set. Believe me, you're not the first tabloid reporter I've caught."

Simone examined Walker—the rumpled hair, the intelligent features. He wore the same clothes he'd had on that morning—white, untucked oxford, faded jeans, Nikes. "You don't look like a security guy," she said.

"I don't?"

"Not at all. Where's the crew cut and the bad sports coat?"

"Hey, *we're* the ones who are supposed to be doing the profiling."

She smiled. "Listen, can I ask you a question?"

"Yes, I voted for Schwarzenegger."

"That's not what I was going to ask."

"I never served in the military. I have a college degree, but yeah, I do read Tom Clancy from time to time. And I box."

"Okay, okay . . ."

"Just wanted to get the rest of the profiling out of the way for you." He winked at Simone, took a sip of his scotch.

"This morning," she said, "what was it about me that gave me away?"

He laughed a little. "For future reference?"

"Yeah. I'm . . . I'm sort of new at this. I need to know these things."

His gaze traveled from Simone's eyes to her mouth, down the borrowed halter top and jeans, all the way to the tips of the heels and back up—a slow and lingering journey that made Simone's face heat up. "Well, first of all," he said, "you are *so* not from Utah."

"You wanna know something?" said Walker. "I really like the *Asteroid.*"

"Now you're just being ridiculous."

Half an hour later, Simone had switched to Coke and was feeling a little less fuzzy-headed, yet she still hadn't mentioned Destiny's name. She'd thought Walker might be a good source, Hollywood security job and all, but she told herself she had to be careful about it—get to know him first so he wouldn't think she was only trying to yank information out of him. She couldn't just blurt out, "Do you know what happened to that stripper Destiny?"

That would be like shooting off with no foreplay.

Besides, Walker was so easy to talk to. She'd told him about going to Columbia, about the *LA Edge* folding, about the financial desperation that forced her into tabloid journalism. The thing was, he seemed more interested in what Simone had to say than her state of intoxication—which was, at the very least, a nice change of pace for tonight.

"I'm serious," Walker said. "The *Asteroid* is my favorite of those rags."

"Well . . . they placed a nicely worded classified ad for the job. I'll give them that."

"So . . . where are you from originally?"

"You've never heard of it."

"Try me."

Simone gave him a long look. "Wappingers Falls."

"No way. I'm from Rhinebeck."

"Stop it."

"I *am*! Astor Road. My folks still live there. I took a girl from Wappingers Falls to senior prom."

"We grew up twenty minutes away from each other?"

"I'm older than you, though. You don't have a big brother or sis—"

Simone swallowed hard. "No."

"Only child, huh? Me too . . . kind of. My brother is fifteen years older than me."

"Really?"

He nodded. "I was what you call unexpected."

She grinned at him. "You still are."

"I'm going to take that as a compliment, Brittany."

"Simone."

"Right. I keep forgetting. The thing is, you look like a Brittany."

"I do?"

"No."

Simone finished the rest of her Coke. On the other side of Walker—in lieu of an ashtray—was a huge nest marked with the words "Pterodactyl eggs." "I hate this place," she said.

He snorted. "As if cavemen hung out alongside T. rexes. Would it kill them to stick to one prehistoric era?"

"Oh, my God, yes! Exactly!"

For a long moment, Walker said nothing, just gazed into her eyes. "You know what I miss most about Rhinebeck?"

"What?"

"Christmastime, when they put all those little white lights in the trees outside the Beekman Arms."

Simone smiled.

"Thing is, I didn't think about those lights at all when I was living there. Christmas was fucking cold and I was always the one who had to shovel the driveway, put the fake reindeer on the roof 'cause my dad was too old to climb up there. It was a pain in the ass. . . . But now, I think of those white lights and it makes me . . . well up a little. Something so *real* about it, you know? White lights on bare trees. . . ."

"Yeah," Simone said. "And bugs in the summer. Don't get me wrong. It's great not having mosquitoes, but it also makes me feel like they know something we don't."

"Ah, yes. Mosquito conspiracy theory."

"I'm telling you, there's something there."

Walker's hand brushed against hers and his expression went serious. "What the hell are you doing in this ridiculous dive, anyway? I mean, I live right around the corner and I have terrible insomnia. What's your excuse?"

Now. Now she could ask him. The sentence formed: *Do you know a stripper named Destiny?* But then it popped into her mind again, the blood in Emerald's sink . . . the shoe in her trash. Matthew had said he'd never had a chance to ask Emerald about that shoe.

Emerald had stormed out in disgust after Elliot told her about Destiny and the steak. . . . "I found Nia Lawson's other shoe."

Walker peered at her. "That actress who . . ."

"Mack Calloway. Yes. The Cinderella slipper."

"Are you sure it's hers?"

"Almost positive."

"That . . . that is incredibly weird."

"Isn't it? I can't believe my boss made me throw it out. He's got something against Nia Lawson. But here's the thing." She leaned in close, lowered her voice. "You're not going to believe where I found it."

Walker's eyes widened, but before Simone could say anything more, her cell phone chimed. She glanced at the caller ID, even though there was only one person who could be calling at this hour. "Nigel?"

"Are you speaking to someone?"

"Yes."

"I want you to leave the bar, go out to your car, and call me back within the next ten minutes for instructions."

"Okay," she said. "But why?"

"I will tell you, but you mustn't react in any way; you mustn't change your facial expression. If you are capable of doing this, please reply simply, 'Yes.'"

"Yes."

There was a slight pause. Walker mouthed the words "Are you okay?" And Simone nodded, keeping her face as blank as she could as Nigel's voice raced into her ear.

"I've just heard from my police source," he said. "Emerald Deegan is dead."

FIVE

Simone didn't play tennis, but she was wearing tennis whites. She was walking a dog that didn't belong to her in a neighborhood she didn't live in, getting ready to act surprised by the one thing she already knew: Emerald Deegan had died of an apparent suicide late the previous night.

Two suicides, one month apart, the first suicide's shoe in the second suicide's garbage. . . .

Simone tried to focus on the world around her, but it was hard. The sunrise bled a kind of gaudy, MAX Factor coral into the lavender sky, and there was that same pasty-sweet smell that melted through Simone's open windows every morning—that mixture of sage and wet driveway and residual, night-blooming jasmine. That, combined with lack of sleep and a blossoming hangover, the tennis garb and this unfamiliar dog—which jerked at its leash so hard it kept gagging—made Simone feel as if she were asleep at her apartment, in the midst of some fever dream.

The facts, as Simone knew them, only added to the feeling. *What connection could there be?* Back at the *Asteroid*, she'd done a few quick Internet searches on

Emerald and Nia. Far as she could tell, they'd never acted in anything together, weren't involved in the same charities, didn't go to the same parties or hang out with any of the same people. They didn't share an agent, a manager, a publicist. . . . Plus, Emerald was on a hit show, while Nia hadn't worked in years. They had absolutely no reason to have ever met. Yet Emerald had that shoe—Nia's bloody suicide shoe—in her possession.

And now they're both dead.

"Ccccccchhhhh," said the dog.

"Heel."

The dog, a fluffy white cockapoo named Madison, paid no attention to the command. "Ccccccccccchh," it said again, its limpid black eyes popping a little. Then it reared up on its tiny hind legs, yanked harder, and made a different sound, like wax paper crumpling.

"Breathe!"

The dog emitted a deep growl, but at least its vocal cords were in use.

Both Madison and the tennis whites had been donated by Kathy, who'd sped over to the *Asteroid*'s office an hour and a half earlier at Nigel's request.

"Will you be coming with me?" Simone had said at the time, trying hard to keep the *Please, I'll do anything* out of her voice. If there was any place on the entire spinning planet Simone would less rather be than the *Asteroid*'s reporters' room at four thirty in the morning with a chardonnay hangover, it was the scene of Emerald Deegan's death, alone.

"Sorry," Kathy had said. "The Hollywood Division cops know me from when I pretended to be Phil Spector's maid."

Simone had searched Kathy's face. Ever since her fellow reporter had arrived at work, she had been doing this, hunting for the faintest hint of emotion within those princess eyes, that placid mouth. Finally, she said, "I can't believe this, Kathy. Can you? I mean, we were just in her trailer, borrowing clothes—"

"All actresses are weird," Kathy said.

"But—"

"Listen, anybody who wants to be famous is nuts. You actually go so far as to achieve it—to become so famous you're trapped in your own home because you can't walk from your front door to your car without a bunch of ass-holes taking your picture. . . . Then you're out-and-out psychotic. And psychotic people do things like kill themselves."

Simone looked at her. "Like Nia Lawson."

"Yes, honey." Kathy cast a quick glance at Nigel, then spoke a little louder. "Now remember, you're a neighbor walking your dog before your morning tennis lesson, and you just happened on all these cars outside the house of that sweet girl, Emerald."

Simone said, "But I won't be able to get any on-the-record quotes if I don't identify myself as a reporter."

That's when Nigel had interrupted. "You are not a *reporter*. You are an *insider*. As in *According to an insider, coke-addicted starlet Emerald Deegan died of a lethal mix of autoerotic asphyxiation and speedballs after finding a secret sex tape of her cheating boyfriend Keith Furlong and seventeen Laker Girls.* Am I clear?!"

Simone's hangover was now in full bloom. Her eye-balls strained against their sockets, and she was so thirsty her tongue could grow fur and it wouldn't surprise her. When Madison tugged at the leash again, she nearly top-pled to the ground.

She closed her eyes, breathed deeply. She tried imag-ining herself at the suicide scene, affecting one of those laid-back California accents as she spoke to police out-side that gate. *I was wahlking my dahg and huhrd this comewtion. Did something hahpen to Umrahld?*

The way she was feeling right now, it was hard to imagine saying anything at all, let alone saying it *in char-acter.*

Would she ever be allowed to tell the truth? Less than

two full days on this job and already she was beginning to suffer from honesty withdrawal.

Simone recalled her last image of Neil Walker, running his fingertips along the edge of that idiotic pterodactyl nest, as she told him with no explanation, "I have to go."

"You do? Why?" He'd looked so confused. But she hadn't said another word; she'd just raced out of Bedrock, like Cinderella at the stroke of midnight. Thinking about it made her wince. Simone didn't like screwing with people's heads. She was not, by nature, a mysterious person.

Madison barked, tugged, and gagged in rapid succession.

"All right already, I'm going, I'm going. . . ."

At the end of the block, Simone turned right on Linda Vista. She looked up the steep street—literally *up* the street—and nearly cried. *Just get it over with. It's not like the house is going to come to you.*

Simone figured she may as well carry Madison. The dog probably didn't weigh much more than a can of peas, and anything beat listening to it gag.

She crouched down, stuck a finger under Madison's collar, and unhooked the leash at the exact same moment she noticed the helicopters buzzing overhead. Then a news van sped by and screeched to a halt several blocks up, near the top of the hill.

That's when Madison took off, heading straight up the hill like an oversized cotton ball shot out of a cannon.

Come back here, Simone wanted to scream as she chased the little dog up the pavement to the end of the block, across the street and one, two, three blocks more, her knees buckling, breath burning into her lungs like astringent. Her face throbbed. She felt a long, sharp pain in her side as if an axe were buried in it, but still she kept moving.

She could not lose Kathy's dog in the Hollywood Hills—not with the coyotes and the rattlesnakes and all those idiots driving Hummers, screeching through intersections without a passing glance at whatever tiny animal might be scurrying in front of their enormous, bone-crushing tires. . . .

Finally, Simone caught sight of Emerald's house. The gate was open, and easily half a dozen police cars spilled out the driveway, along with various unmarked vehicles—belonging, no doubt, to DAs, detectives, criminologists . . . not to mention the three news vans across the street, shooting footage of . . . what were they shooting? The vehicles, the front of the house, the backs of two men in shirtsleeves and dress pants, walking up to the front door, carrying briefcases made of metal.

The house was tall and thin like Rapunzel's tower—only Mexican-style, with red and pink bougainvillea crawling up its face. Madison stopped in front and started sniffing at the curb.

Thank you! Simone caught up to the dog, practically fell on top of it . . . until she skirted under one of the cars and scurried up the driveway.

"Wait," Simone gasped. She was aware of uniformed officers milling on the doorstep. None of them looked at her. Neither did the small group of men and women in suits involved in hushed conversation on the sidewalk, or even the TV reporters across the street, shouting, "Officer!" and "Do you have a statement?" There was too much going on. Too many other things more deserving of attention than a small, sweaty young woman in tennis whites doubled over in pain as she attempted to chase a cockapoo up the driveway, both of them weaving around the cars, both of them making their way to the back of the house.

Emerald's backyard was surprisingly large, considering how closely the houses were jammed together. Simone had chased Madison behind a magnolia tree and through a line of hedges to get here, and now she found herself in a Mexican-style paradise, with painted tile pathways winding through lush green grass dotted with impatiens and blossoming white hibiscus. A tennis court stood beyond the landscaped area, shaded by thick oaks.

At the center of the tile pathway was a bubbling fountain. The minute she saw it, Simone forgot all about Madison, the cops, Emerald's lifeless body in the house behind her . . . everything except the crisp music of water hitting marble.

LA tap water quality, Simone had read, ranked a dismal twenty-second among major U.S. cities. But Simone was too parched to care. She crouched over the side of the fountain, and shoveled water into her face like a lunatic.

When she was finally sated enough to draw breath, Simone felt a moist tickle on her calf and realized Madison was licking her. She turned around, sat on the grass, and picked up the dog, which curled up in her lap as if it were the most natural thing in the world.

A crime-scene-trained cockapoo. God, Kathy Kinney is good.

Simone closed her eyes and put her head back for a few minutes, listened to the water. She felt the sun soaking into her face and thought, *Emerald left all this. Why?*

Simone didn't hear footsteps, but after a few minutes she did notice that someone was standing over her, blocking the sun. She opened her eyes and stood up to face a curly haired woman around her own age in white capris and a pale green T-shirt that read "Peace, Love and *Suburban Indescretions.*"

"Um . . . hi?" said Simone.

The woman's eyes were dry, black stones. "Are you the new tennis pro?"

You are not a reporter. You are an insider. "Yes," said Simone. "I'm the tennis pro."

"I'm Holly, Miss Deegan's personal assistant? She won't be able to meet with you today. I'm sorry. I should have called."

The woman's voice was flat, mechanical. Simone peered into her eyes. She saw that dying shock—like a candle flickering. She said, "You were the one who found her."

Holly opened her mouth to speak, then closed it again. She did this a few times—a kind of strange, sad tic—before tears spilled down both her cheeks, and she turned away and started to sob.

Simone didn't think about what to do. She was exhausted, her emotions pressing up against her skin, so she placed Madison on the ground and took the personal assistant into her arms and just hugged her. "I'm sorry," she said. "I'm so, so sorry."

Holly said, "How did you know?"

"I can just tell these things. It's okay . . . I mean, God, it's not okay. It'll never be okay, but . . ."

Holly cried into her shoulder for quite some time, without saying a word. Simone wished she could do something more, say something to make her pain go away—until she took a few steps back from herself and remembered she did not know this woman and she'd lied her way into the hug. She wasn't a friend. She was an insider.

Finally, Holly caught her breath and pulled away. "It still hasn't really sunk in," she said.

"I'm sure."

"I keep thinking I've got to remind Emerald about Kabbalah class. And she needs a pedicure appointment for this party tomorrow night, and . . ."

"She was planning on going to a party?"

Holly nodded.

"Why . . . I mean . . . did you have any idea why she would have done this?"

She shut her eyes very tightly and said nothing. For a moment, her face seemed to close in on itself.

"Sorry, that was a really stupid question."

Holly said, "No, it isn't." Her dark gaze darted away from Simone's face and scanned the landscape behind her. "Emerald wasn't the one who did it."

"What?"

"Ms. Kashminian," a female voice called out. Simone saw a slim woman in a pale blue linen suit standing at the back door. "Can you please answer a few more questions?"

Holly sighed. "Come with me," she said to Simone. "I could use the company."

Simone scooped up Madison and followed Holly to the back door, through a laundry room and into a large, modern-looking kitchen, where a group of latex-gloved criminologists snapped pictures of . . . what? An open drawer?

Despite the rumble of conversation, the unfamiliar arms around its tiny body and the runny wedge of Brie cheese that stood, untouched, on a platter on the kitchen counter, Madison did not make a sound. (Yes, Kathy Kinney was *that* good.) No one turned to look at Holly, Simone, and the woman in the suit as they passed through the room and climbed a long flight of stairs up to what must have been the master bedroom. The door was half open, and within, Simone could hear the popping of cameras, the whizzing of Polaroid film. She saw a group of dark-clad men and women snapping pictures around the bed. *Like a photo shoot, only . . .*

Simone was aware of that smell, the same smell from Emerald's garbage, just two days ago. *Endangered species*, she thought. Closer to the door, a piece of paper was taped to the floor. On it, a large, handwritten number three. Simone had to peer at it closely to see what the paper was labeling: a small, dark spot on the floor, much like the spot on the silver shoe, the pool in the sink . . . *Blood?*

The woman turned to Simone. "Who are—"

"She's the tennis pro," said Holly. "I brought her for moral support. This is Detective Bianchi. You know, I never got your name. . . ."

"Simone." She couldn't take her eyes off the dark spot.

The woman nodded. "I need to show you something in the master bathroom, Ms. Kashminian." She looked at Simone. "Wait here, please."

Detective Bianchi pushed the door open, and the two women moved past the group and disappeared as Simone stood there staring at the scene, the dog a warm weight, its heart beating rapidly against the crook of her arm.

Two of the criminologists left Emerald's bedside, brushing against Simone as they made their way back downstairs. "Cute little dog," said one of them, but Simone didn't answer.

She could see the edge of the bed. She could see Emerald's hand.

Were it not for the cameras, for that smell, for the deep stain on the sheet beneath it and dried blood crusting the frail, bare wrist, Simone might have thought the hand belonged to a statue. It was that white, that cold looking. That perfectly still. *So much blood, around one small woman.*

She shot herself? Or did someone else . . .

In her mind, Simone could hear those bracelets jangling as Emerald threw the cell phone across the room, Keith Furlong's name on the caller ID. So full of motion she was, so wired and angry and alive. She could hear Emerald's voice, that edge in it, and try as she might, she couldn't reconcile that with this blood, this smell, that unadorned limb like a stage prop on the stained satin sheet.

I intend to live alone until I'm at least thirty.
I intend to live alone. . . .
I intend to live.

Simone's eyes started to water, not from the smell of death but from the *feeling* of it. She held Madison tightly—just to be close to something with a beating heart. That's when she heard one of the criminologists say, ". . . cut her own throat . . ." And for the first time she could remember, Simone's curiosity failed her. She leaned against the wall, waiting with her eyes closed, because she couldn't look anymore, she just couldn't.

"Let's go back outside."

Simone opened her eyes to Holly's face. She looked very pale and Simone saw something in her eyes, a type of dull outrage, as if, on top of everything else, someone had just insulted her. "Okay," Simone said, and followed Holly back down the stairs and out the door, the phrase *cut her own throat* rolling through her head.

Simone remembered the red pool in Emerald's sink. *Actors rehearse.* She pictured Emerald standing at the sink, nicking the skin of her throat, thinking: *Can I do this?*

But that didn't explain the silver Jimmy Choo. It didn't explain . . . *Two cut throats, one month apart, the first victim's shoe in the second victim's garbage. . . .*

As soon as they got out onto the grass, Madison squirmed, so Simone placed the dog on the ground and attached the leash before saying, "Holly, what—"

"I don't want to talk about it."

She stared at her. "What do you mean, you don't—"

"You're going to ask what that detective showed me in the bathroom."

"No," Simone said slowly. "I was going to ask you what you meant when you said Emerald didn't kill herself."

"Oh, that." Holly sighed, her gaze falling on the green grass, then returning to Simone's face. "Sorry, I didn't mean to snap at you."

"No apologies necessary," said Simone.

"Can I . . . Do you mind giving me your number? I can't talk to anybody right now but . . . maybe later."

"Of course."

From her back pocket, Holly removed a piece of spiral notebook paper and a pen, and handed both to Simone. The notebook page had some writing on it. "MUNG BEANS. FLAXSEED BREAD. VITAMIN WATER," it read in neat, block letters, the points of the *a*s sharp, the *e*s made to look like backward threes.

"Use the back," said Holly, and Simone wrote down her cell phone number.

"New York area code," she said.

"Yeah," said Simone. "I . . . um . . . That's where I'm from. Originally."

Holly looked at Simone for what seemed like a very long time. "I can trust you, right?"

Simone felt a stab of guilt, but she nodded anyway. *You are not a reporter. You are an insider. You're not hurting anyone. You're just . . .*

Holly reached into her pocket and took out a business card. "I don't give my number to very many people," she said, as she handed it to Simone. "But, I don't know. I get a good feeling from you. And I could use a friend."

"Thanks." The guilt was spreading like a fresh stain.

Suddenly, Holly shouted, "Get the fuck out of here! Don't you have any decency at all?" She was looking over Simone's shoulder.

Simone turned around. It took a few seconds for her to add up in her head exactly what she was looking at—to make sure it wasn't some sleep-deprivation-induced hallucination.

It was Neil Walker—security expert, Rhinebeck native, the first normal person she had met since moving to this strange city. Okay, maybe he was working security at the crime scene, but he was between two uniformed cops, and they were escorting him out the back door of Emerald Deegan's house. Simone's first thought was, *Please don't give me away, Neil.* Her second, which she said out loud, was, "What the hell?"

"Tabloid reporter," said Holly.

"Tabloid reporter?" Simone practically choked on the phrase. "Are you *sure*?"

"Yep. That one's been thrown off set before."

"He has?!"

Holly nodded. "I hate tabloid reporters."

Simone locked eyes with Walker. He gave her a small, sly smile.

"Me too," she said.

SIX

Like most aspiring journalists, Simone checked the masthead of every publication she read. The size of the staff list, the job titles, the ratio of male to female names . . . that could tell you a lot about whether you'd want to apply for a position there and what your chances were of getting one.

But Simone had never read the *Interloper*. That was too bad. If she had read it—if she had checked the competing tabloid's masthead even once—she would have recognized the name when he'd said it at Bedrock . . .

NEIL WALKER: Senior Reporter

There it was, in bold black letters, smack in the middle of the list. *He didn't even bother to make up an alias.* "Unbelievable," Simone said. "Absolutely unbelievable."

Simone was at the huge outdoor newsstand directly across the street from the *Asteroid*. Nigel had given her money to buy the daily papers once she arrived back at work at ten a.m., after changing her clothes, and dropping the dog off at Kathy's West Hollywood apartment. But she hadn't gotten very far on that assignment. For ten minutes at least, she'd been standing here, the bright sun pressing into the back of her neck, shaking her head at Walker's name.

"You looked me right in the eye and said, 'Security expert.' Right in the eye, without a hint of . . . *Nobody* can do that to me. You're like . . . a world-class liar. You could go to the Lying Olympics."

"You talk to yourself too, huh?" said Elliot's voice behind her.

Simone turned around.

"Suggestion: put your hand over your ear. People will think you're on your cell phone."

"Uh, thanks," said Simone. "Did Nigel send you after me?"

"He thinks you took his money and ran away," Elliot said. "You really can't blame him—it's kind of an epidemic lately."

"Still no word from Destiny?"

"I'm hitting her cans tonight."

Simone frowned at him until she realized he was talking about stealing trash, which made her think of . . . "There's something really weird about Emerald Deegan's suicide."

Elliot's face darkened. "It wasn't because of me."

"Huh?"

"When I told Emerald about Furlong and Destiny and the steak," he said.

"Oh, no, Elliot, I—"

"She didn't even look surprised. Grossed out, yes. Angry. But not like she was going to—"

"That's not what I'm talking about."

Elliot said, "It's not?"

Simone put a hand on his shoulder. "No." She looked into his malamute eyes and saw moisture creeping into the corners, saw the way his thick brows pressed into each other as if they were trying, in vain, to push awful thoughts out of the brain behind them.

"Keith Furlong was a dog, and Emerald knew it," she

said. "One disgusting steak anecdote wasn't going to push her over the edge." Simone wasn't sure whether this was true, but she believed it was. Besides, Elliot needed to hear it.

His face relaxed a little. "What are you talking about then?"

"Emerald's garbage."

"The birds?"

Simone sighed heavily. "The *shoe.*"

"Oh, right."

"Think about it, even if you don't believe that was Nia Lawson's other shoe, and I do. . . . She cuts her throat, and a month later Emerald commits suicide in the exact same way?"

"Hmm," said Elliot. "Could be a trend."

"A *trend*? Cutting your own throat?"

He shrugged. "Hollywood."

Simone's headache was coming back. She closed the *Interloper*, grabbed the *New York Post*, the *Daily News*, *LA Times*, and *USA Today*, and handed them all, plus Nigel's money, to the newsagent.

As she waited for her change, a delivery truck pulled up, its driver carrying a stack of magazines, which he dropped in front of the counter, then rushed back to the truck to get more. Simone glanced at the stack. It was a new men's lifestyle magazine, *Action.* And her sister was on the cover.

Greta wore an old-fashioned fedora with a press card stuck in the band, a trench coat unbuttoned to the waist with nothing underneath. A bright orange cover line swooned across her hips: *Greta Glass: The Journalist We'd Most Like to Be Embedded With.*

This newsstand just got better and better.

"Los Angeles Police Department, Media Relations, how may I help you?"

"I'm calling regarding the death of Emerald Deegan."

"May I have your name and media outlet?"

"Simone Glass. I'm with the *As*—"

Click.

Simone sighed. "That's my fifth hang up in a row."

"Welcome to on-the-record interviews," said Kathy. "I keep telling Nigel we should just change our name to the *Ass*—it's all anyone ever lets us say."

Elliot chuckled. "I work for the *Ass*."

"You work *hard* for the *Ass*," Matthew said. "There's no place you'd rather be than right here, *in* the *Ass*!"

The two of them started giggling like third graders, and before long Kathy joined in: "Where else are you gonna get the inside poop?" she said, making Elliot go into convulsions, as Carl the receptionist walked in with everyone's take-out lunches. "I will *not* pick up the phone and say, 'You've reached the *Ass*!'"

Matthew threw back his shimmering head; he was laughing so hard, tears streamed down his cheeks. "God, you kill me, Carl."

Simone thought, *Could we all use a break or what?*

But a break was not in the offing. The LA staff was holed up in the reporters' room, working the Deegan suicide story until it wrapped. Since Emerald had killed herself late Tuesday night and the *Asteroid* closed its issues on Wednesdays, that meant they had just one day to slap together a cover spread.

Technically, they had less than a day, since it was three hours later in New York. There was no time to think about this frail young woman taking a paring knife out of her own kitchen, bringing it upstairs into her bedroom, and slicing her throat. To them, all that existed was a blank spread—and all they could do was fill it, as fast as possible, and send it to New York.

After Googling Emerald for the background file, Elliot was now creating a list of other famous suicides via cut throat. So far, the only ones he'd been able to find were a manic-depressive silent film actress, a latently gay B-movie producer from the '80s, and, of course, Nia Lawson.

Meanwhile, Matthew, with the help of a psychic he'd interviewed, was crafting a sidebar: CELEB DEATHWATCH: WHO'LL GO NEXT? Kathy had scheduled a phoner with a body language expert for a half-page piece entitled "Was Emerald's Slouch a Cry for Help?" And Nigel had swung an exclusive with world-renowned herbalist Hilton "Mr. Tea" Kleinberg, who had once mixed up a special ginkgo-anise tincture designed to help Emerald memorize lines.

Which left Simone to write the straight news story—*the meat*, as Nigel called it. At first she'd been glad. She could focus on facts. She could get actual, on-the-record quotes from people who mattered. She could organize a real news piece, impress her new boss with her solid reporting skills. But that was before they all hung up on her—Muzzy Schindler, Barry Savage's office, Keith Furlong's office, the coroner, the LAPD. . . .

Simone needed another angle. She cast a quick glance at Nigel, peering over Elliot's shoulder at his computer screen. "That's all the cut throats you can find besides Lawson?" he was saying. "The poof producer and the chubby little actress from the Mesozoic era?"

"Well, there's Robert Clive."

"Who?"

"British conqueror of India. Cut his throat with a penknife in 1774."

"Oh, now *please*."

"Sorry. It's just not a very common way to kill yourself."

Exactly, thought Simone. On her computer screen, she called up Celebrity Service, typed in the *Asteroid*'s account number, and looked up representation for Nia Lawson. Only one name was listed: her manager, Randi DuMonde.

Simone punched in the number, and after one ring, a cheerful male voice answered. "DuMonde Management!"

"Yes, hi," said Simone. "I understand you represent Nia Lawson."

There was a long pause, and the cloudless voice went faux somber. "She's . . . no longer with us."

"I know. . . . Listen, I'm a reporter, and I was just doing a story on Emerald Deegan, and I was wondering if I could get a quote from Ms. DuMonde on the parallels. I don't know if Nia and Emerald knew each other, but—"

"Who did you say you were with?"

Simone braced herself. "I'm with the *As*—"

Click.

"Goddamn it."

Nigel was glaring at her. "Right," he said. "Let's see if the telly can give us anything."

Soon the only sound in the reporters' room was the CNN anchor's voice, punctuated by the shallow click of keyboards. "Why did one of Hollywood's most promising young stars decide to end her own life so violently?" the anchor asked no one. "That. Remains. A mystery."

"Man, this guy's a snooze," Matthew said.

"Agreed." Nigel worked the remote even faster than he spoke. How he could hover on a channel for one-third of a second and know for a fact it wasn't worth watching . . .

"*Legal Tender*'s on now," said Kathy. Simone gritted her teeth. Nigel flipped right to her sister's show and stayed there.

Greta wore a suit the color of dark chocolate, a burgundy blouse, and an expression so serious you'd think she'd lost her entire family. "Hollywood was shaken this morning by the mysterious suicide of one of its most promising young stars. Why did she do it? And why so violently?"

Matthew said, "Now *that's* class."

"I adore that jacket," said Kathy.

Simone glared at her steno pad, at all the potential sources she'd written down and crossed off when they refused to speak to her. "We'll have Ms. Deegan's dear friend and publicist, Muzzy Schindler, on in a bit," said Greta. "But first, via remote, here's the Los Angeles County coroner to tell us exactly what happened."

"Great, just fucking great," Simone muttered.

"Talking to me?" said Elliot.

"Oh, no, I was just—"

"No need to explain."

Greta was speaking to the coroner. "There are obvious parallels with Nia Lawson's suicide. Do you see this as some type of ghastly Hollywood trend?"

Oh no, you did not just say that.

Nigel said, "Finished with that meat?"

"Huh? No, not—"

"Get on it, then. No time to waste."

Simone sighed. She might not have on-the-record quotes—or any quotes at all—but at least she knew the who-what-when-where of the story. She typed: *In the predawn hours of August 25,* Suburban Indiscretions *star Emerald Deegan, twenty-eight, was found dead in the bedroom of her Hollywood Hills home, victim of an apparent suicide.*

According to police sources, she had punctured her own throat with a paring knife that came from her kitchen.

Nigel stood behind her. "What type of style do you call that?"

"AP style."

"It's abysmal."

She turned. "Umm . . . what?"

"Look at it." Nigel poked her screen. "All you have here are facts."

"But it's a news story—"

"I don't care if it's the bloody president you're writing about. I'm not interested in *facts*. I want *details*."

"Details."

"The heartwarming, eye-popping, gut-wrenching details."

"But I can't get anyone to—"

"There is no such thing as can't. If you are unable to get the details from legitimate sources, then *make them up* . . . within legal limits."

Greta's voice emanated from the TV. ". . . Emerald Deegan was somebody's daughter!"

"Like that!" Nigel turned his whole body toward the screen. "Make us cry for her and . . ." He stared at Greta's image. "Nice tits," he said, moving away.

Simone swallowed hard. *Details, okay. . . . Deep breath. . . .* She typed the words: *Emerald Deegan—who was somebody's daughter—was found dead, victim of an apparent suicide.*

She deleted it immediately.

"Don't worry," said Kathy. "We've probably all gotten that speech at one time or another."

"How am I supposed to *make up* details about someone's suicide?" said Simone.

"Didn't you meet anyone at the crime scene?"

Simone cringed. "Yes," she said. "I did." Simone envisioned a line separating what she would and would not have been willing to do for a story just a few weeks ago. And as she took Holly Kashminian's business card out of her pocket and called the number, she could see herself stepping over that line . . . and erasing it.

Holly still had that feeling. She'd had it ever since she'd arrived at Emerald's at four in the morning—with two skinny soy lattes, today's *Suburban Indiscretions* script, and newly filled prescriptions for Emerald's Vicodin and Xanax—ready to prep her boss for her early call to the set.

Holly had been wondering how Emerald's *Asteroid* interview had gone (*fucking Keith and his fucking birds*) when that feeling had crept up her spine, as light and deliberate as spider tracks.

Someone is watching me. . . .

It was nearly twelve hours later. Emerald was dead, and Holly was at home, but if anything, the feeling was more powerful. Holly dug through her messenger bag until she found what she wanted. She ripped open the white paper bag from the pharmacy and looked at both bottles of pills. *Vicodin or Xanax? Painkiller or antianxiety?*

Holly had closed her window shades as soon as she'd gotten home, but still she sensed eyes—unseen eyes, watching those shades, waiting. . . .

Antianxiety it is. She read the instructions on the Xanax label: *.5 milligrams. Take one tablet, three times a day.* Holly walked into her kitchen, filled a glass of water. She took one pill, but still her heart pounded. Still she felt eyes, still she wanted to scream, *Leave me alone!*

She took another Xanax. Then one more.

Holly walked back to the couch. She picked up today's script and thought about reading it—Emerald's last lines ever—but she couldn't focus. She closed her eyes and found herself remembering what that cop had shown her in Emerald's master bathroom. *You knew about these, didn't you, Ms. Kashminian? Why didn't you tell us?*

Holly's jaw clenched up . . . but then a new feeling swept over her—like warm, soapy water, washing most of the tension away. Xanax. No wonder Emerald liked this stuff.

Holly's phone rang. She checked the caller ID and saw the New York cell number of Emerald's new tennis pro. "Hi, Simone." Holly's voice was as mellow as a jazz deejay's.

"Hi. I hope I didn't catch you at a bad time."

"No," she said. "Just taking care of a few things." Holly took a breath, and her eyes started to well. She assumed it was the pills at first, but then she remembered crying on Simone's shoulder, back at Emerald's house. What was it about this woman that made her comfortable enough to cry? *Positive energy.* That's what Emerald would have said. "I'm glad you called, Simone."

"Listen, I can't stop thinking about what you said. About Emerald not being the one who killed herself?"

Holly's thoughts went to Emerald's cut throat, to the knife she'd seen in her hand, so familiar . . . then, to the note. "I still don't think she killed herself." She grabbed a Kleenex out of the dispenser on her coffee table, wiped her face.

"Why?"

"She . . . was not that kind of person. I mean . . . Emerald was into Kabbalah. And suicide's a sin in Judaism."

"That's the only reason?" Simone sounded disappointed.

Holly said, "Listen. Um . . . I've got to—"

"I wanted to ask you something."

Holly's mouth was dry from the Xanax. Her top lip kept sticking to her teeth. "Yeah?" she said.

"I . . . I have a friend. Brittany. She was an extra on *Suburban Indiscretions* yesterday. She told me that Emerald invited her into her trailer."

Holly wanted to get herself a glass of water, but her legs felt weighted. "I didn't meet anyone named—"

"It was while you were gone. You were taking Emerald's clothes to a PETA auction."

"Oh."

"Anyway, she said she went into Emerald's bathroom and she saw blood in the sink. You have any idea what that could—"

"No!" Holly snapped—those words, "blood in the sink," cutting through the medicated calm and echoing. That had been the wrong reaction, she knew. But finding the right one was hard. For a moment, Holly felt kind of desperate, as if she were clawing her way up a cliff that was crumbling. "I mean . . . uh . . ." *Find a reason, find a reason. . . .* "Nosebleeds."

"Huh?"

"Emerald. She got nosebleeds all the time."

"Into a sink?"

"If she couldn't find a tissue, sure," said Holly. "She had a very delicate system."

"But—"

"I don't want to talk about it anymore." Maybe she was wrong about Simone, the positive energy. These intrusive, accusing questions . . . Was it the medication, or was this tennis pro—this stranger—even worse than Detective Bianchi? "I've got to go." Holly started to hang up the phone.

"Wait, Holly," said Simone. "I'm really sorry. It's just . . . the only person I've ever known who died was my grandpa, and that was when I was a baby. Seeing Emerald's body like that. . . ." Simone exhaled. Holly could hear her breath trembling. "I'm just looking for reasons, I guess."

Holly's pulse slowed a little. Some of the calm came back. She thought, *Maybe it's just a New York thing.* "I understand." She heard a rustling outside her window. Something moving through the bushes. A stray cat, a squirrel.

"Holly," said Simone, "this may sound a little weird, but . . . you think it would be okay if I called Emerald's parents and expressed my condolences?"

Shit. Emerald's dad. He knew by now, of course. The cops had called him. But if there was one call Holly was dreading . . . "That's incredibly sweet of you," she said. "It's just her father. Her mom passed away when she was little. I'll get you his number."

Holly grabbed her Palm Pilot, looked up Wayne Deegan's phone number, and gave it to Simone. "Do me a favor and express my condolences, too," she said. "Tell Wayne I'll be calling as soon as I can get it together."

"Of course."

Holly said, "One thing, though. Please don't tell him about . . . what your friend saw in the sink."

"I won't," she said. But Holly could hear the *why* in her voice.

"The thing is, Wayne doesn't . . . he never knew she had nosebleeds . . . and he tends to worry."

There was a pause. "Okay."

"Thanks, Simone."

Holly hung up knowing how ridiculous that must have sounded. *Wayne tends to worry.* The man's only daughter was dead. She was found on her bed with a knife in her hand and more blood on her sheets than inside her body—and Simone was supposed to believe he couldn't handle *nosebleeds*?

She thought about calling Simone back, telling her not to bother with Wayne, it probably wasn't a good idea . . . until that *watched* feeling returned, more forceful than ever. The rustling grew louder outside her window—too loud for a stray cat, too loud for a squirrel. A possum, maybe? A dog? Then . . .

She heard a voice out there, whispering her name.

Holly picked up her cordless receiver and padded to her window, quietly, carefully. She placed a hand on the curtain. "I am calling nine-one-one now!" She hit the three numbers. All she needed was to press the TALK button and she would be connected. Holly held her breath, yanked the curtains to the side, stared out the window. . . .

No one. No one in the bushes, no one in the yard, no one running across the street. Not even a stray cat. In some ways, this was more upsetting than seeing a face pressed against her window. If she couldn't trust her own ears, couldn't trust her own brain . . .

Holly grabbed the Vicodin bottle, took it with her into the kitchen, ran herself another glass of water, and cracked the childproof lid. This time, she wouldn't bother reading the label.

SEVEN

A s Simone ended her call to Holly, she was more perplexed than ever about the blood in the sink. But, she supposed, it didn't matter much. Whether it was from nosebleeds or injecting or Santeria or vampirism, none of it compared to slitting one's own throat. Besides, what Simone had gotten out of the conversation was a lot more valuable. She turned to Kathy. "Emerald's assistant just gave me her dad's home number!"

"That is awesome," Kathy said. "What are you going to do with it?"

"Umm . . . call him up and ask him questions?"

"Identify yourself, get some on-the-record quotes."

"Yes, that would be the plan." Simone started to pick up the phone, but Kathy grabbed her hand.

"Before you make that call, I want you to think about where that approach has gotten you so far."

Simone said, "I can tell where this is going, but—"

"I also want you to think about that assistant. How will she feel if she gets a call from Emerald's father— 'How dare you give an *Asteroid* reporter my number?' Imagine, she's lost a dear friend, she's out of a job, and she gets a call like that, from her dead boss's father?"

Simone frowned. "I'll tell him I got his number some-where else."

"Okay."

Simone started to pick up the phone again; Kathy stuck her hand over the dial pad. "Cut it out," Simone said.

"Bear with me a second," Kathy replied. "I just want you to think about Emerald's poor, poor dad. He lost his son Oz, and now his only daughter, his only *child,* has cut her own throat? Don't you think . . . what's Daddy's name?"

She sighed. "Wayne."

"Don't you think Wayne would rather hear from a *friend* of Emerald's? Maybe someone from her Kabbalah study group, or a PETA pal? You know, someone who could help put her life in perspective? Don't you think Wayne *deserves* that, rather than some *tabloid reporter* calling him up to ask *questions*?"

"Kathy," said Simone, "he deserves the truth."

"The truth is overrated. He deserves kindness." She gave Simone a long, meaningful look. "And you, honey, you deserve details."

Kathy's blue eyes sparkled like a sunlit ocean, and for what was easily the tenth or twentieth time since they'd met, Simone thought, *God, she is good.*

Kathy moved her hand away from the dial pad. "Do the right thing."

"I'm *trying.*" Slowly, Simone tapped Wayne Deegan's number into the phone. After one ring, she heard a man's voice that was so weak, it was as if someone had taken a vacuum cleaner to it, sucked out all its life. "Hello?"

"Mr. Deegan?"

"Yes."

"I . . ." Simone's throat clenched up. She swallowed. "I just wanted to tell you I'm so, so sorry for your loss. I can't even imagine how you must feel right now."

He said, "Who is this, please?"

Emerald's voice floated through her mind. *My dad believed in magic. He still does.*

"Hello?"

"I'm . . . I was . . . I'm Tina. Emerald's Pilates partner."

Kathy gave her a thumbs-up sign.

"I was . . . I'm wondering if I might be able to drop by. I have some flowers, and—"

Deegan said, "I'm allergic to flowers."

"Okay. Listen, I'm sorry to have bothered you." Simone shot Kathy an angry look.

Kathy shrugged her shoulders, mouthed the words "Oh well."

That's the last time I listen to her. Simone figured Deegan must have hung up the phone, and she was about to do the same, until she heard the man's voice again, the faintest hint of life in it. "You know what, Tina? I could use the company."

It wasn't until she was driving to Wayne Deegan's house in Arcadia that Simone's conscience woke up and started tearing at her. Before that, she'd been on a bit of a high. When she told Nigel that Emerald Deegan's father had invited her to his home, he'd looked her in the eye and said, "Well done." He'd even called New York and told Willard about it, mentioning Simone by name.

"Heartwarming, eye-popping, gut-wrenching," said Nigel as she walked out the door. "Get it fast. And don't hit traffic. We're closing the story in six hours."

Simone had sprinted out to her Jeep and taken off, car radio blasting, heart banging against her ribs, the words "heartwarming, eye-popping, gut-wrenching" running through her head like song lyrics. Not once did she feel guilty for telling this man—this man whose only daughter had bled to death that morning—that she was Emerald's Pilates partner. Not until now.

She opened her window and let the dirty air burrow into the side of her face. The Santa Anas had died down, but it was still hot beyond belief, and the heat seemed accusatory—it made her think of hot seats, of white-hot lamps from movie interrogation scenes.

On the car radio, Meat Loaf was wailing about how he'd do anything for love, but he wouldn't do *that*, and Simone wondered, what was her *that* when it came to this job? Did she even have a *that* anymore—or had two days at the *Asteroid* rendered her thatless?

She had lied to a grieving parent.

She glanced into the rearview mirror at the black Saab behind her, peered into the window of the yellow Beetle one lane over, the college girl behind the wheel smearing gloss on her lips. She gazed ahead, at the dirty pickup truck piled with rusted car parts, and in the lane to her right, at the elderly couple riding silently in some kind of Buick, staring straight ahead as if each of them were alone. Who knew what secrets any of these people had? Who knew what lies they were living with, what truths had hurt them beyond repair? Who knew what they were thinking, what played on their consciences, if they had ever betrayed or hurt or even killed. . . .

Simone shook her head. Jobs weren't supposed to pose existential dilemmas, but this one did. She'd received high honors in journalistic ethics and now . . . now she was an *insider*.

She saw the Santa Anita Avenue off-ramp and pulled off the freeway. Wayne Deegan's house was less than five minutes away and she couldn't afford to think about this, not now, when she had to bring back a story that would close in six hours. The story of a frail beauty whose dad no longer believed in magic. The story of a promising young TV star who had slashed her own throat . . . or . . .

I still wish I had a big sister.

Why?

Protection.

Or had been murdered. Did Emerald's father think she'd done that to herself? Or did he have doubts, like Holly?

A few blocks south of Wayne Deegan's street, Simone glanced into her rearview mirror and saw a black Saab.

It was the same Saab from the freeway—about ten years old, dusty, with tinted glass so you couldn't see the driver. *We're just going in the same direction*, Simone thought. But then she replayed the drive in her mind and realized that every time she'd looked in the rearview, the Saab had been there. A car length or two between them, yes, but the entire drive, in the same lane. . . .

Simone sped up so quickly her tires squealed. Just before she reached the stoplight on Santa Anita and Foothill, she put her right blinker on, shifted suddenly into the left lane and started moving into oncoming traffic, horns screaming at her. The black car clung to the space behind her. She felt like something out of an old Bruce Willis movie—this being the part where the Eurotrash with the ponytail leans out the side of the Saab and starts firing the submachine gun.

Her pulse raced; her head brimmed with questions as she powered west on Foothill, away from Wayne Deegan's house. Panicked as she was, she was also horribly confused—which was almost worse.

Who was following her? Why would anyone want to?

When she reached a space between the dividers on Foothill, Simone hung a quick left, tearing up some residential street whose name she didn't bother to check. After a few blocks on the new street, she forced herself to look into the rearview mirror again. No Saab—at least not where she could see it.

Simone made a U-turn and headed East on Foothill, retracing her steps, moving back toward Wayne Deegan's house. No Saab on the other side of Foothill. No Saab in the rearview. The black car was nowhere.

Okay . . . Maybe she'd managed to scare it off. Or maybe it had never been following her to begin with.

She took a deep breath, tried to focus on getting to Wayne Deegan's house. That was the important thing—not some disappearing 1995 compact. She glanced at the directions Deegan had given her. *Left on Santa Anita, four blocks up, another left on Woodland. The house is white brick. . . .*

On the radio, Simone heard a commercial for a new movie, *Devil's Road*, starring Chris Hart, whom she used to have a crush on back in high school. "Chris Hart as you've never seen him," said the solemn male voice-over, "and introducing . . . Dylan Leeds."

Dylan Leeds was apparently a woman—a woman with a thick California accent that, to Simone, sounded oddly familiar. "Please dewnt be thaht way, Dahniel . . . ," she said, her voice choked with emotion. *Who talks like that? Someone I know, or knew. . . .* Simone wracked her brain for a few moments and drew a blank.

It was the film's title that stayed with her, though. It felt prophetic. "Don't go down that road," intoned the voice-over, just as Simone made a left on Woodland—Wayne Deegan's road.

Simone drove slowly down the quiet, residential street, both eyes peeled for white brick. Like most nice neighborhoods in Southern California, everything here had a spit-shined look to it: not just the cars, but the green lawns and deep black driveways, the pink and red camellia bushes with their glossy leaves. All of it so perfect, so clean—as if the residents were trying to compensate for the air quality—or for something else.

Wayne Deegan's house was huge, a white-brick mini-mansion wedged into a lot better suited for a ranch house. Simone found it startling. Over the phone, he hadn't sounded like a mini-mansion kind of guy.

Even the doorbell was louder than she'd expected it to be, a sterile, electronic *bing*. She thought maybe a maid would answer the door, but then she heard a man's voice—the same defeated voice from the phone.

"Is that you, Tina?"

She inhaled sharply. "Yes, Mr. Deegan."

"Okay, just a minute."

Deegan cracked open the door, and she saw them, Emerald's geode eyes, set in the large, florid face of a man in his late fifties. It choked her up so much she had to stare at her shoes. Why was it genetics could be so moving?

"So you were friends with my little girl?"

"Yes," said Simone. "She was . . . just . . . wonderful."

He opened the door wider, revealing the whole of his big frame—the opposite of his daughter's, yet somehow just as frail. His thin gray hair stood half on end, and he wore frayed, navy blue sweatpants, a matching sweatshirt with the Dodgers logo across the front. He smelled faintly of ketchup.

In the geode eyes, she saw not tears but the threat of them, a kind of cloudiness. Her own father's eyes had looked the same when he told Simone and Greta about the death of their grandmother—his mother. It killed Simone that there were still men like this around—men with cloudy eyes who wanted to protect you from their emotions.

"The place is a mess," Deegan said. "Hope you don't mind." And Simone knew this whole Pilates partner thing was not going to work.

Wayne Deegan stopped reminding Simone of her father the minute she stepped into his house. When he'd mentioned the mess, she'd anticipated a little disorder—but not this. She tried to keep her expression neutral, like this was nothing unusual. Just a middle-aged gentleman, living alone. . . .

It was like a cityscape of old newspapers—rows and rows of them stacked up, yellowing and torn, intermingled with magazines, advertising supplements, and telephone books, some of the stacks as tall as Simone, some just one *Wall Street Journal* away from toppling and causing a hideous domino effect. Deegan was a big man, but in Simone's opinion it would be entirely possible for him to fall victim to his own compulsion, suffocated by newsprint, unable to free himself.

Simone tried to keep her tone neutral. "Did Emerald ever visit you here?"

"Oh, sure," he said. "Every Sunday."

"Really?!"

"I'd make her coffee, we'd catch up, listen to jazz records. I'm a collector."

That is certainly true. She tried to picture Emerald roaming through all this detritus in high heels, bracelets jangling. Several paths wound through the stacks of papers, and Deegan took one of the wider ones, his sneakers crunching on errant pages that had drifted to the dusty wooden floors. Simone followed, glancing at a page as she stepped on it—*LA Times.* January 1, 2000.

"Can I get you a cup of coffee, Tina?"

"No, thanks." She followed Deegan into a den, where more newspaper piles loomed over the furniture like disapproving parents. Simone's brain shouted, *Tell him who you really are!* It was bad enough to lie to a grieving father, but to lie to one with an obvious mental illness . . .

Deegan sat down on the couch, which was large and elegant, covered in thick jade silk. It didn't look like something he'd pick out for himself, and Simone wondered if it was a gift from Emerald. She sat down beside him, her gaze shooting to the coffee table, to stacks of *Time, Newsweek, People* . . . not a tabloid in sight.

"You know," Deegan said, "Emerald never mentioned taking a Pilates class."

"Mr. Deegan, I'm so sorry."

He nodded "Thank you."

"No, I mean . . ." Simone looked into those cloudy eyes again. *There is no easy way to say it, so stop trying to find one.* "I'm not really Emerald's Pilates partner."

He gazed at her. "You're not?"

"No. . . ." She took a deep breath, in and out. "I'm a reporter for the *Asteroid.* I lied to get you to talk to me."

Deegan was silent, and so was Simone, and for a while they both sat there, her words hanging in the still air like subtitles.

Simone took a breath. "I met Emerald one time, on the *Suburban Indiscretions* set. I probably spent a total of fifteen minutes with her, but even then, she mentioned you. She said you believed in magic, and I could tell she loved you very much."

She ventured a glance at Deegan, who was closing his eyes tight, pinching the bridge of his nose to stem the flow of tears. "I guess I'd better leave now," she said.

Deegan opened his eyes. "Don't go."

Simone looked at him.

"Hey, you came all this way, I should at least talk to you."

"Really?"

"Why not?" he said. "You're a hell of a lot nicer than the *Times* reporter who called. And like I said before, I could use the company."

By the time they'd been talking for twenty minutes, Simone's microcassette recorder placed on the coffee table atop a 1999 *People*, she had forgotten about the smell of dust and newsprint, the leaning, moldering piles of periodicals, and even the fire threat they posed.

Because, aside from all that, Wayne Deegan was a remarkably normal and humble man—especially for this town. A former sound engineer for a small record company who had lost his wife to cancer, he had tried his best to raise his daughter alone. He told Simone, "It was hard. There were a lot of things, I think, Emerald couldn't talk to me about."

"Like?"

"Boys, makeup, clothes. . . . Emerald's mom died when she was just three, and I never had too many female friends—or friends in general, so . . . she kind of had to figure out that stuff on her own."

Simone leaned forward. "What about Emerald's brother? Were they close?"

He gave her a blank look. "Brother?"

"Yes," said Simone. "When I met her on set, she mentioned a brother named Oz?"

Deegan stared at her, the color draining from his face. She cleared her throat. "Did I say something wrong?"

"She knew his name."

Simone said, "What do you mean?"

"Oz was Emerald's twin."

"But why wouldn't—"

"He was stillborn."

Simone's gaze went straight to the floor. "Oh."

When Deegan spoke again, his voice was slight and faraway, like someone hypnotized, recalling a troubling dream. "I don't know how she learned his name," he said. "She . . . Emerald was a very sensitive person. Too sensitive."

"How do you mean?"

"If Oz was a girl, we would have named her Glinda, but I never told Emerald either of those names. She went through a phase, she was about six. . . . She kept telling me she ate too much of Mommy's food when she was in her tummy. Said she starved her brother to death and Mommy too. I kept trying to tell her that wasn't true at all, that she was the light of my life and . . ." He ran the back of his hand over his eyes, swallowed hard.

"It's okay," said Simone "It's . . ."

"She stopped eating. Didn't eat anything I made her, and I tried everything. I figured she was just picky. Lots of kids are, and she said she was eating her school lunches, but . . . she got real pale and skinny and . . . one day I got a call from the school nurse. She had fainted in class."

"You must have been so scared."

He nodded. "I rushed her to the hospital. They said she was dehydrated. They hooked her up to IVs, and when she got some strength back I took her in to see a shrink that specialized in anorexia. Anorexia at six . . ." Deegan looked at Simone. "But it wasn't like that. It wasn't about how she looked. It was because she felt bad for being alive."

Simone recalled Emerald's thin, thin body, heard her say, *Nerves.*

Deegan ran a hand through his fine, dull hair. "You understand what I'm saying?" he said. "When you tell me she mentioned Oz to you, and then . . . then this morning she . . ." His voice trailed off.

Simone said, "Did Emerald seem unusually upset recently?"

"No," said Deegan. "But the thing is, she *never* acted upset around me. She was always my cheerful girl, never told me anything bad. I've read stuff in the papers—your paper, too—about her boyfriend, Keith . . . running around with other women, not treating Emerald the way she deserved. She said, 'Don't believe what you read, Daddy. Keith and I are great.'" He swiped his face with the sleeve of his sweatshirt and said, "I don't know how to do this."

"It's okay, Mr. Deegan. We can end it now if you like."

"I don't mean the interview," he said. "I don't know how to . . . I don't know how to live without my little girl. This isn't the way it's supposed to go. This shouldn't be something I have to *learn.*"

Simone just looked at him. What could she say to that? He was right.

Wayne Deegan sent Simone off with a microcassette full of details Nigel was bound to love, plus a stack of personal photos—Emerald dressed as a ballerina for Halloween, Emerald as a tomboyish preteen in soccer clothes, Emerald glamorous in her prom dress with her very tall date, both of them smiling nervously for her father's camera.

"She left home not too long after that one was taken," he had said. "'Someday, Daddy,' she said, 'I'm gonna get so rich I can buy you a big house.' Three years later, she bought me this castle."

"She sure kept her promise," said Simone.

He stuck out a big, meaty hand, and Simone shook it. "I hope I was able to help you."

"Oh, you did," said Simone. "I'm pretty sure you saved my job."

"Good. You seem like a nice kid—and don't worry. You got an exclusive. I'm talked out for a while."

She smiled. "Thank you, Mr. Deegan." She started to open the door, then stopped. "One more question, if it's okay?"

"Sure."

"Did Emerald, by any chance, know Nia Lawson?"

He squinted at her. "The gal who fooled around with that congressman and then . . ."

"Yes."

"I don't think so," he said. "Wait, you're not saying there's a . . . connection or anything, are you? Like some kind of trend?"

"No," Simone said. "I wasn't—"

"Because Emerald had her problems. But she wouldn't . . . she wouldn't do this to people who loved her because of a trend."

"I know that."

He trained his gaze on her, his expression very serious. "You can use everything I said," he told her. "But treat my little girl fair, Tina. Okay?"

"I will." Simone took her steno pad out of her purse, wrote down her cell phone number, and handed it to him. "If you think of anything else, give me a call. By the way, my name's not Tina. It's Simone. But please don't tell Emerald's assistant what I do, okay? She thinks I'm Emerald's tennis pro."

He smiled at her, and said, "Sure." As if that were the most normal request in the world.

As she walked out to her car, Simone gazed at the prom photo, at Emerald's eyes. Despite the smile, there was such sadness in them. And something else, something dark and secret. *Maybe Emerald really did kill herself.*

But the thought was interrupted by a tingle of fear, strong and sharp between her shoulder blades. Simone spun around, peered into the bushes that lined Deegan's short driveway. When she saw no one there, her gaze darted up the street and down, searching for that black Saab, because she knew what the fear tingle meant. It was instinctive; there was no mistaking it.

Someone was watching her.

EIGHT

Holly took two Vicodin, slept for two hours, and woke up feeling groggy but a good deal clearer about what had happened at her window. She was not going insane. She was simply stressed out and grieving and, yes, hearing things. As she'd learned in one of her college psych classes, perfectly normal people can hallucinate aurally when under extreme duress.

She just needed to take better care of herself. She needed to eat, to get some rest. That way, the next time she spoke to the police, they might actually believe her.

Holly remembered her last conversation with Detective Bianchi, back at Emerald's house.

I know you don't want to face it, Ms. Kashminian, but your boss was a sad and troubled woman.

You didn't know her. You never saw her alive.

That may be true, but—

Emerald would never kill herself no matter what you think. And the note . . .

We all know how you feel about the note, ma'am.

Holly rolled her eyes. "What a bitch." Not to worry, though. She'd rest. She'd make an appointment to see that detective. And she would prove her point. Emerald had been murdered.

Holly's phone rang, and she picked it up without looking at the caller ID. "Hello?"

She heard nothing but breathing. She looked at the screen: BLOCKED CALL. "Keith?"

"Hnnhhh," went the breath, with no voice behind it.

"Who is this?"

She heard the wet sound of a tongue clicking. Then the caller started to laugh. Holly slammed down the phone, but that laugh stayed with her—a laugh she not so much heard as *felt*, dry and stinging, down the side of her neck.

By the time Simone was back on 134 Freeway, the feeling of being watched had eased a little. But that didn't stop her from glancing into the rearview mirror every three or four minutes, checking for that Saab as she gripped the wheel.

When Simone's cell phone chimed, she nearly swerved into the next lane. She checked the caller ID and her heart rate slowed back to normal. Of course it was Nigel. Who else would it be?

"Details?" he said.

"Yes, Nigel, lots of them. Heartwarming, eye-popping, the works," Simone said. "All on the record. Exclusive to the *Asteroid*."

"Right," said Nigel, in a tone that felt thrillingly close to praise.

Simone had an urge to pump her arm and shout, "Yes!" until Nigel said, "Do you think we could send a photographer over there for a shoot? New York says they're willing to stay late."

Simone cringed, her mind filled with images of those stacked-up newspapers, of headlines about psycho dads and apples not falling far from trees. "He won't sit for a shoot," she said. "I already asked him."

"Right," Nigel said. "Well, at least we've got the exclusive."

"Yes, absolutely."

"Oh, that reminds me, did Emerald's dad mention anything about her doing pornos?"

Simone coughed. "What?"

"Escort work, perhaps? There's been a rumor about for months, concerning her whoring herself around Hollywood before she got her big break."

"No, Nigel. Emerald's *grieving father* didn't mention—"

"We'll make do, then. Very good."

Click.

Simone stared at her phone, thinking, *Was that what he meant by details?* For the briefest of moments, she remembered what Wayne Deegan had said: Emerald bought him that house *three years* after she left home. She was still unknown back then. How could she have made that much money?

Treat my little girl fair.

She forced the thought out of her mind.

The ringtone trilled again, and Simone picked it up, not to Nigel's voice but to a woman's—thick and a little slurry. "He's watching me, Simone."

Her shoulders tensed up. "Holly?"

"He called me. He didn't say anything, but I'm sure it was him. He . . . laughed."

"Who? Who called you?"

"Whoever killed Emerald."

"What?!" said Simone.

For several seconds, there was no response. Nothing but shallow breathing and the faint buzz of static.

"Holly, are you . . . feeling okay?"

"I took a Xanax," she said. "Listen, can I talk to you in person?"

"Well, I—"

"Please. I . . . I don't feel comfortable with phones right now."

Holly wanted to meet at the Green Earth Macrobiotic Café, which as it turned out was located in Beverly Hills, just a few blocks from the *Asteroid*. It was a spartan place with hard, unyielding chairs and lights bright enough to be used for interrogation.

It was also very loud. Because there were no draperies or carpeting or even tablecloths (Were vegans against textiles?), there was nothing at all to muffle conversation, so the minute you opened the door, you were practically knocked back against it by echoing, aggressive chatter.

Simone searched the noisy space until, finally, she caught sight of Holly sitting alone at a corner table, staring into a clear mug of tea. Even from across the room, she looked exhausted, defeated.

It was worse close up.

Holly said, "I hope I didn't drag you away from a lesson or anything."

"No," said Simone. "I'm kind of between lessons."

"Well, thanks for coming. I know this place is out of the way, but it feels . . . safe, you know? Maybe it's the bright lights or something."

"What's this about a phone call?"

"Oh, that," said Holly. "Seriously, if this was yesterday, I would have just thought it was a prank call or the wrong number. But . . . ever since this morning . . . ever since I went to Emerald's, I've felt . . . watched."

"I feel that way too," Simone said.

Holly gaped at her. "You do?"

"Well, not so much now, but earlier I did."

"That must be why I called you," Holly said. "Something tells me you're the right person to talk to about this."

"Intuition."

"Yeah."

Simone recalled Emerald back in the trailer. *I've got good intuition about people.* She felt that stab of guilt again and swallowed, as if to smooth it out, digest it. She eased herself into the chair across from Holly's and said, very quietly, "You think Emerald was murdered?"

"I *know* she was."

Simone's eyes widened.

A waitress the color of skim milk approached. "Can I get you anything?" she said, her voice just as tired and slow as Simone expected it would be.

"Tea," Simone said, just to get her away from the table.

"We have chamomile, Darjeeling, jasmine, ginger-peach—"

"Same as she's having," Simone said. As soon as the waitress walked away, she said, "Did the police say it was murder?"

"The police don't know a damn thing!"

She took a breath. "Okay."

"Sorry. It's just, if I hear one more time about no sign of forced entry, I'm going to scream. They didn't *know* Emerald." Holly opened the messenger bag she'd slung over the back of her chair, removed a thin stack of papers, and placed them on the table in front of Simone. "I want you to look at these."

Simone thumbed through the stack, a series of notes to Holly written on lined paper in the same neat block letters she'd seen on the grocery list Holly had taken out of her back pocket earlier, at the crime scene. "Are these from her?" said Simone.

Holly nodded.

She began to read.

> H—PLEASE PICK UP DRY CLEANING.
> H—WAS CALLED BACK ON SET FOR RESHOOTS. PLEASE CANCEL IVY DINNER RESERVATION.
> H—PLEASE BUY TIFFANY TIE CLIP AND BIRTHDAY CARD FOR DADDY. YOU CAN USE MY VISA.

"Notice anything?" Holly said.

Simone looked up at her. Outside of Emerald's perfect, somewhat anal-retentive script there was nothing remarkable about these notes. "Umm . . ."

"What do they all have in common?"

"They're all written to you?"

"Yes, but that's not . . ." Holly sighed. "Okay. . . . You know those spiral notebooks? They've got the wire coil on the side, and you tear the pages out?" She made a ripping gesture with both hands. "Like this? The edge that's been ripped out, it gets kind of crumbly."

Simone had no idea where she was going with this.

"Look at all these notes," Holly said. "They're ripped out of spiral notebooks, but the edges are smooth. That's because Emerald had a thing about shags."

"Shags?"

"The crumbly edges. Whenever she ripped a page out of one of her notebooks, she had to make sure all the shags were off, and that the edges were smooth. It was like . . . a compulsion."

"Interesting," Simone said.

Holly closed her eyes. Her face went absolutely still. "The note she left."

"You mean the suicide note?"

Holly nodded. "There were shags on it."

Simone stared at her.

"She wouldn't do that." Holly looked up. Her eyes were wet. "She just . . . I know she wouldn't."

"Did you tell the police?"

"Yeah, but they won't listen."

"Maybe . . . maybe they know best, Holly. Maybe people forget things like . . . shags when they've decided to kill themselves."

Holly's gaze went hard. "The police do not know best," she said. "They think she wanted to kill herself because she was a . . ."

"A what?"

"She wasn't completely happy."

Holly's voice sounded small and lost, and in her eyes Simone saw something else, something besides grief and anger. . . . "Holly," said Simone, "what did the note say?"

The waitress came back to the table. "One ginger-peach," she said. "Can I get you honey or—"

"No."

"Maybe some lemon or—"

"*No.*"

The waitress walked away, muttering something Simone couldn't hear, though she was pretty sure she got the gist.

"It's not important what the note said, because Emerald didn't write it. I mean, not of her own free will."

"Still."

Holly exhaled. "It said, 'I love you, Daddy. I'm sorry.'"

Simone searched her face. "That's all?"

"Yeah. No reason why she did it. No instructions, nothing about Keith." Holly sipped her tea. "Nothing about . . ." Her voice faded.

You. There was nothing about you in the note, no "I'm sorry, Holly," and she must have known you were coming in early the next morning, must have known you would be the one to find her.

"Sometimes," Simone said, "people want to hurt themselves so badly, they don't think about who they're taking down with them."

"No," said Holly. "You don't understand."

"I think I might."

"You *don't*." She closed her eyes and started speaking again, her voice tremulous, pained, as if someone were dragging the words out of her. "When I found Emerald, she wasn't wearing her bracelets."

Simone looked at her.

"Do you have any idea how fucking weird that is? She didn't even take them off to shower."

"Maybe . . . maybe she wanted to get rid of worldly possessions."

"Those worldly possessions," Holly said, "were covering scars."

Simone's eyes widened. *You can't help but think . . . What is underneath? What is she hiding?* She recalled the fresh pool of blood in the sink, the way Emerald had acted when she first invited Kathy and Simone into her trailer. Upbeat, but only temporarily. . . . Then, the terror in Emerald's voice as she spoke to Matthew. *I didn't agree to answer questions about . . . my personal choices.*

"She cut herself," said Simone. "She cut her own wrists."

Holly nodded. "The backs of her ankles, too. She said it released the pain. Made her feel more alive." Her eyes glistened. "I'm the only one who knew—I don't even think Keith . . . Her dad can't find out. It would kill him, I swear to God it would."

Simone recalled the blood dripping down the heel of the shoe—the shoe she'd assumed was Nia Lawson's. *The backs of her ankles.*

"My third day working for Emerald, I walked in on her . . . bleeding into her dressing room sink," Holly said. "She was so ashamed. I promised I'd never tell anybody."

"And you kept your word."

She nodded, stared at her hands. "She needed help, probably. She was a self-mutilator, and that kind of thing can escalate. I've read up on it. But you know . . . you make excuses. You rationalize. The cuts weren't that deep. It was her business, not mine. Everybody has secrets. . . ." She looked at Simone. "It's amazing what you tell yourself, just to avoid doing the right thing."

Simone cringed a little. "Yeah." She took a sip of her tea and held it in her mouth—the tang of peach. It made her think of summer in Wappingers Falls, of fruit stands and mosquitoes and thick, humid air . . . of going through a whole day with nothing to hide. "What if it *did* escalate—the cutting?" she said, finally. "What if Emerald slit her own throat because—"

"She didn't."

"How do you know?"

Holly exhaled. "Emerald had a secret collection of knives. No one knew about it except me. They were surgical knives." Holly held Simone's gaze. "She was killed with one of those knives."

"I thought it was a paring knife."

"That's what I told the press. You understand?" said Holly. "Emerald didn't want *anyone* to see those knives, didn't want anyone to know about them. Ever. If she used one to kill herself, everyone would know. Everyone would see. The police. Her father . . ." Holly's eyes were pink-rimmed and teary, her pupils dilated from whatever pills she'd taken. But Simone had to admit, she had a point.

"She didn't ever want her father to know about the knives," Holly said. "She didn't ever want her father to see the scars."

Simone nodded. "I understand."

"Please," said Holly, "don't tell anyone."

Simone said, "I won't. I promise." And she meant it.

As she left the restaurant and headed back to her Jeep, Simone saw that image once again—Emerald's white hand on the bed, the frail, bare wrist crusted with blood. Holly could be wrong, she knew. Emerald was a cutter—a fragile, unhappy woman who had just found out that her boyfriend of two years had betrayed her yet again. If ever there was someone who fit a suicide profile . . . But as Simone recalled that lifeless hand, one unanswerable question entered her mind . . .

What had happened to Emerald's bracelets?

Destiny's finger was very swollen. The top part looked as if someone had shoved an air pump in and inflated it 'til it was ready to burst. She couldn't move the finger. It was bruised close to black, plus it throbbed and throbbed—an alarm going off. She couldn't do much about it, though, not now. Maybe once she got hold of her eight thousand dollars, once she found a bus and then a plane and traveled far from here, far from him. Then she could take care of the finger. Of course, by that point she might need to have it amputated.

When Destiny had first arrived here, at this crappy hotel, she'd knocked on her neighbor's door. The neighbor was a skinny woman with steel-wool hair and terrible meth mouth, what few broken teeth she had clinging to her gums like shards of glass. Her eyes had that dullness that people's eyes get when they're ill, that overcooked look. At first, the woman had only cracked the door. But when Destiny had held up that finger, the crack had gone wide open.

"Holy shit, who did that to you?" The woman gave Destiny three plastic bottles of vodka to wash her wounds, a half-eaten bag of Doritos, and a six-pack of Coke—everything she had, she explained. Then she pushed her out, as if the finger were contagious or something.

Destiny wasn't sure the vodka had been a good idea. It had burned so bad it made her scream, and after she was through cleaning it, the finger throbbed as much as ever. But what was she going to do? It wasn't like she could check herself into Cedars-Sinai. She had no money, no insurance. And anyway, she couldn't risk being seen. Not with him out there. A powerful man—a VIP—looking for her.

She was afraid to use her phone because he might be able to trace it, but she didn't have a choice. She had made one call—to her friend Leticia. Leticia was not a Pleasures girl. She was a specialty performer, and the only person Destiny knew who could keep a secret . . . she kept so many of them.

Leticia had an extra key to Destiny's house. Whenever Destiny went away for a few days, Leticia would collect her mail, water her plants. She was like that. Trustworthy.

So when Destiny called Leticia and asked her to use her key, go into her bedroom, remove the sealed envelope from her underwear drawer and bring it, at midnight, to the Starbright Hotel in East LA, she knew Leticia would do it just as Destiny said, no questions asked. She knew Leticia wouldn't mention the blood on the floor unless Destiny said something about it first. And when Destiny added, just before hanging up, "In the kitchen, you'll see a picture of me and Snow White from when I was a kid. Can you bring that too?" she knew Leticia would, without telling anyone anything.

She had specifically said, "Don't call back." That's why it was scary when Destiny heard Nick Lachey's "What's Left of Me"—her ringtone—slipping out of her purse. In her head, she started coming up with other things it could be—the neighbor's radio, her imagination. She didn't want to believe it was really her cell phone. Destiny communicated with everyone via Black-Berry. Very few people had her number. Very few. Her breathing shallow, she pulled the phone out of her purse, thinking, *No, no, please, no. . . .*

Leticia's number was on the screen.

"Hey," Destiny said. "I told you not to—"

"I'm sorry, baby," Leticia said, "but I checked your panty drawer, and there was no envelope in there."

"There *wasn't*?"

"I checked all the other drawers, just in case you made a mistake, and it wasn't there either."

Destiny bit her lip. *He took my money.* "Okay, well, did you—"

"I didn't find any Snow White picture in the kitchen either."

"What?!" He had taken her mom's picture. For some reason, that hurt even worse than the money. Tears sprung to her eyes. She didn't want to start crying, not on the phone with Leticia, plus she needed to end the call fast. She made her voice cheerful. "No worries. Thanks for trying."

"No problem, baby."

I have no money. I can't leave. "You rock, Tish."

"Anything else I can do?"

"Nah. Listen, I gotta run. See you soon." *Please let him forget me. Please, please.* . . .

"By the way, Dessy, do you have a new boyfriend?"

"No. Why?"

"Nothing really." Leticia chuckled. "It's just . . . I've never seen your place looking so clean before."

NINE

Writing up "the meat," as Nigel called it, Simone avoided all mention of scarred wrists and secret compulsions, focusing only on her on-the-record interview with Wayne Deegan. While questions still pulled at her—*What happened to Emerald's bracelets? Why would she cut her throat with one of her secret knives?*—Simone was able to put those questions aside, keeping her promise to Holly as she crafted Wayne's anecdotes into a six-hundred-word piece.

If she did say so herself, the piece was good. The headline read EMERALD'S SECRET TRAGEDY: THE BROTHER SHE NEVER KNEW with an "exclusive" banner across the top. When Kathy read it, she got tears in her eyes and said, "That's beautiful, honey." Elliot said the article got him, much like Duran Duran's "Save a Prayer" got him, "right in the heart." And Matthew told Simone, "You're fantastic," in a way that made her turn the color of a good Merlot. Even Carl the receptionist wanted an advance copy to take home to his mother.

Best of all, Nigel said, "Nice work."

Nice. Work. The entire drive home, Simone savored

those two words like Belgian chocolate, rolling them over and over in her mind. She felt so proud of herself, she almost called Greta and told her everything—the *LA Edge* folding, her terrible month, her interview at the *Asteroid,* stealing garbage—just so she could brag about "Nice work." But by the time she got into her apartment, she'd reconsidered.

Instead, Simone stopped in the kitchen, opened the Napa Valley pinot noir she'd bought at the Vons down the street, back when she was floored by the fact that they sold all types of alcohol at LA grocery stores. Simone had bought the wine for a special occasion and, though she'd been thinking more along the lines of a hot date, "Nice work" qualified. Anyway, if her first month here was any indication, this stuff would turn to vinegar if she saved it for a hot date, or even a tepid one.

She took a wineglass out of her cupboard, poured herself a nice-sized serving. The wine was smooth and dry and luxurious on her palate and it soothed all the way down, like an internal massage.

She sat down on the sofa bed, which was more of a love seat, actually. She'd found it at Ikea and had it shipped—the one piece of furniture she'd bought for her life in LA—because the color had stirred something in her. It was a soft, sweet red, like construction paper valentines.

Simone took another sip of wine. Sometime in the course of stopping back at her place this morning after Emerald's, changing out of the tennis whites, showering, dressing, and going back to work, she'd straightened up her apartment, making and folding up her bed in the process. Damned if she could remember any of it, though. So much had happened since then.

She flipped on her TV. The local news was on. One of those live, televised police car chases they were always showing out here. (Something Orwellian about those, too. Or *Mad Max*ian. Or something.) An overhead shot—three squad cars chasing a stolen Escalade, an announcer breathlessly intoning, "He's never gonna get away. He does not stand a chance." And that, for some reason, made her think of Emerald. Simone had borrowed clothes from her one day, seen her lifeless body the next. How vulnerable that bare hand had been, how sad. A frail woman who made herself bleed, just so she could feel alive.

She did not stand a chance.

Back at the office, Simone had seen a photo of Keith Furlong. He was very tall, and not so much handsome as pretty, the type of pretty that takes hard work. In the picture, he was standing in front of his club with Emerald, wearing a pink wife-beater, baggy shorts with hula girls all over them, and an entire jar of gel in his hair. His eyebrows were tweezed, his chest waxed. His muscles bulged in that globular, gym-rat way that spoke more of artfully placed scar tissue than of actual strength. Emerald was gazing up at Keith, an adoring look on her face. He was grinning at the camera.

Not a chance.

Was Keith missing Emerald now? Was he grieving like Holly, like Wayne? Had he seen it coming, her death—the violence of it? Or was he out partying with Destiny right now, showing off those bleached teeth and spending her eight thousand dollars, saying things like, "Life goes on"?

"They're heading off the Escalade!" cried the announcer. "It is the end of the line for our thief!"

Simone turned the TV off. She could hear crickets outside her window, the only bugs she'd encountered in LA. And somehow, she found their chirping more lonely than silence.

She brought the glass into the kitchen and poured the rest of the wine back into the bottle. She needed to turn in. She had work tomorrow, and it would be another big day. She and Kathy were set to pose as cater-waiters at a party for that movie she'd heard advertised, *Devil's Road*. As Nigel would probably say, no one would take hors d'oeuvres from Simone if she had dark circles under her eyes. And regardless, she didn't much feel like celebrating anymore.

Later, as Simone lay in bed, lingering in the last moments of consciousness with those sad crickets chorusing outside her window, she found herself thinking of Wayne Deegan . . . alone in the house Emerald had bought him, wandering the paths between his newspaper towers. How long would he last without her Sunday visits, without his little girl?

She thought of Holly. Would she find another job, move on, recover? Or would all of it stay with her, like a pin stuck in her finger, hurting just as much whenever she looked at it directly: That awful creeping certainty that her boss had not killed herself, she had been murdered. That *watched* feeling . . . and most of all that powerlessness, knowing that no matter what she told the police, they wouldn't believe her.

What if Holly was right?

TEN

Ring . . .

Simone jolted awake, her eyes seeking out the clock by her bedside: *6:00.* Her phone rang again, and she groaned. Was Nigel going to do this every morning? She checked the caller ID. It wasn't Nigel. She picked up the phone, her heart pounding. "Mother?"

"You're still asleep?"

"It's six in the morning. Is everything okay? Is Dad—"

"Oh, honey. I'm so sorry. Yes, yes. Daddy's fine. I forgot about the time difference."

Simone exhaled hard.

"Shall I call back later?"

"No," she said. "That's okay. I've got to get up soon anyway."

"Well, I think you'll be glad I called, because I have some very exciting news."

Simone rubbed her eyes. "What is it?"

"Your sister has been nominated for a Glory Award."

"A . . . a what?"

"A Glory, dear," she said. "It's one of journalism's highest honors."

"It is?"

"For broadcast cable journalism, yes. Anyway, Greta has gotten tickets for all of us. The ceremony is a month from now in New York City, and it's televised!"

"But—"

"Don't worry about plane fare. Your father and I will send you a ticket."

"I just . . . I don't know whether I can get the time off."

"You just tell them your sister has been nominated for a Glory and they will definitely give you the time off," she said. "They're journalists, aren't they—the people you work for?"

"Uhhh . . ."

Simone's mother's voice went soft. "I'm sorry, Simone. I didn't even ask. How are things going at the *Side*?"

"The *Edge*, Mother."

"You doing all right? You need us to send you anything?"

"No."

"Are you sure? I know the cost of living in Los Angeles is not—"

"I'm fine. . . . Terrifyingly fine."

"I am so glad to hear that."

"And I can afford my own plane ticket."

Simone said good-bye and hung up the phone quickly, thinking about how, in the past few days, she'd probably told more lies than she had in her entire adult life. But out of all of them, the lies she'd just told her mother were the ones she couldn't imagine taking back.

Simone arrived at work to Matthew looming over Carl's shoulder, both of them staring intently at the receptionist's computer screen. "Did he just call her his breakfast, lunch, and dinner?" Carl said.

"Better dialogue than *Alexander*," said Matthew.

"Yes, and for a celebrity sex tape, it's well acted, too!"

Simone peeked at the screen, saw what looked to be Colin Farrell . . . quite a bit of Colin Farrell. If Simone were watching this with Matthew Varrick's lips inches from her ear, she definitely wouldn't have enough breath left in her to answer phones in a professional manner. Carl had to be straight. Like a Kinsey 1. That was the only logical explanation.

Simone cleared her throat. "So I guess that's considered work-related research?"

When Matthew and Carl turned to look at her, their smiles disappeared. "Hello, Simone," said Carl. His eyes were big with concern.

"What's wrong?" she asked.

"It will pass."

Simone hurried back to the reporters' room. Elliot and Kathy were both there, involved in a hushed and animated conversation that ended—immediately—when Simone walked through the door.

"What the hell is going on?" said Simone.

Kathy shook her head.

Elliot said, "No offense, but I'm really glad I'm not you."

Before she could say any more, Nigel stormed into the room, his lips a crack in his face, the anger in his eyes so pure it bordered on murderous.

She expected him to explode—literally—but when his voice came out it was witheringly quiet. "Tell me why I should ever trust you again."

"I . . . I . . . *what*?"

On the desk nearest Simone, Nigel carefully placed a layout from next week's *Interloper*. "We have a spy there," he said, "who faxed this to me this morning."

Simone looked at the page. All the air seemed to rush out of her body at once.

The headline read, EXCLUSIVE! EMERALD'S DAD: MY SECRET BATTLE WITH HOARDING DISORDER. The page was filled with photos of Wayne Deegan in his worn Dodgers sweats, standing in various rooms of his house—surrounded, sometimes enveloped, by those threatening stacks of newspapers.

"You told me he promised us an exclusive!" Nigel bellowed. "You told me he wouldn't sit for a photo shoot! You never even mentioned he's a nutter!"

Simone read. The article was both candid and respectful—especially for something printed in a supermarket tabloid. In a first-person piece that read as if Wayne were speaking out loud, he detailed his lifelong struggle with OCD—the hoarding aspect of which had only become prevalent in the last several years—and bipolar disorder. "It's hereditary," he told the reporter. "I think Emerald may have had it, too. I sure know there have been times when *I* wanted to kill myself. I yearn for my only daughter—for the grandchildren I will never have. But the truth is, I can relate. I know the pain she must have felt. I know it because I have felt it, firsthand."

Simone winced. Nigel had every right to be angry. Compared to this, the piece she'd written was a bedtime story for toddlers.

"As of now, you are on probation," said Nigel. "If I do not get something brilliant from you by the end of the week, do not bother to come in on Monday. Your trial here is complete."

He left the room. Kathy and Elliot looked at Simone as though she'd just been given two days to live. She picked up her cell, tapped in Wayne's number, and tried to control her anger. He was still a grieving parent, after all. You can't scream, "What the fuck?!" at a grieving parent.

"Mr. Deegan?"

"Hi, Simone."

She cleared her throat. "Listen . . . I know it's a terrible time for you but—"

"You heard about the *Interloper*."

"Yeah, I mean . . ."

"I know. I promised you the exclusive. I hope you didn't get in too much trouble."

"To tell the truth, I did."

"I'm really sorry. It's just . . . about five minutes after you left, this really nice young man showed up. We got to talking and . . ."

He kept speaking, but Simone was having difficulty distinguishing the words. She was too busy staring at the small byline at the bottom of the page. *Reported by Neil Walker.*

". . . and *his* father had hoarding issues too. . . ."

"Do you." Simone's voice came out a full octave higher than its usual range. She took a breath. "Do . . . you . . . happen to know if this reporter was driving a black Saab?"

"He was!" he said. "Saw it when I walked him out to his car. Do you know him?"

"No," said Simone. "I do not know him at all."

She was aware of Nigel's voice out in the hallway stammering into his cell phone. "I . . . I know. . . . Yes, Willard, he did promise an exclusive . . . but . . . but . . . but . . ."

Simone said good-bye and hung up the phone, still glaring at Walker's byline.

As Simone and Kathy drove to the *Devil's Road* party, another *Devil's Road* commercial played on the radio.

"That's good luck," Kathy said, somewhat lamely. "Hearing a commercial for the movie whose party we'll be infiltrating."

Simone said, "Not a superstition I'm familiar with."

Over Kathy's speakers, Dylan Leeds said, "Please dewnt be thaht way, Dahniel." Again Simone thought, *Where have I heard that voice?* And again she drew a blank. The announcer then mentioned that the film had been directed by Jason Caputo. The son of the deceased Oscar-winning director Terrence Caputo, Jason was getting a lot of press as a wunderkind, a talent, a *"hot find."* But come on. . . . With a name like Caputo, how hard could it be to *find* him? Some people had all the luck. The announcer listed the film's other stars: Garrett Durant, Miranda Boothe, Blake Moss.

"Ooh, Blake Moss," said Kathy. "Now there's a naughty boy."

She was right. The star of a huge sex scandal around eight years back, Blake Moss was known more for his kinky tastes and wild, bacchanalian parties than he was for his movie roles. Simone perked up. Maybe she would get some dirt at this event. Maybe her job would be saved.

"Don't hold your breath," said Kathy.

"Huh?"

"Blake Moss won't go to a party unless he can snort cocaine off some starlet's ass crack."

Simone's spirits dropped. "That's pretty impressive," she said, "that whole mind-reading thing. Have you always been able to do that, or did you take a class?"

"Santeria," said Kathy.

"Ah. Should've known."

On the radio, Ray Charles sang "Busted." Simone wondered if that, too, was good luck—or if he was simply reading her mind.

The *Devil's Road* event was being held at the Beverlido Hotel, a former eyesore on Sunset Boulevard that some supermodel's architect husband had restored to all its 1950s Copacabana-ish glory. Kathy and Simone were getting ready in the women's staff locker room. As Kathy helped her with her red bowtie, it hit Simone anew, the futility of it all. "I don't even know why I'm bothering," she said. "I'm out on Monday, anyway."

"Don't be that way," Kathy said, which made Simone remember Dylan Leeds's line from the radio ad, and at last she felt it wash over her—the relief of recognition.

"Julie Curtis," she said.

"Huh?"

"Nothing. I was just thinking about Dylan Leeds—from the movie. She sounds exactly like this girl I went to high school with. . . ."

For one frozen moment, Simone was in eleventh

grade again—sitting on the couch in Julie's living room in Wappingers Falls, splitting a can of Budweiser they'd stolen from the fridge and watching Nirvana singing "Lithium" on *MTV Unplugged*. Simone could taste the beer, cold and bitter, could hear that strumming guitar and that pain-filled voice, and then she could see the tears running down Julie's face . . . tears for Kurt Cobain. Ten years later, Simone felt the same strange emotion she'd experienced back then . . . that combination of awe and envy. *Julie feels everything so strongly. She's a little more alive than everybody else.*

Amazing how memories worked—how something that happened so long ago could just flip back in front of you like a dog-eared page, as bright as ever. "I wonder what she's doing," said Simone.

"Voodoo, obviously," Kathy said. "She gets paid to do love scenes with Chris Hart."

"I wasn't talking about Dylan Leeds. I meant Julie, from my high school." Simone stepped back and smoothed her red butcher's apron, dropping her microcassette recorder into one of the pockets. "You know, you've mentioned voodoo three times since I've known you."

"Yeah, well, it's rush week at my coven."

Simone smiled.

At the end of the bank of lockers stood a full-length mirror. Simone and Kathy moved toward it and checked out their reflections. "You've really got a great look for this job," said Kathy.

"Please."

"I'm serious," she said. "Even the punk haircut works. It's like, you don't want to be sweet. But, try as you might, you just can't help it. Know what I'm saying?"

"Not really."

Kathy patted her on the back. "Nigel can't fire you. I won't let him."

Simone said, "You're a really nice person, Kathy."

"No way. I'm a huge bitch."

As they started out the locker room door, Kathy said, "Oh, by the way, have you ever cater-waitered before?"

"No. Why?"

She grimaced. "Never mind. You'll see."

"For the fifth time, the vegetarian pot stickers go on the green trays and the shrimp pot stickers go on the pink ones," said Erika James, the owner of Erika's Edibles. Her face was inches away from Simone's, like some kind of tiny drill sergeant with an unnatural food obsession. "Green! Vegetable! Pink! Shrimp! Is that too hard for your itty-bitty mind to grasp?"

Frustration was worming its way into Erika's every feature. Beads of sweat dotted her hairline, and the tips of her glossy black pixie cut were starting to curl. Her skin was as pink as one of the shrimp trays.

Yes, Simone was a bad cater-waiter, but it wasn't the fifth time she'd been told about the trays. It was the second; third, tops. Regardless, Erika was overreacting.

Technically speaking, she was working for Simone, not the other way around. A former acting school classmate of Kathy's, the caterer had agreed to "hire" the two women for the night's event, in exchange for three thousand in cash.

So she had no right to complain. Zero.

The other cater-waiters kept giving Simone pitying "I'm so glad I'm not you" looks, but they didn't know the half of it. She had around ten dollars in her bank account on a good day, and now she was about to lose her second job in a month—probably the last journalism job she'd ever have—all because she'd crossed paths with Neil Walker, a world-class, picture-on-a-Wheaties-box-level liar. Before long she'd lose her lease, and her bank account would sink to negative numbers. And she would have to tell her family.

Some bribe-accepting bitch telling her where to put the shrimp? That was the least of Simone's problems. . . .

"Let me ask you something," said Erika. "Do you have to work *hard* to be so stupid, or does it just come naturally?"

But it didn't make things any easier. Without a word, Simone placed the three errant pot stickers onto a pink tray and moved out of the kitchen. "Where do you *think* you're going?" Erika said.

"Bathroom," Simone said between her teeth. "Be right back."

Simone swung open the kitchen door and walked into the ballroom, with its pale pink walls, mammoth chandeliers, and black-and-white-tiled dance floor, sleek and gleaming. To walk through this room was to walk into a time capsule—she half expected Ricky Ricardo to hop up on the bandstand and sing "Babaloo"—and Simone would have been impressed, had she not just let go of the last, frayed thread at the end of her rope.

Her footsteps bounced off the hard tiles—*click, click, click*—as she made her way to the far end of the room, where Kathy was setting up one of the open bars.

"I have to leave," Simone said.

"Erika's being mean, huh?"

"That's the understatement of the century. It's like a scene from *Mommie Dearest* in there."

Kathy removed the last bottle of Swedish vodka from a crate and placed it on the black bar. "It's not you," she said. "I know Erika, and she's just . . . she's a guilty john."

Simone looked at her. "A what?"

"You know. The guy who hires the prostitute, fucks her up, down, and sideways, and then slaps her around and calls her a filthy whore."

"Oh."

"Erika's betraying her clients and she feels guilty as hell. So what does she do? She takes it out on you. She blames the poor hooker."

"Okay, I get it. Wait . . . hooker?"

"But let me tell you something, sister. You're not going

anywhere. You're gonna do our pimp proud today. You're gonna unclamp those knees of yours and start screwing like a champ. And guess what? He's gonna stop beating the crap out of you. He's gonna tell you he loves you and buy you some nice bling."

Simone had to smile a little. "You really know how to work a metaphor, Kathy."

She pulled a piece of paper out of her red butcher's apron and unfolded it. "I got the guest list," she said. "Let's go over it, see what kind of leads we can look for. Whatever news we pick up, you get all the credit."

"Oh, Kathy. You are so ni—"

"Yeah, yeah. You told me."

The *Devil's Road* party was being hosted by Chris Hart and his wife, Lara Chandler—or as the media referred to them, Clara. They were major A-list talent, but Z-level tabloid fodder. Married for eight years, they were considered Hollywood's happiest couple. "Believe me," Kathy said. "I once spent two weeks in my car, staking out Clara's house with binoculars from seven a.m. to seven p.m. every day. Nigel wanted one fight. One lousy little *spat*, and I couldn't even get that."

She moved a manicured finger down the printed list. "Let's see," she said. "Looks like there's a bunch of humanitarian types here. Clara's way into the Big Picture these days. You saw them both on *Nightline*, right?"

Simone nodded.

"Nelson Mandela. Boring. Coupla senators . . . Schwarzenegger . . . Meryl Streep . . . Come on, where are the stars?"

"No reality show people?"

She shook her head. "I hate this class-act bullshit. Wait . . . Jason Caputo!"

"The director?"

"Oh, right. For a second I thought he was that new guy on *One Tree Hill*. . . ." Her eyes scanned the page.

"I wish Blake Moss was coming," Simone said.

"I hear he's having a party tonight," said Kathy. "Now

that I would like to infiltrate. Get this. Blake's fuck palace used to belong to Mary Pickford! There's something almost . . . blasphemous about that, don't you think?"

Holly's voice popped into Simone's head. *And she needs a pedicure appointment for this party tomorrow night, and* . . . "Emerald Deegan was supposed to go to a party tonight," she said. "I wonder if it's the same one."

"Let's not talk about Emerald," said Kathy, "or any members of her family."

"Agreed." Still, Simone couldn't help but think about Emerald's deepest, darkest secret. If she had betrayed Holly, if she'd written up a story about Emerald cutting herself, about the knife collection, the scars . . . the *Asteroid* would have had a *real* exclusive. It would have blown Walker's "Hoarding Disorder" story out of the water.

Simone couldn't believe she was thinking this way, even for a second. She could hear Deegan saying, *Treat my little girl fair* . . . and she wished she could slap herself. Then she wished she could slap the next awful thought out of her mind: *Did you treat me fair, Wayne?*

Maybe it was for the best that Simone was about to lose this job.

Kathy was reading the list. "Quincy Jones, Dylan whatsherface, couple of designers, Miranda Boothe. She always wears something trashic, but we need more than fashion police stuff. . . . Oooh. Dale Waters."

"Who?"

"You know, the hottie from that boy band . . . um . . . crap. I can't remember their name, but one of them is gay. They're white. Kinda hip-hop, but very sweet and earnest? You know which band I'm talking about, right?"

"No."

"Well, trust me, they're way big. Let's see . . . George Clooney."

"Really?"

"Don't hold your breath, he's shooting right now. Brad Pitt—same." Kathy folded up the list. "Let's just hope

Dale does something spicy. I'll make his drinks extra strong."

Simone said, "Kathy, this is hopeless."

"No, it's not."

"I have this feeling like my head's on a chopping block. The blade's hanging over me, and no matter what I do, no matter how hard I try to impress Nigel, it's just a matter of time before it falls."

She raised an eyebrow at her. "Now who's working metaphors?"

Simone tried to smile, but she couldn't. She heard the kitchen doors swing open, and Erika shrieking, "That is *not* the bathroom!" And she didn't even bother turning around. She kept walking, straight and deliberate, out of the ballroom toward the hallway that housed the staff elevators.

"Where the *hell* do you *think* you're going?!" Erika called after her.

Simone didn't reply. She just hit the elevator button and walked in, wondering if there was any point in ever coming back.

"Chris, Chris, Chris!"

"Lara!"

"Lara, over here, love!"

"You guys look great!"

"How does it feel to be Sexiest Man Alive?"

"Are you pregnant?"

Simone hustled past the crowd—paparazzi and newspaper stringers and eager young reporters from the glossy celebrity weeklies, pushing and shoving and flopping all over each other as they jockeyed for quotes, glances, anything at all out of Clara.

From where she was, she couldn't see the superstar couple, just the backs of all the press people, which made the scene all the more desperate and bizarre: a feeding frenzy with no food.

Staring at the writhing bodies, she couldn't help but

wonder if one of them belonged to Neil Walker. But that wasn't his style, was it? Why do real work when he could wait in the parking lot, jump one of the reporters, and swipe her tape recorder?

Simone shook her head, walked past the red carpet toward the parking lot. *You win, Walker. Hope you're happy.* Times like this, Simone wished she smoked. It would have given her something to do, something else to think about as she stood away from the sparkling gowns and popping cameras and those inane, shouted questions, at the entrance to the dank, hot alleyway behind the hotel. It would have given her something to focus on besides her thoughts.

Like a slap, she felt it again . . . that chill sensation at the base of her neck, that feeling of being watched. But before, it had been Walker, and now . . . What would Walker be doing back here? She turned, searched the alleyway, then listened. . . . There was no sound, save a faint rustling in one of the rusted Dumpsters lined up against the windowless brick. Rats? Clearly, this was the Beverlido's bad side.

She turned back around again, gazed down the block at the parking lot . . .

"Simone."

It came from directly behind her, a hissing whisper in the alleyway. But when she spun around and looked, no one was there.

"Simone!" The whisper was more insistent now, like a ghost shouting her name.

"Over here." It was coming from the Dumpsters. She moved into the alleyway, and when she got to the middle bin, she saw the lid was cracked open, saw those malamute eyes peering out of the dark space. "Elliot?!"

"Hi."

"What are you *doing* in there?"

"Nigel," he said. "He heard some heroin rumor about that boy band kid, Dale Waters? This alleyway is where everybody likes to shoot up, so . . ."

"So he's making you stake it out . . . from *there*?"

"Best view in town," he said. "Plus, while I'm at it, I can look for needles."

"God, you're a . . . good sport," she said. Even from outside the bin, the fumes were getting to her. And the longer she stood in front of it, the worse they got—the rotting corpses of uneaten meals. "How can you stand this?"

He held up a gloved hand, the tin of rose salve clasped between his thumb and forefinger. "Man's best friend," he said. "What are you doing outside the hotel?"

"Getting a little fresh air," said Simone, which under the circumstances was pretty ironic.

"Well, I'm glad I caught you. Listen," he said. "I feel really bad about what happened to you with the Deegan story."

"Yeah, well . . ."

"I wish I could help you get on Nigel's good side. But I don't think he has a good side."

Simone smiled. "That's okay."

"So . . . anyway . . ." Elliot cleared his throat. "I, uh, I got you a little something. To cheer you up."

"You didn't have to—"

"Hold out your hand."

He slid the other arm through the narrow space and dropped something into Simone's waiting palm, something light and cool and surprisingly delicate.

It was a silver bracelet, dotted with six large square-cut rubies.

Simone gasped. "Elliot . . . I can't—"

"Sure you can," he said.

"But this must have cost—"

"Didn't cost a dime."

"What do you mean?"

"Found it in Destiny's trash."

Simone cringed.

"I sterilized it," he said. "Don't worry."

"I don't know, Elliot," she said. "It's beautiful and all,

but . . . wearing jewelry out of someone else's garbage . . ."

"Don't knock it," he said. "One time, I was going through Madonna's cans. Found a Cartier watch. Sold it on eBay for ten thousand bucks."

Simone held the bracelet up to the light. "They're real rubies, huh?"

"Yep."

She remembered her phone conversation with her mother. *I can afford my own plane ticket.* Even though she could afford *nothing*; even though she was about to lose her new job before it even began. She fastened the bracelet on her wrist. It *was* beautiful. Probably the nicest thing she'd ever owned. And whether or not it came out of a stripper's garbage, it might just pay her rent for a few more months. "Thank you, Elliot."

"Nothing dead in her cans, by the way. In case you were wonder—"

But he stopped when he heard approaching footsteps, a man's voice saying the word "alley."

"Shit. Someone's coming," said Elliot. "Get in."

"What?"

"Get in!" Without another word he was opening the Dumpster lid, and Simone was pulling herself up and in, holding her breath all the while.

ELEVEN

Too bad she couldn't hold her breath forever. Simone had never sat in on an autopsy, but to her way of thinking, there was no way it could smell worse than the inside of this Dumpster. Plus, it was hot in here—a good twenty degrees hotter than the ninety-degree day progressing outside, which *baked* the stink, making it even more unbearable. Like Elliot, she was standing up, overstuffed garbage bags huddled around her feet. She hoped none of them were leaking; she did not want a souvenir.

Elliot handed Simone the rose salve, and she rubbed a glob of it under her nose. They both stood there, quiet, Simone trying not to audibly gag as the footsteps neared, and the man's resonant voice said, "What is going on with you, babe?"

"Nothing," a woman's voice replied. "I just . . ."

Carefully, Simone and Elliot cracked the Dumpster lid.

"You just what?"

"I'm tired of sneaking around."

In perfect sync, Elliot and Simone pressed their bodies against the metal, peered through the crack.

The woman said, "I feel dirty, Chris," and Simone

registered what she was looking at: Chris Hart gazing intently into the eyes of someone who was not Lara Chandler . . . not even close. The woman's hair was light blond, the virtual negative of Lara's famed raven tresses. She wore a strapless gold lamé dress, revealing a tattoo on her left shoulder blade. And that voice, that accent . . . Simone reached into her apron pocket, plucked out her microcassette recorder, and turned it on.

Hart said, "You don't look dirty to me, Dylan."

Dylan Leeds.

"You know what I mean."

With his free hand, Elliot slipped a camera phone out of the pocket of his cargo vest and took three pictures, *Click, click click.*

"Did you hear something?" Dylan said.

"Don't think so."

Noiselessly, they closed the lid of the bin and slipped down, Simone clutching her recorder.

Hart said, "Do you have any idea how perfect you are? How perfect *we* are?"

"But . . . what about Lara? If we're so damn perfect, why can't we just *tell* her and—"

"You know why."

"But what if it comes out anyway? Chris, famous people can't have secrets."

"Yes, they can."

"But with the movie, the paparazzi—"

"Relax, Dylan. Come closer."

"But . . ."

"Closer. Look into my eyes."

Dylan said something neither one of them could hear.

And then Hart replied, "I want you. More than anyone else."

Elliot mouthed: *Jesus Christ.*

Hart's and Dylan's footsteps moved away from the Dumpster, out of the alley, out of earshot. Just to make sure they were really, truly gone, Elliot pulled himself up and peered over the edge of the Dumpster. He stared out in every direction, then slid back down again.

Simone rewound the tape a little and hit PLAY.

"Chris, famous people can't have secrets."

"Yes, they can."

She and Elliot said it at the same time: "No, they can't."

"You do the honors," he said.

"Really?"

"Sure." Elliot grinned. "I think this ought to get you off probation."

Simone's pulse raced as she pulled out her cell phone and tapped in the *Asteroid*'s number, ready to give Nigel the biggest shock of his whole shock-laden life.

By the time Simone had spoken to Nigel, washed off the Dumpster stench, and returned to the ballroom, the event was in full swing. She spotted Kathy at her bar, pouring a glass of wine for Nelson Mandela, and sprinted across the room to get to her, practically knocking over Meryl Streep, the head of the African Children's Relief Fund, and poor Lara Chandler in the process.

When Simone finally reached the bar, Kathy took one look at her, grinning like a lottery winner, and said, "Did you get laid out there?"

"Better." Simone pulled her fellow reporter away from the bar and into the nearest bathroom and, after checking every stall, after making absolutely sure that Neil Walker was not hiding in the recesses of the women's restroom, she told Kathy everything that had happened in the Dumpster—and then played her the microcassette.

After she finished, Kathy stared at Simone for several seconds, then threw her arms around her. "I'm so proud of you!"

"Thanks."

"Tell me again what Nigel said."

"He said I'm off probation."

"For all eternity."

"For all eternity, yes."

"Man," said Kathy. "I was all excited to tell you that Blake Moss is actually here. I'm thinking, 'Where the hell is Simone?' I'll tell you where she is! She's listening to Chris Hart *cheating* on Lara Chandler!"

Simone glanced around the room again. "Elliot deserves the credit. If he hadn't been in the Dumpster . . . oh, my God. Did you see this bracelet he gave me? He found it in Destiny's trash."

A shrill voice said, "I cannot *believe* this!"

Simone turned to see Erika James standing in the bathroom doorway, her tiny body vibrating with anger, her eyes aimed like death rays directly at Simone. "You have been gone for more than ten minutes! What the *fuck* do you *think* you're doing?"

Her voice bounced off the tile walls, echoing for several seconds after the sentence was complete. Simone took a good long look at her. *Bring it on, bitch. I'm off probation.* Then she cleared her throat, strolled up to Erika James, and used the two inches she had on her to their full advantage. "If you don't like me talking to Kathy," Simone said quietly, "I could talk to Chris and Lara instead. I bet they would *love* to hear about the little deal you made with my *real* employers."

Erika's eyes went as wide as poker chips. "You . . . you can't."

"Sure I can." Simone gave her a bright smile. "Listen: 'Hi, Chris. Hi, Lara. I'm a tabloid reporter. For just three thousand bucks, Erika let me put on this cute outfit and hang out with you guys!' "

"I'll tell them you're lying."

"Good point." Simone paused for a moment, scratched her chin thoughtfully. "Well, if they need proof, I'm sure my *real* boss would be happy to provide the cashed check."

Kathy guffawed. "The kid's right. He would."

For the first time since Simone had met her, Erika was at a loss for words.

Simone sighed. "Anyway, I'm going to get out there and see if I can meet Dylan Leeds. You got any pot stickers you want me to pass, Erika? I think my itty-bitty brain might be up to it now."

Simone made her way through the glittering, perfumed crowd. She kept her eyes peeled for blond hair, for a strapless, gold lamé dress, but people kept wanting hors d'oeuvres, which slowed her down considerably. They expected her to stop, to give them napkins, a somewhat unwieldy procedure.

Out of the corner of her eye, Simone spotted a swath of gold fabric leaning out from a cluster of the tuxedos and black cocktail dresses. But when she made her way toward it, she bumped full-on into the back of a tall man, spattering soy sauce onto his tux.

The man spun around, and Simone recognized him as Blake Moss. And as she looked up at that chiseled face, those devilish eyebrows, she recalled a lot more things about him than the wild parties and the raunchy reputation. He had a taste for theatrical S&M. He owned several ball gags, a cat-o'-nine-tails. He paid hookers extra if they agreed to play dead. Amazing that Simone would know such bizarre, intimate details about someone she'd only seen on movie screens, but she did. Everyone did, thanks to a 1998 tell-all piece in *Vanity Fair*. Like Dylan Leeds had said, *famous people can't have secrets*.

"I'm so sorry, Mr. Moss." She handed him a stack of napkins. "I'll get some seltzer."

His brown eyes glinted in a way that made her want to put on more clothes. "You don't have to do that."

Blake had been talking to a lean bespectacled guy with floppy brown hair. It was Jason Caputo—the physical opposite of his famously bald, rotund father. Simone recognized him from the cover of *Entertainment Weekly*'s "Young Guns/Big Shots" issue. "Really," Simone said to Blake Moss, "it's no trouble."

Caputo looked at her. "Blake likes to be, uh, spilled on, if you know what I'm saying."

"Actually, I have no idea what you're saying."

"Cut it out, Jase." Moss touched a finger to Simone's earlobe. "Virgin ears."

Simone took a breath. "Are you sure you're okay, Mr. Moss?"

"Blake," he said. "After you've spilled on me, we should be on a first-name basis."

Caputo snickered.

Simone was about to leave when Moss said to Caputo, "So Holly Kashminian called, demanded I cancel my party." She froze.

"What did you say?" Caputo asked.

"I told her Emerald wouldn't have wanted me to."

Simone heard herself say, "That *was* your party."

He stared at her. "Huh?"

"Oh . . . I'm sorry. I just . . . Holly Kashminian goes to my gym. She mentioned . . . you were one of Emerald Deegan's friends."

"Poor Emerald," Caputo said.

"Yeah, it's tragic," said Moss. "But I can't say I didn't see that one coming."

Simone said, "Holly didn't see it coming at all."

Moss rolled his eyes, nodded. "Emmy was a sad little camper," he said. "Holly was her number-one fan. Sweet girl. But not what you would call a reliable narrator." He turned his attention back to Simone. "Anyone ever tell you you've got beautiful hands?"

Caputo said, "Put the waitress down, Blake."

"I'd better get back to work." Simone started to turn, but noticed Blake Moss was still watching her, his gaze now fixed on her neck.

"Nice meeting you both," she said.

Caputo nodded. Moss gave Simone a look she recognized from his films—a sneaking half leer of a smile that clung to her skin. "I really like your hands," he said.

An unreliable narrator. Simone wasn't sure how good a judge of people Blake Moss was, but his description of Holly made sense. She *was* Emerald's number-one fan. And she was the only one who seemed to think her death wasn't a suicide. Maybe Emerald *was* a sad little camper—a self-mutilator who could no longer find relief. . . .

Stop thinking about Emerald and find Dylan Leeds. Simone veered toward the gold lamé, ignoring the five or six people who asked her for sashimi bites. She couldn't afford to waste any more time cater-waitering.

When she finally reached Dylan's group, Simone hesitated long enough to read the tattoo on the starlet's shoulder blade—two Japanese letters, the phrase "Living on a Prayer" underneath.

Bon Jovi?

Dylan Leeds turned around.

"Sashimi?" Simone said, but then she got a good look at Dylan's face, and Dylan gaped at her and said, "Simone Glass?" in that thick California accent, and Simone almost dropped her tray.

"Julie Curtis," she said.

"I can't believe this!"

It took a few seconds for Simone to get her jaw unlocked. "Me neither." Julie Curtis, Simone's best friend from junior year at Wappingers Falls High, was about to take the *C* out of Clara.

"I mean," Julie said, "I thought you'd be a big-time reporter by now."

One of the suits turned around—tall and baby-faced, with thick, sandy hair and kind-looking eyes. "Who is this, Dylan?"

"Friend of mine from high school," she said. "Simone, this is Nathaniel—my manager's assistant."

"Hi."

"She isn't always this rude," Nathaniel said. His voice sounded familiar.

"Rude?" said Julie.

"Uh . . . 'I thought you'd be a big-time reporter by now'? Not what you'd call tactful, sweets."

"Shit, I'm sorry," said Julie. "Seriously, some of my best friends are cater-waiters. You just always seemed so . . . I don't know. Driven."

"I did?"

"Personally?" said Nathaniel. "I respect cater-waiters a lot more than reporters."

Simone said, "Who do you work for, Nathaniel?"

"Randi DuMonde."

And she remembered where she'd heard the voice. *She's . . . no longer with us.*

"Nia Lawson's manager," Simone said. "I . . . uh . . . I saw her on TV."

"You know, Simone, I'm actually Randi's *associate*, not her *assistant*. I even have my own roster of talent. But Dylan here has a little trouble with us working stiffs."

"I can't believe this," Julie said. "Seriously, Nathaniel, Simone and I were best friends for like . . ."

Six months. "I can't believe it either," said Simone.

"I love your haircut, by the way," Julie said. "Very retro."

"Thanks."

Julie said, "There are about fifty billion things I want to ask you about."

"Me too," said Simone. "Maybe sixty." *And that's not even counting Chris Hart.*

Julie laughed, but before she could say any more, Hart was next to her, along with some woman who must have been a publicist, telling her the *People* writer was here and wanted to "touch base."

Hart gave Simone a quick glance. "Hello," she started to say, but she saw ice in his eyes, and went silent.

"I'll call you!" Julie said, as Hart, the woman, Nathaniel,

and several other suits whisked her away like a feather-light set piece.

By the time Simone realized they'd never exchanged numbers, Julie was long gone. *I can't believe she's having an affair with Chris Hart.*

Simone felt a tap on her shoulder, heard a man's voice say, "Excuse me, miss." *Oh great. Another hors d'oeuvres hog.* But when she turned around, she found herself looking at Keith Furlong.

He was even taller in person—and somehow, his height felt intrusive, as if he'd grown that big on purpose. Furlong was wearing his version of formal wear—black tux with velvet lapels, silver vest, and in lieu of a bow tie, an ascot with a diamond stickpin. It looked like something a pimp would wear to the Oscars—not to mention his hair, which was stiff enough to draw blood.

He wore contacts the same green as a Ping-Pong table, but despite that flash of color, the eyes were dead. They reminded Simone of sharks' eyes—no emotion, just purpose. Not the eyes of a man who had lost his love less than two days ago.

"Sashimi bite?" said Simone.

He shook his head. "Where did you get that bracelet?"

Shit. It's from Destiny's trash. "My mom gave it to me," she said. "College graduation."

He stared at her. "Nice mom."

She stared back. "You're Keith Furlong, aren't you?"

He smiled. The eyes perked up a little. "You recognized me."

"Yes," Simone said. "Listen, I'm so sorry for your loss."

He blinked a few times. "Emerald," he said.

"Yes."

"It is awful. But, you know . . . I truly believe she is in a better place."

"If you don't mind my asking," said Simone, "why are you here?"

"Bedrock. We're doing the afterparty for the *Devil's*

Road premiere next Friday." Furlong caught sight of Blake Moss. "Yo, dawg!" he shouted, and pushed his way to where the movie actor was standing. "Party's at ten, right?"

Simone heard Moss say, "Bringing Dessy? I *like* her."

As she moved in the other direction, toward Kathy's bar station, Simone wondered if any woman, anywhere, could be missed less by her man than Emerald Deegan.

The mask was feeling too tight. It was always uncomfortable at events like this—promotional parties where he had to shake hands and crack jokes and smile. But at this one, at the Beverlido, it felt tighter than ever. He did not want to be here. He hated this hotel. His mother used to love it. It was soaked in memories.

He smiled at the group of people he was with, pretended he was listening to what they were saying. But all he could think about was the next one—part three in the Project. He knew where she was now, he knew how to get there, and he knew exactly what he was going to make her do. . . . He'd rehearsed it in his head so many times. Already, he had marked her. But instead he had to be here with these people, the smile mask as tight as a vise. It was not fair.

A woman approached his group, an actress. He had met her before, but her name eluded him. "You look so handsome," she said.

"Right back at you," he replied. "Of course, you're always drop-dead beautiful." The actress grinned while his brain repeated the phrase. *Drop dead.* It brought Nia Lawson to mind . . . Nia at the very end—Nembutal Nia, head drooping, stinking of vomit, delirious.

It hadn't gone the way he'd envisioned it, back in his office, when the Project took shape. He had wanted Nia scared. Shamed. But she wasn't alert enough for that, so he had to settle. He would never settle again. He hadn't settled with Emerald—even though Holly Kashminian was making people think he had . . . telling the world it was a paring knife. Really, what kind of shame could come out of a kitchen?

The third time, though. . . . The way he had it planned. He knew it would be the most perfect of all.

It made the mask more bearable, rehearsing the third time in his brain. And so he imagined, through countless conversations with business contacts and politicians, with agents and publicists and studio executives, what it would be like to shame number three, to hurt her, to hear her weep and then, to cut her open. He imagined it while talking to pristine-looking actresses, smiling at the idea of them reading his mind.

But when he saw that waitress, his visions crumbled. The rehearsing stopped. He had never met her before, yet she was wearing it. The bracelet. *How?* The word swirled in his mind. *How? How?*

After he spoke with her, he stared at the waitress from across the room, watched her every move like he would watch a dumb pet, unknowing in its cage. He watched who she smiled at, how she walked, the way her mouth moved when she spoke. He watched her hand, the way the bracelet clung to the thin skin of the wrist. And again he thought, *how?*

Until he had an answer, he would keep watching her. And if the answer was a good one, maybe after.

TWELVE

Throughout the rest of the party, Keith Furlong watched Simone. She'd be talking to Kathy, serving hors d'oeuvres, reaching into her apron pocket, making sure her microcassette recorder was working, and she would catch him looking at her. They creeped Simone out, those Ping-Pong-table green eyes of his, examining her every move.

It was because of the bracelet. That much was obvious. Keith knew that bracelet. He may have even bought it for Destiny. And he couldn't figure out what it was doing on the wrist of some cater-waitress he'd never seen before.

During the ride back to the office, Kathy talked and talked, while Simone stared at her wrist, at this bracelet that could pay her rent for months. Had Keith really given this rare object to a seventeen-year-old stripper? It didn't even look like his taste—it was too elegant, too subtle for a man who'd wear a diamond stickpin to a late-afternoon movie party.

Even more puzzling, Destiny had *thrown it away*. If Keith had given it to her and she was mad at him, she could have at least tried to sell it on eBay. Yes, Destiny was just a teen, but she was a *practical* teen—a teen willing to sell details of her sex life for eight thousand dollars. *You'd think she'd be willing to sell a ruby bracelet, no matter who gave it to her.*

"Yo!" said Kathy. "Where'd you go?" They were on the 105, a sharp, twisting freeway that cars always took too fast when it wasn't packed with traffic. The sun had set, and night urged itself against the Audi's windows, each passing set of headlights holding the threat of a pileup.

Simone was pretty sure Kathy had been saying something about Chris Hart's rumored "tantric sexpertise," but she wasn't sure enough to fake it. "Sorry," she said. "I was just thinking."

"About what?"

"This bracelet."

"See, now I wouldn't have guessed that in a million years. My psychic powers must be going."

Simone looked at Kathy. "Seriously," she said. "If you were Destiny . . . or even if you weren't, would you throw a bracelet like this out?"

"No, but like I said, stars are psychotic."

"Destiny isn't a star," said Simone. "She's a kid who takes her clothes off."

"But she *wants* to be a star. She *wants* to be famous. That's the psychosis right there."

Simone sighed. "I guess."

"I mean, come on," Kathy said. "Look at Nia Lawson. She wasn't a star anymore. Christ, she was living in *Inglewood*. Yet she kills herself in that sick way . . . somehow her shoe gets into Emerald Deegan's trash, and don't even get me started on all things Deegan. Famous people are nut jobs, I'm telling you—"

Simone's heart sped up. "What did you just say?"

"I said, 'Famous people are nut—' "

"Not that," said Simone. *Two cut throats, one month apart, the first victim's shoe in the second victim's trash. . . .*

And the second victim was missing *all her bracelets.*

Simone grabbed her cell phone out of her purse and started tapping in Holly Kashminian's number.

"What are you doing?" said Kathy.

Simone said, "Can you do me a huge favor?"

Holly lived in a small bungalow at the bottom of Linda Vista. As Kathy pulled up in front of it, Simone understood how tangible it was for Holly—the lack of Emerald. If the street weren't so prohibitively steep, Holly's boss's house would have been within walking distance, less than a minute away from her own.

"Emerald's *assistant* lives here?" said Kathy. "Dollars to donuts Em was paying her rent. A nice little place like that, in the Hollywood Hills?"

She thought of Wayne Deegan's castle of a house. "You're probably right."

"Okay, so I'm going to drive around the block and—"

"It won't take any longer than that, I promise."

Simone hurried up to the bungalow's door, rang the bell. She could hear Holly moving across the room and regarding her through the peephole before unbolting a series of locks.

Holly stood in the doorway wearing khaki shorts and a tank top that read "Bebe" in sequined letters. She seemed tired and sad, and her hair looked like she'd slept on it funny, but her pupils weren't quite as dilated as they'd been before. "What's up?" she said.

Simone held out her wrist. "Do you recognize this bracelet?"

Holly's face went white, and Simone had her answer.

"It's Emerald's, isn't it?"

Holly said, "The ruby closest to the clasp. Turn it over."

Simone did. It had a silver backing, an inscription. And when she read the inscription aloud, Holly said it with her:

"Love, Luck, Long Life."

Holly stared at her. "Emerald's father gave her that. It was her favorite."

Kathy's Audi rounded the bend and pulled up to the curb. "I've got to go," said Simone. "You mind if I keep this a little while? I need to show it to someone."

"Okay," said Holly. "But, wait. Where did you find it?"

Simone didn't want to upset Holly, didn't want her any more involved than she already was. "A friend found it," she said, "in a Dumpster . . . outside the Kabbalah Center."

Holly stared at her. "You have interesting friends."

"I know."

"If Emerald threw that out," said Holly, "maybe she really was getting rid of . . ."

"Worldly possessions."

"Yes." Something stole into Holly's black eyes, played across her sad features—something calm and sweet.

Hope, thought Simone, who was not feeling any.

"Let me get this straight," said Kathy, as she pulled the Audi into the *Asteroid*'s parking lot. "Destiny tossed out Emerald's bracelet, so therefore she's going to turn up with a cut throat."

"I don't think she threw it out," Simone said. "I think someone—Emerald and Nia's killer—might have put it in her trash."

"You know what I think?" Kathy said. "I think you've been hanging out with that crazy assistant Holly too long. I think Keith swiped Em's bracelet and gave it to his lover because he's freakin' cheap. I think the lover found out, and got so pissed off she threw it in her garbage."

Simone had to admit: "When you say it out loud like that . . ."

"It makes more sense than your garbage man–slasher theory?"

Simone nodded. "But it would put my mind a lot more at ease if we could just *find* Destiny. Ask her. Has anybody reported her as a missing person yet?"

"Her boss at Pleasures," said Kathy. "Elliot swung by there last night, after he hit her cans. But you know what Elliot said?"

"What?"

"Her boss wasn't all that surprised. My guess is, the kid's in Mexico right now, buying eight thousand dollars' worth of margaritas." Kathy turned off the car, unfastened her seat belt. "Forget about Emerald and Destiny, okay? You got us the best story we've had in years. Nigel wants to have your babies." She opened her door and got out. "Do me a favor and bask in your own glory."

By the time Kathy and Simone arrived at the office, Elliot, Matthew, Carl, and Nigel had already killed a bottle of Veuve Clicquot. Nigel said, "Not to worry, ladies. We saved the Dom for you!"

After they popped open the champagne and Nigel toasted Simone, Elliot, and the next issue, he brought them into his office, where, as proud as a new father, he presented a completed cover story layout, faxed in from New York. At the center of the layout was a picture of Chris and Lara, split in two by a lightning bolt, and a neon-bright headline that read TROUBLE IN CLARADISE!!

"Excellent headline, right?" said Elliot.

"Great font color too," Kathy added. "Nothing says *naughty* like hot pink."

"We're getting photos of the home wrecker by tomorrow," Nigel said. "And the brilliant part is, we're getting them cheap because no one knows she's the *home wrecker yet!*"

Simone stared at the layout—at the large gray box, set in the middle of the two columns of type. It was the box where Julie's picture would go, and there was already a caption underneath: *Dirty Dylan!*

In the lower right-hand corner of the page was a larger box reserved for the camera-phone photos with a smaller headline: EXCLUSIVE! THE SECRET TALK THAT ENDED HOLLYWOOD'S HAPPIEST MARRIAGE!

She had a vision of Julie in high school laughing

her head off at a joke Simone had made. "Do . . . do we have to call her Dirty Dylan?"

"It's a pun on their conversation, love," said Nigel. "She told Hart she felt dirty."

"Oh. I get it." The layout glowered up at Simone from Nigel's desk. She'd get over it, she knew. After all, Chris and Lara were public figures and so was Julie . . . well, so was Dylan Leeds, anyway.

Nigel said, "I'm taking all of you out to dinner at Tom Cruise's favorite restaurant."

"Get out!" said Kathy.

"You deserve it." He looked at Simone. "Especially this one here, with her microcassette. She deserves it all."

"Thanks, Nigel," she said. "But if it's okay with you, I think I'm going to go home."

Simone drove home feeling like she hadn't done enough, and like she'd done too much. Not enough for Destiny, too much for Julie . . . *or against Julie, as the case may be.*

Yes, Dylan Leeds was having an affair with a famous married man. But Julie Curtis was the coolest new girl ever to enroll at Wappingers Falls High. Julie was the future movie star who'd come all the way from California. And for six months—until she hooked up with varsity quarterback Todd McKenna (and who could blame her for that?)—Julie was the best friend Simone had ever had.

Dylan Leeds may have been dirty, but Julie Curtis never was.

The price of fame, Simone thought, which made her remember Destiny—disappearing Destiny and her eight thousand dollars. If Simone could just find Destiny, show her this bracelet. If she could hear her say, *Keith gave me that. It was Emerald's, so I threw it out.* If she could hear Keith say, *Before she killed herself, Emerald gave me her bracelets. She was getting rid of her worldly possessions, but I didn't want 'em, so I gave them to Destiny. . . .* If she could just hear either one of them say either of those things, she could stop worrying.

If not, she needed to find Destiny, warn her.

Simone checked her watch. It was just about ten right now. Blake Moss's party was starting. Keith would be there, and maybe . . .

Bringing Dessy? I like her.

Simone wished she could get into that party—wished that at least she knew where Blake Moss lived. . . . Then, as she crossed Sunset, made her way onto Coldwater Canyon, Simone suddenly remembered what Kathy had said back at the Beverlido.

Blake's fuck palace used to belong to Mary Pickford!

"Yes!" said Simone.

She knew that stupid Map of the Dead Stars' Homes would come in handy.

Blake Moss's house—compound, actually—was at the top of Coldwater Canyon, Mulholland Drive West. Mulholland was more view than street. It was both stunning and dangerous, like so many things in this city, and Simone had driven its length once before, to see for herself the panorama found in nearly every movie that takes place in LA.

That had been in daytime, though. Now it was night, and as she peeled down the winding mountain road, the city lights spread out in front of her like a bath of sequins. And, for a brief moment, Simone was here only to admire.

Then she found the address. Without rehearsing a way in, she pulled up to the gate and pressed the button. A woman's voice, older and accented, answered, "Yes."

"I'm here for the party."

"What is your name?" she said. "Did you receive an invitation?"

"Listen," said Simone, "I need to see one of the guests. Her name is Destiny. Dessy. It is very important I see her. It could . . . be a matter of life and death."

There was a long pause, during which Simone heard nothing but chatter and, experimental jazz. The woman came back. "There is no one here by that name," she said.

"Are you sure? What about Keith Furlong? I think she might be with—"

"If you do not have an invitation, I will need to ask you to leave."

"You don't understand!" said Simone. "This is urgent."

Silence.

Great. Simone was just about to roll up her window and drive away when she heard another voice. Younger, Californian. "Simone? Is that you I see through the surveillance camera?"

"Julie?!"

"What are you doing here?"

"Um . . . well, I'm looking for . . ."

"Kidding!"

"Huh?"

"You are such the ace reporter, tracking me down!" Julie said. "Now stop talking to that box and get your ass in here."

The 1998 *Vanity Fair* article that exposed Blake Moss's sexual exploits was called "Secrets of Desire," and it wasn't even *about* Blake Moss. It was an in-depth profile of a high-priced Hollywood hooker named, of course, Desire. In it, she outed several of her A-list clients—two or three rock stars, an action movie hero, an already-fallen televangelist—but Blake Moss. That was the bombshell.

The star of the family-friendly sitcom *Corey Next Door*, Moss was considered clean-cut inside and out—the type of actor who would, and *did*, thank Jesus Christ for his People's Choice Award.

When Moss's fans saw Desire's revelations, it was as if they'd been told there was no Santa Claus. (Simone could still remember Greta calling her at her college dorm, crying, *"Corey Next Door is a pervert! I've lost all faith in humanity."*) Before long, *Corey* had exited the airwaves and the onetime poster boy for family values had become a Hollywood casualty—a victim of his own unyielding image.

Simone had felt sorry for him—until around three or four years ago, when Jason Caputo had cast him as the villain in his breakthrough film, *Bad*. Blake Moss was reborn. In the tabloids, the phrase "bad boy" was permanently affixed to his first name, and he became known for his wild, bacchanalian parties. When he thanked Jesus for his Best Supporting Actor Oscar, everyone knew he was being ironic.

As Blake pointed out in a *Playboy* interview, he could now do whatever he wanted to whomever he wanted, wherever he wanted, with *all the bells, whistles, and ball gags*—and it only increased his bankability: *I wouldn't have said so at the time, but Desire was the best thing that ever happened to me.*

Greta was probably the only person in America who had never gotten over the scandal. If Simone were to call her sister right now and tell her she was poolside at a Blake Moss party, watching Blake's agent doing body shots off a *Playboy* centerfold, Greta would have hung up on her without so much as a follow-up question. She almost did feel like calling her sister—just to describe this scene out loud.

Simone felt as if she were trapped on the set of an NC-17 version of *South Pacific*. There were tiki torches everywhere, strange, prehistoric-looking plants, neon-bright parrots screaming from the trees, scantily clad women and men chatting, drinking, making out . . . some of the more inebriated ones actually *going at it* atop overly picturesque rock formations. Whether they were famous or not, most everyone here *looked* it—poreless, close-up-ready creations made for billboards and movie screens.

Destiny was nowhere in sight, though Julie said, "I'm pretty sure Keith Furlong should be here at some point."

So Simone opted to hang out with her old friend, to take in the bizarre scenery, to keep her eyes peeled for Keith Furlong and an AWOL stripper.

"You know," Julie was saying now, "except for the hair, you look exactly the same as you did in high school."

Simone took a sip of her rum and Coke and looked at Julie's face—the powder blue eyes, the button nose and full mouth, the tiny capsule-shaped mark on her left cheek—a pencil lead that had been trapped there when she was six and was too dangerous to remove without scarring her. On anyone else the mark would have been a little gross, but on Julie it somehow added to the mystique. It was a deep, sapphire blue, and Simone could remember a college boy, mooning over Julie at some party they were at, telling her the pencil lead brought out the color of her eyes.

"You look the same too," Simone told Julie.

She shook her head. "I've aged." She turned her gaze away from Simone and back to Blake's agent and the centerfold. They were on a raft in the middle of the pool. She wore nothing but a thong, and he was licking salt off her breast, taking another swig off the tequila bottle. Her body was perfect—so toned and surgically enhanced that she seemed a step higher on the evolutionary ladder, while Blake's agent had the look of an oversized baby, his baggy white swim trunks only adding to the effect. "How can she *stand* that?" whispered Simone.

"Are you kidding?" said Julie. "That's Lazlo Gant. He's one of the most powerful agents there is." She smiled at Gant—a knowing, hungry smile. And Simone thought, *You're right. You have aged.*

A large hand slipped around Simone's waist, almost making her drop her drink. When she turned, there was Blake Moss. His hair was damp and he had on a terry-cloth robe with, Simone was willing to bet, nothing on underneath.

"Hi, Blakey," Julie said.

"Dyl." He took Simone's hand, held it up so the bracelet glistened in the torchlight, and brought it to his lips. Then he gazed at the other hand, the one grasping the rum and Coke. "Lucky drink."

"Blake," said Julie, "this is my dear friend Simone."

He grinned. "Yes. This is."

Simone said, "Do you know if Destiny's coming tonight?"

He raised an eyebrow at her. "You know Destiny?" He kissed her hand again, and someone shouted, "Put the waitress down, Blake!" It was Caputo, who was standing with Miranda Boothe from the movie, a few supermodels, and a guy who may have been Charlie Sheen. "Get over here—I want to introduce you to somebody."

Blake sighed. "Excuse me, ladies."

Simone realized he had never answered her question.

"I think he likes you," Julie said.

"I think he likes anything with a pulse." She remembered the *Vanity Fair* article, the details . . . "Or without a pulse, as the case may be."

"God, you're as picky as ever."

"What do you mean?"

"Come on, Simone. You had some really nice guys into you back in high school. You wouldn't give them the time of day."

"You mean those football players? The ones you and Todd kept trying to set me up with?"

Julie flinched at the name. "Todd McKenna. I haven't thought of him in ages."

Simone looked into her eyes. She knew she was lying.

There was a lull in their conversation. A good, long one that maybe lasted several minutes. Simone welcomed the silence. It eased the tension, kept her from worrying about saying something she shouldn't, something that might reveal what she really did for a living. Something that might reveal next week's story. . . .

Was Julie feeling this way too? Was she thinking about Chris Hart, and guarding secrets of her own?

Simone took a big swallow of her rum and Coke and surveyed the scene again. A group of men were talking to a large woman in a red silk dress, one of them saying something about Nextel stock—as, less than three feet away, a shipping heir was leaning against a thick palm tree, getting serviced by a wasted female pop star. The shipping heir's head snapped back in ecstasy and his body began to convulse. Simone couldn't remember his name, but she'd seen him on some reality show where they sent rich kids to boot camp. The pop star was wearing cutoffs and a bikini top, and she was on her knees. Her name was Lynzee de la Presa, and last year she had won seven Grammy Awards. Simone couldn't believe she was watching this. Didn't Moss's house have *rooms* in it?

"That's my manager," Julie said.

"Huh?" It took a few seconds for Simone to register that she was referring to the large woman in the red silk dress. "Oh . . . really?" She glanced at the group again, recognized Randi's associate, Nathaniel, who was now discussing the huge hit his IBM stock had taken at the end of July. "Had to give up the Malibu place, but I love my new pad," he said. "Needed to downsize anyway." The rest of the group stood there listening, so sober, so oblivious to the shipping heir, who was now zipping up his pants as Lynzee de la Presa, winner of seven Grammy Awards, stretched out on the grass and closed her eyes.

Honestly, how long did it take people to get that unshockable?

Julie said, "Randi's great. I almost cashed it in last year when I hit the big two-five, but she talked me out of it. Sure enough, she was right."

"The big two-five?"

She laughed a little. "For actresses—well, actresses who are my type, anyway—turning twenty-six is sort of like the clock striking midnight. You hit that age and you're not Scarlett Johansson yet, you're screwed. You'd better find yourself a husband fast because you are not an ingénue anymore. Thank God I met Chris Hart."

"*What?!*"

"Hello? *Devil's Road*?"

"Oh, right."

"I never would have gotten that part if it wasn't for him."

Simone examined Julie's face. "I used to have a huge crush on Chris Hart back in high school."

Julie shrugged. "Not when I knew you. It was all about Brad Pitt. Man, how many times did you force me to watch *Twelve Monkeys* with you?" Her face gave nothing away.

Lazlo Gant jumped off the raft, making enough of a splash to drench the centerfold, and swam over to the side. "Stick a fork in her, she's done!" he said as he pulled himself, dripping, out of the pool.

"You want to meet Chris?" Julie said. "He's here."

Simone gulped down the rest of her drink. "Sure."

They walked away from the pool, up a small hill with a gazebo on top. Torches lined their path, as if they were on their way to a tribal ritual of some sort. . . . Human sacrifice, maybe. The phrase "Dirty Dylan" snuck into Simone's head, and she tried to tamp down that stab of guilt. "Julie," she said, "are you sure you're ready to be famous? I mean . . . those paparazzi can be pretty brutal. And the press . . ."

Julie turned to her, smiled her dazzling smile. "If there's one thing I know how to handle," she said, "it's attention."

Chris and Lara were standing under the gazebo—Lara in a flowing white linen dress, Chris in khaki pants and crisp white shirt. As Simone and Julie approached, they were no more than a foot apart, involved in an intense conversation. The way they were looking at each other smacked of déjà vu. *Where have I seen that?* Simone wondered, for about three seconds before it hit her. She was looking at a mirror image of Chris and Julie in the Beverlido's alley. It was as if Hart were auditioning the same scene, opposite different actresses. Simone heard Lara say, "I know you so well."

Julie tapped Chris on the shoulder. He turned, and instantly the intensity dissipated. "Oh, hi, Dylan." He couldn't have sounded calmer.

"I'd like you to meet my old friend Simone—from Wappingers Falls," she said. "She had a total crush on you in high school."

Simone felt herself blushing. "Thanks, Dylan."

"Nice to meet you, Simone," said Hart, who clearly had no recollection of her from the *Devil's Road* party, hours before. He held his hand out to her, but as she shook it, he looked not at her face but at her hand, her wrist. "Pretty bracelet." He held Simone's hand up, showed his wife. "Do you like that, Lara?"

She nodded. "What is it, Loree Rodkin?"

"Not sure." Simone coughed. "It was a gift."

"From who?" said Chris.

Julie said, "Nosy," her tone a little too familiar, too teasing, for its own good.

Lara said, "Did Dylan tell you what she did to get the part in *Devil's Road*?"

"Uh . . . she, um . . ." Simone looked at Julie. "You said if it wasn't for Chris, right?"

"Thanks a lot," Lara said.

"Huh?" said Simone.

Lara sighed. "When Chris decided to produce this film, he showed me the script, and asked if *I* wanted to play Delilah," she said. "I didn't really think it was the right part for me—she's a little young, for one thing. And she really should be a natural blonde. Dylan and I have the same manager, and I immediately thought of her. Chris didn't want an unknown, but I marched her right into his office. I had her memorize one of Delilah's monologues, and without even introducing herself first, she recited it. He was sold."

"I was so nervous, I cried in the middle," said Julie. "Had to catch my breath."

Chris smiled. "That's what sold me."

Simone stared at Julie, headlines shooting through her mind: HART-BREAKER: DYLAN WAS LARA'S BEST PAL! LARA'S TRAGIC MISTAKE: "I TRUSTED DIRTY DYLAN!"

Hard to believe that for six months in high school Simone had known Julie so well that she could predict what she was going to say before she said it. They told each other their most secret daydreams and their darkest fears and their most embarrassing crushes. They spent all day in school together and talked for hours on the phone every night. They found the exact same things hilariously funny—Chris Rock, the stateroom scene in *Night at the Opera*, the way their math teacher Mr. Hansen's butt always shook when he wrote on the chalkboard.

When I'm a famous actress, Julie once asked her, *will you write my life story?*

Of course! Who knows you better than I do?

But now, as Simone watched her old friend Julie talking so calmly to the new friend she'd betrayed, Simone wondered if she had ever known Julie Curtis at all.

By three in the morning, a lot of the more exhibitionistic guests had either left or passed out on the grass, and the party became smaller, more low-key. Chris and Lara went home, as did Caputo, Randi DuMonde, and most of the others whose jobs required them to wake up in the morning. Not Simone, though. After three more rum and Cokes, she was feeling nothing but love for her high school friend. Even if she was screwing the husband of the woman responsible for her big break, Julie was still a hell of a lot of fun.

At this moment, the two of them were sitting on the edge of Blake Moss's pool, dangling their feet in the water, Julie leveling Simone with the celebrity gossip she knew.

"But that doesn't even make sense," Simone was saying now. "There isn't enough room in a bathroom stall for her to be doing that with one guy, let alone a whole boy band."

"Yoga," Julie said.

Simone burst out laughing.

Julie said, "I'm serious," but she started laughing too, and Simone said, "How do you know all this stuff?" and Julie said, "You'd be surprised how much I know." And then, just like that, the laughter died in her throat.

Simone looked at Julie's profile as she gazed at the water, her pale blue eyes reflecting the pool lights. Julie inhaled sharply, then stopped, as if she was going to say something but thought better of it.

Simone thought, *She's going to confess*, and she almost told her, *Don't do it. Don't tell me, because then I'll have to confess too. I'll have to tell you my real job, and that's gonna put such a damper on this evening. . . .*

Julie said, "I know why Nia Lawson killed herself."

Simone stared at her. "What do you mean?"

"It wasn't because of what happened with her and that congressman. I mean, it's sad and all, but that was doomed from the start, and she probably knew it."

"Are you talking about all the bad press she got?"

Julie shook her head. "It was what happened after the press died down. How everyone . . . just stopped caring."

Simone recalled what Nigel had said. *She died a month ago, and she couldn't even move issues then.* "But why now? She'd been over for years."

"Randi had just met with Nia Lawson, a few weeks before she did it. Randi was . . . she was pretty convinced she could find work for Nia, maybe she could make a comeback. And then . . ." Julie pulled her feet out of the water and hugged her knees to her chest in a way that made her look very small, like a child. "I think Randi saying that stuff to Nia brought everything back. I think she killed herself because she knew the comeback could never happen." She took a breath and looked at Simone. She could tell Julie wasn't talking about Nia Lawson anymore. "I don't think she ever got over being ignored."

"Julie," she said, "you don't ever have to worry about being ignored."

"I hope not. Like I said, I can handle attention. But the *lack* of it . . . that's what scares me."

Like an answer, a deep voice cried out, "It's not fucking fair!"

Julie and Simone turned around and saw Blake Moss apparently trying to calm down a man in baggy orange shorts, who was pounding his fist into the thick trunk of a magnolia tree. "Take it easy, man. Calm down," Moss was saying.

"Don't you fucking tell me to take it easy!" The man's voice was choked, agonized. Simone and Julie stood up, moved a few steps closer, and the man slipped out of the shadows. Keith Furlong.

How long had he been here?

His face was red and contorted, a tear glistening on his cheek. "You have no idea what I'm going through!" he howled. "Get away from me. You have no fucking idea!" Then he took off, rushing past the women, the smell of his sweat mingled with heavy cologne, lingering in the air as he headed off toward the front of the house. "You have no idea how much this *hurts*!"

Blake Moss stood beside Julie and Simone, all three of them listening to the screech of Furlong's tires. *Emerald's death. It has finally sunk in.*

Blake said, "Now there is a dude who needs to get a grip on his emotions."

Simone turned to him. "Don't you think that's a little unfair?"

"Unfair?"

"Well, *yeah*. He just lost someone he loved very much."

Moss turned to Julie. "Shit, she's adorable."

"Yeah, she's always been like that."

Simone said, "What do you mean?"

"He's not freaking out over Emerald, angel. He's mad because he lost the *Devil's Road* premiere party." Moss rolled his eyes. "Your friend Destiny talked to one of the tabs about his private life. That and the whole Emerald thing . . . the studio doesn't want the picture to be associated with that."

Simone said, "That . . . that's why he was *acting* like that? That's why he was punching the tree?"

"Well, it *is* his livelihood." He gave Simone a long, steady look. "Good thing Dessy never showed," he said. "I've a feeling she would have gotten it a lot worse than my tree."

Destiny tried very hard not to make noise. She never put her TV on, barely used the water faucets, and padded around her room very softly, like a cat. Her finger throbbed worse than ever, but she never cried, never made a sound. What if he was in the hallway, listening? He could be. He could be anywhere.

Just two days ago, Destiny had dreamed of being famous. She had pictured her name in headlines, people recognizing her in the street, asking for her autograph. Now all she wanted was to disappear.

Terror was with her always now—a constant, draining terror, like she was treading water in the middle of the ocean. Every so often, she'd think, *Sooner or later, the shark will get you.* . . . She hated that thought.

She never opened her window shade, but sometimes she peered around it, just so she could see what time of day it was. She did that now.

Outside it was dark—not that it made any difference. But it was as good a time to sleep as any. Destiny kept her clothes on. She switched off the lights. Then, carefully, she got in bed and eased onto her side. She rested her hand against her hip, felt the pulse beating into that enormous black finger. She didn't mind it so much now, the finger. It reminded her she was alive. She felt the rough pillow pressing into her cheek. There were no sheets here, no bedding at all. It made her own little house seem like a luxury condo, the type of place where one of Them would live. Where he would live.

She closed her eyes and let the finger throb and hated

her house, herself, her life. Most of all, she hated him. She wanted to cry. *Think good thoughts, think good thoughts. . . .* She brought Mom to mind, that day at Disneyland. She didn't care so much about princesses anymore, didn't care about Snow White or Fantasyland.

So instead, Destiny remembered something from later in the day. . . .

The sun is setting and they are on the riverboat ride, watching mechanical Indians dancing around a fire.

Destiny—Sara—looks at them for a while, but she finds the fake Indians boring. Their movements are so small, so predictable. It would be much more interesting if they just had real people pretending to be Indians.

Sara turns away from the robots and looks straight ahead, at the water reflecting the pink and orange sky. This makes her gasp. It is beautiful. She imagines herself spinning around in a dress of those colors. "They make prettier sunsets here," she says. And Mom puts her arm around Sara and laughs, unaware of the tumor beginning to form in her brain. Mom holds Sara close and kisses her cheek, and says, "You are my most special girl." Sara says nothing, just smells Mom's shampoo, which she knows for a fact is what love smells like.

Moments later—or was it hours?—Destiny was back in her bed. Her mom stood over her, stroking her hair. *Stop treading water, Sara. Come with me.*

I want to, Mommy, but I'm scared.

Destiny heard her own voice saying the words and woke up. *Talking in my sleep.* Her eyelids drifted open, and it took several seconds for her gaze to focus. There was something on the pillow, next to her face. A photograph. She picked it up.

It was the picture her mother had taken. Sara and Snow White. *I must still be dreaming. I left that in the kitchen, and then it was gone. . . .* But how could she be dreaming when she could feel it between her fingertips? How could she see the picture so clearly when . . .

The lights were on.

Destiny's mind screamed, *Who turned on the lights?* And from behind her came the answer . . . a latex-covered hand sliding over her mouth. "Hello, Destiny," said his voice, so calm, so certain. "Time to pick up where we left off."

Destiny closed her eyes tight, tears leaking out the corners. Her body convulsed and she felt her bladder release, hot liquid pouring down her legs. Her throat welled up with a thick, choking sob, because she didn't want it to be true, didn't want this to be happening, but it was. It was real.

The shark had come.

THIRTEEN

Simone walked into the office at twenty minutes after ten with a raging rum and Coke hangover and Nigel rushing out into reception to greet her as if she were the queen. "If it isn't the best insider we've ever known!"

Simone said, "It was more Elliot than me."

"Maybe," said Carl. "But Elliot didn't go to high school with Dirty Dylan!"

Simone stared at him. "How did you know?"

"Kath told me," Nigel said. "Wait. You weren't planning on keeping that from all of us, were you?"

"No, of course not."

Simone made it to the reporters' room in three angry strides.

As she stormed in, she heard Matthew saying, "So, was she the school slut or what?" Simone ignored him, ignored Elliot, and headed straight for Kathy's desk.

Kathy was pecking away at a sidebar: IS DIRTY DYLAN PREGNANT? She continued typing, maddeningly cool.

Simone took a breath, in and out. "Okay, first thing. How did you find out?"

"IMDb," Kathy replied. "I'd noticed you talking to Dylan at the party, but you never told me about it. And then you suddenly got that attack of the guilts, didn't want to celebrate. I remembered you mentioning your high school friend, and sure enough, the Internet Movie Database says Dylan Leeds was *née* Julie Curtis."

Simone gritted her teeth. "Okay, fine."

Kathy kept typing. "IMDb rocks. I can't believe we used to have to use clip files. You don't know how lucky you have it. Reporting was a bitch before the Internet."

"Kathy," Simone said, as calmly as she could manage, "why did you *tell*?"

Kathy stopped for a moment, gazed up at her. "You can't keep stuff like that from Nigel, honey," she said. "Number one, he'll find out and get pissed. Number two, it's not fair to *us*. This story is the best break we've had in years. It could save our jobs—our homes, our health insurance. Hell, Matthew's planning on getting married over Christmas. This is his future you're talking about."

"Matthew is getting *married*?"

"If you have an inside connection to that story, you need to be open about it." She gave Simone a pointed look. "It's the *ethical* thing to do."

"But . . . she's my friend."

"Your *friend* is breaking up Hollywood's happiest marriage. It's going to be a cover story for us for weeks, months maybe. So you're either going to wind up sitting around the office making up stories about what a whore your friend is or you can hang out with her as an insider and give us something more balanced." She raised an eyebrow. "Something closer to the truth."

Simone moved away from Kathy's desk.

"She's right, you know," said Matthew.

Simone said, "No. She's just damn good."

"You're the good one." He winked at Simone, and predictably she blushed.

"You're getting married?"

Matthew shot a look at Kathy. "Yep, Ms. Kinney is not the best person to trust with a secret, is she?"

"Who's the lucky—"

"You'll get an invite, don't worry," he said. "But right now, I'd rather show you exactly how good you are."

Simone's pulse sped up a little. "Um . . . what?"

Matthew moved past her, turned on the TV.

There was Meredith Vieira, sitting in front of an image of Chris and Lara, the words "Golden Couple: Tarnished" underneath. He flipped the channel: one of the camera-phone photos of Chris and Julie with the *Asteroid*'s logo stamped over it, a voice-over saying, "A tabloid has un-earthed exclusive details of . . ." He switched again: foot-age of Clara, holding each other on the Beverlido's red carpet, waving to the cameras. "Get all the juicy details in next week's *Asteroid*."

Try as she might, Simone couldn't get her jaw to close.

"I'd say you are very damn good," Matthew said.

Kathy said, "Agreed."

"How . . . how do they know so soon? The story isn't out 'til next week."

"We posted a teaser on our Web site," Matthew said. "Plus our PR department leaked the camera-phone pics." He grinned. "Check out next week's *Asteroid* for the real untold story."

Elliot said, "Bet you feel like talking to yourself. I know I would."

Nigel strolled in. "Which station are you on?" Elliot asked him.

"Fox."

Matthew flipped to the local Fox affiliate, and sure enough there was Nigel in a dark blazer and tie, speaking a mile a minute, his eyes darting from the photogenic fe-male anchor to the camera, as if he expected one—or both—to draw a gun when he wasn't looking.

"What can we learn from all this?" the anchor asked him.

"Do not trust a soul. Or should I say a *soul mate*."

"Strong words."

"Strong but true." Nigel took a breath. "Think about

it. If the beautiful Lara Chandler isn't safe from betrayal, is anyone safe? Is anyone really?" He stared into the camera, his pupils pinging back and forth. "Remember, more exclusive photos in next week's *Asteroid* . . . plus a transcript of Chris and Dylan's dirty Dumpster tryst!"

As the anchor shifted to another story, Elliot turned to Nigel. "That 'Is anyone safe?' bit. . . . That gave me chills."

"Thanks. I'm rather proud of it myself."

Matthew flipped stations to a bemused-looking Caputo. "They were friends—that's all," he was saying. "Lara was on set a lot, too. Chris is a devoted husband."

"Look at that little smirk," said Kathy.

"He is so loving this," Matthew said. "This movie's going to be bigger than all his dad's films combined."

"God, yes," said Kathy. "If Terrence were alive, I'd call him for a quote."

Matthew flipped the channel again, and at last Simone saw Julie. . . .

As a voice-over described the "stunning young newcomer who rocked the foundations of Hollywood's happiest marriage," the camera showed live footage of Dylan Leeds walking from an office building to her car, a group of reporters shouting at her. Despite the heat, she wore a dark trench coat, huge sunglasses over her eyes.

"A star is born," said Matthew.

Was Simone just rationalizing, or did Julie look pleased with herself? Her hair gleamed in the sun; she'd obviously had it together enough to get it washed and styled that morning. Her makeup looked perfect too—the innocent pink lipstick . . . and . . . was she smiling, just a little bit?

"All right, back to work," said Nigel.

Kathy said, "Can't we at least see Greta Glass's take on this?"

"Oh, all right."

His cell phone trilled. He headed into the hallway.

Simone was staring not at Julie but at the shouting reporters. Among them was the *Interloper*'s Neil Walker.

Like Julie, Walker wore dark sunglasses. But unlike Simone's high school friend, he was not smiling at all.

Simone thought, *Maybe I am good.*

But as Simone sat down at her computer, she felt that bracelet on her wrist and she closed her eyes, unable to think of *Asteroid* sales or Julie's newfound stardom or even Walker—though he had looked so wonderfully annoyed. All she could think of was Keith Furlong the previous night, his red contorted face as he punched that tree . . . and the fact that Destiny had been nowhere in sight.

Nigel swept back into the reporters' room, folded up his cell phone, and said, without preamble, "Were you at the Blake Moss party last night?"

Simone cleared her throat, shook the image of Keith out of her head.

"Well, were you?"

"Uh, yeah, I . . ."

"Should have told me. Yes, you should. My source tells me both Clara and Dylan were in attendance?"

Simone sighed. "Yes."

"Well," he said, "what do you have for me?"

LARA'S TRAGIC MISTAKE: "I TRUSTED DIRTY DYLAN!"
"I . . . um . . ."

"Out with it."

"You wouldn't believe what I saw Lynzee de la Presa doing with that shipping heir from the TV show."

Nigel rolled his eyes. "Lynzee blows random blokes in public every time she drops a little X. Claims it helps warm up her vocal cords. It's old news, and we're a family publication." He peered at her. "I want to hear about Chrylanara."

"Seriously, Nigel. There isn't much to tell. Wait! Jul—Dylan gave me some hot leads about other stars. Get this, in the women's bathroom at Hyde—"

"Not interested. You're telling me you didn't even notice any palpable tension between Chris, Dylan, Lara, or all of the above?"

"No." She honestly hadn't. And as for Julie backstabbing Lara, she couldn't bring herself to tell Nigel. There was something so hypocritical about it—betraying someone to reveal a betrayal.

She had to draw the line somewhere.

"Right, well, ring her up now then. The *Interloper* is going to be all over this. We need more in this issue, and we need it to be exclusive."

"But . . . who knows if she'll say anything?"

"Make her." He glared at her. "Call her up and let her know how sodding, pissing awful you feel about all the bad press she's been getting."

Simone rolled her eyes. "All right." Before she'd left the party, Julie had given her a card with her home phone and cell number on it. She may as well call. Odds were she'd get voice mail, leave a message. *I've seen the news. How are you holding up?* What was the harm in that?

She took the card out of her wallet. *Dylan Leeds, Actor,* it read in feminine gold script. She'd call the cell number first, then the home phone. She'd leave messages at both places, and Nigel would be satisfied.

But when Simone called Julie's cell, she answered after one ring. "Thank God it's you, Simone."

"Hey, uh . . . I'm so sorry about all this bad press."

"I'm on the corner of Beverly and Pico. How fast can you get here?"

Simone looked at Nigel. "I guess I can be there in about . . . ten minutes?"

He raised his eyebrows at her and mimed applause.

"Great," said Julie. "Look for a black limo."

Simone shoved the business card into her back pocket, threw her microcassette recorder into her purse, and hurried out the door.

Exactly ten minutes later, Simone pulled up to the corner of Beverly and Pico, but she didn't see a limo anywhere. She parked her Jeep, got out and walked to the edge of the sidewalk and waited, staring out from

the residential street corner as if she were peering over
the edge of a cliff, looking for a ship that was lost at
sea.

She did say Beverly and Pico, didn't she?

A thought slithered into her mind: What if this was
some kind of trap? What if Julie had found out that she
worked for the *Asteroid* and she'd lured her here to . . . to
what? Paranoia. It was an occupational hazard, wasn't it?
No wonder Nigel was the way he was.

Simone's cell phone trilled.

She looked at the caller ID. "Holly?"

"You still have that bracelet, right?" Holly's voice was
sharp, agitated. She didn't sound like she'd slept, but at
least she wasn't slurring her words.

Simone crossed the street, looked up and down again.
Nothing. "Yes."

"Okay, listen," Holly said. "Do you know anyone,
maybe at the tennis club or something, who has any connections with the media?"

Simone gulped. "Why?"

"I know who murdered Emerald."

"What?"

"It's Keith, Simone."

Simone felt the name like ice against the back of her
neck.

"The police still won't listen to me, but I know it's
him, and I need to get it out there."

"How do you know?"

"He hates Wayne, hated that Emerald loved her dad so
much, and he hated that bracelet most of all, because it
was Emerald's favorite."

Simone remembered the *Devil's Road* party, the cold
way that Furlong had stared at her wrist. *Where did you
get that bracelet?*

"It would be just like him to kill Emerald, take her
bracelets, and give his other girlfriend the bracelet he
hated the most."

Good thing Dessy never showed. I've a feeling she

would have gotten it a lot worse than my tree. "Holly," said Simone, "did Keith ever get violent with Emerald?"

Three blocks up, a black limo screeched into view, just as Holly breathed, "He scared her."

"I gotta go," said Simone. "But you'll be around later, right?"

"Yeah."

"Good," she said, "because I do know somebody in the media you can talk to."

Just as she ended the call, the black limo pulled up beside Simone and jolted to a halt. From the same direction the limo had come, Simone saw a huge SUV traveling at top speed. The limo's back window cracked open to reveal Julie's face. "Get in fast," she said.

FOURTEEN

F orget about fastening her seat belt. Simone barely had time to close the door before the car was careering down Beverly, then hurling into a series of sharp right turns that made her regret the buttered bagel she'd eaten that morning. "Sorry," Julie said. "It's the paparazzi." Simone peered through the back window, saw a long black telephoto lens aimed out the window of the SUV. "What do they want pictures of?" she said. "The back of the car?"

"Really, what a bunch of freaks." Julie was still wearing the black trench coat and shades. On the other side of her sat a dark tower of a man who appeared to have been molded out of iron. His head was shaved and gleaming. His hands looked as if they could crush bricks with ease. "Simone, this is Maurice," Julie said. "He's Chris's bodyguard, helping me out for the day, right?"

Maurice gave Simone a slight nod, which struck her as more polite than dismissive. He was so powerfully built that his every gesture carried a slight threat; obviously, he was aware of that.

"Hi." Simone looked at Julie. "How are you holding up?"

"Good as can be expected. I mean, I figured maybe after the movie came out I'd start getting recognized, but . . . not this, you know what I mean?"

Simone hadn't planned on saying it, but looking at her onetime classmate in those black oversized sunglasses, she couldn't stop the question from coming out. "Julie, between you and me . . . is it true?" She could practically see Nigel applauding. *Brilliant, love. Between you and me. Earn her confidence.*

Julie took off the shades. Her eyes were calm and dry. "Let me tell you something, Simone," she said. "I don't screw men who belong to other women."

Someday, she is going to win an Academy Award.

The limo made a U-turn so sharp it was more like a V, and the SUV was history. It sped back up Beverly again. Simone groaned. "Where are we going?"

Julie gave her a halfhearted smile. "I'll buy you lunch afterward, okay?"

Eventually, the limo pulled into the parking lot of a Century City building. Maurice stretched, then began to slide out of the car. As he unfolded his large body, it was much the same effect of someone snapping together a submachine gun.

"Nice of Chris to lend Maurice to you," Simone whispered.

Julie rolled her eyes. "You don't even know."

Simone looked at Julie. "Can I ask you something?"

"Do I have a choice?"

"Why would you want to get mixed up with Chris Hart?"

"I told you," she said. "I don't screw men who belong to—"

"Be honest with me, Julie. Please."

Julie waited for Maurice to leave the car, and then she spoke so low that Simone strained to hear her. "Me and Chris. It's different than you think."

"What do I think?"

But then Maurice was back, holding the door open for

them, saying in his deep voice, "We don't want to be late."

"I'm really sorry about this, Simone," Julie whispered. "But I need a friend right now."

Simone nodded. What else could she do? They were standing on a small, hastily constructed wooden stage outside the Century City offices of Julie's manager, Randi Du-Monde. And they were about to hold a press conference.

On the other side of Julie stood Randi wearing a red linen suit and a facial expression that could intimidate cops, dictators, serial killers. Simone hadn't really gotten a good look at Randi at the party, overwhelmed as she'd been by the spontaneous porn going on behind her. Now, though, she saw that Randi was a spectacle in her own right—a perfectly coifed, expertly made-up, aging pageant queen of a woman, who carried her two-hundred-plus pounds with a scary grace. Large as she was, she was the type of person you couldn't imagine ever breaking a sweat. She was that cool, that in control. "Randi, meet my friend Simone," Julie said. "We went to high school together."

Randi's grip was viselike, and when Simone looked into her eyes, she saw fire. To say she was up for a fight would have been a terrific understatement. Randi was lit up like a chandelier at Caesar's Palace. She turned to Julie. "Ready to kick butt?"

"Yes, Randi."

"Good girl."

Also onstage were Maurice, a few publicists and lawyer types, and, next to Simone, Nathaniel. "Bet you wish you were passing dim sum to Nelson Mandela right now," he said.

Simone nodded. "God, yes," she said. "You do a lot of these things?"

"Press conferences? A few. It's like standing in front of a firing squad, only it takes longer and you can't smoke."

Simone looked down at the bank of microphones and TV cameras, at the print reporters gathering directly in front of the stage, shoving cassettes into their recorders, testing the microphones. She gulped.

Nathaniel said, "Why do I feel like I should be holding a bucket of chum?"

Simone's gaze passed over the logos on the TV cameras. She saw *Legal Tender* on one and backed up, so she was standing partly behind Julie.

"Let's get this party started," said Randi.

She walked up to the microphone and thanked everyone for coming. Simone watched her, speaking so clearly in that red suit, all coiled power. Simone leaned into Nathaniel. "She's loving this, isn't she?"

He nodded. "More than life itself."

As Randi continued to speak, Simone checked out the print reporters. Matthew was there. She locked eyes with him for a moment, and he winked, which put her a little more at ease . . . until she saw the man standing next to him.

Neil Walker. He winked, too.

Randi said, "If the *Asteroid* opts next week to run this libelous story, Ms. Leeds's legal team is prepared to take action."

Simone glanced again at Walker. He gave her a pleasant smile.

"And now, Ms. Leeds would like to read a prepared statement."

Julie walked up to the microphone. She had removed the trench coat and was wearing a sleeveless linen dress the color of peach yogurt. She moved with studied tentativeness as she took the typed page out of her purse and unfolded it, her hands trembling slightly. When she cleared her throat and spoke, her voice was soft, fragile. Simone remembered how Julie had looked at Blake Moss's agent— that calculated desire—and thought, *She can definitely act.*

"I am deeply shocked and saddened by an upcoming tabloid article linking me romantically with Chris Hart," Julie said, each word punctuated by what sounded like a thousand popping flashes. "I . . . respect and admire Mr. Hart. I would never do anything to break up a marriage, let alone a marriage as close and solid as his and Lara's."

Julie wiped a tear from her cheek.

The reporters were riveted; every eye in the group was fixed on her face . . . every eye, that is, except for those of Neil Walker. When Simone met his gaze, he held it, engaging her in a staring contest that—ridiculous as it was—she refused to lose.

"Questions?" Julie said. A few dozen hands went up, including Walker's.

You wouldn't dare.

The first question came from a *USA Today* reporter, who said, "Miss Leeds, what were you and Mr. Hart talking about behind the Beverlido?"

Julie cleared her throat. "Work," she said. "The film we're in, *Devil's Road*, hits theaters a week from today."

"But why would you be having a business discussion in an alley?"

"It was a sensitive business discussion." Julie brushed away another tear.

Simone thought, *She is better than Kathy Kinney.*

Then Julie pointed to Walker.

"Ms. Leeds," he said, "despite what you are going through, you look absolutely beautiful."

Oh, give me a break.

"Thank you. What a lovely thing to say."

Walker said, "Can you please tell us the identity of the young woman standing next to you?"

Simone stopped breathing.

"This is my manager, Randi Du—"

"No, ma'am. We all know Ms. DuMonde. I'm talking about the woman on your other side."

"Oh, this is Simone. She's one of my oldest and dearest friends, and she's here for moral support."

"So, you're saying she isn't a member of your legal team." His gaze probed Simone's face. "And she's not with the press."

"No," said Julie. "She's not." A pause followed—probably only a few seconds long, but it may as well have lasted days, weeks, centuries.

Walker smiled at Simone, a challenge of a smile that made her grit her teeth.

Julie called on the next reporter, a woman from *People* who wanted to know if Julie had spoken to Chris and Lara since that morning. By the next question, Simone felt calm again. She wondered why Walker hadn't outed her as an *Asteroid* reporter, but not for too long. She didn't want to think about why he did anything.

Later, back at the office, Nigel announced, "We will all be working through the weekend to keep our momentum going." And no one complained.

Simone wrote up a rather nebulous but intriguing story called INSIDE THE WORLD OF CHRIS'S NEW LOVE. Though nothing in it pointed directly to Simone, it did include Dylan's insistence "to friends" that she didn't steal other women's men and her wild car chases with the paparazzi (whom Nigel insisted Simone refer to as "fans"). The article also detailed Chris's protective feelings for his beautiful mistress, as evidenced by the fact he'd lent her his strongest bodyguard in order to shield her from legions of Dylan-haters.

The whole time, Simone couldn't stop thinking of her last phone conversation with Holly. And, at nightfall, she sped over to the personal assistant's bungalow.

Just as Simone was about to ring the bell, she sensed something odd. A rustling, as if someone were moving through the bushes around the side of the house. The hairs stood up on the back of her neck and her mouth went dry. "Who's there?" she said. The rustling stopped. She stepped away from the door and peered around the house. She saw nothing, no shadows. Still, she wished she had a flashlight because she could have sworn she heard something else . . . a whisper of a laugh.

Stop it, Simone. You're imagining things. She leaned on the bell.

Holly said, "Simone?"

"Hi."

Holly opened the door. She looked pale and gaunt, but her eyes and voice were clear—drug-free—and when Simone walked into her living room, it was neat and orderly. Her floors gleamed and her potted plants glistened with beads of water and everything smelled of pine cleanser. She may not have been able to leave her house, but she'd certainly been able to clean it.

Holly brought out two glasses of water and they sat down on the couch—jade green silk, identical to Wayne Deegan's. "I love your sofa," Simone said.

"Emerald," said Holly. "She had wonderful taste. She gave me this, too." Holly plucked the necklace she was wearing out of her T-shirt. Simone moved closer and looked at the pendant at the end, a large, single emerald cut in the shape of an *H*. "That is beautiful."

"I never take it off," said Holly, and Simone glanced at the bracelet on her own wrist, the bracelet Emerald had never taken off.

"So," said Holly, "is your media friend going to meet us here?"

Simone took a deep breath. This was harder than she thought it would be. She closed her eyes for a moment, then opened them again.

"Is something wrong?"

Simone thought of holding her breath and jumping into cold water, she thought of doing the right thing, she thought, *Holly deserves the truth.* Until finally she was able to make herself say the words: "I'm the media person, Holly."

"What?"

"I'm a reporter," she said, "for the *Asteroid.*"

"What?!"

Holly glared at her. In her black eyes, Simone saw the same anger and disgust she'd seen two days ago, when the police escorted Neil Walker off Emerald's property. "I'm sor—"

"You lied to me."

"I didn't know what to—"

"Get out."

"Holly."

"Get out!"

"No!" Simone's voice was louder than she'd intended. It bounced off Holly's walls and through her windows, a piercing shout. But Simone couldn't help it; she needed to be heard. She took a breath. "Look," she said, "you have every right to be angry."

"You bet I—"

"But consider this. Yesterday, you told me that Emerald was a cutter. That is *huge* news. But you asked me not to tell anyone—I gave you my word. I didn't tell a soul. I wrote up an on-the-record piece with Wayne Deegan, who gave a better story to the *Interloper*, and I almost lost my job. But still I didn't tell anyone, Holly," she said. "Still I kept your secret."

Holly stared at her, her eyes softening a little.

"So you can throw me out of here if you want, you can cold-call *People* or the *LA Times*. But I think that would be a big mistake." Simone took off the bracelet. "I may be a tabloid reporter," she said, "but I believe you. And I'm the best friend in the media you're ever gonna have."

For a long time, Holly sat on her couch, twisting her emerald pendant between her fingers and watching Simone, as if she expected her to say more. Finally, she took a breath. "Wayne is giving tabloid interviews?"

Simone nodded.

Holly took a sip of water, set the glass down on the coffee table next to a stack of *Suburban Indiscretions* scripts and a cluster of framed photographs—an elderly woman with Holly's large black eyes; a chubby-faced baby; Holly and Emerald in ski outfits, pink from the cold, beaming at the camera. "Okay then," she said quietly.

First, Simone called Nigel. "I have Emerald's assistant here, and she wants to go on record saying she believes Keith Furlong killed Emerald."

"Sounds brilliant," he said. "So long as it makes it through Legal."

"We've got the go-ahead," Simone told Holly. But the more she spoke to Holly, the less convinced she was that the article *would* make it through Legal. Yes, Keith had an anger management problem. Simone had seen it herself at Blake Moss's party. Yes, he was an obvious narcissist, and no, he didn't seem to care at all that Emerald had died in such a horrible way. As for motive, he *was* very pissed off that Emerald had talked to the *Asteroid* about him, but as Holly revealed, those were *his* malnourished, illegally poached birds. If Emerald had been trapped into discussing his cheating, he had no one to blame but himself. To Simone, the most incriminating thing was the bracelet. But while it was strange that a piece of Keith's girlfriend's jewelry would wind up in his lover's trash, that's all it was, strange. And strange was nowhere near enough to satisfy a tabloid's lawyers.

"You said Keith scared Emerald." Simone took a sip of water.

"Yes."

"Tell me about that."

Holly peered into her own glass. "She said he had secrets."

"You mean, like, with Destiny?"

"No. She said there was a part of him she didn't know. A dark side. Sometimes he'd disappear, wouldn't tell her where he was, and if she asked, he'd get this look in his eye . . ."

"Like a shark."

"Emerald just called it mean." She flicked off Simone's tape recorder. "That's all I've got."

Simone said, "Can I ask you something off the record?"

"Sure."

"Do you have any reason to believe Keith would have known about Emerald's knife collection?"

"Not really," she said. "She hid it from everyone. And

they each had their own bathroom. . . ." Holly picked at a finger. "You . . . you don't think there's a story here, do you?"

Simone sighed. "We'll figure something out."

"Thanks," she said. "You don't even know how many reporters I called—they don't care. I guess all anybody is into now is the whole Chris-Lara-Dylan thing, huh?"

Simone grimaced. "I guess."

"I just wish I could get the police to listen, but no."

"Why won't they, Holly?"

She sighed. "Emerald left a note, there was no sign of forced entry, no sign of a struggle, she was a cutter with a history of depression. And Keith had an alibi."

"He did?"

Holly nodded. "The manager, Cole, says he was at Bedrock that whole night."

Simone's spine straightened. "He wasn't."

"What?"

"I was at Bedrock that night," she said. "I talked to Cole. And I'll tell you one thing. If there's one place Keith *wasn't* the night Emerald died, it was Bedrock. And Cole knew it."

Holly's gaze sharpened. "So why did he lie to the police?"

"That," said Simone, "is a very good question."

As Simone left the bungalow and walked out to her car, headlines auditioned in her mind: KEITH LIED, EM DIED. EMERALD'S LAST NIGHT: WHERE WAS KEITH? *That might work*, she thought. Implying without out-and-out accusing. She would need a police quote. . . .

Simone pulled out her cell phone, tapped in the number Holly had given her, and heard the voice mail of Detective Louise Bianchi, Hollywood Division. "Detective Bianchi," she said, "my name is Simone Glass and I'm with the *Asteroid*. I wanted to talk to you about Keith Furlong's possible role in the death of Emerald Deegan. I would like a statement from you, but I also have some new evidence. Oh, yeah, and I can dispute his alibi." She hung up. *That should merit a callback.*

She folded up her phone. When she put the key in the Jeep's door, she felt a hand on her shoulder. She opened her mouth to scream, but no sound came out—a response that would have troubled her if she weren't so overtaken by terror. . . .

Which wilted when she turned and saw that the hand belonged to Neil Walker.

"Hi!" he said.

"What are you doing here?"

"Sealing the deal."

"What deal?"

"In case you don't remember, I spared your under-cover ass today. I do a good deed like that, I want something in return."

"What do you have in mind?"

He moved closer, brushed a lock of hair out of her eye. His burning gaze lingered on her face, and Simone thought, not for the first time, that he was very good-looking—in a smart-ass kind of way. "I think," he said, "you need to start sharing a little."

Simone felt a rush of color to her face. "Hey," she stammered, "I don't know what kind of women you hang around with, but . . ."

"Take it easy. I want to share Chrylan leads."

She cleared her throat. "Chrylan?"

"Yeah, you know. Chris, Dylan. The new Clara."

"You want to . . ."

He grinned at her. "What did you *think* I wanted?"

"Nothing!" *God, how embarrassing.* "Nothing . . . just . . . I don't share leads with the *Interloper.*"

"Oh, yes," he said. "Yes, you do." He was looking at a business card, holding it up to the light. "Unless you'd like me to place a call to Randi DuMonde, or . . ." He smiled at the card. "Hmmm . . . Dylan Leeds, Actor . . . Well, that's debatable. But I bet the contact information is accurate."

Simone stared at him. "Where did you get that?"

"You."

"When?"

"Just now. Got it out of your back pocket."

"How did you—"

"Know it was there? I didn't. Just exploring."

"You are . . . *unbelievable*."

"Come on, Simone. This arrangement can work for both of us. We can be like . . . a secret team. You give me the Dylan stuff you don't use, and I'll run it. And vice versa. I'll give you a piece of my leads. Our editors will think we've got great new sources. No one will ever know."

She leveled her gaze at him. "That sounds good," she said. "Except for, you know, all of it."

"Hey, I'm doing you a favor."

"Oh, really? What kind of leads do you have? I mean, other than the ones you steal from me."

"You'd be surprised, sweetheart."

"Yeah, right."

"Seriously. I'll give you one right now. I happen to know for a fact that Keith Furlong was cheating on Emerald Deegan."

"Wow, that's hot," she said. "Next you're going to tell me Elton John is gay." Surreptitiously, she slipped the bracelet into the side pocket of her purse.

Walker took a step forward, which put his body so close to hers she could actually feel the heat it emitted. "Look," he said softly. "We can make this easy . . . maybe even fun. Or I can force you into it. It's your choice."

Her chest tightened. A gasp escaped from her lips. "I don't trust you."

"The feeling is mutual."

Simone felt it again—the start of another ridiculous staring contest. *I don't have time for this. I really do not.*

But she did it anyway. She stood there, stock-still next to her Jeep, staring into his eyes, refusing to budge. What was it about him? No matter what was going on in her life, he made it more important to get the last laugh. *You have no idea*, she thought as she stared into those gas-flame irises. *You have absolutely no idea how badly I'm about to kick your butt with this Keith Furlong story.* She grinned up at him, eyes sparkling. For a second, Simone thought she saw something else in his eyes . . . something that may not have had anything to do with competition or Chrylan leads or . . .

Maybe she was just imagining.

A smile played across his lips. "What," he said, "is on your mind?"

She started to say something, but then she stopped, and then a sudden burst of mechanical sound put their staring contest to an end. Simone jumped a little, confused. Until she figured out it was both their cell phones, ringing at once.

Simone and Walker answered their phones in unison, doing a weird sort of dance as they attempted to hear each other's conversations while digesting their own, and speaking as quietly and cryptically as possible, so as not to be overheard. At one point, Simone realized she was following Walker and trying to get away from him at the same time.

This had to stop. Now.

It was Nigel on the phone, and Simone needed to focus on what he was telling her. Because what he was telling her made the blood freeze in her veins.

By the time she hung up with Nigel, Walker was already in his car. "I've got to run. We'll talk later," he said. But she didn't reply. All she could do was get in her Jeep and start it up and drive, to where Nigel had told her to drive—to the Starbright Hotel in East LA. All she could do was turn on the radio, try not to think too hard about what Nigel had said—his speech slowed to normal from shock. *"They found Destiny. She is dead. Her throat has been cut."*

FIFTEEN

According to Nigel's police source, Destiny's estimated time of death had been four thirty in the morning. Simone had been home already, sleeping off the rum and Cokes from Blake Moss's party—the party she'd supposedly gone to in order to try to find Destiny.

She hadn't tried very hard.

Simone had barely asked a few people where she might be—this missing seventeen-year-old girl with a dead woman's bracelet in her trash. . . . She'd spent most of the night hanging out with her friend, drinking, ogling celebrities, gossiping.

Simone could have saved Destiny. At least, she could have warned her—if she hadn't made excuses. *The kid's in Mexico right now, buying eight thousand dollars' worth of margaritas.*

Even as Kathy had said it, Simone had known it wasn't anything more than a pretty picture for her mind. And yet she'd told herself, *That makes sense.* Because she'd *wanted* it to make sense.

The shoe, too. Ever since Holly had told her that Emerald cut the backs of her ankles, Simone had thought that the Jimmy Choo in her trash—and the blood on it—must've belonged to Emerald. But it hadn't. . . . *And somewhere inside her, she'd always known.*

The first victim's shoe in the second victim's garbage. The second victim's bracelet in the third victim's garbage. . . . Three dead young women, their throats all slashed. Connected by what someone had forced them to throw away.

Their favorite belongings, their secrets, their lives. Trashed.

Simone remembered a journalistic adage that was a favorite of her features writing professor: Two's a coincidence. Three makes a trend.

Will it stop at three?

She turned on the car radio. A hyper-animated deejay, talking about Chris and Dylan, who suddenly seemed part of the distant, soft-focused past. "Lara Chandler!" he yelled. "I mean, come on. You get to hit *dat* any time you want, and . . . well, like this tabloid dude says—coming to you courtesy of our Fox news affiliate . . . *If the beautiful Lara Chandler isn't safe from betrayal . . . is anyone safe? Is anyone really?* My thoughts exactly, tabloid dude. Is *anyone* safe?"

The cars in front of Simone started to slow down and, several blocks up Sunset, she saw the flashing lights of police cars. "My thoughts, too," she said.

When Simone reached the Starbright, she saw Walker's black Saab parked a few blocks up and across the street. *Of course that's what his call was about.* She pulled behind it and parked just as he was getting out. She wasn't sure why. There were closer spaces. But somehow, it was better to be near him—even if he was the competition, even if he had lied to her, stolen her leads, threatened to give her up to Julie.

It was better to be near anyone right now.

He walked up to her window. "You drive fast."

"Yeah, well."

"So . . . you knew about Destiny and Keith Furlong?" he asked.

"Of course I did."

"And the steak."

"Yes, the steak, too."

Simone pictured the bracelet coiled in her purse like something lethal, something poisonous.

"What's wrong?" Walker said.

She was unable to get the thought out of her mind: *Whether or not Keith Furlong put that bracelet in Destiny's trash, the person who killed Emerald did.* "I want to tell you," she said, "but I can't."

He nodded. "I can understand that. Odds are, I wouldn't be able to tell you either." She got out of her car, and they both stood still, staring at the flashing jam of police cars. All that attention for one dead girl.

Walker said, "You want to call a truce for tonight? I mean . . . we're both here. We may as well . . ."

"Infiltrate together?"

"Yeah."

"I'd like that," Simone said quietly.

He turned away, looked up the street. "Good."

As they started walking toward the hotel, she said, "But, you know . . . don't expect me to share anything I get in there with you."

"Like I need you to share. I've been doing this since you were trying out for the cheerleading squad."

"I never tried out for the cheerleading squad. And it seems to me, about twenty minutes ago you were *begging* me to share."

"Chrylan leads. That's all I want from you, and that's what you're gonna give me." He gave her a sidelong glance. "Oh, and just FYI, I don't beg. For anything. Ever."

Simone stifled a smile. They crossed the street. At the hotel's entrance, a curly-haired blond guy was involved in a heated discussion with two uniforms. "I'm telling you," one cop was saying, "we have no statement at this time."

The blond said, "How long is *this time* gonna last?"

"Quite a while, sir."

"*Enquirer* reporter," Walker said, between his teeth. "Annoys the hell out of me."

"Walker," said Simone.

"Yeah?"

"I don't trust you."

He nodded.

"But I don't hate you, either."

He stopped walking and gazed at Simone's profile. "Same," he said.

The *Enquirer* reporter was still arguing with the cops as Simone and Walker approached. *They're never going to let us through.* She hesitated a little, trying to think of a plan, but Walker put a hand on her back and urged her past the group, and sure enough, they went right through the door. Behind them, Simone heard the reporter say, "There is such a thing as *freedom of information!*"

"Man, that guy is irritating," said Walker. "One on-the-record with Howard K. Stern and he thinks he's Woodward and Bernstein rolled into one."

They were about five feet away from the elevator. "I think we're actually going to make it," Simone said.

"Of course we are," Walker said. "All you have to do is act like you know where you're going."

He hit the button on the elevator just as a deep voice said, "Wait!"

Simone turned and saw a large ruddy-faced man with a thick shock of white hair. The man wore a dark suit, a loosened tie. And, as if he needed one, a detective's badge around his neck. "Wait!" he said again.

The elevator door opened and Simone jumped in, pulling Walker with her. She hit the CLOSE button, but Walker shoved his hand in front of the electric eye and held the door open for the approaching detective. "What the hell are you doing?" Simone said.

Walker didn't have time to answer before the detective was in the elevator with them, breathing hard, saying, "What's the matter, Neil? You forget how to say hi?"

Simone's eyes went big.

Walker smiled. "Act like you know where you're going—that is important," he said. "But it also helps if the lead detective knows you can beat the crap out of him."

The detective, whom Walker introduced to Simone as Ed Sandiford from Robbery-Homicide, hit the button for the fifth floor. "He's obviously trying to impress you," he said.

"You mean to tell me I *can't* beat the crap out of you?"

"I mean to tell you it's irrelevant, considering I have a Glock forty-five."

Simone said, "How do you guys know each other?"

"Neil and I met at a press conference a couple of years ago," Sandiford said. "We wound up at the same bar later, and I got to telling him about my son. He's a smart kid, real skinny though, and he was having this bully problem at school. Neil says, 'I can teach him how to box.' Turned out he wasn't lying."

Neil turned to Simone. "I generally don't lie to people carrying Glock forty-fives."

"Gotta get me a Glock," Simone said.

"Very funny."

"Anyway, thanks to this guy, my kid now kicks butt. So, to pay him back, I give him leads every now and again."

"You *do* box," Simone said to Walker. "You were telling the truth about that."

"Of course."

"So, are you really from Rhinebeck?"

Walker shook his head. "San Diego."

Unbelievable.

As the elevator climbed, Walker looked at Sandiford. "Another cut throat, huh?" he said. "Was it suicide?"

Sandiford's gaze went from Walker to Simone and back. "Off the record," he said, "it has been made to look like it. But, deep background, we're not buying it this time."

Simone stared at him. "Why?"

They reached the fifth floor. The doors opened. "You'll see," he said.

Cops and criminologists spilled out of the crime scene into the hallway. Two uniforms began moving toward Sandiford. He turned to Walker and Simone. "Make yourselves as invisible as you can," he said quietly. "And whatever you do, do not ask questions."

They stood behind Sandiford, following him past a group of crime scene photographers and into the room. The room Destiny had died in. The walls were yellow and cracked, and the carpet was so stained you couldn't determine the actual color. But what hit Simone worst was the smell—like the smell in Emerald's room, only stronger, so much stronger. . . . Her stomach seized up. She put a hand over her nose and mouth, tried to focus on sounds—the pop of cameras, the rustle of polyester uniforms, the murmur of voices . . . *Age of victim, seventeen and a half . . . Fully clothed . . . Cause of death appears to be a severed jugular . . . left index fingertip has been severed as well, right index finger severely infected, as the result of an older injury . . . contusions to the . . .*

"You okay?" said Walker.

She made herself say, "Yes."

In front of them, the group shifted as Sandiford and the two uniforms moved to the back of the room, giving them a clear view. Simone turned away for just a few seconds. *Okay. Ready, set . . .*

She turned back. She looked at the bed. Her breath died inside her.

It was lying on the bed—the thing that used to be a seventeen-year-old girl, arms and legs akimbo. The throat was deeply slashed, blood clinging to the neck, the face, the shoulders, fanning out from beneath the head like a dark halo. The face was so bruised it was impossible to tell her natural skin color, so contorted it was impossible to tell her age. It was impossible to tell what she had looked like at all in life, except for the strawberry blond hair now crusted with blood, and the eyes, gaping open in permanent terror. They were light green, her eyes, flat and cloudy, like sea glass. And her mouth . . . what was that jammed into her mouth? Some kind of gag, now drenched in blood.

"Are you all right?" said Walker. "Should we . . ."

Simone looked closer at the gag, at the thin, stacked edges, some of them green. . . . It was a wad of money. "Eight thousand dollars."

"What?"

One of her hands gripped a knife—thin, serrated, with a wooden hilt. As a criminologist moved toward the hand to photograph it, Simone thought of that raw steak as she said the words, "Steak knife."

She remembered the bracelet in her purse. "Where's Detective Sandiford?" She needed to talk to him, to give him the bracelet, but most important she needed to get out of that room, away from that smell, that destroyed body . . . that hate.

"I think he's in the hall," said Walker, and then Simone was out, Walker following her, saying in a low voice, a voice that wasn't his, "What do you think that meant?"

Simone didn't need to ask what he was talking about. She knew. He was talking about the two words written in blood on the wall over the bed.

Snow White.

SIXTEEN

In the hallway, Simone gave Sandiford the bracelet and told him it had been found in Destiny's trash. She also told him some of what Holly had said but, since Walker was standing next to her, she left out the more print-worthy details. Sandiford listened to her intently, wrote everything down on a steno pad.

Then she told him about the Cinderella slipper, and Walker's voice came back to her: *"You found Nia Lawson's shoe in Emerald Deegan's garbage?"*

Sandiford said, "Where is the shoe now?"

"My boss made me throw it out."

"Figures," Walker said.

"Regardless," said Sandiford, "I'm going to suggest we open up those other two suicides, start looking into the possibility of serial murder." He glared at Simone and Walker. "And that is not for publication under penalty of *death.*"

Simone said, "But—"

"I'd like you to run the bracelet story, though. Might bring him out of the woodwork. I mean . . . if there *is* a him. Or a her, or an anyone. It still could be three suicides."

"Not *three* suicides," Walker said. "How could Destiny have . . ."

"She did," Sandiford said.

"Huh?"

"The writing on the wall. Snow White. That's what you're talking about?"

Walker nodded.

"I don't know who cut the tip of her finger off, or if anyone forced her to do it. But there were paint flecks from that wall inside the wound," he said. " 'Snow White' was written by her, with the blood from that finger."

Simone and Walker rode the elevator down together in silence. As the doors opened, Simone glimpsed his profile, so pale, his jaw tense, and she knew he was thinking the same way she was, those same images stuck in his mind. That horror. It was not so much the thing on the bed, the inanimate body, but what the girl had to do in order to become that thing. *I don't know who cut the tip of her finger off, or if anyone forced her* . . . Simone thought of those pale green eyes, wrenched open forever, and she knew. Someone had forced her. . . .

They walked through the lobby without saying a word, passed the blond *Enquirer* reporter, who was no longer complaining to anybody. They moved beyond a few paparazzi standing outside, one of whom shouted out, "Hi, Neil!"

He didn't reply.

He walked Simone to her car, and for a second she thought he would just leave her there, as if they had never met at all. But instead he said, "I hope you don't mind this." And he took her in his arms, and the two of them held each other, saying nothing, for a very long time.

Simone felt like she might break down, or maybe *he* would . . . break down and cry for all that blood, all that hate, for that poor, torn, seventeen-year-old girl. But neither of them did. The silence, the warmth—they were enough.

Finally, Simone pulled away.

Walker said, "If you tell anyone about this, I will deny it."

"Who am I going to tell?"

"Good point. Anyway, truce is over. I'm stealing that bracelet story."

"You can't do that! Emerald's assistant gave me an exclus—"

"Kidding." He smiled at her—a small, sad smile. "It's all yours."

"Really?"

"But starting tomorrow I'm officially back on your ass. And you're giving me those Chrylan leads."

"Don't hold your breath." As she put the key in her door, her hand trembled a little.

"Simone?" Walker said.

"Yeah?"

"Are you okay?"

She looked into his eyes and decided to be honest. "I don't know."

"Me neither."

She nodded. "Good night, Neil."

"'Night."

As she drove home, Simone turned on the radio. Ludacris was bragging that he could "stay harder than a cinder block," and normally the line would have made her smile. *Thank you for that valuable information, Ludacris. It is duly noted.* But she couldn't listen, couldn't think about anything other than what she'd seen on that bed. She turned the radio off.

She remembered three days ago, when Nigel had given Elliot those camera phone photos of Destiny and ordered him to show them to Emerald.

Simone wished she had seen those photos, if only to have another image to remember her by—this girl, this torn, broken teenage girl.

Had Keith Furlong done that to her? Had he stood

behind her as she faced the wall, shaking and bleeding? Had he forced her to write those words? Was he capable?

Simone heard a sound in her car, the whistle of a dropping bomb, a mechanical explosion. It was her cell phone, the ringtone she had chosen for text messages. Who was text messaging her after midnight? Simone's skin froze as she recalled Holly telling her about the call she'd received from Emerald's killer . . . the laughing.

At the time, Simone had thought Holly was delusional, thought it was the Xanax talking—Xanax and sleeplessness and grief. But now, now . . .

Someone had made her write "Snow White" in her blood.

She grabbed her phone out of her purse, flipped to text messages, and looked at the screen. It was from Greta. Simone exhaled and opened the message:

Saw u at press conf! How do u know Dylan? Call me.

Simone hadn't felt close to her sister for years—but now, it was as if they lived on separate planets. She turned her gaze back to the road, and she knew she couldn't go home, not now. She couldn't pull out her bed, couldn't change her clothes, couldn't brush her teeth and lie down and sleep. She couldn't say to herself, *I'll work on the story tomorrow.* Not now, with awful questions burning in her mind. She needed to talk to someone, anyone, who knew Destiny alive.

She looked at the time: 12:20 a.m. *Not too late*, she thought. She hit END, tapped in 411, and asked for the address of Pleasures, in Hollywood.

Years earlier, Simone had read an article in *Cosmo* titled "Strippers' Sexy Trade Secrets," which stated, "Purple or red lights make cellulite disappear!" Pleasures obviously subscribed to this theory. The place was awash in purple light and mirrors. As she walked in, Simone looked down at her hands, which were glowing violet, and felt as if she'd stepped into someone else's strange dream.

The air was thick with perfume and baby oil, Fergie's

"London Bridge" blaring over the speaker system. Three women, naked and shaved, writhed on the horseshoe-shaped stage, clinging to polls, then slipping to all fours, playing to the men at the tables below. Fergie's voice moaned, "Make you go down," and other women slinked through the crowd in flimsy negligees, beaming at customers, mingling. Since California state law prohibited alcoholic beverages in top-less/bottomless strip clubs, there was a juice bar at the back of the room. For some reason, Simone found this more per-verse than anything else: fully dressed men sipping orange juice and vitamin water while talking to women wearing nothing but see-through swaths of fabric. If the men had been getting sloppy, make-an-ass-of-yourself drunk, at least, humiliation-wise, it would have made for a more even play-ing field.

Simone walked up to the bar, Destiny's dead green eyes in her mind. She ordered a glass of seltzer, well aware of how the bartender looked at her, a woman alone, wearing jeans and sneakers in a strip bar. "Is Pellegrino okay, ma'am?" he said, a tinge of sarcasm in his voice.

Simone nodded, her gaze scanning the room for a girl to talk to. A few seats down, a very tall, voluptuous redhead in a filmy black slip was talking to two middle-aged con-ventioneers in suit coats, one with a terrible comb-over, the other still wearing his "Hello my name is" sticker. Simone took her bubbly water and moved closer.

The conventioneers may not have been drinking at Pleasures, but they'd certainly had a few earlier, and it showed all over their sweaty pink faces, advertised itself in their slurred speech. "If you give my friend a lap dance and I, uh, watch," Comb-over was saying, "then I don't have to pay, right?"

"Sorry, sweetie, private dances are private." The red-head stared him down hungrily. "I wish I didn't make the rules. I'd take you both. For free."

His friend grinned at her. "My name is Frank," he said, the silliness of that comment amplified by the sticker on his coat. *Must be really proud of his name.*

The redhead winked at him. "Charity."

Simone said, "You can say that again."

"Huh?" said Frank.

Simone asked her, "Can I talk to you, in private?"

Charity turned, stared Simone in the eye. "I love girls," she said. "Does your boyfriend want to watch?"

"No boyfriend."

Charity gave her the exact same wanton look she'd just bestowed on Comb-over. "Thirty dollars for fifteen minutes."

Comb-over said, "Can I watch? *Please?*"

Simone leaned close to Charity. "I don't want a lap dance," she said. "I want to talk to you about Destiny."

Instantly, the hungry glint evaporated. "Are you a cop?"

"No," said Simone. "I'm . . ." *A reporter? Friend? Pilates partner?* "I'm worried."

Charity stared at her, saying nothing for what could have been a full minute. Then she grabbed Simone's hand and said to the conventioneers, "Sorry, boys. This is going to be one on one."

Charity took Simone into one of the back rooms, a small space with a velvet banquette, one hard chair, and a wall full of mirrors. *If it weren't for the red lights, you could hold dance classes in here.* And in a way, that was appropriate—pure theatrics.

Charity closed the door, urged Simone into the chair, and kneeled in front of her—all for the benefit of the surveillance camera. Then she said, "I'm worried too."

"Do you know what—"

"Some cops were here a little while ago. Told us what happened. Suicide. Yeah, right."

Simone looked at her. "So, you don't think she killed herself either."

"No way," she said. "There was nobody happier than Destiny, especially in the last week. She had some deal going on, said she was going to be famous."

The image flashed in Simone's head, the wad of

blood-drenched bills shoved in Destiny's mouth. "When was the last time you saw her?"

"Four days ago." She gave Simone a long, steady look. "How about you?"

"Huh?"

"When was the last time you saw her?"

"Well . . ."

"You didn't know her, did you?" said Charity. "You *are* a cop."

She shook her head. "Reporter."

Charity rolled her eyes. "Jesus." She started to get up.

"Wait," said Simone. "Please. I know how it sounds. But this isn't . . . it's not for publication."

"Give me a break."

"I know it wasn't suicide," she said, "because I saw her tonight. I saw what was done to her."

Charity stopped. "Really?"

She nodded. "I was at that hotel. With the cops, and I saw. It was . . . horrifying."

Charity brought a hand to her own neck. "Cut."

"Yeah, but there was more." Simone stared at her. "You don't want to know."

"God," she whispered. "The poor . . ."

"I meant what I said. I am worried. I'm worried for whoever is next because—"

"Next?"

Simone said, "I'm afraid the same person who killed Destiny killed Emerald Deegan. Nia Lawson, too."

Charity half collapsed on the floor and looked up at Simone, her pale skin reflecting the red lights in a way that made her seem bruised. "My God," she kept saying. "My God, my God . . ."

"I'm just . . . I'm trying to make sense of this. And to do that, I've got to know what Destiny was like when she was alive. . . . What she was into."

She said, "What do you need to know?"

"Did she do drugs? I'm wondering if maybe a dealer . . ."

"No drugs. She said they ruined your looks. She didn't drink either."

"Did she have a boyfriend? Anybody who . . . maybe seemed a little weird?"

Charity examined her long red nails for a drawn-out moment. "It's probably because we're so close to the studios, but we get some VIPs here," she said. "A lot of them liked Destiny."

"Why?"

She tilted her head to the side, gave Simone an appraising look. "If you were interviewing me for your newspaper, I would tell you it was because she had a sort of light around her—a natural charisma that they were drawn to, like she was one of them."

Simone said, "What if I wasn't interviewing you? If this was all off the record. What would you tell me then?"

Back to the nails. "I would tell you that VIPs tend to be freaks," she said softly. "Destiny was willing to . . . do certain things. Plus, she was discreet."

Until recently. . . . "Was there anybody in particular?"

"There were lots of them. They'd take her out to the hot clubs, parties. Promise her stuff if she did things in return. Golden showers, B and D, light torture . . . Destiny wasn't into any of that but, you know . . ." Charity's lips curled into a small, bitter smile. "She called it 'paying her dues.'"

Simone winced. *Say his name.* "Have you ever met Keith Furlong?"

"Yes," she said slowly. "I know Keith."

"What do you think of him?"

Charity was quiet for so long that Simone almost repeated the question. "Keith Furlong," she said finally, "is a very important person."

After Simone left the back room, she tried her luck with a few other strippers. She didn't get very far, though. She was clean out of cash, having given it all to Charity—but that probably didn't matter much anyway. For most of them, Destiny's name was enough to cut off all conversation before the cost of alone time ever came up. Simone's eyelids were starting to drift shut. She knew she had to get home or risk falling asleep at the wheel.

She walked out to her car, taking in the strangeness of this night. Five hours ago, she had thought Emerald's death was probably a suicide after all. She'd gone to Holly's out of kindness—guilt, maybe—but her main concern had been Chrylan. Now Chrylan was the last thing on her mind, so overtaken was it with images of three young, dead women.

Simone heard footsteps behind her. That *watched* feeling slithered up her back again. And then, on her shoulder, she felt the weight of a hand. *Walker.* Without bothering to turn around, Simone said, "Are you sure your name isn't *Stalker*?"

"I don't get it," said the voice. It wasn't Walker.

Simone spun around. The dim lights of the parking lot illuminated the face, the Ping-Pong-table eyes of Keith Furlong. "Looking for a job?" he said.

"I . . . uh . . ."

"Because you aren't quite Pleasures material."

Don't look afraid. Don't act afraid. "Can't blame a girl for trying."

Furlong said, "Who do you work for?"

"What?"

"You heard me"

"I don't . . . I don't know what you're talk—"

He took a step closer to her, bent down, put his face so close to hers that when he spoke she could smell his mouthwash, his thick cologne. It sickened her, the closeness. But she would not move, would not make room for him, she would not . . . "You are a reporter," he said. *"Who do you fucking work for?"*

Don't back up. Don't look afraid. Don't think about Destiny's face. "Why did Cole lie for you, Keith?"

"What?"

"The night Emerald died. Cole told the police you were at Bedrock. Why'd you have him do that?"

"I didn't have Cole do anything," he said between his bleached teeth. "You didn't answer my question."

"Where were you that night? What were you really doing when Cole said you were at Bed—"

His hands went around her throat, thumbs pressing against her voice box. He did it lightly, but she felt it in his thick fingers—the potential. "You have any idea how easy it would be?"

"Get your hands off me."

"Who do you work for?" The thumbs pressed a little harder.

He is just trying to scare you. Don't let him. Scare him back. . . . "Go ahead and ask Detective Sandiford where I work," she said. "He knows."

"Bullshit," he said. But the hands dropped away.

"I'm on my way to meet Ed now," Simone said. Her voice pitched a little higher, but she kept it steady enough, considering. "Do you want me to have him call you? Because I can."

Furlong said nothing. He just stood there, breathing hard, his fake green eyes filled with hate. Very quietly, he said, "I'm watching."

As calmly as she could, Simone turned and headed toward her Jeep. But the whole ride home, her heart thumped against her ribs, those two words lingering in her head like a recent nightmare. *I'm. Watching.*

SEVENTEEN

At work on Saturday morning, Simone wrote up two stories: "Was Emerald Murdered?" and "Keith's Secret Lover Found Dead!" According to the Legal Department in New York, the *Asteroid* could not point the finger directly at Furlong in either piece, though the Emerald article could include on-the-record quotes from Holly, in which she described Keith as "heartless," "an egomaniac," and "only after Emerald for her money."

For the "Secret Lover" article, Simone got a quote from Sandiford in which he claimed they were still considering the death a suicide—though she did get him to admit, on the record, that Furlong's connection to both dead women was "suspicious."

Strongest of all was the sidebar, "The Mystery of the Bracelet," complete with the photographs Simone had taken with Holly's camera phone. But, while she was allowed to ask in print why Emerald's bracelet had been thrown in Destiny's trash on the evening of her death, Sandiford asked her not to dispute Furlong's alibi for that night. "We don't have enough on him," he explained. "If he is guilty, that could make him run."

Simone wished she could stick it to Furlong a lot worse than that. Frightened as she was by the previous night's run-in, she thought she'd be safer from him if he were implicated in print. Under public scrutiny, he would want to lay low, act as innocent as possible. He would want to stay away from the reporter he'd threatened. But this way, with his guilt only hinted at . . .

I'm watching.

On the positive side, Emerald's and Nia's death investigations had been officially reopened, the division detectives turning them over to Robbery-Homicide. This morning, Holly had told Sandiford about the phone calls she had received and about her deep, growing suspicion of Keith Furlong.

"You want me to call Loverboy for comment?" said Kathy.

"That would be great."

Simone finished the mystery sidebar and stretched. Except for whatever comment Kathy was about to get from Furlong, all three of her articles were done.

Her cell phone chimed. Walker. Her face flushed a little. She covered up his name on the screen and said between her teeth, "You realize I'm at work right now."

"Just wanted to let you know," said Walker, "I meant what I said last night."

"About . . ."

"Being officially back on your ass. Today."

"Oh, now, please."

"One hot Chrylan lead, by the end of the day, please," he said.

"At least you said please."

"Don't think I'm gonna take it easy on you because of that hug," he said. "I still have this business card, and I'm not afraid to use it."

"But—"

"By the end of the day, please." *Click.*

Simone put her head in her hands, rubbed her eyes. *You wouldn't dare, Neil, would you?*

She got up and moved behind Elliot.

The final sidebar on the spread was historical—the one Elliot had originally prepared for the Emerald suicide story, then called "Look Who Else Cut Their Own Throats!" Interestingly, it now *worked*. Thanks to the paucity of examples, the sidebar supported the theory that Destiny, Emerald, and even Nia had been murdered. The new title: "It's the Least Popular Form of Suicide!"

Simone read over Elliot's shoulder. *Manic-depressive silent movie queen Magda Adair slit her throat with a diamond hat pin after discovering her husband in bed with the housekeeper. Schlock movie producer Reginald King cut his jugular with a hunting knife after gay rumors surfaced in a tell-all book, penned by his wife . . . But other than those two famous cases, suicide by cut throat has been practically unheard of.*

Elliot said, "Not happy campers, huh?"

Simone nodded.

Kathy hung up her phone. "Man, Furlong is an asshole."

"What did he say?"

" 'No fucking comment, bitch.' *Through his assistant!* I wish we could run the quote just like that."

Elliot chuckled. " 'No fucking comment, bitch,' said Keith, through a spokesperson."

Simone smiled a little. "Where's Matthew, by the way?" she asked Kathy. "I haven't seen him all morning."

"He and Carl are out choosing china patterns. Nigel gave them the morning off."

"Wait. *Matthew and Carl?*"

She nodded. "They're getting married in Massachusetts."

Elliot sighed. "Why didn't they choose Hawaii?" he said. "Provincetown is going to be freakin' freezing in the wintertime."

"Matthew *and Carl*?" Simone said again.

Nigel stood in the doorway. "I need to speak with you."

The room went quiet. Simone glanced up from her

computer and saw that he was talking to her, the same hard glint in his eyes as had been there days earlier, when he'd nearly fired her over Wayne Deegan. "What's up?"

"Please come into my office."

Simone got up from her desk, thinking, *Please?*

"Sit down," said Nigel. He closed his office door.

"What did I—"

"It has come to my attention," he said, "that you have been associating with the enemy."

"What?"

"You've been spotted with Neil Walker, from the *Interloper.*" He spat out the name. "That is instant grounds for dismissal."

Simone's heart dropped. She started to say, "I don't know what you're talking about." But midsentence, she realized there was no point.

She thought of the paparazzo shouting, "Hi, Neil!" Of all the police officers she and Walker had passed. Of course someone would have noticed them and told Nigel. Nigel had police sources, he knew all the paparazzi. He had spies everywhere—even at the *Interloper.* "We were . . . we were both covering Destiny," Simone said. "We couldn't really avoid each other."

"My source saw you walking across the street together, into the hotel, leaving the building still together. My source said you were publicly intimate."

"I was not *intimate.*"

Nigel glowered at her. "So you are saying that the rest of it is true."

"Okay, yes. We showed up together. He had been trying to blackmail me into sharing leads."

"With what information did he blackmail you?"

"He was at the press conference, Nigel. He saw me with Dylan Leeds. He threatened to tell her I'm with the *Asteroid.*"

Nigel's scowl darkened. "Right," he said. "Well, in that case I have one question for you."

Simone waited.

"How the fuck did he know you work for the Aster-oid*?!"*

She grimaced. "Because . . . I told him."

"You—"

"He kicked me off the *Suburban Indiscretions* set. I thought he was a security guard, I swear. I thought . . . I don't know what I thought, but he's a really good liar, and I'm so, so sorry. I promise it will never happen again."

"You're fired," Nigel said.

"But I'm telling you the truth."

"I've no doubt of that."

Simone stared at Nigel, and he stared right back. Slowly, she got up from the chair and left his office.

Simone opened her desk drawer, removed her micro-cassette recorder, her pens and steno pads, and collected business cards and matchbooks—souvenirs of less than one week on the job—and shoved them all into her purse.

"What are you doing?" Kathy said.

Simone couldn't look at her. She couldn't speak.

"Simone?"

Simone unplugged her phone charger and put it in the bag with everything else. She noticed three new messages on her cell phone and listened to them there, just because she couldn't bring herself to walk out the door.

The first was from Holly. "Things went great with Detective Sandiford," she said. "Thanks so much for everything—I have new respect for the *Asteroid*."

Simone sighed and hit SAVE.

Elliot said, "What happened with Nigel?"

The second message was from Greta. "Hi, Monie! I hope things are going great at the *Edge*. Listen, I don't know if you got my text message, but I saw you on TV with Dylan Leeds. I've been trying to get an exclusive interview with Dylan and I'm wondering . . ."

Simone hit ERASE.

Kathy said, "Simone. What is going on?"

Simone hit END after the next message, a hang up from "restricted." Strange, but at this point she didn't care. Tears were beginning to creep into her eyes, but she wouldn't cry. Not here, not in front of everyone, not over this damn job.

She thought about Walker. What if that had been his plan all along—getting her fired? What if Destiny's death hadn't leveled him the way it had leveled her? What if he'd only hugged her like that so the paparazzi could see them, so they could report back to Nigel?

That was probably far-fetched, but the fact was, Walker had won. She had lost her job. She was no longer an insider. The staring contest was his.

"I'm fired," she said.

"Oh, my God," said Kathy.

Simone's face was hot. She felt tears welling up again and bit them back, hurried out the door without bothering to check and see if she'd left anything. On the way out, she passed Carl and Matthew walking in together with bags from Neiman Marcus. "Congratulations," she said.

"Where are you going?" said Matthew.

"What's wrong?" said Carl.

But she was already in the elevator. Already going down.

Emerald sat next to Holly on her jade green couch, bracelets clinking as she raised a glass of champagne. "This, my dear, is cause for celebration!" she said.

"Do you mean the Asteroid *article?" Holly said. "Or the police investigation?"*

"Neither." Emerald clinked Holly's glass. "What I mean is," she said, "you're finally sleeping."

Holly's eyes opened. She was in bed. After she returned from Detective Sandiford's office and put in a call to Simone, Holly had changed into a big T-shirt, gotten under her covers, and, for the first time since Emerald's death, she had slept without the aid of pills, and she had dreamed. Yet another thing to thank Simone for.

She stretched, looked at her clock. Two in the afternoon. She'd only slept for four hours, but to Holly it felt like days. Normally she hated napping; it made her feel groggy and lazy, but now she was energized. She needed to call Wayne Deegan. Emerald's body had been cremated; there would be no funeral. But she and Wayne needed to plan a memorial service. She'd already received calls from Emerald's *Suburban Indiscretions* cast-mates asking about that. And she hadn't known what to tell them—hadn't been able to return their calls. Now she could. Now she could do anything.

Holly got out of bed and walked into her living room. She sat on her couch, reached for her phone, and started to tap in Wayne's phone number, fingering the emerald pendant that hung from her neck. But she stopped when she noticed a manila envelope on the floor, her name written across it in neat block letters. Someone had slipped it under her door.

She walked across the room, picked up the envelope, and opened it. There was a piece of spiral notebook paper inside, and when she turned it over, when she saw what was on it, she collapsed onto the floor, the blood thrumming in her neck, her face.

And then she started to cry.

It was a cartoon drawing of a naked Emerald, ribs protruding, eyes huge and pleading, mouth wrenched open in a silent scream. Scars were drawn on the cartoon Emerald's abdomen and wrists, and blood spurted out of its neck. Above the head hovered a thought bubble, the sentence inside it written in the same block letters: SHUT UP, HOLLY!

At the bottom of the page in smaller letters were the words "I am watching."

All the shags had been carefully removed.

During the drive back to her apartment, Simone tried

not to think about the fact that tomorrow and the next day and the next, she would have no reason to climb Coldwater Canyon. She would have no reason to worry about Keith Furlong either, because before she knew it, she would be on her way back East again, her journey across the country deemed an official failure. Who knew if Kathy, Elliot, and Matthew would pick up her leads on Destiny, Emerald, and Nia? But odds were, the story would die. After all, none of those women moved issues like Chrylanara. Speaking of which, who would be the *Asteroid*'s Chrylan insider now? Would Kathy try to befriend Julie? Would Matthew charm her to distraction as Elliot dug through her trash? Or would they try for that closeness and fail and ultimately fold as New York went through with its plan of shutting down the West Coast bureau . . . all because Nigel couldn't handle a reporter talking to the competition. Seriously, when you thought of it in those terms, Nigel's reasoning was ridiculous. What did he say she was doing? *Associating with the enemy*? Please. What was this, an episode of *Survivor*?

Of course, none of that made her feel any better. She'd reached the bottom of Coldwater Canyon and was driving through Studio City when her cell phone rang. She answered it. "Hi, Julie."

"What's wrong? You sound awful."

"Huh? Oh . . . I'm just tired."

"Well, I hope you're not too tired. I'm meeting Randi and a bunch of *Devil's Road* people at Swifty's tonight at nine. I want you to come with me." She added, "Your high school crush will be there."

"Who?"

"Chris Hart, silly."

Yeah, right, that's what Chris Hart is known as these days. "Okay."

"Great. Text me your address, and I'll pick you up in the limo."

"Looking forward to it," she said, even though she

wasn't looking forward to it at all. Simone was getting tired of *Devil's Road* people, tired of VIPs. Charity was right—they were a bunch of freaks. But Julie was still so hard to say no to.

Just as Simone was pulling up to the curb in front of her apartment building, her cell phone chimed again. She glanced at the caller ID, and her heart beat a little faster. "Nigel?"

"Hello, love," he said. "Listen, I've been thinking about it, and I've decided you're not fired."

"I'm *not*?"

"Have you heard today from Dirty Dylan?"

She winced at the name. "Yes. We're getting together tonight. At Swifty's."

"Brilliant." Simone could hear the smile in his voice. "I believe I've found a way to make the situation work in our favor."

From her apartment, Simone phoned Desert Ranch spa in Palm Springs and reserved a room under the name of Britt Gleason. Then she called the West Coast bureau of the *Interloper* and asked for Neil Walker. When he picked up, and she said, "Hi, it's Simone," he said, "I was just going to call you."

"Yeah, well, I've got your Chrylan lead."

"So I guess I won't be calling Dylan, then," he said. "Too bad, because this is a *very* attractive business card."

"It is," she said. "But this lead is much more gorgeous."

"You're killing me here. Out with it."

"Are you sitting down?"

"Yes, yes. . . ."

"Dylan's pregnant."

"What?!"

"She just found out, and she is freaking. Says she needs to get away from it all, figure things out."

"I can't believe this."

"Believe it. She's checking into Desert Ranch tonight, and I wouldn't be surprised if Chris heads down there too."

"Are you . . ."

"On my way, yeah." She sighed heavily. "I promised I'd meet her. But I bet you anything Chris shows up and tries to talk her into having the baby."

"Jesus," he said. "This is huge!"

"Oh, I almost forgot. Dylan is traveling under the name of Britt Gleason."

"See you there," he said.

"Just don't give me away."

"Wouldn't think of it," he said. "You know, one good turn . . ."

She felt a jab of fresh guilt, and she tried to ignore that, tried to ignore everything except that she had her job back. She looked at the clock. It was five p.m. Plenty of time before Julie would pick her up in the limo. But she may as well get ready—take a shower, make herself something to eat. The shower, in particular, was sounding good. She started to unbutton her shirt, then stopped as she thought of Walker again. No doubt he was in his car right now, driving all the way down to Palm Springs. It was a good plan, yes. And the fact was, he'd threatened her first. *One Chrylan lead by the end of the day.* Who did he think he was? Still, she felt bad about it.

Some things couldn't be ignored, no matter how hard you tried. . . .

The phone rang. At first, she thought it might be Walker, saying, *I can't believe you thought you could put one over on me.* But when she glimpsed the caller ID screen, Holly's name was on it. Simone picked up the phone. "Hi, Holly," she said. "Sorry I didn't call you back, but I had this problem at work and—"

"Simone." Holly's voice was small. "Is there any way you can pull that story about Keith?"

Her breath caught. "Has he been threatening you?"

"No, no . . . nothing like that. I just . . . I've changed

my mind. That's all." She sounded as if her whole body was trembling.

Simone breathed into the phone, and said, "Holly, I'll try. But I don't know if I can."

Holly didn't reply. She had already hung up.

EIGHTEEN

Swifty's was the VIP lounge of the Beverlido Hotel, but years ago, "back in the day," as Julie told Simone, "it was just the Lounge. Everybody used to come here—Dino, Frank, Marilyn . . . but also girls like me, who wanted to get discovered."

"I'd say you've been discovered, Julie."

She laughed a little. "Yeah, really."

The two of them were sitting at a corner table—one of the most sought-after spots in the small, dimly lit room, which was, in turn, one of the most-sought-after spots in all of LA. Like everything else in the Beverlido, Swifty's had undergone a sort of retro face-lift. With its dark wood paneling, Tiffany light fixtures, and elaborate 1930s-style ashtrays (those important enough to get in were certainly allowed to smoke), the bar was designed to make you feel like you'd stepped into an unusually glamorous time capsule. It was, as they say, art directed to death.

On a purely professional level, Simone knew how lucky she was to get into this place—it was an eavesdropper's dream come true. But much as she tried to enjoy the setting, she couldn't stop thinking about Holly, how frightened she had sounded. Why? What had happened?

Simone had phoned Nigel, asked if they could retract the Emerald story, or at least take Holly's quotes out of it. But no, he said. According to the New York office, the article had shipped. When Simone had called Holly back, she had said, "That's okay." But not like she meant it. She had said it in a tiny, lost voice that made Simone think, *It is not okay at all.*

Julie was talking now, something about Shirley Temple drinking Shirley Temples in this very seat.

Simone said, "Sounds cannibalistic."

Julie smiled. "You're still funny," she said, her gaze floating around the room.

"Not my best line, but thanks." Simone's eyes drifted to the pencil lead in Julie's cheek and it hit her yet again, how surreal this all was. Julie Curtis, in her life again, and unbelievably famous. When they had first come in, Julie had pointed out four major studio execs, and on her own Simone had recognized Will and Jada Pinkett Smith, Cate Blanchett, Lynzee de la Presa and that shipping heir. Involved as they were in their own conversations, they all gaped at Julie as if she were a goddess. Or a nine-car pileup. Either one.

Julie didn't seem to notice. She had said it herself: *If there's one thing I know how to handle, it's attention.*

"Oh, good, they're here," she said. Simone looked across the room and saw Randi DuMonde and her associate, Nathaniel, followed by Jason Caputo, a pouting brunette who had to be a model, Blake Moss, Chris Hart, and his bodyguard, Maurice. They approached the table, and greetings were exchanged, Caputo introducing the woman as Ila. *Why aren't these women ever called Debbie or Pam?*

Of all of them, Simone was probably happiest to see Maurice. There was something so soothing, so safe in that calm, lethal presence. She recalled her confrontation with Furlong in Pleasures's parking lot. How differently it would've gone down had Maurice been by her side. Fleetingly, she thought, *Maybe, once I get to know him better, Chris can lend me Maurice, too.* But then she remembered she was not a friend but a tabloid spy. And odds were, Julie would learn that fact long before Simone got to know Chris at all. She shuddered. She didn't want to think about that, but it did seem inevitable.

How would it happen? Would Julie ever forgive her?

"Hi, angel," said Blake. He took Simone's hand and kissed the inside of her wrist—an uncomfortably intimate thing to do, considering he didn't even know her last name. "What happened to your pretty bracelet?"

Simone coughed. She looked at Caputo, waiting for him to tell his villain to put the waitress down, but he was too busy ordering Grey Goose and sugar-free Red Bull for Ila, Cristal for everybody else.

Once the waitress left, Caputo turned to Randi. "You look like hell."

"How do you expect me to look?" she said.

"Randi," Nathaniel explained, "was at the police station for a couple of hours today."

Simone's gaze snapped onto him. "Why?" she and Caputo said at the same time.

Moss asked again, "What happened to your bracelet?" He was still holding her hand. This bothered her.

"Clasp broke," she said. "It's at the jewelers."

Hart said, "How are you, Dylan?" and Simone was caught between probing his face for emotion, trying to hear Nathaniel explain to Jason why the police had been questioning Randi, pulling away from Blake, and attempting to see around Ila, who sat statue-still between Simone and Julie—a beautiful, placid obstruction.

"I'm fine, Chris," Julie said.

"Are you sure?"

"Yeah, don't worry, I'm—"

"I need to talk to you," he said. "In private." His voice was calm, but very cold, even angry, Simone thought. Odd. Why would Chris be angry at Julie?

"*Now,* Dylan." Chris stood up and walked to the far end of the room without even looking back, Julie trailing after him like a pet. Maurice started to get up too, but Chris gestured at him to sit back down.

Simone wanted to exchange glances with Maurice, to ask him, "What was *that* about?" But clearly the bodyguard was not interested in gossip. From the inside pocket of his tailored suit coat, he produced the latest issue of *Forbes* and started to read, as if he were sitting in a doctor's waiting room next to a bunch of sick people he had no desire to know.

Nathaniel said to Caputo, ". . . and the detective showed her pictures."

Randi's eyes were downcast. Though she was wearing another bright red outfit—this time a high-collared knit dress that clung to her large body in a what-are-you-looking-at sort of way, with matching high heels that put her several inches over six feet, her face didn't match the power ensemble. She looked tired, defeated, a little bit ill, even. Simone thought, *Pictures of what?*

"Damn, Randi," Caputo said. "I'm sorry. I had no idea. I've just been so wrapped up in the whole promotion thing for the film, I . . . God, that's just . . ."

Simone nudged Ila. "Do you happen to know what they're talking about?"

"New client of Randi's?" she said in a thick Russian accent. "She has killed herself?"

Simone could feel the blood rushing out of her face. "Which client?" she asked, from across the table.

Randi looked at Simone, then took a huge swallow of champagne and glanced sidelong at her associate, as if cueing him to speak.

"You probably haven't heard of her," Nathaniel said. "Her name was Destiny."

Destiny was a client of Randi's. Nia Lawson was a client of Randi's. . . . As soon as she could, Simone excused herself from the table and headed for the narrow hallway where the restrooms were located. There were four of them, all single-seaters, which was good—she needed the privacy. She waited for one of them to become free, locked herself in, pulled her cell phone out of her purse and called Holly.

No reception. *Damn.* She had to do the next best thing, which was to jam her body into the corner at the end of the hallway, face the wall, and call Holly from there.

Holly picked up after one ring, her voice no longer tiny and scared. Worse. Full of pills. "Simone."

"Holly, you need to tell me what's going on."

"Nothing," she said. "Nothing . . . is going . . . I was just . . . sleeping."

Simone looked at her watch: nine thirty. "Oh," she said. "I'm sorry. You're probably making up for lost—"

"You need anything? Because . . ."

"Right." Simone closed her eyes. She felt a bug on the back of her neck and brushed it away. "Just a quick question. Was Emerald ever represented by Randi Du-Monde?"

On the other end of the line, there was a heavy stretch of silence. Holly said, "What the fuck is that supposed to mean?"

"What? I was just asking because—"

"What are you insinuating, Simone?"

"Nothing!"

"I can't believe this."

"Look, is this about the article? I'm sorry, Holly. I tried to get Nigel to pull it, but . . ."

Click.

Simone stood there for a while, staring at her phone, waiting for it to ring again. Had Holly really hung up on her? That couldn't have just happened.

The bug was back again. Maybe it was some kind of sign—the first annoying summer bug she had encountered since moving to LA. She slapped her palm against the back of her neck. But this time, it didn't fly away. She realized it was not a bug—it was a finger. A thick finger running up and down the back of her neck. Simone froze. Slowly, she turned around . . . until she was looking into the face of Blake Moss.

How much of that conversation did he hear?

"You are not a waitress," he said.

For several seconds, Simone forgot how to breathe. She forced a smile. "Actually," she said, "what I really want to do is direct."

He didn't smile back.

Simone said, "I . . . don't know what you're talking about."

"Dylan told me," Blake said. "You went to Columbia School of Journalism. You're looking for reporting work."

He spat out the word "reporting" like it was a bad piece of meat, but still, Simone breathed a quiet sigh of relief. "Found me out."

Blake cupped her chin in his hand, tilted her face up, forcing her to look into his hungry brown eyes. "Why would an angel like you want to be something as sleazy as a reporter?" The other hand stroked the back of her head, crawled into her hair. *Man, this guy is not one for personal boundaries.*

"Excuse me," she said, "but what makes you think you can touch me like that?"

Moss bent down, bringing his face nearer—a face so famous, it seemed like a caricature—and Simone had the oddest sensation, as if she were being harassed by a close-up. "I can do anything I want," he said. The hand that had been cupping her chin moved to her throat—the second man to take hold of her throat in twenty-four hours, though Moss's grip was looser than Furlong's, less overtly threatening. He slipped his index finger under her jaw. "Your pulse is getting faster," he whispered, his breath pushing against her skin. "I can tell. You're not as clean as you look."

"Get away from me."

Blake Moss took a step back, but his gaze stayed

locked on hers as he grinned his famous grin, that slow, predatory leer. "Soon, angel," he said, "I will know all your dirty secrets."

Simone told Blake she needed to use the bathroom and went back to the table a few minutes after him. She didn't want to walk next to him, didn't want to be that close to him, even for the amount of time it took to walk back to the table. He gave her a weird feeling. Maybe it was all the press he'd gotten, or the type of roles he always took, or, more likely, the nonstop, inappropriate touching—but there was something about Blake Moss. . . . Every time she spent more than two minutes next to him, Simone felt like she needed a liquid nitrogen bath.

When she got back, Chris and Julie had returned and were sitting at opposite ends of the table. Every eye in the room was on them, and they seemed hyperaware of this. They acted as if they barely knew each other, Chris saying things like, "What did the test audience think of the new ending, Jason?" and "Maurice is an awesome golfer, aren't you, Maurice?" and "Randi, why so freakin' quiet?" without casting so much as a glance at the woman he had told two days ago, *I want you. More than anyone else.*

Every so often, Julie would smile at something Chris said, but the smile always went unreturned. It was the closest Simone had ever seen anyone come to ignoring Julie Curtis. And it was a little worrisome. She could understand lying low, but this bordered on cruelty. She glanced at Julie listening to Caputo dissing *Devil's Road*'s most recent test audience, her eyes glistening in a way that wasn't in keeping with the conversation. She was holding back tears.

Caputo was oblivious. "But like my dad once said," he was telling her now, "the masses are asses."

Nathaniel said, "I don't think your dad invented that saying, Jase."

A few people chuckled, but not Randi. Randi said

nothing. She stared into her champagne glass, her face perfectly still, as if she did not want to disturb the bubbles within. Simone understood, though. She knew what Randi had seen in those police station pictures. "Randi," she said, "I'm very sorry about your client."

Randi locked eyes with her—blue eyes, cold and pale and as hard as ice. But for a few seconds, Simone saw in them a frailty. "She was just a kid," Randi said. "I probably shouldn't have signed her in the first place."

Nathaniel said, "She was mixed up with a bad crowd. Something like that was bound to happen sooner or later."

"Nathaniel," Randi said, "I saw the pictures. Something like that . . . It is never *bound* to happen."

"Sorry."

Blake said, "I'll tell you who I feel sorry for."

"Who, Blakey?" said Jason.

"Furlong."

Simone stared at him. "Why?"

"With a track record like that," he said, "he'll never get laid again."

Everyone at the table laughed, except for Simone and Randi and Ila, who seemed to have a limited knowledge of English to begin with. Julie was laughing just as much as anyone else. Her gaze was riveted on Chris Hart, and she laughed exactly as hard as he did, her laughter dying down at the same time, as if she were following his lead in some new, complicated dance.

"Speaking of Furlong," Hart said, "he's uh . . . here, you know."

"No fucking way." Jason peered around the room.

Hart smiled. "Not here," he said. "The hotel. He checked in under the name Cole Whitney. Isn't that nuts? Guy wants to lie low, he checks into the damn Beverlido—*and* he makes the reservation under his own manager's name!"

Simone's eyes went wide.

Nathaniel said, "If he wanted to lie low, he could have stayed in my pad."

"C'mon, Nathaniel," said Caputo, "there are limits to downsizing."

"I introduced him to Destiny," Randi said. "I introduced him to . . ." She took a breath. "I am never introducing Keith Furlong to anyone again. Ever."

Nathaniel put a hand over hers—a surprisingly personal gesture, Simone thought, for a young man and his older, female boss. "It is not your fault," he said softly.

Randi yanked her hand away.

"Let's find out what room he's in," said Blake. "Send him up a girl. A brave one."

Caputo said, "You are awful, dude."

Simone stood up. "Excuse me for a minute. I think I left my cell phone in the bathroom." To the left of the narrow hallway where the restrooms were located stood a set of double doors that led into the hotel lobby. Simone bypassed the restrooms and pushed through those doors, moving through the lobby as fast as she could. As she walked, she punched a number into her cell.

"Hi, hon."

"Kathy," said Simone, "I need your advice. Furlong is staying at the Beverlido under an assumed name. I know the name, but not what floor he's on, and I don't necessarily want to talk to him, but I want the scoop fast. . . ." The elevator doors opened, and Simone hurried in.

"Ninth floor," said Kathy.

"How do you know?"

"That's the VIP floor. You won't be able to access it without a key. Just hit floor eight, take the stairs up. You dressed cute, honey?"

Simone had on a sundress, platform sandals. "Yes! I actually am!" She pushed the button for the eighth floor.

"Awesome. Walk down the hallway like you know where you're going and find yourself a maid. Chat her up, give her money, whatever it takes. Make that your *new* mantra: Maids know all."

"Thanks, Kathy," she said. A family was getting on the elevator with her, the baby crying, the mother cooing, the father searching for the key as the sullen teenage son slid in and hit floor eleven.

"Good luck," Kathy said. "But don't forget about Chrylan, okay? That's our paychecks."

"Don't worry, Kathy, I won't." Simone hung up.

The doors started to close, but then a hand jammed itself between them and a man got on, keying the slot for the ninth floor. The doors finally closed, and then the man turned around and gave Simone a stare that could freeze lava.

Simone gulped, visibly.

The man was Neil Walker.

NINETEEN

"Walker."

He gave her a curt nod. "Gleason."

"Neil, I—"

"Wait. Let me save you the breath." He raised his voice an octave. "'I'm sooo sorry. *Nigel* put me up to it. I'm small and clueless and cute, and my mean old boss *forced* me to screw you royally.'"

He narrowed his eyes at her as the sullen teenage boy watched, rapt. "Save it, sweetheart. Those are stale groceries. I'm not buyin' 'em, I'm not baggin' 'em."

Simone looked at him. "You really think I'm cute?"

"Not funny. So not in the *vicinity* of funny that I am ending the conversation now."

The elevator stopped on eight. "Your floor," he said.

"Neil . . ."

"Your. Floor."

Simone exhaled. Slowly, she got out of the elevator. But as soon as the doors closed, she raced to the end of the hall, opened the stairwell door, and rushed up the stairs. When she opened that door, Walker was standing in front of it, talking calmly into his cell phone. "Hello, security? I'd like to report an intruder on the VIP floor."

"Oh, now come *on*." She grabbed the cell away from him. It wasn't turned on. "Hilarious," she said.

"You know what's really hilarious? I knew about Furlong checking in here this morning. Remember when I said I was going to call you? Well, I was, and I was going to tell you *that*. I figured you were calling to tell me about Chrylan going to Swifty's because Swifty's manager had already told me they made a reservation. She's a good friend, the manager." He gave her a pointed look. "Unlike some people."

She leveled her eyes at him. "You're pretty high and mighty for someone who masqueraded as a security guard and threw me off a—"

"I didn't know you then," he said. "I was probably better off."

"Neil, please—"

"*Anyway*, I'd already booked this room when you called. I figured, hey. I could get the Furlong scoop, you could talk to Chrylan, we could meet up in my room, share leads, order up some champagne and omelets on the *Interloper*'s tab, watch a little HBO . . ."

Simone looked at him, feeling a little wistful. *That sounds like fun.*

He shook his head. "Too bad you missed your chance."

"Wait, we can still . . ."

"Oh, no, we can't. My maid."

"What?" said Simone.

"*My* maid."

At the end of the hall, a small elderly woman in a uniform was pushing a cart of towels. "She's mine," said Simone. "I speak Spanish!"

Walker took off after her, with Simone close behind him, shouting, *"Señora! Espera un momento!"*

As they got closer, Simone said, *"Hola. Me llamo Simone."*

The maid gave her a blank stare.

Simone said, "English?"

She shook her head.

Walker said, *"Ola. Muito prazer em conhecer. O meu nome e* Neil."

The woman's face lit up. *"Ola!"*

Walker glanced at Simone. "Portuguese," he said, and proceeded to have an animated five-minute conversation with the woman, the only word of which she understood being Furlong's alias, "Cole."

The woman then left, shaking Walker's hand and giving him a grandmotherly peck on the cheek.

Simone studied him with her hands on her hips.

"Interesting," he said.

"What?"

"Furlong's pregnant. He's checking into the Desert Ranch spa under the name of—"

"All right, all right."

Walker whispered, "He's coming up behind you."

Simone was about to tell him to cut it out, she got the point, when she felt it—that heavy hand on her shoulder. She turned around. Keith Furlong was standing so close to her she could see the tiny errant hairs sprouting between his plucked eyebrows. "What the fuck are you doing on my floor?"

Walker said, "I see you guys know each other."

Furlong was wearing a gray wife-beater and huge black shorts, and he had an added greasiness, as if he hadn't showered in a few days. A smell clung to him, a mixture of gin, hair gel, and stale sweat. "I told you," he said, "I'm watching. I've been watching you. Now I *know*."

"What do you know, Keith?" she said.

His face went pink, then purple. She saw beads of sweat on his upper lip. He wasn't wearing the contacts now, and his real eyes were a dull, wet brown. Hard to believe that for two years this man was known to all as the suave, successful live-in boyfriend of *Suburban Indiscretions* star Emerald Deegan. *This is what it looks like under the mask.*

"You wreck people's lives," he said. "You're tabloid scum. You're better off dead."

Simone's eyes widened. "How do you know that?"

"I told you. I'm watching." Furlong balled his hand into a fist and hurled it at the side of her face—but before he was able to make contact, Walker's hand shot up, clamped around the wrist, and held it there.

Furlong grimaced.

"You want to fight somebody," he said, "fight me."

Walker let go of the wrist. Furlong came at him. Walker's fist flew up, connected with his jaw. Furlong fell to the floor, then struggled to his feet, but Walker came at him again. And so he threw his hands up in a kind of truce. "I've got nothing against you, man," Furlong said, rubbing his jaw.

"Why not?" Walker said. "I'm tabloid scum, too."

Furlong glared at Simone.

"What were you doing Tuesday night, Keith?" she said. "Why did Cole say you were at Bedrock?"

He lunged at her, but Walker took a step forward and Furlong slunk back. "I'm going." He headed away from them, down the hall to his room.

Simone caught her breath, trying to get it out of her mind; the way he had looked at her. That hate. *I am watching.*

"You okay?" Walker said.

"I think so."

"Good." She sort of wished he would hug her, like he had after they'd seen Destiny's body. But that was obviously too much to expect.

"Sandiford was right," she said, just to keep him from walking away. "You weren't lying about boxing."

"I don't always lie, Simone." He took his wallet out of his pocket, removed Dylan Leeds's business card, and gave it to her. "See? You don't have to worry. Your cover is safe."

"Neil. I'm sorry." She looked at him. "No excuses. Just . . . just that, okay?"

"Better head back downstairs to Chrylan," he said. He stared into her eyes for a few moments. And then, without saying good-bye, he walked down the hall to his room.

Simone was left remembering the look in his gas-flame eyes—the same look she'd noticed outside Holly's house. It was so serious, this look, yet so oddly tender. Simone could feel it in her toes . . . but like before, it disappeared long before she could figure it out.

By the time Simone returned to the bar, Chris Hart had left, along with Randi and Maurice. Julie was deep in discussion with Caputo, Nathaniel, and Moss. *Great, now my Chrylan story is gone*, thought Simone, who couldn't, as it turned out, hold on to anything tonight.

Ila had migrated across the room and was now sitting in the lap of one of the studio executives.

As she approached the table, Simone was about to ask what had happened to Chris, but the tension in the air made her stop before anyone noticed her. All the men were looking at Julie, whose expression seemed stolen off the face of a different, less fortunate woman.

"You're not angry at me, are you, Jason?" Julie was asking.

"Why would *I* be angry?"

"I'm telling you, I'm just as upset about all this as he is. Neither one of us wanted it to come out now."

"Dylan, it's none of my damn business."

"It's nobody's damn business," said Nathaniel. "I mean, if you decided to talk to the tabs, then—"

Blake noticed Simone first. "Angel, what took you so long?"

"Turned out I left the phone in my car."

Julie narrowed her eyes at Nathaniel, her speech fuzzy from champagne. "I didn't leak the story," she said. "And you know what? I don't give a damn whether you believe me or . . ." She glanced toward the door, where Sheryl Crow and Jennifer Aniston were greeting a group of friends—a group that included Lara Chandler. "Oh, great," Julie said.

Lara Chandler was wearing a clinging purple dress that played up her slim body and her shining black hair—her "hot and single look," as they would no doubt refer to it in the *Asteroid*. She peered around the room, and once she caught sight of Julie, Chandler promptly excused herself from her girlfriends and made her way to their table.

To say all eyes in the place were on her would have been a major understatement.

Lara ignored all the men and stared Julie in the eye. But instead of averting her gaze, or mumbling an apology—which is what Simone probably would have done—Julie stood up, looked right back at her, the friend she had betrayed . . . and smiled.

"What do you want, Lara?"

When the actress spoke, her voice was surprisingly measured. "You don't know what you're getting yourself into," she said. "I feel sorry for you."

Julie's smile dropped away.

Lara left the table and then the bar, taking her girlfriends with her. Julie watched her leave, pain settling into the corners of her mouth. "Whatever," she whispered.

Simone realized: *I have my story for the night.* But there was no joy in the thought. None at all.

Once they were back in the limo, Julie popped open another bottle of Cris. Simone said, "You're doing wonders for my liver, you know that?"

"Come on," said Julie. "Help me celebrate."

Simone took a sip to keep the bubbles from spilling over. "Celebrate what?"

"My first movie, you giant dork!" Julie put on that grin she often wore—plaster-bright, too perfect to be believed. Never in her wildest dreams had Simone thought she'd feel sorry for Julie Curtis, but right now, she did. Could Julie ever stop acting and tell the truth?

Of course, Simone was acting right now, too, and she wasn't even an actress. . . .

Maybe lying was part of the atmosphere here, in this city where everyone wanted to act or write or direct—to make up stories and play them out. Maybe fiction was in the air like smog, and there was no avoiding it.

Simone heard herself say, "What happened with Chris? Why did he walk out?"

"Nothing. He gets in moods sometimes."

"Julie," she said, "if you don't mind my saying, why Chris? I mean, you could have anybody you want, and he's . . . I'm sorry, but he doesn't seem . . . he doesn't seem like he's in love with you."

"I told you before," she said, "it isn't what you think." She looked at Simone for a good long while. "Would you like to see my house?" she said. "It's right around here."

As tired as Simone was, Julie was hard to say no to. "Sure."

"I lived in an apartment for ages, but last year, when I got the part in *Devil's Road*, the first thing I did was I made the down payment on this place. I used to drive by it all the time and it was like . . . You know how it is, when you see a guy you really want, but you're too shy to talk to him?"

Simone nodded.

"Like that."

The car headed east on Wilshire until it hit La Cienega. Then it headed north for a few blocks, then east again, on a peaceful, modest residential street. A few more blocks, and the limo pulled into the driveway of a small, '60s ranch house with a trimmed square lawn and a tidy garden. "This is it," Julie said.

"Really?"

There was no gate, no security camera, no thick line of hedges even. Nothing to put any distance between the house and the street. It was late now, quiet. "But . . . aren't you worried about security?" Simone said.

"I wasn't," Julie replied. "Until yesterday."

Simone cringed.

"I don't give a damn, though. Pretty soon, Lynzee de

la Presa will do something crazy. The paparazzi will move on, and I'll still have this fab house." She looked at Simone. "No matter what happens with Chris, I'm keeping it."

Simone said nothing, that sentence taking root in her mind. Since their first meeting at the *Devil's Road* party, that was the closest Julie had come to admitting the affair. *No matter what happens with Chris.* She waited for Julie to say more, but all she added was, "You've got to see my plants. I have a green thumb. Who knew?"

Simone looked at the house. Beyond the lack of security, it was such an odd home for a celeb to fall in love with. It couldn't have been more different from Blake Moss's compound, or Emerald's tower or any dead celebrity's mansion Simone had seen on her Map of the Stars' Homes. It was so . . . *normal.* There was something else about it too, something that set it apart from the other houses on the street.

As they got out of the limo, Simone noticed the four pink rosebushes that clung to the side of the white house. She breathed in their scent, then looked down at the brick walkway bordered by purple and white impatiens. Then she remembered. Julie's mom's garden. She studied the red door and matching shutters, the window box overflowing with multicolored pansies. "Julie," she said, "this looks exactly like your old house in Wappingers Falls."

Julie grinned. "I know! Isn't it amazing?"

Once they were inside, Julie took Simone on a tour. Proudly, she showed her old friend the floral-print couch, the wicker furniture, the dozens and dozens of houseplants—"They give you so much, and all they ask for is water"—and the huge wooden *J* mounted on the wall, which Simone remembered from Julie's room back in high school. She checked out the small kitchen with its '60s-style electric range and potted herbs lined up on the tile counters. While Julie's bedroom, too, was sweet and basic, it did house the only extravagant item in the entire space—a huge gilded antique mirror, shaped like a heart, that Julie had hung over the dresser. "Randi gave me that," she said. "Not something I would have picked out myself, but . . ."

"I can see that," said Simone. Slipped into the corner of the mirror was a snapshot: Julie and Todd on senior prom night, 1998. By then, Julie and Simone had drifted apart. They'd say hi to each other when they passed in the halls, sometimes study for tests together, but that was about it. Simone didn't resent it. She had other friends, and besides, Julie was in love—real, knock-you-off-your-feet-and-take-everything-you-own love.

Simone still had an image of them after Spanish class, of Julie pushing Todd up against a bank of lockers, murmuring, *"Da me un beso,"* again and again. How she'd marveled at the look on Todd's face—pure ecstasy. *To change a guy's face like that,* Simone had thought. And then, again: *To be Julie Curtis, just for one day. . . .*

She recalled Julie and Chris, the stern way he'd said, *"Now,* Dylan," and how she'd followed him across the room like a puppy, how she'd laughed when he'd laughed, the way she'd smiled at him, so expectant, receiving nothing in return. Yes, in high school Simone had had a crush on Chris Hart. There were a few months there when she'd taped his "Sexiest Man Alive" photo to the inside of her locker.

But she did not want to be Dylan Leeds. Not even for a day.

"Simone," Julie said, "do you ever feel . . . like someone is watching you?"

She turned around, stared at her. "What do you mean?"

"It's probably nothing, but . . . for the past couple of days, when I've been asleep, I've had to get up, make sure the shades were drawn."

"Julie," said Simone, "you should always have your shades drawn, and your doors locked. You're famous. In fact, it wouldn't be such a bad idea to get a bodyguard of your own."

"It's not that," she said. "It isn't the fame thing. It's . . .'watched' is the wrong word." The blue eyes gazed into Simone's, and she saw something in them that made her turn cold. "I feel . . . hunted," Julie said.

Simone stared at her, unable to say a word.

Then Julie burst out laughing.

"What . . ."

"Not bad, huh? I've got a horror film audition coming up. Thought I'd practice on you!"

Simone exhaled hard. "That was really mean!"

"I'm sorry," she said. "But you'll forgive me when you see the surprise I have for you!"

"What?" said Simone.

Julie pulled her into the living room. "Okay," she said. "Sit on the couch and close your eyes." She did, and when Julie told her to open them again, she'd cued up a DVD on her small, flat-screen TV. She hit PLAY.

"Oh, my God," said Simone. "It's *Night at the Opera!*"

Julie skipped to the stateroom scene, and together they watched it, laughing until tears ran down their faces. When it was over, Julie gasped, "One more time?"

"Sure!" said Simone, because she hadn't laughed that hard in months. Still, an image nagged at her, and it was hard to brush off. It was the look in Julie's eyes, the depth of the fear when she'd said, *I feel hunted*. She was a good actress, yes, but not *that* good.

TWENTY

H is initial idea had been a trilogy. The Project
would consist of three events, because three was
the most perfect number. He knew that from
movies. You want an image to make an impact, you
show it three times. In real life as well, three told you,
*No coincidence. You're not imagining things. This is
really happening.* Three put fear in your heart.

Three would put fear in *her* heart.

So that night two months ago, when he had walked
into his home and taken off the mask and felt rage ripping at his skin. The night he decided to *do something
about it.* That night, he had thought: *Three.*

Nia Lawson would be one. That was a given. She was,
after all, the source of rage, the final straw, the inspiration.
Two, Emerald, who was more than deserving. He'd
known that for a while. Three, he had thought, would
come in time. Months, years from now. It didn't matter.
He would see her, and he would know.

He hadn't expected her to come so soon. Destiny was
so perfect, so deserving of shame. Perhaps the most perfect of all. In movies, the third appearance of the chosen
image should be the strongest, the most memorable.

And it was.

The Project was a success. He had shamed Nia, Emerald, and Destiny, as he had been shamed. He had ended them, as he had been ended. Everyone knew it wasn't a coincidence. And, best of all, he had put fear in *her*.

The only problem: He wanted more. He thrived on it now—finding them, marking them, bringing their shame out into the open. He told himself, *Wait, be patient.* And, as luck would have it, he found two more.

Probably three, but he needed to research that one.

It was eleven o'clock on Sunday morning. He was sitting in the front seat of the car he used for the Project. After all these years, the car still smelled like his mother—cigarettes and Shalimar. The smell used to make him gag, but now he liked the symbolism.

He was still tired and achy from last night at the Beverlido, but he leaned forward in the vinyl seat. He smelled his mother and he watched her house, number one of the second three. Her shadow moved past the window. Before, he had thought Holly Kashminian wasn't right. After all, the only thing she'd done was lie about the knife. That was nowhere near close to what one, two, or three had done. But now, now . . .

Holly had been talking. Talking to the police, and more tellingly, to the press. She had called the *Times*, *People*, *Entertainment Tonight*—and those were only the ones he knew about through his contacts. They weren't listening, of course. They thought she was crazy. Nonetheless, Holly Kashminian was distinguishing herself.

A messenger van pulled in front of Holly's house, and the driver hurried up to her door, a manila envelope in his hand. *What's this?* He watched the driver ring the bell, wait on the step . . . No answer. Too scared to answer her own door. He smiled. Clearly, his messages had made an impact.

After a minute or so the driver stepped away from the door, rolled the envelope, and shoved it into the mailbox. Then he got back in his van and drove off.

Holly's mailbox was located in front of hedges. It was not visible from her house. Calmly, he got out of his car, walked up to it, removed the envelope and brought it back to his car. The envelope was not taped shut or sealed. Just a twist of the brad and it was open.

Inside was a large Xeroxed newspaper article folded in half. When he unfolded it, a note fell out, but he didn't bother picking it up. For now, he needed nothing but to stare at this page—a page from the *Asteroid*, dated next week. He read each article, growing angrier and angrier until the rage pierced his skin, until it made him quake.

He looked at the picture of the bracelet. Then he read the small, boxed article and the blood coursed through his veins so hot it stung.

Holly. Is. Deserving.

This one would be soon. His rage would not let him wait, not this time. He could not be patient. He would drive home, he would assemble a kit. He would mark her. And then she would be his—the most deserving one yet. Carefully, he folded up the article, placed it back in the envelope. He didn't return it to the mailbox. It would be part of Holly's kit.

The note was still on the floor of his car. He picked it up and read it:

> *Dear Holly,*
> *Enclosed is an advanced copy of the spread, faxed from New York. I hope you are feeling better about this. I think it turned out very well, and you should be proud. Please call me when you can. I am worried about you.*
> *Simone*

Simone. As he stared at the name, he started to laugh. *How about that*, he thought. No more research was needed. He had his three.

* * *

"Holly? It's Simone. I just wanted to make sure you got the spread. It'll be out Friday, and I had it messengered this morning. Okay. I guess you're not picking up your phone. Please call me when you can."

Simone hung up. She was calling from the reporters' room. But while she was supposed to be writing an article about Dylan and Lara's confrontation at Swifty's, she kept thinking about her phone conversation with Holly, how strange she had sounded, how cold. *What are you insinuating, Simone?*

Then she had hung up on her—hung up on the person, the *friend*, whom, one night earlier, she had trusted with her deepest-kept secret. *And all I did was ask . . .*

"Kathy," she said, "what can you tell me about Randi DuMonde?"

Kathy glanced up from the piece she was writing: "Lynzee de la Presa's Lesbian Secret!" "Dylan's manager?"

Simone nodded.

"Outside of her being a bitch on wheels? Not a lot. She reps some hot stars, but the only one she deals with around here is Nigel—and that's just to scream at him." She looked at Simone. "Why?"

"I asked Emerald's assistant if she was ever with Randi, and she got really mad and hung up on me."

Kathy stopped typing and looked at Simone. "Honey, you did a fab job on that spread. The bracelet thing was genius," she said. "But you've got to let it go. Leave it to the real newspapers. You're our Chrylan girl."

Simone winced. *The real newspapers.* She stared back at her screen, the headline shouting at her: DYLAN AND LARA FACE OFF! *You are not a reporter. You are an insider. Your job is not to save people. It is to betray them.* Simone remembered the previous night, sitting on Julie's floral-print couch—the couch not of a brazen movie star but of somebody's kindly old aunt. She remembered laughing with her over the Marx Brothers and seeing how she'd still kept her prom picture and thinking, *Deep down, Julie is still my friend.*

Then thinking, *Deep down, I am not her friend at all.*

"You're saving our jobs," said Kathy. Simone hadn't said anything, but it wasn't hard to look at her face and know what was on her mind.

At least she was trying to do away with the phrase "Dirty Dylan." In this piece, the one she was writing, Simone hadn't used it once—nor would she, in any future Chrylan stories. Yes, it was a little like making sure your hostage got three square meals—the least you could do. But it was something. Wasn't it?

Simone's cell phone rang. Julie. Of course it was Julie. She took a breath, got herself together. *You're her friend. Her loyal, cheerful, guilt-free friend.* "Hi, Julie."

"Everything about you reminds me of you. Except you. How do you account for that?"

"Huh?"

"Groucho. *Night at the Opera.* Remember?"

"Oh," said Simone. "Right."

"I know. Celeb impersonation is not my strong point."

"No, Julie." Simone read at the words she'd just typed on the screen: " '*Lara didn't back down,*' said an insider. '*She looked Dylan straight in the eye and said . . .*' "

"No, that was good."

"Man, somebody is hurtin' today. Listen, I'll let you go, but I want you to come to another party with me tonight."

"*. . . straight in the eye and said, 'I feel sorry for you.*' " "I . . ."

"I'm taking that as a yes. The limo and I will be at your place at six p.m.," she said. "And come hungry because there'll be lots of sushi."

"Wait," said Simone. "Where is the party?"

"Beverly Hills," said Julie. "Randi's house."

Simone was outside, clearing her head. She had taken a lot of breaks today, fresh-air breaks in the hot sun and smog—

so many that it had caused speculation among her coworkers. Kathy had asked if she'd started smoking. Elliot had said, "You're talking to yourself, right?" And Matthew, a knowing smile crossing that face, had said, "I can think of many more interesting things to be doing out-of-doors."

Lucky Carl, Simone had thought, despite the jumble of questions in her brain. *Lucky, lucky, lucky Carl....*

Simone walked down to the corner of Beverly and Wilshire, then she turned around and started back to the office. Shiny cars drove by, motorists gawking at her. Walking in LA, she noticed, always generated this type of response. *Oh, my God, do you see that woman? She's ... she's using the sidewalk! She's outside, in the atmosphere!* It had been disconcerting at first, but now she was used to it, and at the moment she couldn't care less. Let 'em stare. There was too much else on her mind.

She had called Holly two more times, once on her home phone, once on her cell, and left messages on both. At this point, she didn't expect a callback. What was it she had done to offend Holly so much? It couldn't have been mentioning Randi. There was something else going on with Holly. It had been going on ever since she'd asked her to retract the article. Was she scared of something? Or was she just tired, and wanting to be left alone?

Simone could relate to that. There was a part of her that wished Julie would leave her alone. A part that wished Julie would find a guy who really loved her and blow Simone off, just like in high school. She didn't want to go to Randi's party tonight. She didn't want to spend time with VIPs anymore, and she sure as hell didn't want any sushi. Mostly, she didn't want to spy on Julie.

Simone didn't want to be here, either, walking in this bright, hurtful sun, every single driver on this needlessly wide street gaping at her as if she were walking a tightrope, nude and painted blue. Where *did* she want to be?

She knew the answer to that one, too, and it made her cringe in protest—all the way from the inside out: She

wanted to be in a hotel room on the VIP floor of the Beverlido, having champagne and omelets, watching a little
HBO. . . .

Her cell phone rang. She looked at the caller ID. *Unbelievable.* "Walker?"

"I know what you're thinking," he said.

"You *do*?"

"You're thinking, *I wish I knew what that maid said
last night. Damn.* And you know, you're right to wish
that because she gave me some *very* interesting information."

"What did she say?"

"Oh, no. . . . See, I'm just bringing it up for gloating
purposes."

Simone smiled. She couldn't help it. "Well," she said,
"I am *very* glad you called. Because you would not *believe* what went down in Swifty's."

On the other end of the line, a pause. "Nope," he said.
"Not falling for it. Sorry, sweetheart, I know bluffing
when I hear it."

"Buy the next *Asteroid*. We'll see who's bluffing."

"I never buy that rag."

"I thought it was your favorite."

"Okay," he said. "Much as I love listening to your
feeble attempts to ride my ass, I actually called you for a
reason."

Simone said, "I'm listening."

"Are you related to Greta Glass?"

A noise escaped from Simone's mouth—a strange,
sickly hack.

"I'm taking that as a yes."

"No!" Simone said. *"Of course I'm not related to
her!"*

"Man," he said. "Switch to decaf."

Simone took a breath. "I'm just . . . not much of a fan
of hers. Why . . . why do you ask?"

"She called me."

"She *did*?"

"Well, her producer did, and I thought, *Hey. Greta Glass. Same last name as Simone. Same shape mouth.*"

"Why did Greta . . . Greta Glass's producer call you?"

"He said she wants to interview me as an expert about Chrylan. So what is she, first cousin?"

Simone said, "I have never met her before in my life."

"God, you are *so* untrustworthy. You lie so much, it's almost a turn-on."

"Don't do the interview."

"Under penalty of what? You gonna banish me to Palm Springs again?"

"Neil. . . . Listen, you and I bust our asses on these stories, and then people like Greta Glass, they sit there in their air-conditioned studios, reading from teleprompters and using all our information. And they get called *real* journalists and get nominated for awards and—"

"She's your sister."

Simone took a deep breath. She started to lie again, but thought better of it. What was the point? "You're the only one who knows."

He said nothing, but Simone could *hear* the grin.

"Can . . . can you please keep this under your hat? Greta doesn't even know where I work and—"

"Let's see . . . Don't tell Dylan you work for Nigel. Don't tell Nigel you've been talking to me. Don't tell anybody you're Greta Glass's sister, don't tell Greta Glass where you work." He exhaled. "You know what? I'm gonna need a bigger hat."

"I'll make you a deal."

At that, Walker laughed. He laughed for a long time. And when Simone said, "Walker," and "Come on," and "I'm serious," he just kept laughing. He laughed so long that she nearly said, "Forget it" . . . until finally, he stopped. "Okay," he said. "What's the deal?"

It took three of Emerald's Xanax, two Vicodin, and an Ativan to get Holly to sleep these days. But it worked, and she was glad for that. There wasn't much else to do in her house, her cage, other than sleep, or lie in bed chasing thoughts away—waiting, hoping for sleep to come. That last message—the picture of Emerald, bleeding, begging Holly to shut up—that had done it. It had shut her up good.

Mission accomplished. You win.

But that wouldn't be enough for him, she knew that. The *Asteroid* would come out, and he would know she had talked. Or that detective, Ed Sandiford, would question him, tell him the things Holly had said. And his anger would grow. He would find her and he would . . .

Once, she had seen Keith Furlong take one of those birds of his, those illegal birds that had gotten Emerald in so much trouble. He had been mad for one reason or another, probably a low-money night at his club. He had yelled so loud, called Emerald such despicable names, that Holly couldn't bear to hear them in her own head, even now. He had called her those names and then he had taken that bird—that pretty, frail bird. He had pulled it from its cage and squeezed the life out of it. He had thrown it at Emerald's wall and it had slipped, all the way down, leaving a trail of blood.

She remembered the faint red stain on the white wall and the look on Furlong's face. She knew how much he enjoyed ruining small things.

So Holly stayed inside. She locked all five of her high-tech bolts—bolts she'd initially installed to ward off robbers in her rich neighborhood—and she kept the cordless in her hand at all times, 911 predialed so all she had to do was hit TALK.

For a while, she didn't answer the phone for anyone except friends, and then she stopped answering the phone at all. She lived off Lean Cuisines and filtered water and Emerald's pills and she slept, taking enough pills to ensure that her sleep would be deep, dreamless.

Holly was waking up from a sleep now, waking up to a ringing telephone. She heard Simone's voice floating out of the living room answering machine saying something about the article. She put the pillow over her head. She didn't want to hear it. Holly probably shouldn't have hung up on Simone like that. Odds were, Simone didn't know the rumors about Randi DuMonde. Very few people did. Holly had heard from Rico Valdez, Cambria's gardener on *Suburban Indiscretions*. And what he had told her, he had told her in deepest confidence. What he had told Holly had to do with Randi DuMonde and Emerald. Holly didn't believe it. She refused to believe it. But now. . . . What had Simone said? *Was Emerald ever represented . . .*

Holly got out of bed and took the box out of her closet—a box of Emerald's things from years ago, long before she had gotten the part of Cambria. Long before she and Holly had ever met. Holly knew what was in it, though. After she found out about the cutting, Emerald had given her the box, and said, "You may as well be the keeper of *all* my secrets."

Emerald had asked her not to show the box to anyone. And, if for any reason Emerald were to die or disappear or if she wound up in a hospital, Holly was supposed to destroy it. She hadn't destroyed it, not yet. She hadn't been able to.

"Sorry, Emerald," Holly whispered. Then she opened the box. It was filled with stacks of spiral notebooks, which may have explained Emerald's disgust of shags. Holly pulled out the top one and opened it. It was a journal. They were all journals.

She read, eyes unblinking, breath going shallower with each page. "I can't believe this," she said. "Why didn't you tell me?"

To think Holly had yelled at Rico over this. "How can you spread such an awful rumor?!" *Rico was right.* After a few more pages, Holly had had enough. She was about to put the journal away when something fell out of it, a folded, yellowing magazine article. She picked it up, unfolded it.

It was that famous 1998 *Vanity Fair* piece: "Secrets of

Desire." She read it through, even though she'd read the piece before. She read it through for clues. But when she saw what was attached to the piece, she had no need for clues anymore. It was as if the cumulative effects of the pills she'd been taking took flight, leaving Holly behind, clearheaded. More clearheaded than she'd been in years.

It was a contract. A ten-thousand-dollar freelancer's contract from *Vanity Fair*, made out to Emerald Deegan, a.k.a. Desire.

Holly didn't want to think about what all this meant. She was through thinking. Now was the time to start asking questions. She went into the living room, found her phone book, and looked up the number of DuMonde Management.

TWENTY-ONE

As Simone and Julie arrived at Randi DuMonde's Beverly Hills mansion, Simone's first thought was, *Randi must have some well-paying clients.* After the enormous wrought-iron gate swung open, the limo pulled up a long winding driveway to a wasteful showpiece of a house, full of sleek angles and cathedral-sized windows and wood probably carved right off northern sequoias. "One person lives here?" Simone said. "I mean, does she at least have a dog?"

Julie laughed. "Randi is a fan of excess."

"I'd nominate her for fan club president," said Simone. But she couldn't look at Julie. She'd been having trouble with that the whole ride here, even though her friend didn't seem to notice. Simone's head felt like a box of lies. As she smiled at the back of the front seat, trying to focus on what Julie was saying—about the film opening Friday, about Randi, about the party—that box threatened to burst.

There was so much going on in her mind, so much she couldn't tell Julie. . . .

She was still worried about Holly. Simone had tried calling her once more, right before the limo picked her up. She had told her again about the article, asked her to please call. No response. Again. She kept wondering: *Should I go to her house? Knock on the door? Or would that be an intrusion?*

Also, she had arranged to meet Walker. In exchange for his not telling a soul that she was Greta Glass's sister, Simone had said she'd meet him at his apartment whenever the party ended and give him a *true* Chrylan scoop. If her leads proved accurate *for a change*, then he, in turn, would reveal what Furlong's chambermaid had said.

If Nigel finds out, she told him, *I'll lose my job for sure.*

He won't. I promise, Nigel does not have spies in my apartment.

So on top of everything else, Simone was now a tabloid double agent. Queen of Duplicity, with a box of lies for a head. How had this happened to her, in only a week?

". . . and Jason said, 'Screw you, we're keeping the murder at the end!' Can you imagine? To the head of the studio! I swear, if it weren't for his last name, he would have so been fired. Where are you, Simone?"

"Huh?"

"I'm monologuing here."

Simone turned and looked at Julie's face, the pencil lead picking up the color of her clear blue eyes. Honest eyes, no matter what she was doing with Chris. The limo pulled up in front of the house.

"Julie," said Simone.

"Yeah?"

What kind of a job expects you to do this to a friend?

"What is it, Simone?" The driver got out of the car, opened the door.

"I . . . I don't like sushi."

Julie widened her eyes in mock horror. "Why didn't you tell me that earlier? Oh . . . now I can never speak to you again!"

"Yeah, well . . . sushi party and all. I didn't want to hurt your manager's feelings."

As she started to get out of the car, Julie patted her hand. "At least," she said, "there are no more secrets between us."

The inside of Randi's house was arty intimidating, like a museum. The mammoth door opened onto an indoor Zen garden, with blue slate floors and bonsai trees and an enormous pile of glossy, multicolored stones with water trickling down the sides.

There wasn't a chair in sight.

Nearly every guest, in this area at least, was tall, breathtakingly beautiful, and female. It reminded Simone of one of those old *Star Trek* episodes, where the *Enterprise* lands on the Amazon planet and even Spock starts to feel his logic getting fuzzy.

She wondered if they were all Randi's clients, because, stunning as they were, none of their faces were famous, or even familiar looking. *Randi must specialize in the up-and-comers.* And just like that, she recalled Destiny's eyes, the wad of money shoved into her mouth.

Why would a Hollywood über-manager sign a seventeen-year-old stripper? Why would she introduce that stripper not to directors or producers, but to a club owner?

Simone looked at Julie, her powder blue gaze roaming around the room, searching, no doubt, for Chris Hart. She remembered Lara saying that she, too, was a client of Randi's. How could the same manager rep a seventeen-year-old stripper and a superstar like Lara Chandler?

Julie stopped and peered through one of the area's large windows. Simone looked in that direction and saw Chris Hart, Lara-less, motioning for Julie to join him. "Come on, Simone," she said. But when she started to pull her out, Hart shook his head, and mouthed the word "Alone."

Julie said, "Sorry, I . . ."

"No problem. Go ahead."

Julie hurried through the cluster of guests and out into the landscaped grounds, leaving Simone to fend for herself in the Zen garden.

A cater-waiter walked up to Simone with a tray of sushi. "Sea urchin?"

"No, thank you." She watched him leave, wondering if maybe he was a tabloid reporter.

"Simone." It was Randi DuMonde, looming over her in a sleeveless bright red cocktail dress. Simone was beginning to wonder whether the woman owned clothes of any other color.

"You remembered my name."

"That's my business," she said. "Remembering names." Randi was at least a foot taller than Simone, and up close, she saw how large she really was—her eyes, her shoulders, her teeth, her feet. Randi didn't just intimidate Simone, she made her feel lower on the food chain.

"How are you holding up?" Simone said.

"Excuse me?"

"You know . . . Dest—" *Shit.* Would it make sense for Simone to remember Destiny's name? How many times was it mentioned at Swifty's? "Your client. The young girl who—"

"Destiny, yes," she said. "The police are now thinking it might be drug-related. She smoked crack, which . . . well, if I had known that I never would have signed her."

No drugs. She said they ruined your looks. Why would Charity have lied about that? Simone looked at Randi, looked deep into her eyes, and knew. It was she. She was the one who was lying. "So you don't think Keith Furlong—"

"What?" she said. "I never said anything about Keith Furlong."

Salt-N-Pepa's "Push It" started to play.

"A classic," said Simone.

"My ringtone." Randi answered her cell as Simone stood there, shifting from foot to foot, wondering whether or not their conversation had ended. This was a whole new dimension of awkward. "How did you get this number?" said Randi. "I see." She looked at Simone. "Excuse me, I'm going to have to take this."

She walked away. Simone stood there for a few minutes, trying to figure out what had changed Randi's mind about Keith Furlong, why she was claiming that Destiny smoked crack. Right next to her, a supermodel type leaned against a wall, listening raptly to a balding man, the top of whose head barely cleared her collarbones. "So I told Marty, 'Stop it with the costume dramas. What are you, PBS?'"

The model gaped at him for a few minutes, then began laughing hysterically.

"So," he said, "you want to, uh . . . you know . . ."

"I have been dying for you to ask me that."

The look in the model's eyes—that hunger—made Simone think of Charity. But Pleasures was a strip club and Charity was a stripper and that hungry look was part of the performance. She glanced around the room and saw that same look on the faces of so many other beautiful women. *Up-and-comers.* Was this what all young actresses had to do? Was the casting couch really so pervasive? Or did this have something to do with the managerial style of Randi DuMonde? She remembered Julie, the way she'd looked at Blake Moss's agent. That same hungry look. . . .

The short, balding friend of Marty's trailed the model to the end of the Zen room and through a hallway. Simone kept her distance, but followed.

She passed some kind of marble spa with a massage table, a Jacuzzi, and a sink full of black healing stones, then an entertainment area with a pool table, vintage jukebox, and a cinema-sized plasma screen, then a yoga room with nothing in it but windows and mats, all spotless, all with doors wide open, but not a party guest to be seen anywhere. The model and Marty's friend seemed to have disappeared. *Where did everyone go?* Simone wondered . . . until she saw a series of closed doors.

She tried one. It was locked, but when she pressed her ear up against it, she heard the model's throaty voice saying, "And I sing a little too. You want to hear me sing?"

Marty's friend said, "Let's see what else you can do with your mouth."

"Ooh, okay . . . Mmmmmm . . ."

"God . . . Wait, slow down, I'm gonna . . ."

Simone winced, backed away from the door. *Okay . . .*

She tried another door. This one opened. Inside, she saw a chiseled, middle-aged man with his pants around his ankles, a blonde on all fours in front of him, while a dark-skinned woman grasped his shoulders, wearing a strap-on . . .

She closed the door quickly.

"Like what you see?" said a voice behind her as a big hand slipped around her waist. She recognized the voice, the hand, before she turned around—and for once she was glad to see him. "Blake," she said. "What's the deal with Randi?"

Blake smiled. "Perceptive girl," he said. "But what would you expect from Columbia Journalism?"

"You mean she really. . . . ?"

"No, but I can see why you'd think that. Come with me, angel. We'll talk."

Blake Moss took Simone's hand and led her back into the spa room, closing the door behind him. "Talk to me," said Simone.

"Wait." He drew the shades on the enormous window and switched on the lights. "Now," he said, "we have some privacy."

And his eyes went cold.

Simone cleared her throat. "So, is Randi a—"

"I don't want to talk about Randi." He moved toward Simone. Within seconds, she was pinned against the tile wall, one of his hands pushing her shoulder against it, the other grabbing her hip. Moss's face was inches away from hers, his voice low, threatening. "I want to talk," he said, "about what you do for a living."

Simone's heart pounded. His breath was hot in her face and his eyes glared into hers.

"What do you mean?" she whispered.

"I knew you weren't as clean as you look," he said. "But I didn't know you were *that* dirty." When he spoke again, it was like a nightmare come to life, everything within her giving way, crumbling with each word. . . . "You're tabloid scum, angel. You've been spying on your friend, getting her into all kinds of trouble with Chris, printing all her secrets."

Tears sprung into Simone's eyes. "No," she whispered.

"You ought to be ashamed of yourself, angel."

A tear leaked down the side of her face.

Blake said, "Are you, angel? Are you ashamed?"

"Yes."

He moved closer, shook his head. He clicked his tongue at her. *Click, click, click . . .*

"Does . . ."

"Does Dylan know?" he said.

She couldn't speak, couldn't breathe.

"No. Right now, the only one who knows is me."

Simone exhaled. Her breath was raw, shaky.

"And if you like," Moss said, "we can keep it that way."

"You mean . . . you won't tell her?"

He loosened his grip on her a little, but his eyes still drilled into hers. "I mean I won't tell her . . . *if*." He grinned. That snaking half leer of a grin, and he didn't need to tell her if *what*. "You're disgusting," he said softly. "You ruin people's lives. You need to be shamed." He brought his hands up to her shoulders, pressed down hard until her knees hit the tile floor. "Deeply shamed."

Simone closed her eyes. She felt his hand on the back of her neck. "Play dead," he murmured, and she thought of Julie laughing like a kid on her floral-print couch. She thought of Kathy telling her she'd saved all their jobs, and Matthew and Carl with their wedding plans and their bags from Neiman Marcus, and Elliot . . . Elliot willing to spend a day in a Dumpster, hunting for spent needles, just to be able to keep working at the *Asteroid*.

Moss's grip tightened on her neck and the other hand ripped at the top of her blouse, popping buttons, and she heard his breath go fast and ragged. "You sick bitch." As Moss pulled her to him, Simone realized that she, too, would spend a day in a Dumpster to keep her job at the *Asteroid*.

But she wouldn't do this. This was one line she could not cross.

She yanked Moss's hands away and pushed him back. "I . . . am going to tell Dylan."

"I don't care. Just leave me alone."

He leaned against the massage table, wheezing, his belt buckle undone. Simone pulled her shirt together and fell against the door, pushing it open, heading back through the hallway into the Zen room, practically knocking down Nathaniel as she passed. "Where's Dylan?" she said.

"By the pool with Chris," said Nathaniel. "What happened to you?"

Simone didn't answer. What was the point? Before long, no one around here would ever speak to her again.

Randi DuMonde's swimming pool was the size of a small lake, with a natural-looking waterfall rushing over slick rocks to feed it. It was surrounded by tiki torches, which reminded her of Blake Moss's party. *How long ago was that? It feels like years.*

Simone glanced around its perimeter, until finally she caught sight of Julie standing near the waterfall, engaged in what looked like a friendly conversation with Chris Hart. But she couldn't hear what they were saying over the other guests' voices and the rushing water, or the steel drum band playing calypso at the far end of the garden.

When Simone got closer, though, she heard. "I cannot trust you," Hart was saying. "And if I cannot trust you, I don't know how you expect this to—"

"No, I swear. I—"

"Why, Dylan? Why did you?"

"I *didn't*. I don't know where they got their information, I swear, I . . ."

"I wish I could believe you."

Hart stormed off. And before Simone could say anything, Julie was off too, shouting at him to wait, please wait, yet not getting what she wanted.

Simone stood on a grassy hill near the pool watching Julie run into the cabana, closing the door behind her. She took a deep breath, thought about leaving, just turning around and leaving, calling a cab to pick her up. But then she saw Blake Moss standing across the pool and staring at her with frost in his eyes, and she knew. She had to be the one to tell Julie.

She walked down the hill, past a female sitcom star she recognized talking to a heavy comedian and one of the LA Lakers—something about a recent trip to Paris—and Simone thought, *Maybe Randi is just a regular manager.* But it didn't make any difference. It was her job—not Randi's—that was the point.

All the lights were off in the cabana, save the dim electronic glow of Julie's cell phone. She wasn't talking to anyone on it, just holding it between her two hands, like a child holding a toy. Simone's eyes adjusted to the dark room just as Julie began to cry. She was sitting on the floor, and Simone sat down next to her. "What's wrong, Julie?"

"Oh, thank God it's you," she said.

It broke Simone's heart.

"I just can't do this anymore," Julie said. "The movie comes out in less than a week, but . . . I don't like this. I don't like anything about it."

"About what?"

"Being famous. Being with Chris. Being me."

"I thought you wanted all that," Simone said. "You said you could handle the attention."

"I didn't know," she said. "I had no idea Chris was such a control freak. He keeps saying I'm talking to the tabloids. I'm not, okay? I'm not. But what if I was? What difference would it make whether people found out now or . . ."

Simone stared at her, wanting to say, *Found out what?* And hating herself for wanting to say that. What was wrong with her? Her friend's world was falling apart. Simone was the cause. Simone was about to tell her she was the cause, and still . . . still she was searching for a lead.

Julie wiped a tear from her cheek. "I . . . got this message on my machine this morning. Just a hang up, but it made me feel scared. So much is beyond my control, Simone. Pretty much everything, actually."

Simone gritted her teeth. She felt a lump in her throat, swelling. "Julie, I have to tell you something."

"Me first," she said. "Remember last night, when I told you I was auditioning for a horror movie?"

Simone nodded.

"There is no horror movie," she said. "I really do feel hunted."

Simone thought of Blake Moss, of Keith Furlong. "Me too," she said.

"Really?"

"Julie, I know you're not talking to the tabloids, and soon everybody else will know that too."

"How can you be so sure?"

"Because it's been me," she said. "I'm a reporter for the *Asteroid.*"

"That's not funny."

"I'm serious. I was just posing as a cater-waiter at that *Devil's Road* event. There's a lot of things—private things you've told me that I haven't passed on, but the big stuff . . . I . . . I thought you liked the attention. I thought we were making you a star. . . . I'm so, so sorry."

Julie stared at Simone for a good minute, reading her

face. Her eyes were soft and glowed a little in the darkness. "Leave," she said, "or I will call security."

Simone did as she was told. She had no other choice.

As she walked out the door, Julie said, "You're disgusting." The second time she'd been told that. But now the words stuck to her, sunk in.

TWENTY-TWO

Simone walked out of the cabana, beyond tears, beyond thought. She noticed Jason Caputo, who was now talking to the sitcom star and the Laker. He nodded at her when she passed, but she looked right through him even as he said, "Hey, who died?" She looked right through Nathaniel and Randi, involved in an intense conversation, Nathaniel saying, "You can't leave your own party."

"All right then," Randi replied. "First thing in the morning."

As she reached the end of the lawn and headed back through the glass doors she heard a smirk of a voice behind her. "Angel? Do you need a ride home?"

Her back stiffened, but she did not turn around. She moved through the Zen garden, where Marty's friend was talking to three new models, the singing one nowhere in sight. She pushed open the massive door, walked down the driveway. The gate opened for her, and she headed out to the sidewalk. She walked up half a block and plucked her cell phone out of her purse. She started to call 411 to find the number of a cab company, then she realized she had no money; she'd left her credit card at home.

And she started to cry.

She collapsed on the sidewalk, deep sobs wracking her body, feeling awful and defeated and completely alone. She heard a car pull up, but she didn't look up. Why bother? Who knew her around here, in Beverly Hills?

Then the driver said her name.

The car was a black Saab. She gasped. "What are you doing here, Walker?"

"Staking out the party," he said. "I didn't trust you to come to my place, so I was going to follow you home and . . . this isn't really important. Get in."

Simone got into the front seat.

Walker said, "What happened to you?"

She pulled the top of her shirt together. "Blake Moss sort of attacked me."

"Are you serious?"

"Yeah."

"That's terrible."

She shrugged. "I survived," she said. "Oh, and Dylan now knows where I work."

He stared at her. "How?"

"I told her."

"You did? Why?"

"I was forced into it but . . . I don't know. I probably should have done it a long time ago, before . . . She was so hurt, Neil."

She started to cry again, and Walker said, "Oh, shit. Please don't do that." He put his arms around her and held her tightly and said, "I hate it when women cry."

"I'm sorry." She said the words into his neck, and he pulled her closer.

"Don't be sorry. Just . . . cut it out. Please."

"I just feel so . . . terrible about . . . everything."

"You have nothing to feel terrible about."

"Oh, come on."

"Why do you think I've been stalking you ever since you started work? Because I find you attractive?"

She looked at him.

"Okay, so that's part of it. But you're also a really good reporter. You're sharp, you're perceptive. You know how to find the right angles. And you earn people's trust. Your second day on the job, you had Emerald Deegan's personal assistant *crying on your shoulder.* I mean . . ."

"Julie told me I'm disgusting."

Walker tilted her chin up and looked into her eyes. "Julie is Dylan, right?"

She nodded.

"Okay. In your professional opinion—as an observer— does she love Chris Hart?"

"No."

"How about him? Does he have it bad for her? Does he wanna be with her no matter what, let the chips fall where they may?"

Simone rolled her eyes. "God, no."

"So, correct me if I'm wrong about this. Here's a woman who screws a married guy—a guy she doesn't love, who's not even all that into her—just so she can play a bimbo in a Jason Caputo movie."

"There might be other reasons," she said weakly.

"And *you're* disgusting." He shook his head. "What a stupid world."

"I don't know, Neil. You ever feel like you've got so many lies in your head you can't keep them all straight?"

"Yeah, but I've got this great pocket organizer."

"I'm serious," she said. "I'm tired of lying. If Nigel doesn't fire me over this, I might have to quit."

"And do what? Find a job at a *legitimate* paper, print whatever crap the mayor's publicity department gives you? I've done that. That was my first job, and I practically shot myself in the head over it. Believe me, sweetheart, you are better than that." He gave her a long, serious look. "You're more truthful than that."

"Really?"

"Not to *me.* You lie to me, constantly."

"You should talk."

He held a hand up. *"But,"* he said, "even though you lie your ass off in everyday conversation, everything you write for the *Asteroid* is gospel. Why do you think everyone's so pissed off at Leeds for talking to the tabs? Because the tabs have the *truth*," he said. "Not whatever illusion Hart and his handlers were trying to feed them about his perfect, happy marriage. Not that press conference, which was laughable. . . . The whole world has the *truth*, Simone—including that sister of yours—and it's all because of *you*."

Simone felt herself smiling. "You're good," she said.

"I mean it. The *Asteroid*'s lucky to have you." He moved a little closer, brushed a finger against her cheek, still damp from tears. "Anybody would be lucky to have you."

She didn't look away. She just gazed into his eyes—so serious—as his finger moved from her cheek to the curve of her jaw, to the center of her closed lips, parting them. . . .

"What the hell am I doing?" he said. "I'm sorry."

"That's all right."

He cleared his throat. "I'll . . . I'll drive you home, okay?"

She shook her head. Gently, she put her hands on either side of his face, and she pulled him to her and kissed him softly, then a little harder as the need grew and she began to melt.

"Go home," she whispered. "Take me with you."

Walker peeled away from the curb. His apartment was fifteen miles away, but he made it there in just under four minutes.

Walker's apartment was on the eighth floor. Somehow, Simone managed to get through the gate, then the front door, through the lobby, into the elevator, up all seven flights, into his apartment and onto the floor in front of his couch without once taking her hands or mouth off of him, even for a second.

How Walker was able to get keys into doors during all

of this, how he was able to see where they both were going—that was one for the ages, though he was nothing if not coordinated. She might ask him about that later, or maybe not. For tonight, at least, she gave up planning questions—gave up thinking altogether—in the elevator, when he lifted her and her legs went around his waist and his hand went from her throat to the remaining buttons of her blouse.

All she could do was want him.

She kissed him hard and pressed herself against him, and still she wasn't close enough, she needed to be closer. Simone had wanted men before, of course, but nothing like this . . . this feeling of being consumed by it from within.

Not until she heard the apartment door slam shut behind her, not until she felt the smooth planks of the wood floor against her back and the hard weight of Walker's body on hers did she know that soon, she would be close enough.

Later, much later, when they were lying side by side on Walker's floor, holding hands and breathing, he uttered the first sentence to come out of either one of them since they'd entered the building: "I'm relatively sure you just told me the truth."

Simone smiled. "Repeatedly."

"Really?"

"I'm not that good an actor."

He rolled onto his side and kissed her lips. "You have many other talents."

Simone's cell phone chimed. She saw Nigel's number on the screen and the whole night came flying back at her, the talk in the cabana. . . .

"Nigel?" Simone said.

Walker murmured, "Bet you're glad you don't have a picture phone."

"Right," Nigel said. "Dylan Leeds knows who you are."

Simone grimaced. "I'm sorry."

"Hart's assistant phoned, said she was going to file a restraining order against all of us—silly cow." He actually chuckled.

"You're . . . not mad at me?"

"Of course not. It was bound to happen sooner or later. Always does."

"How did Chris find out?"

"I've no idea. The assistant didn't feel like opening up about it." He chuckled again. "At any rate, chin up. We'll restrategize tomorrow. In a way, it's good news, what with that fuckwit Neil Walker following you about. He'll get nothing more from you."

Simone said it. She couldn't help herself. "I am so not fired!"

Walker mimed applause.

"Get some rest, Simone," Nigel said. "You sound like a wally."

After Simone hit END, she looked at Walker. "He called you a fuckwit."

He draped an arm over her waist and looked into her eyes. "At least someone around here is behaving predictably."

It was getting late, and Simone had no desire to put her clothes back on, let alone take a long cab ride home. So Walker took her into his bedroom, where they made love once again on surprisingly lush and comfortable sheets.

When Simone commented on them afterward, Walker said, "I don't buy anything with under a three hundred thread count. It's the one thing I'm a snob about."

Simone raised an eyebrow at him.

"I'm kidding. My mom gave me the sheets as a housewarming gift. The hell I know about thread counts?"

Simone let her gaze drift to the entertainment center next to the bed and began reading his CD titles.

"Okay," he said. "I know where this is going."

"*Miss Saigon, Wicked, Les Miz* . . . *Pippin*? You even have *Pippin*?"

"I happen to enjoy Broadway musicals."

Simone rolled over onto her back. "So let's see," she said. "We've got three-hundred-count sheets. We've got show tunes. We've got . . . well, of course, we've got your job, which is *gossip writing*. . . ."

"I'm gay," he said.

"I knew it."

"Except for the whole wanting-to-have-sex-with-women thing."

"Right."

"That is where I diverge."

Simone moved on top of him, held his gaze. "Walker?"

"Mmmmm?"

"What did the maid say, at the Beverlido?"

He grabbed her around the waist. "Good strategy you got there."

"Come on," she said. "You said you would tell me."

"I guess I did."

"So?"

"She said she understands English, even though she doesn't speak it. I told her Furlong's room number, and she said she was cleaning in there once, and apparently he was talking to another guy. I'm guessing his lawyer. The guy was telling him to get rid of some videotapes. And Furlong said, 'No. We're screwed if I get rid of those.' Something about the cops. And the other guy said, 'I don't care. I want them destroyed.'"

"That's weird," said Simone.

"Isn't it?"

"No, I mean it is, but . . . I was there, and I didn't hear her mention the *name* Keith Furlong."

"Right," he said. "I guess she knows him by the name he checked in under, Cole Whitney."

Simone had a different thought, but something kept her from bringing it up. *I'll tell him later. But for now* . . . "What do you say we explore that divergence?"

He grinned. "Only if we can listen to *Pippin* afterward."

Simone fell asleep in Walker's arms, thinking, *How can I ever leave this place?* It was his fault, all of it—him, and those sheets. The mattress wasn't bad either. . . .

She sunk into a deep, sated sleep, calm and dreamless and safe. At around three in the morning, Simone slipped out of REM and saw a brief, fevered image of Julie sobbing in front of a mirror. She jolted a little, and Walker held her tighter, and then the vision slipped away as quickly as it had come, replaced once again by velvety black.

The first pink rays of sunrise were pressing through Walker's bedroom window. Simone's eyelids fluttered and opened, and she reached out to touch him, but she felt only the pillow. When she rolled over, she found herself alone in the bed. She heard his voice, low and muffled, in the other room. "When are they bringing him in? Robbery-Homicide, right? Okay. . . . In the front or the back of the building?"

Quietly, Simone got up out of bed, went into the bathroom, and turned on the shower.

Minutes later, Walker was back in the room. "Up already?"

"Yeah," she called out over the running water. "I thought I'd get an early start."

"Not too early, I hope. I was just gonna run out and get us some coffee and bagels. Be here when I get back, okay? I'll, uh, make it worth your while."

"How can I refuse?" Simone said.

She listened, heard Walker hurry out of the apartment. Then she turned off the water, left the bathroom fully dressed, rushed outside and across the street to the Four Seasons hotel. There, she got money out of the ATM and paid the bellman to call her the world's fastest taxi.

Forty miles away, Holly Kashminian was freshly showered and dressed and her mind was clear. She had taken no pills in more than twelve hours and for the first time in days she was anticipating something other than sleep. *Answers.* That was what she wanted, that was what she would get. And then, maybe then she could put Emerald to rest; maybe then she could move on. She heard a knock on her door and sprung up from the couch, thinking, *She's early.*

Holly didn't mind. She appreciated early people. She was one herself. She unlatched the bolts. "Randi?" she said. And without waiting for a reply, she opened the door.

TWENTY-THREE

Simone arrived at the Robbery-Homicide division in downtown LA at seven thirty a.m. She had the cab drop her off in front, where Ed Sandiford was waiting next to Neil Walker. When Simone got out of the cab Sandiford said, "Hi, there. Neil's friend, right?" while Walker looked at Simone as if she were holding a two-foot-long machete to his neck, then uttered a sentence that was unintelligible to humans.

"No," said Simone. "He is not my friend."

Sandiford shot Walker a look. "Blew it, didn't you?"

Slowly, he nodded.

"Detective Sandiford," said Simone, "who are we waiting for?"

As she said it, a squad car pulled up to the curb. Simone peered into the back—and saw Keith Furlong. "We're questioning him," Sandiford said. "Man fitting his description was seen leaving the Starbright near Destiny's estimated time of death."

Simone nodded. She stared at Walker. He would not look back. An officer got out of the front seat of the car, opened the back door, and Furlong stepped out. He was wearing the same wife-beater and shorts he'd worn at the

Beverlido. His hair stuck to the side of his face. He was working on a five-o'clock shadow that crept down his neck, and his skin looked pale and blotchy. If Simone didn't know Keith Furlong, she might have even felt sorry for him. He looked that broken, that pathetic.

Walker held out a cassette recorder: "Do you have a comment for the *Interloper*?" He glanced at Simone, then added, "And the *Asteroid*?"

"I am not guilty of this awful crime," Keith said flatly. "I am confident that the truth will come to light." His mud brown eyes moved from Walker to Simone. Very quietly, he said, "You will pay."

Police brought Furlong into the building, and Sandiford started to follow. "Either of you guys want to call me this afternoon, I'll give you a statement," he said. Then he patted Walker on the shoulder. "Good luck to you," he said, before walking inside.

Simone stared at Walker.

He forced a smile "So, can you believe Furlong was—"

"I don't want to talk about Furlong."

The smile left his face. "I know," he said. "I'm sorry."

"That isn't good enough, Neil. Last night . . ." Her vision started to blur. *Oh, no, you will not cry now.* She closed her eyes, composed herself. "Last night . . . I don't usually . . ." She tried again. "Last night should have changed things between you and me."

Walker said, "It did."

"Obviously not enough." Strange, but on the cab ride over, Simone had come up with a whole speech about trust in relationships, and where there's no trust, there's no respect, no caring. It had to do with feelings—real, honest feelings, and how they should always outweigh the job, the scoop. At the time, she'd been so angry she finally understood expressions like *He makes my blood boil.* But now, looking at Walker standing silent, his blue eyes dulled and cloudy, she couldn't feel anger. She couldn't feel anything but sad.

She turned and walked up the block, took her cell phone out and called a cab, wishing more than anything she had one of those memory-erasing sticks from the *Men in Black* movies—anything to yank last night out of her mind.

"Be patient with me, Simone," Walker said. "Please. I'm still learning."

But he was standing alone on the sidewalk. Simone had already left.

Randi DuMonde was used to throwing money at people, just as she was used to people throwing money at her. That's what her business was, really. The continuous tossing back and forth of large bills—for beauty, for protection, for fame, for privacy. . . .

She got that. It was basic. And unemotional. She was not one for emotions . . . or at least not the show of them. It embarrassed her, those wet tears, that weakness.

So, when Emerald Deegan's assistant had called in the middle of her party, asked to meet with her and talk about Emerald and Randi's former association, she had thought, first, of money. Write Holly Kashminian a check, shut her up. Clean and simple.

Admittedly, when Holly had first explained what she'd found, Randi had gone pale. It was bad enough to have been in business with two of these girls. But three—to have that brought out in the open—that was terrible. Not to mention Desire. What would Blake say when he got those calls from the police, from the press?

Holly had to know that. Odds were, she was a smart girl. They were all smart out here. After listening to what Holly had to say, Randi had taken out her checkbook and said, "Where can we meet to discuss this further?"

"My house," Holly had replied. "I can't leave my house." And then she had lost it, weeping into the phone.

This came as a shock to Randi, an unwelcome shock. "Now, now," she had told Holly lamely. "Now, now, dear," thinking, *Dear God, make her stop*. Holly had asked her to come over immediately and at first she'd agreed. But as Nathaniel pointed out, Randi couldn't leave her own party. So she'd called Holly back. "I can't leave here tonight. How about seven thirty in the morning?"

"That sounds perfect," Holly had said, all business this time, not a trace of emotion in her voice. *Either she's got split personality disorder or this girl could teach a graduate-level course in screwing with my head.*

That morning, Randi got dressed in flowing red linen pants, a matching silk T-shirt, and red pumps. She shoved her checkbook into her purse along with a huge wad of Kleenex, hoping, praying that Holly would not cry again. Randi could negotiate. She could bargain and she could bend. She could write a check. But comforting—that was not one of her skills.

Randi got into her Mercedes-Benz and drove to the address Holly had texted her—a pretty little bungalow down the street from where Emerald had lived. She parked in front of the house and walked up the path, clutching the purse. She noticed how nicely mowed the lawn was, how neat the garden was. *This is all a good sign*, she thought as she rang the bell. *Where there is order, how can there be disorder—mental or otherwise? Does that make any sense?*

There was no answer. Strange. She'd figured Holly for the type that would open the door when she was still coming up the walk. Randi rang the bell again.

Still no answer. Just for the hell of it, she tried the knob. And to her surprise, the door drifted open.

Why would a girl who was afraid to leave her home leave her door unlocked?

"Holly?" she called out.

No response. The living room, like the yard, was nice and neat. Another good sign. Maybe the girl was just a sound sleeper. Randi moved through the living room, across a short hallway, to an open door that had to be the bedroom.

"Holly? Are you asleep? It's Rand—"

For a moment, Randi lost the ability to speak. Everything in her froze—her bones, her muscles. Her lungs stopped breathing. . . .

The bed was awash in bright red blood. Lying on it, a girl who had to be Holly. She had what looked like a wadded-up newspaper jammed into her mouth, and her throat . . . her throat had been slashed, from ear to ear. Randi stared at her, thinking, *Oh, dear God, no, not like that, no, no, no. Not again. No . . .*

Then the girl's eyes blinked.

Randi grabbed her cell phone out of her purse, called 911, screamed something into the receiver about a cut throat—she couldn't even tell what she was saying, but the paramedics would find her. That was their job, it was what they got paid for. Randi yanked the newspaper out of the girl's mouth and her lips started moving, she made a gurgling sound. Randi realized she was trying to speak. "No," she said softly. "Rest, Holly. Okay, please just . . ."

The bloody mouth formed a word: *"Trash."*

Then the eyes closed and Randi heard sirens and the paramedics arrived, rushing around Holly, going to work. Randi backed up for them with that image in her mind: the girl's eyes on her, the ruined mouth. The word. *Trash.*

The paramedics had Holly on a stretcher now. They carried her through the bedroom door and Randi followed.

Next to the door was a small wicker wastebasket lined with a plastic bag. As Randi passed, she saw a solitary item inside. A picture of some sort. *Trash.* On her way out, she grabbed the picture. She didn't look at it until she got out of the house and the paramedics were loading the stretcher into the back of the ambulance. "Do you want to ride along?" one of them asked her.

"That's okay," she said. "I'll follow in my car." And then she looked at the photograph. Randi knew it. She had seen it before: a little girl with strawberry blond hair and a big smile, standing next to Snow White at Disneyland.

Randi fell to her knees, and started to scream.

* * *

Once the cab dropped her off at her apartment, Simone showered fast, shoved a few pieces of bread into her mouth and stared into her closet, Kathy's voice in her head. *You're young and cute. Feel it. Work it.* She chose a short sleeveless plaid dress from the Gap—not exactly that skimpy Brittany ensemble, but it would do. She put on the dress, her platform sandals, and checked herself out in the mirror. *Not bad. A little makeup, I'll have something to work with.*

Of everything that had happened between her and Walker the previous night, Simone was glad of only one thing: When he had told her what the Portuguese chambermaid had said, she hadn't revealed what she'd been thinking.

Walker had assumed the maid was referring to Furlong by the name he'd checked in under. But that didn't make sense. Chambermaids dealt with room numbers, not the names given to the front desk. The maid had told Walker about a conversation she'd overheard between two men, one of whom was named Cole. Why would Furlong's lawyer call him by an assumed name?

Sure, maybe it *was* Furlong and his lawyer, who was calling him Cole for the benefit of eavesdropping maids. But what Simone thought was this: The maid had overheard a conversation between Furlong and *Cole*. Maybe the manager wasn't exaggerating back at Bedrock when he told Simone he was Furlong's silent partner, his Karl Rove.

She recalled what Walker had said: *The guy was telling him to get rid of some videotapes. And Furlong said, "No. We're screwed if I get rid of those." And the other guy said, "I don't care. I want them destroyed."* But Walker had thought Cole was Furlong. When you switched it around, it actually made more sense: Furlong, asking his reluctant "number two" to dispose of some incriminating tapes.

Simone looked at her clock. Ten a.m. She had already

called Nigel, told him she'd be late for work, but it should be worth it. She headed outside and got into her Jeep, thinking about what Cole had said to her on the night Emerald had died. *He's not around, I run the show.*

Well, Cole, let's see how well you run it.

Simone started up her car, headed up Ventura Boulevard toward Coldwater Canyon and West LA, where Bedrock was located. She turned on the radio, flipped the dial past some guitar rock station, Phish singing, "Each betrayal begins with trust . . ."

Each betrayal.

She banished them both from her mind: Walker and Julie, betrayer and betrayed. Right now, she was not a friend or a lover. . . . She was simply a reporter. And life was only about Cole—what he was hiding.

To Randi, this was surreal, like something out of a bad dream, something out of her past. She was crying—crying for the first time she could remember, tears drenching her cheeks, her nose running—*crying* over some girl who'd been trying to blackmail her.

She was sitting in the ICU waiting room at Cedars-Sinai while doctors operated on her blackmailer. She was talking to that detective, to Sandiford. He was asking her about her business, and she was trying to do what she always did, tailor the truth, just a bit . . . but it was hard to do that and think and worry and cry all at the same time.

"Are you a madam, Ms. DuMonde?"

"Huh?" She blew her nose into a Kleenex, wiped her eyes.

"Are you a—"

"I used to be. Not now. But I never liked that term." *Sniff.* Some of Randi's girls, they could cry at the drop of a hat. They wore their emotions close to the surface—it was what made them so good at their jobs. Not her, though. Not Randi. She was better at burying than releasing.

"I'm not in Vice, Ms. DuMonde. I'm looking for a serial

killer, and anything you tell me about the victims, their relationship to you . . . anything that could—"

"A serial killer."

"Yes."

"God."

"So," he said. "You understand the importance."

She breathed in and out. Breathed until she could
function again. "Destiny," she said. "Little girl in the
Disneyland picture."

"Yes?"

"I set her up on a few dates. After she signed with me.
They were purely social. I am a manager, Detective. I get
professional acting roles for my clients. My roster in-
cludes—"

"I don't need your résumé, ma'am." Sandiford's gaze
was calm, serious. "Who did you . . . fix Destiny up
with?"

"I have a list of names. Back at my office. I can have
my associate fax them to you."

Sandiford raised his eyebrows at her. She knew what
he was thinking. "I am very organized," she said. "I keep
records of everything, including . . . blind dates."

A doctor stepped into the doorway, and everything
else in the room fell away. The doctor looked at Randi as
if she were Holly's mother. And in a way, that's what she
felt like. A mother. How strange. "Do you happen to have
phone numbers for her family? Friends?"

"Oh, God," she said, the tears coming again. "God,
God, God."

Sandiford took over. "We have Ms. Kashminian's cell
phone," he said. "We can check her apartment as well."

"That would be a good idea."

Sandiford said, "Is she . . ."

The doctor shook her head. "Ms. Kashminian is stabilized," she said. "But she is in a coma."

Randi exhaled hard. Stabilized. That was a good word.
People came out of comas all the time, you heard about it
on the news, you . . .

Why was this affecting her so strongly? But even as she wondered, Randi knew. Long ago, Randi had had a husband. *You can let go of the past*, her ex-husband used to say. *But the past won't let go of you.* Wise man, Randi's ex.

She glanced at Sandiford. "Are you through with me, Detective?"

"For now, ma'am, yes."

"In that case," she said, "I'd better go home. I could definitely use the rest."

TWENTY-FOUR

Bedrock looked even cheesier by the light of day.
Simone had heard somewhere that, in its previous
life, this supposedly hot nightspot had been a bud-
get chain restaurant, and you could still see that side of
it—the glittery glass mixed into the stucco, the bright
blue wooden beams framing the door. There was a metal
flag holder, too, and while there was no flag in there now,
it seemed the perfect place for a giant banner reading
"IHOP" or "HoJos" or some other homey set of initials.

She'd much prefer this place if it were an IHOP. As it
was, the best thing she could say about it was it made her
hungry for pancakes.

The door was open, and so she walked in. It took her
eyes a while to adjust. Even in daytime, it was close to
pitch-black, just a few mood lights in the windowless
space. She looked around, at the glow-in-the-dark cave
paintings, the big bowl of pterodactyl eggs.

Truth be told, the place reminded her of meeting
Walker, and that made her reluctantly wistful. She thought
about the previous night and was struck by a vision of
Walker's face above hers as they made love, his eyes looking deep into her own. . . .

Stop it.

And then she heard a man's voice say, "Who's there?" And she saw Cole at the bar, pulling bottles out of a crate.

Simone pasted a smile on her face. She channeled Kathy. *Feel it, work it.* "Hi, Cole," she said. "Remember me?"

He smiled. "Sure I do . . . uh . . ."

"Brittany."

"Right!"

Simone could tell he had no idea who the hell she was. She looked at him. "Destiny's friend."

"Oh, my God. Right. Hey, listen. I'm so sorry."

Simone swallowed. "I've been pretty freaked out about it," she said.

He unloaded three more bottles. "Yeah," he said, "I could imagine."

Simone noticed something. Ever since she'd said Destiny's name, Cole refused to look at her, his eyes darting everywhere else—the bottles, the fake brontosaurus, the signs for the bathrooms. But her eyes, her "exotic" green eyes, as he had called them . . . Cole was avoiding them at all costs.

Forget young and cute. It's time to be direct. "Cole, I have to level with you."

"Yeah?"

"I'm a private detective." *Okay, maybe direct isn't the right word.*

He stopped unloading the bottles, looked into her face. "You are?"

"I'm working with Ed Sandiford now, and—"

"Shit."

"Ed told me that witnesses saw Keith leaving the Starbright—"

"No."

"On the night that Destiny was murdered."

"Oh, fuck me." He leaned over the bar, put his head in his hands.

"Cole?"

"Goddamn it."

"Did Keith kill Destiny and Emerald?"

"No, of course he didn't—"

"What was he doing at the Starbright?"

"He wanted to talk to her. To tell her . . . something."

"How did he find her there?"

"I tracked her down for him. Leticia—"

"Who?"

"Nothing."

"You tracked Destiny down because Keith wanted to talk." Simone stared at him. "I saw her body, Cole. That was some conversation."

"I swear to God he just wanted to talk. He . . . he found her and he was . . . horrified."

"But he didn't call the police about it? Why?"

He looked up at her, pleading. "Because they would ask him what he'd gone there to talk about." He put his face in his hands again. Simone waited, but he said nothing more.

She shook her head. This was going nowhere. "I don't know if you know this, but if you're covering up for him, you could be implicated as well. You could go to jail, Cole. *Look at me.*" She put a finger under his chin, tilted his face up. "Picture yourself. In jail. With those long, pretty eyelashes." Simone had no idea where this was coming from—that edge in her voice, that menace. It was as if every unpleasant encounter from the past few days—Furlong, Moss, Julie, Walker—every last one of them had balled up inside Simone, mobilized her against this one dimwitted guy.

May as well go with it.

His doe eyes sparked with fear. "He didn't kill anyone," he said. "I swear."

"What did he want to *talk* to Destiny about?"

"He wanted to make sure she didn't tell about the . . ."

"About the what?"

"Nothing."

"About the what?"

"When he found her body there like that, he freaked out, he didn't know what to do. He called me, and—"

"About the what, Cole?"

His gaze went back to his hands.

"Look at me."

He looked. His eyes glistened. He was actually about to cry.

"About the videotapes?" she said. "Is that what you were going to say?"

And like that, all the color drained out of Cole's face, like sand out of an egg timer. One tear slipped down his cheek. "Do you still have them, Cole?" she said.

He nodded. "I couldn't throw them out, no matter what he . . ."

"Are they here?"

"Yes."

"I want to see them."

"Trust me," he said, "you don't."

"Yes," she said, "I do."

Quietly, he led her into Keith's office.

"By the way," she told him. "Ed knows I'm here, and expects me back downtown in exactly forty-five minutes."

"Uh, okay." She could tell he didn't know what she was talking about. How weird that of all the bad guys she'd encountered, the bulky Neanderthal was the one who wouldn't think of laying a hand on her. He removed a box from under Keith's desk, set it down on top. Simone looked inside, at several videotapes, each one with a date on the side and a set of initials.

"This is probably the one you're interested in." He removed a videotape with the initials *LC* on the side, and the date: 8/24. The date of Emerald Deegan's murder. Simone looked at him. "What does LC stand for?"

He winced. "You'll see."

There was an entertainment center at the end of the room. Simone slipped the tape into the VCR. "This is his private collection," said Cole. "You . . . you'll see why he doesn't want any of this getting out, but . . . I couldn't throw them away."

She hit PLAY. There was a date and time in the top corner. August 24, eleven thirty p.m. Within an hour of Emerald's death. The camera panned down, slowly. Simone's pulse sped up. She said, "Is this your indie film project?"

"Yeah," he said. "Keith pays me a lot of money . . . to shoot these. He knows he can trust me," he added as the image appeared on the screen. An enormous mountain of a woman—naked and holding a giant diapered baby in her lap. "Mama," said the baby, and began suckling a breast that resembled a king-sized pillow.

"That's Leticia Chase," said Cole.

"LC."

"Yes."

The baby was Keith.

"Destiny introduced Keith to Leticia," Cole said. "She knew her through some of the Pleasures girls. She's a specialty performer and . . . Keith just . . . He knew Des was talking to the tabloids, and he didn't want her talking about *this*."

Simone was absolutely speechless.

"You see," said Cole, "why he didn't want this to get out. It would ruin his rep, his business. But I couldn't throw it away. It's his alibi."

Finally, Simone got her voice back. "That's one hell of an alibi," she said.

Of all of them, Holly was by far the least perfect. She fought back. She asked questions. She was not shamed, not at all. Sitting in his office, he felt a sting on the back of his neck, a terrible souvenir. He touched that scratch and he heard her voice, like smashed glass in his ears. *How dare you?*

In retrospect, he probably should not have chosen Holly. Yes, she had talked. She had shamed men (she had even shamed *him*!), and, in that respect, she was Project material. But she wasn't a whore, and that made her different. She was uppity, entitled, less likely to obey. *Whores obey. It is part of their job.*

On his plasma screen at home, he had an image cued up. It was from the press conference three days earlier. Originally it had been a close-up of the speakers' line, but he had manipulated the image, over and over, so the camera cut closer, then closer, then closer still. By now, it was so close that all you could see were a jumble of pixels, peach, waxy beige, pink, brown. When people came to his house, they would look at the screen, think maybe it was abstract art.

But he knew. It was the faces of two and three. The area around the jawbones, he thought, though he wasn't sure. What he did know was this: It was Dylan's skin and Simone's skin. Dylan's and Simone's tainted blood running underneath. Dylan = two. Simone = three.

He knew this as well: Two and three were whores. They would be much easier.

Before she left, Simone had Cole call Sandiford, tell him everything. The detective said he was on his way to Bedrock to pick up the tapes, and Cole went whiter than ever, though he received repeated assurances they'd be kept in strictest confidence. "Keith will thank you," Simone told Cole after he hung up. "No matter what, it's better than being charged with murder."

On her way to the office, she phoned Nigel and told him exactly why Keith Furlong was no longer a suspect in the Emerald and Destiny murders. There was a long stretch of silence on the other end of the phone.

"Hello, Nigel?"

"That," he said, "is *brilliant.*"

Simone practically drove off the road. "We're going to run *that* story?" she said. "I thought you said we were a family publication."

She almost felt sorry for Keith Furlong until Nigel

said, "We aren't going to *run* the story, love. We're going to *use* it."

Two seconds after she hit END, Simone's cell phone trilled. She looked at the screen. She almost didn't answer, almost turned the phone off and let voice mail do her dirty work. "Hi, Neil."

"Simone, I'm so sor—"

"I know." She kept her tone cool, businesslike. "Listen, before I forget, Furlong is no longer a person of interest."

"Simone . . ."

"Don't mention it. Professional courtesy. Since you told me what the maid said, it's only fair. FYI, he has an incredibly disgusting alibi."

"Please listen to me."

Simone said nothing. She just looked at the road.

"I'm sorry. I promise. I'll never do anything like that again."

Simone took a breath, willed the emotion out of her voice. "Yes, you will."

"No, I . . ."

"You will, Neil. You can't help it. It's the way you are."

"Simone . . ."

"I'd be really awful if I stayed angry at you for it. It's like being angry at someone for having brown eyes. Dishonesty . . . it's a part of your nature."

"That isn't fair."

"Isn't it? I know how it is. There's a lot of my nature that's not admirable. Hell, I tried to send you to Palm Springs just because my boss told me to."

"And I forgave you."

"It's not a matter of forgiving. I forgive you," she said. "And deep down, I'll always think you're the cat's ass. But I can't *be* with somebody and have to sleep with one eye open."

He was quiet.

"You understand?"

"Yes," he said. "I just don't think I'll ever find another woman who'll tell me she thinks I'm the cat's ass."

Simone smiled. "Good-bye, Neil."

" 'Bye, Simone."

She hung up. And then she let herself cry.

As Simone walked into the reporters' room and got situated at her desk, Kathy turned to her and said, "Three words regarding Keith Furlong. Can you guess what they are?"

Simone pondered for a moment. "Major oral fixation?"

She laughed. "True, yes." She raised an eyebrow. "But not quite *news*worthy. Think about that, and I'll give you another guess."

Simone thought. It clicked. "Checked into rehab!"

"Ding ding ding! Little lady gets the stuffed bear, thank you for playing!"

Matthew said, "Was that not the fastest rehab check-in ever? I mean . . . by the time the cops got the tape cued up, he was already doing his first support group."

"America's Speediest Twelve-Steppers," said Elliot. "Good sidebar."

Simone turned to him. "By sidebar, do you mean there's going to be an article?"

Elliot nodded. "On the record: 'Emerald's Cheating Boy-Toy: My Secret Battle with Sex Addiction.' "

"With no mention of the . . ."

"Baby pictures, no. Nigel swung that one pretty easily. Plus, for a later issue, a confessional on discovering Destiny's body."

"That'll get us tons of press," said Matthew. "Nigel says New York is thrilled."

"Isn't that funny?" said Kathy. "There's no one who hates tabloids more than Keith Furlong. And now he's going to be spending hours and hours with us."

Nigel walked into the room. "You're back." He stared at Simone, his eyes cold and hard and as serious as a gun scope, and she thought, *He knows I was with Walker last night.*

Simone got ready. "Did I do something wrong?"

He cleared his throat; his gaze dropped to the floor. "It isn't you," he said. "It's your friend. It's Holly."

TWENTY-FIVE

"**D**ylan. Again." It was the first time Julie had ever gotten ice from Nathaniel. Sure, he was full of attitude—he teased Randi's clients constantly. But the ice. The brush-off. That was new. "Randi is *still* not here."

She put a smile in her voice. "Hey, is that any way to talk to your big moneymaker?"

The ice melted. "Sorry, hon. It's just, to tell the truth, I don't know where Randi is any more than you do—and I *need* the bitch." Julie could hear him typing e-mails as he spoke. Always the multitasker. "You understand, I use the word 'bitch' in only the most affectionate and empowering way."

"Of course you do."

"Oh, hey," he said. "Long as I have you on, I need you to clear up your afternoons for the next few days. Soon as I get hold of La Randi, I want to schedule another press conference. All of us, plus Chris. Talk about this whole Simone Glass thing. Still can't *believe* she was undercover for the *Asteroid*. You must have been shocked when she told you."

Julie's stomach flopped over. "Do we really have to—"

"Trust me, it'll make you look awesome," he said. "Poor, sweet girl from a small town stabbed in the back by her best friend. You know how attention spans are. By the time *Devil's Road* opens, no one will even remember Dirty Dylan anymore. You'll be the victim."

"Nathaniel," she said, "I don't . . . I don't want to be the victim."

"Sure you do. Victims rock. Victims get sit-downs with Barbara Walters and People's Choice Awards."

"But—"

"Gotta run. Important call coming in. Talk soon." *Click.*

As she hung up the phone, Julie flashed on a call she'd received from Simone, a week before the beginning of senior year.

Did you forget or something? I've been waiting for half an hour. The movie already started and . . .

Oh, shit. I did forget. Todd came over and . . .

Long pause. Oh. Okay.

I am so sorry, Simone.

Don't be sorry. It's Todd McKenna. I'd do the same thing.

The movie had been *Night at the Opera*. A perfectly restored print. One night only at Upstate Films in Rhinebeck. Simone had been talking about it for weeks.

So weird, but with everything that had happened in the past eight years, with all the ways she'd aged and changed and compromised, with all the lines she'd crossed, the things she'd done that would look so wrong on paper, blowing off Simone for Todd was one of the things she still felt worst about.

Julie had never wanted to be the girl who forgot her best friend when she fell in love, and that's what she became, and when she saw Simone at the Beverlido party, looking exactly the same except for the uniform and the hair, she had thought: *Here's my chance. I can make it up to her. I can be a good friend.*

What were the odds that Simone would be a cater-waiter

at Julie's first promotional event? *Maybe*, she had thought at the time, *everything does happen for a reason.*

So much for that. Julie collapsed on her bed, stared up at the ceiling. *At least I gave her some good scoop. And the funny part is, she doesn't even know the half of it.* Her vision was blurry, but for some reason Julie didn't realize she was crying. Not until she felt the tears, hot on her face.

Julie's phone rang. Chris. She grabbed some Kleenex out of the dispenser on her bedstand, mopped up her cheeks, took a deep breath. "Hi, honey."

"Dyl, I'm sor—"

"I know. You're sorry for doubting me. You know now I can keep a secret." She got out of bed, wandered over to her giant gold mirror.

Chris said, "I . . . just can't say it enough."

Julie made herself smile. "It means a lot." She looked at the prom picture stuck in the corner of her mirror and felt the tears coming again. She bit them back. "Listen, Chris? Can you maybe come over or something? I . . . I don't really feel like being alone right now."

"Later, sure," he said. "Listen, though. I want to talk to you about something. I have this idea. Kind of a project."

Minutes after Nigel told Simone that Holly had been found with her throat slit and the advance layout of the *Asteroid* that Simone had sent her shoved in her mouth, seconds after he said she was on life support in Cedars-Sinai ICU, Simone received a call from Ed Sandiford, who told her the same thing, verbatim. Still, she couldn't get it to sink in.

Then Ed told her about the picture of a four-year-old girl and Snow White in Holly's trash, a girl who turned out to be Destiny, and Simone collapsed in her chair and put her head down and the room actually started to spin. The air around her crushed into Simone's ears, her face, so loud that it drowned out Matthew and Elliot asking, "What's wrong?" and Kathy saying, "Glass of water?"

"You there, Simone?" Sandiford was saying now.

She took a breath. Gradually, everything shifted back into focus. "I should have gone to Holly's earlier. She didn't call me back and I felt like something was wrong. But I just . . ."

"I know you did," said Sandiford. "We got all your phone messages. Listen to me, Simone. Every time you called her, she was there. She was fine. She wasn't attacked until this morning, and she was still alive when she was found."

"Is . . . is she seeing visitors?" Simone closed her eyes. *She's not seeing anything.* "I mean, can I go to her?"

"Not right now," he said. "They're only allowing family into ICU. But her parents are there, and her brother and his wife."

She has a family. That's good.

"What I'd like you to do, though, is stop by the crime scene, answer a few questions."

"Randi is a madam?" said Simone, who was asking a lot more questions than she was answering. She was in Holly's living room with Ed Sandiford, the beautiful green couch coated in fingerprint dust, personal photos— everything personal—having been removed from the premises. When Simone had first arrived, Sandiford had asked her to walk around, see if the furniture all seemed to be in the same place.

It was. But still she felt as if she were in a different house than the one she'd interviewed Holly in, a house that held another reality.

Emerald was Desire. Simone still couldn't believe it. Years before she was *Suburban Indiscretions'* youngest, skinniest housewife, Emerald Deegan was one of Hollywood's most-sought-after call girls. That was how she'd bought her father that house. Servicing televangelists. Wearing ball gags. Playing dead for Blake Moss.

And Randi was her madam.

"She isn't *exclusively* a madam," Sandiford said. "Not

anymore. What happened was, years ago she set up this brothel, only she called herself a manager, and the girls were her clients. She hired all gorgeous wannabe actresses, and then they started getting real acting jobs and she became their manager for real. Before long, she started getting up-and-up clients and her business became legit in spite of itself. It's like, you're running numbers out the back of a candy store, and all of a sudden everybody wants the candy."

Simone thought of the rooms at Randi's house, the locked doors. "I think," she said, "she's still running a few numbers."

Sandiford nodded. His gaze traveled to the floor. "I'd like to tell you something. Deep background. And I'm only telling you because Neil says you've spent time with Randi and you might be able to help."

"I'm not spending time with Randi anymore . . . or Neil either," she said. "But I'd love to help."

"We'd thought the killer had something against the press. That still might be true. But I'm thinking these murders might have more to do with Randi DuMonde." His eyes went back to Simone's face. "The numbers part of her business."

"You mean . . ."

"Randi signed Nia Lawson a month before her suicide. Told me she was planning a big comeback for her, was working on getting her auditions. But her bookings file looks exactly like Destiny's. Lots and lots of 'blind dates.'"

"You think the killer is going after Randi's prostitutes."

He nodded. "Possibly."

"But what about Holly?"

"The assault on her was different than the others. It was messier, faster. He put the picture in her wastebasket—it wasn't in the trash outside, meaning he probably brought it with him at the time of the killing, rather than days before. There was no note, no writing on the wall," he said. "And he left without completing the job. He saw she'd talked to the *Asteroid*, the bracelet article. I think that just . . . set him off. He wanted her gone."

Simone's stomach clenched up. "If I had never talked to Holly, then she'd . . ."

He waved her off. "She was calling every media outlet in town. If it wasn't the *Asteroid*, it would have been somebody's damn Web site," he said. "What I want to know from you is, have you come in contact with anybody who may have it in for Randi . . . for the numbers part of her business?"

She shook her head.

"Anybody who seemed a little strange?"

She looked at him. "Blake Moss."

"The movie star?" He rolled his eyes. "Yeah, he's strange all right. Just reread that *Vanity Fair* article."

"No, he . . . he found out I worked for the *Asteroid* and he . . . he tried to . . . cut a deal with me," Simone said. "He was threatening."

Sandiford nodded. "I'll look into him," he said. "Just so you know, though, we don't think the killer is sexually motivated. The victims are always clothed, there's never any DNA. We don't even know if it's a man who's doing this." He looked at her. "Plus, I'd think if the killer were a famous movie star, somebody would have spotted him at one of the crime scenes."

"Good point."

"That's why they pay me the big bucks," he said. "Anyway, you've got my number. Call if anything comes to mind."

Simone glanced at the couch again, and for a second she could almost see Holly on it, staring into her glass of water. *You . . . you don't think there's a story here, do you?* She thought of Holly, her throat cut open, the spread from the *Asteroid* shoved into her mouth, and wished, so deeply, that there had never been a story.

Sandiford walked Simone back to her car. As she got in, he said, "Neil Walker is a total pain in the ass."

Simone's chest tightened a little at the sound of his name. "True."

"He doesn't always think before he does things."

"True."

"But, I'll tell you something. He's got a good heart."

He walked back to the crime scene, leaving her there. Simone started up her Jeep and said to no one, "True."

"ICU."

"Yes, I'm calling to ask about the condition of—"

"Holly Kashminian's condition is still the same, Ms. Glass."

"You recognized my voice."

"It's the third time you've called."

"I'm sorry."

"Don't be sorry, Ms. Glass. Being worried is nothing to feel sorry about."

Simone hung up her phone and stared at her blank computer screen, thinking, *Being worried is probably the only thing I don't have to feel sorry about.* Holly was in a coma. Emerald Deegan and Destiny were dead. Julie Curtis—her best friend, whose life story she had wanted to write—was now a national pariah. All because of the *Asteroid.* And mostly because of Simone.

The one decent thing she'd done was telling Julie the truth. . . . The only reason she had done it was that she didn't want to play dead for Blake Moss. So, if everyone now knew how the *Asteroid* was getting its information, if Julie was now back in Chris Hart's good graces, she had Blake to thank for that—not Simone.

And there was still a killer out there.

Simone knew Sandiford was questioning all of Randi's clients—both "numbers" and "candy"—and even though Julie was candy, she had to be scared.

Simone looked at Elliot, busy researching the "Speediest Twelve-Steppers" sidebar for the Keith Furlong interview. "Hey," she said to him, "you're hitting Dylan Leeds's cans, right?"

"I would," he said, "but I can't locate her address. Can't run a DMV check on her because she rides around in a limo."

Simone thought of Julie's peaceful little house, the replica of her high school home that she'd fallen in love with at first sight. "I know where she lives."

"You do? Then I'll hit 'em tonight. Nigel wants us all to pick up the Chrylan slack, now that . . . you know."

Simone nodded. "Just do me a favor. If you find anything unusual in there? Something that obviously doesn't belong to her? Can you let me know right away?"

"Sure," he said. "I'll even send you a pic."

Nigel stepped into the room, asked Simone to come into his office. "I've got an assignment for you," he said. "I think you're going to like it."

Simone stared at Nigel without saying a word.

"I'm asking you because you're the only one who's small enough," Nigel said. "Kath's already posed as a chambermaid at the Chateau, so she's ineligible."

"But . . ."

"We need to pick up the Chrylan slack, love. What better way to do it than exclusive photos of their first hotel tryst?"

"You want me to hide in a closet. With a camera phone. And take pictures of them."

"Under the bed is fine, too."

"I . . . I can't do that."

"I would not ask you to do anything I wouldn't do myself," he said. And sadly, Simone had no doubt that was true.

Logic. Use logic with him, and maybe that will work. "I can't break into a hotel room. I'll get arrested."

He looked across the desk, slid Simone a card key. "That comes from my top secret source as well."

Damn.

"Arrive at the bungalow at nine thirty. Go immediately

to the bedroom, assume your position. Chrylan, the source tells me, will be in the room at ten or later."

Simone looked at him. "Nigel. What if I tell you I refuse to do this?"

"Then I will be forced to hire a very expensive, five-foot-tall paparazzo I know of . . . and you will be suspended from your job indefinitely."

"So they're getting photographed either way."

"Come hell or high water," he said. "Yes."

As Simone walked into the reporters' room to get her bag, Kathy said, "I heard all that. You gonna be okay?"

"Sure," Simone said. "Stabbing my friend in the back was fun, but humiliating her . . . that'll be priceless."

Matthew was on the phone and Elliot was running a search on his computer, but Kathy pulled Simone out of their earshot anyway, and walked her up to the street-facing windows.

"When I first started here, the *Asteroid* was big on AIDS stories," Kathy said. "Always hoped and prayed I wouldn't get one of those. I mean, cheating is one thing. But if a guy wants to keep it a secret that he's dying . . ."

Simone nodded. "I get that."

"So the day finally came, I got one. It's this sweet, older leading man. He's been in the closet his whole life. Through my connections, I pose as a masseuse, give a home massage to his wife, an actress—killer boob job, by the way, I got her to tell me who her surgeon was—"

"Anyway . . ."

"Anyway, this poor woman must not have too many girlfriends, because within like, ten minutes, she's crying all over the table, telling me her husband is dying. Yeah, she's his beard and their marriage is a *faux*mance. But he's also her best friend in the world and she loves him and she doesn't know what she's going to do without him."

"God. That's terrible."

"Then she swears me to secrecy. An undercover tabloid reporter. She says, 'If anyone ever finds out, it'll kill him and me both.'"

"What did you do?"

"Reported the story."

"You *did*?"

"Yep," she said. "Told the world about the wife's boob job. Far as Nigel knew, she didn't give me jack about AIDS." She gave Simone a long, meaningful look. "You see what I'm saying? You're in the hotel closet, honey. You call the shots."

Simone looked at her. "Nobody's going to fire me if the camera phone breaks," she said. "I gave it my best try."

"Exactly." She winked. "Do us proud."

Getting into the Chateau Marmont bungalow had been surprisingly easy. Simone had used the card key and walked into the room reserved for Hollywood's hottest cheating couple without earning so much as a second look from the hotel staff. Nigel's "top secret source" must have been very well connected.

But standing in the closet—just a couple of feet away from the king-sized bed, her phone turned to vibrate like some kind of panting voyeur—that was not easy. Even though Simone had no intention of taking pictures, that didn't make her feel any better about being here, bringing new meaning to *tabloid scum*.

The door to the bungalow creaked open. *Showtime*, thought Simone. There were no voices, no giggles, no murmured sweet-nothings or anything else you'd associate with a tryst. Just pure, thick silence. And then, footsteps.

The footsteps moved through the living room area, coming closer, into the room with Simone. She'd left the closet door open a crack, just so she could get some air, and she peered through it now, holding her breath.

There was only one person in the room. Chris Hart. *Well, that explains the quiet.* Hart sat down on the bed. He took off his shoes, but nothing else. Simone didn't want to look too hard at Hart for fear he'd feel someone watching, but she couldn't help but notice the expression on his face. Bored, slightly annoyed. Like a man on a business trip.

Her cell phone vibrated. She backed up in the closet, looked at the screen, and saw she'd received a text message. She opened it up. It was from Elliot: *Found in DL's trash.* Simone clicked on the photo attachment icon, and a tiny picture filled her screen. A picture of an emerald pendant, cut into the shape of a letter *H.*

Holly's necklace was in Julie's trash.

"Oh, dear God." Simone said it out loud. She pushed open the door and ran through the room.

"Where the hell are you going?" yelled Chris Hart. But she didn't care, didn't care if he saw her, didn't care if he chased her down or screamed at her or sued the *Asteroid.* She pushed open the door and headed out for the parking lot, breath cutting into her lungs, hoping, praying she'd get to Julie's in time.

TWENTY-SIX

From her car, Simone called Sandiford and left a frantic message on his voice mail. She kept remembering what he had said, about the killer targeting Randi's prostitution business. *Why Julie?* she kept thinking as she sped to Julie's house. *She is candy, not numbers.*

But in the back of her mind, she knew. The *Asteroid*. Even though Julie hadn't spoken willingly to the press, the killer still thought she had. Simone screeched to a stop in front of Julie's house—her simple little house, without a gate, without security, without so much as hedges blocking it from the street. She lunged out of her car, whispering, *Please don't let me be too late. Please don't let me be too late*, again and again and again. She ran up to the front door and hit the bell.

No answer. Maybe Julie was on her way to the hotel to meet Chris. *Please.* Simone tried the door. It drifted open. Unlocked. If Julie had left the house, she would have locked it. *No, no, no . . .*

"Julie?" Simone's voice was a bleat.

There was no reply. The living room was undisturbed, and as Simone moved through it, toward the bedroom, the air felt like water, holding her back. That stale, metallic odor drifted out of the bedroom and she ran in whispering, "No, no, no," even though she knew, knew by now what that smell was.

"No, no, no . . . ," she said, the nos getting louder when she saw what she did, and then they became screams, sobs. She pushed 911 on her cell phone, but when the operator answered, all she could do was shriek into it, not wanting to believe her eyes, her brain. . . .

Julie was lying on the bed, her throat cut, a butcher's knife in her hand. She was wearing a white dress, but the dress, her hands, her feet, her face, were clumped with dirt—dirt from her many potted plants, now upended, strewn around the bed, as dead as the owner who had taken such pride in them.

On the wall, over the bed, two words had been written in her blood. And when Simone read the words, she fell to her knees and heaved, feeling as if she could never stop, would never be able to catch her breath.

The words on the wall: *Dirty Dylan*.

Simone kept thinking of two words as she sat in one of the interview rooms in Robbery-Homicide, an untouched glass of water in front of her, a blanket that the beat cops had given her still draped around her shoulders.

The words were "my fault."

She hadn't talked since the cops arrived. After all that screaming and sobbing and heaving, her voice box had shut down, her brain unable to formulate any words but those two: *My. Fault.*

If it hadn't been for her, there would be no Dirty Dylan. Clara would still be Hollywood's happiest couple, and Julie would be an up-and-comer. Not as famous, but not hated. Not by the murderer. *Alive.*

Ed Sandiford walked in and said, "I'm sorry, Simone." And just seeing him there made her lose it again. She started weeping, though she was quieter about it now. Sandiford waited for her to catch her breath and said, "We're not gonna question you now, kid. We're gonna let you go home."

Simone's voice came out, a low, pained croak. "I don't think I can drive."

"I know," he said. "Someone wants to drive you."

He moved aside, and Neil Walker stood in the doorway, his eyes cloudy, waiting. "I'm afraid you have no say in this," he said. "I'm driving you home whether you want me to or—"

Simone went to him and lifted her arms around his neck and buried her head in his chest, and he never finished the sentence. He just held her.

Walker drove Simone to her apartment, went with her to her door, and waited for her to open it. He walked in with her, turned on all the lights, made sure she was safe.

He said, "I guess you want me to leave."

"I don't know what I want."

"I can stand here," he said. "Wait for you to figure that out."

She looked at him. "It might take a while."

"That's fine," he said. "I don't have to be anywhere."

Simone and Walker sat on the couch all night. For the first part of it, she was unable to do anything other than cry, and he let her. He held her and told her it would be all right and rubbed her back as she caught her breath, then pulled her closer when she started sobbing again.

Finally, she felt as if she could talk. And he let her do that too, let her tell him everything that had happened, every detail. He asked few questions, just nodded mostly, until she told him about Julie's body—what had been done to it.

"Oh, my God," he whispered.

"I thought you knew. Thought maybe Ed had told you."

He shook his head. "I didn't ask him for details."

She met his gaze. "But . . . it's going to be the biggest story of the year."

"I didn't care," he said quietly. "I only cared about you."

Simone's eyes started to well up, and her throat clenched and she said nothing, too moved to speak. She waited for him to crack a joke. To say something like, *But as of tomorrow, I'm back on your ass.* But Walker didn't say a word. He just looked at her. She put her head on his shoulder. And she closed her eyes.

Simone didn't know she'd fallen asleep until her ringing phone jolted her awake. She looked at the caller ID: Chris Hart. *Chris Hart?*

She picked it up. "Chris?"

"You could have gotten some awesome photos," he said.

"What do you—"

"Problem is, you were in the wrong closet!" He started to laugh, the laughter growing louder and louder until it became a shriek. The shriek of a murdered woman.

Simone jolted awake. Walker said, "Wha . . ."

They had both fallen asleep, sitting on the couch with all their clothes on. Simone looked at her watch: four a.m. "Nightmare," she said.

"What did you dream?"

She waved him off. "Not important."

"Okay." He closed his eyes again, put his arms around her shoulders. But when Simone closed her eyes, she realized the feeling remained. That odd feeling about Chris Hart. How cold he'd looked, taking his shoes off on the hotel room bed, not a shred of anticipation in his entire face. And what was it he'd said when Simone had run out of the room?

The phone rang, and for a moment she expected to fall into another nightmare, but this time when she looked at the caller ID, she saw her sister's name.

"Greta?" said Simone.

Walker raised his eyebrows.

"Sorry, I know it's four in the morning there."

"Is everything all right?"

"Listen, I just got to the station and your friend Dylan's murder is on the wires and I wanted—"

"I've got no comment."

"What?"

"You heard me."

"Simone, I wasn't calling to ask you for a comment," she said. "I just wanted to tell you how sorry I am."

Simone swallowed. "Oh."

"I had no idea she was Julie Curtis," she said.

"You knew Julie? When we were friends, you'd already graduated. You were living in Atlanta."

"Yeah, but I came home for a visit, and I went to your spring musical. *Hair*, remember? Julie played Sandra. Mom told me she was your best friend. Really beautiful girl."

Simone said, "You've got a good memory. She was great, huh?"

"To tell the truth," she said, "the only thing I really remember about that show is that you were stage manager, and I spent the whole time worrying about you back there. *Hair* is really hard to stage manage. All those cues. . . . Well, I was really impressed."

Simone felt herself smile a little. "You're probably the only person in the audience who was watching the stage management."

"Yeah, well. You're my baby sister. I care."

"That's sweet," said Simone. She meant it.

"Anyway . . . it's really late. I'll let you get back to sleep."

"Wait, Greta?"

"Yeah?"

She closed her eyes, took a breath. "I . . . I'm not at the *LA Edge*. That folded."

"I knew that a month ago. I was waiting for you to tell me."

"I work for the *Asteroid* now."

There was a long pause on the other end of the line, during which Walker asked, "Did she hang up?"

Simone started to nod when she heard Greta say, "I could never work there."

Her jaw tightened. "I know. Sleazy, huh?"

"No," she said. "I mean . . . you've got to have guts to work for a tabloid. No one talks to you, you need to go find leads on your own . . ."

"I didn't think you'd see it that way."

"Simone, I know you think what I do is silly."

"No, I—"

"But I never wanted to be a journalist. I just wanted to be on TV. You . . . well, you've always been the brave one."

Simone felt herself smiling. "I have?"

"Yeah," she said. "But I'm still bigger than you and I can still kick your butt."

Simone said, " 'Night, Greta. And thanks."

"Good night, Monie."

After Simone hung up, she looked at Walker. "She says I'm brave."

"Leave it to a cable anchor to state the obvious."

Simone smiled, and settled back into his arms, and soon they both fell back asleep.

It wasn't until she woke up in the morning that she remembered exactly what Chris Hart had said when she ran out of the room. *Where the hell are you going?* Not, *What the hell are you doing here?*

Where the hell are you going? As if he knew she would be there. And he wanted her to stay.

Simone let Walker sleep on the couch as she took a shower and got dressed, thinking of Chris Hart the entire time. There was something strange about him—the way he treated Julie, that lack of emotion, that coldness—as if she weren't a person but an object, a prop. Like the killer, he seemed to despise the media, tabloids in particular. Most of all, there was that look in his eyes. . . .

Chris, famous people can't have secrets.

Yes, they can.

If Simone were to suggest this idea to Sandiford—the idea that Chris Hart, *Chris Hart*, America's most popular leading man—had brutally murdered four women and critically injured one, he would tell her to get some rest, she was obviously in shock. And that may have been true. But still, she couldn't let go of the idea.

When she walked out of the bathroom, Walker was awake on the couch, checking his BlackBerry. "There's a press conference this afternoon at the Beverly Wilshire," he said. "DuMonde Management, Jason Caputo, Chris Hart, Lara Chandler, and the rest of the *Devil's Road* cast, expressing their sorrow over Dylan."

Simone looked at him. "I've got a weird feeling about Chris Hart."

"That's interesting," he said. "Because I've got a weird feeling about Randi DuMonde."

Simone searched his eyes. "You have an idea," she said.

"You do too."

"Let's collaborate," she said. "Freelance."

Walker didn't reply. He simply picked up his cell, called in sick to work.

TWENTY-SEVEN

I f one year at the *Anaheim Sentinel* and ten years in tabloids had taught Neil Walker anything, it was that press conferences, all of them, were a complete waste of time. It didn't matter whether it was the mayor of Mission Viejo or the chief of police or the cast of *Devil's Road*, anybody who is knowingly standing on a stage in front of fifty reporters is not going to say a damn thing worth printing.

But this one, the Dylan Leeds memorial press conference, this one was going to be worth Walker's while. It would be worth his while because it was being held twenty minutes away from the offices of DuMonde Management—meaning it would get Randi DuMonde and her boy-toy assistant out of there for at least an hour in the middle of the day, when the rest of the building would be open.

DuMonde Management was on the twenty-fifth floor of a Century City high-rise. Without having to look it up, Walker knew exactly how to get there. He'd easily been to a dozen press conferences held right in front of it, a baker's dozen if you counted the one with Simone. As he parked the Saab in the garage and took his ticket, he remembered the way Simone's face had looked when she realized he was one of the press corps. He felt himself smile a little.

Walker took the elevator up to the building's marble lobby, then got into another elevator, hit the button for the twenty-fifth floor. Suite 2504. Walker had only been in these offices once before, trying in vain to squeeze a few quotes out of the boy-toy. But that was enough for him to know it was a tiny place, with just two desks in it—and it had a combination lock, the same kind as the *Interloper.*

The thing with number combination locks, they were always significant dates. Much as you didn't want anybody breaking into your office, you also wanted to be able to get in yourself, so you weren't going to choose some random number that would just slip out of your mind.

If you were a bigger company, you'd choose a national holiday, something the whole staff could remember. With smaller businesses, though, the date could be something more intimate. Special. Before driving over, Walker had called up the DuMonde Management Web site on Simone's laptop and learned that DM had officially opened its doors on April 8, 1995. This he found interesting. They could have just said the business has been around since 1995, or that it was a ten-year-old company, but no. DuMonde Management had an actual anniversary. Walker imagined that every April 8, Randi threw a party for her clients, or maybe she just took the boy-toy out for dinner at La Scala.

So, when he reached suite 2504, Walker didn't even bother with 1995. He keyed in 0408 and bingo, the door opened. He smiled. He was good at combinations.

The office looked even smaller with no one in it, though the huge window did give it some class. He was glad it was a manageable space because he could get in and out relatively quickly, once he found what he needed. He estimated that the press conference had begun close to half an hour ago, which gave him fifteen minutes of safety at the most.

Randi's desk was huge and minimalist, nothing on it but a flat-screen computer and some fancy paperweight that was probably an award. The boy-toy's desk, however . . . that was a disaster area. Papers everywhere, mostly head shots and résumés in the poorest excuse for piles Walker had ever seen. He saw three drafts of the press release announcing today's conference. Kid obviously did most of the work around here.

He went straight for the boy-toy's computer. He scrolled through the Word files and saw that most of them were actresses' first names. Then he hit the icon marked "My computer" and did a file search on the names Dylan and Julie. Nothing. That didn't surprise him much. This type of search only applied to *existing* files.

Another thing Walker's work experience had taught him: You could learn a lot about a person from what they chose to throw away.

Did you throw her away already, Randi? A few keystrokes and the names of the boy-toy's most recently deleted files popped up on-screen like fresh ideas. Most looked to be press releases and old company newsletters. But amidst those files, he spotted one called "DylanL." He slipped the blank diskette he'd brought with him into the computer's A drive, copied "DylanL" onto it, stuck it in his shirt pocket and shut down the computer.

He looked at his watch. That had taken longer than he'd anticipated. As he slipped out the door, he heard the ping of the elevator, so he headed into the stairwell, just to be safe. By the time the elevator doors opened, Walker was already a flight down, thinking once again about how useful press conferences could be.

After she wished Walker good luck and kissed him good-bye, Simone got into her Jeep and headed over to Chris and Lara's house, or, as they called it in the office, Chez Clara. Getting the address had been easy. She'd simply called Elliot, who kept a file of DMV-obtained addresses for can-hitting purposes. At the end of their conversation, Elliot had said, "I heard about Dylan. Anything I can do?"

And she'd known he meant it. It had choked her up a little. Just over a week of knowing these people and they already felt like old army buddies. "Actually," Simone had said, "can you transfer me to Kathy?"

As it turned out, Chez Clara was a white Beverly Hills mansion that used to belong to the head of Paramount Studios back in the '40s. In front of the house loomed a line of tall hedges. Simone pulled up to the end of the driveway, peered through the ornate wrought-iron gate.

The driveway wound up to the mansion—it was showy, but with an old-Hollywood hipness, like the Beverlido, like Swifty's. *Cool place*, she thought.

She pulled out of the driveway and drove to a side street that gave her a good view of the whole block. Then she put the Jeep into park.

Kathy may not have seen one single spat during the two-week Clara stakeout she'd told Simone about when they were cater-waitering, but she had learned an awful lot about Chris and Lara's daily schedule. As Simone had figured, Kathy had kept a list of the mansion's comings and goings, a list she had been able to dig up for Simone when she'd called her at the office.

At two o'clock every afternoon, a van arrived at the gate from Hampton's Linen Service. It was now one fifty. Chris Hart was at the press conference, expressing his sorrow over the tragic loss of his leading lady, with Lara onstage beside him, showing her support. And Simone was in her Jeep, engine running, waiting for Clara's towels to show up.

Sure enough, a van marked Hampton's Linens pulled around the corner at one fifty-five. Quick as she could, Simone threw the Jeep into drive and zoomed up Chris and Lara's street. She swerved in front of the van, cutting it off before it reached the mansion.

"What the hell are you doing?" the driver shouted as Simone breathed hard, collecting herself. Then she got out of her Jeep.

The driver, a youngish surfer type, said something along the lines of, "Dude, what the fuck?" But he stopped when he saw the tears Simone had managed to work into her eyes. "Uh . . . you okay?"

"I'm so, so sorry," said Simone. "I just . . . I'm a little shaken up. I feel terrible about this."

His expression softened. "No worries," he said. "You didn't hit me or anything."

Simone cleared her throat. "Look," she said, "I'm going to level with you. I know you're going to Chris Hart's, and I really need to get onto that property."

A tinge of worry entered his eyes. "Uh, are you like an obsessed fan or something?"

"No, nothing like that," she said. "I'm a reporter."

He laughed a little. "You're kidding, right?"

Simone said, "Do I look like I'm kidding?"

"Dude, no way! I could lose my job."

Simone tilted her head to the side, then reached into her purse and removed her wallet. "Are you *sure* I didn't hit you?" she said. "Because I just went to the ATM and I see about . . . what? Eight hundred dollars' worth of damage to your van."

He looked at her for several drawn-out seconds. Then he said, "Nine."

Walker had told her she'd need a lot of cash. Good thing she'd let him lend it to her. Simone smiled at the van driver. "You're right. I didn't see that scratch over there. Nine hundred it is."

Minutes later, Simone had parked her Jeep up a side street and was riding in the back of the van among stacks of towels and sheets and comforters, all wrapped in paper the color of Tiffany boxes. After the driver pulled up in front of Clara's gate, Simone heard him identify himself to a servant at the intercom. As the gates opened, he said, "You better not get me fired, dude."

"I promise," said Simone, "to keep a very low pro-file."

The van pulled up in front of the house. She heard the driver speaking to a maid. "We're using a new fabric softener," he told her. "Boss wants to know what you guys think."

He opened the back of the van and removed two of the wrapped packages, his eyes not registering on Simone, who was fully visible, though pressed against the passenger's-side seat. After he left, Simone grabbed another package and walked with it into the house, a mask of boredom on her face. *Low profile, low profile, low profile.* The maid—a young, squat woman with shiny black hair—leaned against the doorway. "New fabric softener, huh?"

"Yep. Old stuff was giving people allergies." *Where the hell did that come from?*

"That's too bad," she said. "I liked the fragrance."

Simone glanced at her. "Umm, I forgot where the sheets go."

"Linen closet's upstairs," she said. "Between their offices."

Chris's office. "Wonderful! I mean, thanks."

Simone trudged up a long spiral staircase, passing the driver, who was heading back to the van for another trip. He gave her a look of both surprise and annoyance as he passed, and she half expected him to say it out loud: *You were supposed to stay outside!* But he didn't, of course. For his own good, the driver didn't blow Simone's cover.

Lara's and Chris's offices were located down a hall-way as long as a hotel's. After Simone ripped the tur-quoise paper off the stack of sheets she was carrying and placed them in the linen closet, she took a look at both rooms. They couldn't have been more different, and it was easy to guess which office belonged to whom. Lara's—she *hoped* it was Lara's—was all white: shelves, desk, couch, wicker chairs, flat-screen computer. On the wall hung a white canvas with a thick white frame. She couldn't imagine setting foot in here without inadvertently leaving a mark. The decor was its own security system.

Simone walked into the other office, which reminded her of a '30s gentleman's club—floor-to-ceiling shelves lined with screenplays and rare books, oxblood leather couches, a leather-topped desk bordered with brass studs. There was a black flat-screen computer on the desk, and when Simone booted it up, a breathy Bond Girl voice intoned, "Hello, Mr. Hart."

Shit. Simone jumped back, then put her hand on the optical mouse as the computer's gunmetal desktop came into view. *First, I need to find the mute icon.* But she couldn't do that, couldn't do anything. In the hallway, Simone heard footsteps—two sets of them—moving closer to the office. And two male voices, one of which belonged to Chris Hart.

Walker headed back up Beverly Drive to Coldwater Canyon, his heart beating against the diskette in his shirt pocket. For him, this was one of the best parts of tabloid reporting—slipping the bag of garbage into the trunk, figuring out the combination lock, talking the assistant into giving you those key photos. *Getting in.* Or, in this case, *getting out*, without anyone seeing.

But now, he realized, there was something even better. Better than getting in, better even than learning the information. Because while he couldn't wait to slip that diskette into the laptop and find out what was on it, he was more excited about showing it to Simone—Dylan Leeds's deleted file, straight from Randi DuMonde's office. He knew that when she saw it, her face would light up, and it made his chest tighten, just picturing that.

Weird. He'd had a lot of girlfriends, but this was new. This wasn't lust so much as . . . an overwhelming desire to make her face light up.

Okay, lust too.

Too bad she lived in North Hollywood, though. He

hated Coldwater Canyon. The Saab had trouble with the steep climb up and the sharp turns, and to make it worse, he always got tailgated, no matter how fast he drove. Like this Impala. Right now. This ridiculous land shark from the '80s with the paint chipping off, and even *that* was riding up his ass. Was he *that* slow a driver? He sped up some more. He was going seventy now, up a mountain. *That satisfy you, douchebag?*

He felt a thud on his back bumper. The Saab jolted forward. He opened his window, yelled, "What the fuck?" There was a glare coming off the Impala's windshield. He couldn't see inside.

Like most reporters, Walker had a microcassette recorder. He kept his in the change holder of the Saab, and now he pulled it out, hit PLAY and RECORD and said, "Chevy Impala, late seventies, early eighties. Light green."

Thud. It hit him again. Walker leaned on the horn, jammed his foot on the accelerator, pulled up ahead of it for a few seconds. . . . The Impala lurched forward, and as it did, Walker caught sight of its front license plate: "247CDR," he said into the recorder, shoving it into his pocket with the diskette. The Impala sped up and pulled next to his car.

He looked into the car and saw a figure wearing a hood. *Jesus.* Metal scraped against the thin driver's-side door as the Impala plowed into it. He spun the wheel away.

The Saab skidded off the road, and for one frozen moment he was airborne, all four wheels hovering over the dusty canyon.

I'm going to die, he thought. Then the Saab landed, his body flying off the seat and his head socking into the ceiling, then slamming back down again, the seat belt like ropes against his neck and chest. He got his hands on the wheel and tried to steer, but what was the point of steering when the car was bouncing down a canyon like a roller skate, the tires shot, rocks flying into the windshield?

The Saab skidded, flipped onto its side. Walker heard a crack like a gunshot and knew it was the passenger's-side mirror breaking off, and then the window shattered. He closed his eyes and felt thousands of stings on his face, as if he were being attacked by bees.

Stupidly, he thought about this Saab he'd bought used ten years ago, how it was just the type of car to roll down a mountain and catch fire, how with the money he made he could afford something newer, something safer—a Volvo. Weren't they the safest cars? And he was mad, mad at his brain for betraying him like this.

The car rolled, and his head slammed into the ceiling and he felt something beyond pain, a type of *crushing*, and then he flew into the driver's-side window and noticed the warm wetness of blood trickling down his face.

He smelled heat and dust, and when he opened his eyes for a second he saw motes of canyon dirt swirling, the thick red stain of his own blood on the ceiling.

This is it.

Something big and slick socked Walker in the face. He thought, *About time the fucking air bag deployed.* And as everything went black and his breath began to falter, he wished, so much, that his last thought had been sweeter.

Chris Hart kept a vintage smoking jacket in the closet of his office. It was made of heavy silk and stunk so strongly of bay rum it pervaded the whole space, making Simone's eyes water. Of all the places to hide from Hart, the closet of his office probably wasn't the most ideal, but she hadn't much choice.

She heard the voices louder now, and then the two men walked into the room.

Chris Hart said, "I don't remember leaving my computer on."

Simone gritted her teeth.

"You're scattered," said the other voice, deep and calm. Simone peered through the crack, then eased back again. It was Hart's bodyguard, Maurice. "You need to relax."

"How can I relax?" said Chris. "The tabloids—"

"Don't know a damn thing. Nobody knows a damn thing, Chris, except you and me and the lamppost."

There was a pause, then, "Fucking lamppost."

Maurice laughed.

Hart did too, but the laughter died fast and Simone heard nothing but breathing and someone, one of the men, pacing around the room.

"Least you still got your sense of humor," said Maurice.

"I'm just so scared. . . . About getting found out and—"

"Don't be scared," said Maurice. "I will protect you, always. I will guard this secret with my life."

There was another long pause. And then Hart said, "Hold me."

Simone threw a hand in front of her mouth to contain a gasp.

She put her eye up to the crack in the door and saw Maurice cradling Hart in his arms, Hart whispering, "I don't ever want this to end."

"It won't."

"I want our secret to be safe."

"It will." Maurice pressed Chris Hart to his powerful body and kissed him, deeply.

This was Chris Hart's secret. Not murder.

As Chris lay back on the leather couch, pulling his bodyguard to him, Simone cracked open the closet and stole out.

"Did you hear something?" said Maurice.

Simone dropped to the floor, behind the desk.

"No," said Hart.

"You sure?"

Simone held her breath. *Stay still. Stay perfectly still. . . .*

"Yeah."

She peered around the desk and saw Maurice moving on top of Hart. Staying down, she crept to the door as noiselessly as she could.

Slipping through the door, she heard Chris say something, and her breath caught in her throat. She hurried through the hallway. It wasn't until she reached the stairs that she realized what he had said: *I love you.*

She ran down the stairs. The maid said, "Get lost up there?"

"Yeah," said Simone.

"Easy to do," she said. "I think that guy left without you, though."

By the time she got outside, the van was heading through the open gate. She tore out after it, but the driver peeled away. *For nine hundred bucks, he could wait.*

At least she was outside the gate. She sprinted back to the side street and got back into her Jeep and collapsed onto her steering wheel, thinking, *Great job, Simone.* She'd wanted to help capture a killer—the killer who had taken the four lives, including her best friend's. But all she'd done was to yank a leading man out of the closet, and uncover a club owner's baby fetish.

Simone closed her eyes. She didn't know whether to laugh or to cry, so she did neither, just breathed.

Her cell phone rang. She picked it up. An unfamiliar woman's voice said, "Simone Glass?" The voice was efficient and mechanical, and something about it made Simone start to tremble.

"Yes?" she said.

"I'm calling regarding Neil Walker," said the woman. "I'm afraid I have some bad news."

TWENTY-EIGHT

W alker had been rushed to Valley Memorial Hospital after a passing police officer spotted his Saab upside down in Coldwater Canyon and found him inside, bleeding and unconscious. The woman, whose name was Dr. Marshall, told Simone all of this in a monotone that bordered on robotic. "We found your number in his cell phone," she said now. "I hope I'm calling the right person."

"You are."

"Because if you're just someone he's called a lot, a business associate, maybe, I don't want to trouble you with—"

"You are calling the right person."

"Good," she said.

Simone was rocking back and forth in front of her steering wheel, desperately trying to get her thoughts in order. She had heard about people collapsing from sheer stress. She had never quite understood that, but now . . . now she felt as if she were on the verge. "What is his condition?"

"Serious but stable."

"What does that mean?"

"He's had twelve stitches in his head and lost quite a lot of blood," said the doctor. "He has a severe concussion, edema in the—"

"But what does it *mean*? Is he going to be okay?"

"He's no longer critical."

"No *longer* critical?"

"He's been weaned off the respirator."

The blood pounded in her ears. She wanted not to cry, but to bawl like a baby. "Is he going to be okay?" she said.

"I can't tell you that, ma'am. I'm not psychic."

Simone said nothing.

Devoid of emotion as she was, Dr. Marshall must have known Simone was about to lose it, because she put her on with a nurse, who gave her directions to the hospital.

Simone drove there, numb beyond tears, phrases running through her mind that she didn't understand: *Serious but stable, no longer critical, weaned off the respirator. . . .*

After Simone arrived at the hospital, the nurse at the front desk told her that Walker was in ICU on the third floor. She ran down three different hallways looking for the intensive care unit, feeling like she was trapped in a maze in a terrible, endless nightmare.

When she finally found ICU, she picked up the phone next to the locked door and said, "I'm here to see Neil Walker."

"Your name?" said the nurse.

"Simone Glass."

"Relation to the patient?"

She heard herself say, "I'm his girlfriend."

"I'm sorry, ma'am, we don't—"

"Please!" Her voice came out choked, desperate.

The nurse said, "All right. But just for a few minutes."

Except for the bandage around his head, and the oxygen tube in his nose, and the IVs, Walker might have been asleep. He looked very pale, but peaceful, calm, breathing deeply. Simone gazed at his chest, going up and down under the clean white sheets, and thought, *Weaned off the respirator. Good for you.* She touched his face, felt the coolness of his skin. "You better not go away," she whispered.

"I'm going to have to ask you to leave now, ma'am," said the nurse.

"Two more minutes?"

She sighed. "Okay."

Across from the bed was a metal closet, and when she opened it and saw the clothes he'd been wearing that morning, Simone crumbled inside. She put her hand on the shirt and her eyes blurred. She stole a quick glance at the door, then hugged the shirt to her, like some war widow in a corny old movie.

One week ago I didn't even know Neil Walker.

As she let the shirt go, she felt something in the front pocket . . . a microcassette recorder. Simone pulled it out, along with a diskette, the blank one he'd brought to Randi's that day. She looked at the diskette now, and saw Walker's handwriting on it. "Dylan Leeds File," it said. Simone smiled a little. "Nice work, Neil," she whispered, as the nurse came back in.

On her way out of ICU, Simone met Dr. Marshall, who, despite her unfortunate voice, was a surprisingly attractive blonde whose hair was cut in a sophisticated bob. "Sorry we couldn't let you stay longer, but he's still in serious condition and you're not family," she said, like one note on a piano, played over and over.

"I understand."

"I'll call if there's any change in his condition."

"Thanks."

Simone headed down the hallway to the ICU waiting room. It had been empty when she first arrived, but now she saw one person sitting there—Nigel.

Simone said, "What are you doing here?"

He glared at her. "I might ask you the same thing."

"Nigel, he's my friend. He's in serious condition. Can we please just cut the crap?"

Nigel sighed. "Well, I'm chuffed he's not critical anymore."

"What," Simone said, "are you *doing* here?"

He opened his mouth to say something, then closed it again. "Oh, what's the point," he said. "Neil Walker is my spy."

She gaped at him. "Your *Interloper* spy was . . . Then why did you—why did you fire me?"

"Just because a bloke is your fucking spy, that's no reason to trust him with your reporters." Nigel raised an eyebrow. "Probably *less* of a reason to trust him, isn't it?"

"He never said anything to me about it."

"Right, well, he isn't proud of it," he said. "Only reason he spies for me is Nia Lawson. He feels guilty."

"Everyone told me you had something against Nia Lawson."

Nigel exhaled heavily. "If I tell you this, you must promise never to mention it again."

"Of course."

"I have your word."

"Yes, Nigel."

"Right then," he said. "Neil used to work for me."

"At the *Asteroid*?"

He nodded. "Brilliant reporter. Bit of a . . . conscience problem, though."

"What do you mean?"

"Neil was posing as a bartender at an event. He started chatting up Nia, they exchanged phone numbers, became friends. . . . To make a long story short, she told him about her and Calloway *months* before it was reported anywhere else. How does he respond? Not only does he reveal that he works for a tabloid, he agrees not to tell anyone. Because she *begged* him not to, and he felt *sorry* for her. Months later, Nia Lawson is gassing off to every Tom, Dick, and Harry in the tabloid media—except us!"

He shook his head. "Willard almost fired me because of Neil Walker's crisis of conscience."

Simone stared at him. *Neil has a conscience.*

Nigel stood up. "I am chuffed he's no longer critical, though," he said.

Before he left the room, Simone thought of another question for him. "Nigel, your top secret Chrylan source. The one who gave you the card key."

He looked at her.

"It was Chris Hart, wasn't it?"

"I'm not even going to ask you where you got that information."

"It was though, right?"

"No comment," said Nigel. Then he walked out the door.

At six p.m., Dr. Marshall stopped into the waiting room and told Simone she may as well go home, she'd call her with any news. The whole way back, she thought about Walker, and his crisis of conscience; how maybe he was sort of like an overused teddy bear—dirty, frayed, worse for the wear, but deep down full of clean, white stuffing. Maybe she was the same.

It wasn't until she pulled up in front of her apartment that she remembered the Dylan Leeds diskette—not to mention the microcassette tape, which she played as she was booting up her laptop. She heard a whoosh of air and realized it had been recorded in a car. Then she heard Walker's voice. *"Chevy Impala, late seventies, early eighties. Light green."* The screech of tires, then a thud, then Walker again. *"Shit! 247CDR."*

Simone's stomach clenched up. *It wasn't an accident. He was run off the road.*

Simone called Sandiford and Elliot, left voice-mail messages for each of them with the plate number, the car description, and asked Elliot to run it with the DMV for her. Sandiford could do the same thing, of course, but she didn't want to depend on him to call her back. And she needed to know who that car belonged to.

Her computer booted up. She had a couple of e-mails, but she decided to check those later. She had a diskette to read. She slipped it into her computer, and its contents popped up on her screen: one file, called "DylanL." She double-clicked on it, and then the screen read "Dylan Leeds, actress," with three files underneath: "Movies," "Roles," "Dates."

Dates?

Simone got "Movies" out of the way first. There was only one listed: *Devil's Road*. There would be no more.

Next, she clicked "Dates" and saw a long list of men's names. Most were unfamiliar, but she recognized a few: Lazlo Gant. Instantly, she recalled the way Julie had looked at him, this oversized cherub of a man, at Blake Moss's party . . . Blake Moss's name was on the list too. Simone clicked on it, saw a series of dates, times, dollar amounts reaching into the thousands. . . .

"God," Simone whispered. "She was numbers."

She found herself remembering a high school sleepover at her house, how she and Julie had stayed up until four in the morning, talking mostly about the future.

. . . so right after graduation, I'm going back out to LA, staying at my cousin's. She's already said that's fine.

But, Julie, graduation isn't for another year and a half.

I know. But an actor prepares. Get it?

Umm . . .

That's the name of Stanislavsky's book. It's like the acting bible. I've read it three times.

Cool.

My cousin works at Amblin'.

Where?

Steven Spielberg's company. She's a production assistant. She totally says she can get me an agent. Of course, I don't plan on signing with the first one I meet. You have to be smart about these things.

What had happened to Julie in LA? How had she gone

from Stanislavsky to "dates"? Simone wished she could ask her that, wished she could look into those guileless eyes and just ask, *Why?* Simone's deepest secret had cost her Julie's friendship. But Julie had taken her secret to the grave.

Simone clicked on "Roles." She expected to see the *Devil's Road* character, Delilah. But listed instead was: Partner/Wife.

And when she double-clicked on that, she saw a legal document with signature spaces for Dylan Leeds and Chris Hart. It was binding, promising Julie $5 million up front, with an additional $8 million for each year she stayed "partnered" to Chris. There was a $20 million bonus upon legal marriage, with an additional $10 million for each child "born within wedlock."

The contract lasted eight years. And when Simone clicked on an icon at the bottom of the page, she saw a similar contract, with slightly higher prices, between Chris Hart and Lara Chandler.

Simone's jaw dropped open and stayed there.

She thought of what Chris had said to Julie in the alleyway, and the conversation took on a whole new meaning. *I want you. More than anyone else. Do you have any idea how perfect we are?* He wasn't sweet-talking a mistress. He was telling an actress she was perfect for the part.

Me and Chris. It's different than you think.

Simone thought of that prom picture of Julie and Todd, those smiles of excitement, anticipation. And Lara's words finally made sense. *You don't know what you're getting yourself into. I feel sorry for you.*

Poor Julie, thought Simone. *Poor, poor Julie.*

Simone put the diskette away and checked her e-mail. There was one from her sister:

> Hi Monie. In case you missed the De-
> vil's Road press conference, they an-
> nounced that the premiere will take

place as scheduled, on Friday at Mann's
Chinese. As a "tribute" to Julie, they're
not canceling. Touching, huh? (Yeah,
right . . .)
Love,
G
PS. Attached is an invitation to Julie's funeral tomorrow. I can't fly out
for it, but I thought you might like to
go.

Simone smiled. "I missed you, Greta," she said to the
screen. "Welcome back to my planet."

Simone noticed another e-mail, the return address of
which was SwampDemon@yahoo.com. She assumed it
was spam, but the subject line made her wonder: "Your
boyfriend . . ."

Sure, it could be a Viagra ad, but the ellipses bothered her. She opened it. The message began with more
ellipses:

. . . is out of the way!

The rest of the screen consisted of a photo, and as she
waited for it to load, Simone felt that horrible tingle of
fear sliding up and down her back, pressing into her
neck.

And when she finally saw it, she didn't gasp, didn't
scream—she just thought, *I knew it.* It was a photo of a
black Saab, upside down in Coldwater Canyon.

Simone triple-bolted her door, left another voice mail for
Sandiford about the e-mail message, and slept on the
couch fully dressed, clutching her cell phone. She slept
soundly, as only someone thoroughly exhausted could do,
but as soon as the sun eased its way through her closed
curtains, Simone was awake, and thinking about that
e-mail.

SwampDemon. What did that mean? Who was this person in the green Impala? And why did they want Neil out of the way? An answer to that last question popped into her head, but she didn't want to think about it very hard.

At eight the next morning, her phone rang. It was Sandiford. He had gotten her messages. He thanked Simone for the information, told her not to worry, said that every day his office was following up on leads. He told her he would learn who sent that e-mail if it killed him. He told her he would ask the North Hollywood Division to patrol her street, and in the meantime, "Please lock your doors, close your windows, check your garbage every day."

Simone hung up more frightened than she'd been in the first place. Cops and doctors had a way of doing that, comforting you by way of terror. Simone was making herself coffee when Elliot called.

"I ran the DMV check on those plates," he said.

Her mouth went dry. "Who does the car belong to?"

"Someone named Dolores King."

"A woman?"

"Looks like it. Name sounds kind of familiar, doesn't it?"

"Not really."

"Maybe it's just one of those names that sounds like it should belong to a famous person." She could hear Elliot drumming his keyboard. "I'm gonna IMDb her, just for the hell of it." About five seconds later, Elliot said, "Oh, my God!"

"What?"

He took a breath. "Okay. Now, I'm not sure it's the same person in that Impala, but there was apparently a B-movie actress back in the eighties called Dolores King," he said. "She did a bunch of straight-to-video movies. Then she disappeared. Without a trace."

"Okay," Simone said slowly. "But why the 'Oh, my God'?"

"Again, I'm not sure if this is the same Dolores, but

remember my sidebar? 'Cut Throats Through the Ages' or whatever we wound up calling it?"

Simone's heart pounded. She knew.

Elliot said, "The wife of the schlocky director, Reginald King . . . the one who wrote the tell-all about him . . ."

"Her name was Dolores," Simone guessed.

"Right. But like I said, I don't know if it's the same one."

Simone closed her eyes. "The movies she was in. What were they called?"

"Let's see . . . *Vampire Brides*, *Zombie Bloodbath*, *Swamp Demon*."

Simone felt a hard chill, a horror. "It is the same Dolores King," she said.

TWENTY-NINE

Simone looked through her wastebaskets. Then she put on some rubber kitchen gloves, went outside to the Dumpster in the alley next to her apartment building, pulled out every bag and searched through them, looking for something that might have belonged to Julie Curtis. She did this without hesitation, careful only with broken glass.

Amazing that just ten days ago, digging through Emerald Deegan's trash was probably the most horrific thing she'd ever done. Now she didn't even notice the smell.

After she finished searching through the last bag, she threw out the gloves, went back into her apartment, and took a shower. *Nothing*, she thought as the water ran over her. *Nothing of Julie's in the bags. Does that mean I'm safe?* She had no idea. No idea about anything anymore.

She tilted her face up, felt the hot water on it, rubbed shampoo into her hair and washed it out. After everything that had happened, it felt weird to be doing something so normal. She lathered soap into the washcloth and began cleaning her face, her hands, her body. When she finished, she didn't feel clean enough so she did it again, lathering the cloth, rubbing her stomach harder,

harder until the skin stung and went red, and still, she couldn't get clean enough.

Finally, she collapsed onto the floor of her tub, hugged her legs to her chest, her forehead on her knees as the warm water poured over her head, her back . . . and she couldn't help it. She envisioned Julie hugging her legs at the side of Blake Moss's pool, looking young, lost . . . with just four more days to live.

She had to do something. She had to, or else she would spend her whole life in a fetal position on a shower floor, scrubbing and scrubbing but never getting clean.

Simone turned off the water knowing what she needed to do. First, and most important, she would pull herself together. She would eat something, then call the hospitals, check on Holly and Walker. After that, she would get dressed—put on something nice. It would have to be nice. She had a funeral to go to.

The funeral took place in Forest Lawn, the biggest, most elaborate-looking cemetery Simone had ever seen. When she was in junior high school, Simone had visited France with her parents and Greta, and in some ways it reminded her of the grounds of Versailles—only stretched out over three hundred acres. There were bubbling fountains and Greek statues and lush topiaries and rolling green hills, all dotted with graves, some in the open, some hidden behind walls or within private gardens.

It was impossible to find your way around this place without a map. Fortunately, one had come with Greta's invitation, and Simone used it as she drove through the sprawling grounds, passing two other funerals until she found it . . . Julie's grave site. It was surrounded by rose-bushes, which made Simone think of the pink rosebushes lined up against Julie's house, the rosebushes in her mother's garden back in Wappingers Falls. She wondered if Julie's parents would be here, if she would recognize them if they were.

But Simone wasn't looking for Julie's parents. She

wanted the killer. She wanted to look into his eyes—or *her* eyes—and know. There were parking areas all over the grounds, and Simone pulled into the nearest one, made her way to where a group stood, all in black. As she reached the site, Simone saw Julie's white casket resting next to the pit. It was a closed casket. Of course it was closed. She let her gaze pan over the growing, black-clad group of mourners and thought, *Where are you, Dolores King?*

"Hey," said a man next to her. She turned, and saw it was Ed Sandiford. Relief shot through her. It made her realize how tense she'd been.

"Man, am I glad to see you."

"Don't show it too much," he said. "I'm undercover."

"Looking for Dolores?"

"I see you ran a DMV check too."

Simone nodded.

"There are six undercover here. I'm not gonna tell you who."

"I'm not going to ask," said Simone.

There were chairs lined up on the grass. Everyone started to take their seats. Simone chose one in the back and scanned the crowd . . . Chris and Lara, holding hands next to Caputo, Maurice stoic in the seat behind them. *I guess*, thought Simone, *Lara re-upped.* Blake Moss, in sunglasses, stood next to Julie's other *Devil's Road* costars. . . . A few rows to the right, she saw an elegant, slender woman in a long black shift and realized it was Kathy. Infiltrating. She turned for a moment, and the two women locked eyes. Almost imperceptibly, Simone nodded. *I won't give you away.* She searched the group some more. Where was Randi?

Simone thought she might have skipped the funeral, but then, in front and on the aisle, she saw Nathaniel, his arm around a large middle-aged woman who save for her size did not look like Randi at all. She was wearing black, not red. Her broad shoulders were slumped, her head lowered. Her big arms were wrapped around her stomach, as if she were trying to keep everything in—the secrets, the guilt, the grief . . . and she was crying.

Simone had expected a confrontation—Randi or Chris or Moss shouting her down, calling her tabloid scum, telling her Dylan's death was all her fault and she had her best friend's blood on her hands, they hoped she was happy—all for the benefit of the paparazzi in the parking lot.

But there was no confrontation. This was a very public funeral, with local politicians and newscasters and celebrities Julie had probably never met, unless for a "date," and Dylan's nearest and dearest were, above all, professional to the end. After the brief ceremony was over, they headed back to their cars, talking to each other, hushed and serious, as the paparazzi snapped them with their telephoto lenses.

As Simone neared Chris Hart, he put his arm around Lara as if to shield her, and they both moved away, followed by Maurice.

Randi, her tears gone, brushed past Simone with her head held high, while Nathaniel gave her the same type of glance he'd have given something unpleasant stuck to the bottom of his shoe. Simone glared right back at him, thinking, *What you both did to her was no better than what I did.*

Blake Moss wouldn't go near Simone. She knew he'd spotted her, yet he stayed as far away as possible, never looking in her direction. Then he rushed to the parking lot like a man being chased. Had all these people gotten a directive from Randi to keep away from her?

Simone spotted Jason Caputo on the periphery of the site. He looked calm, relaxed. He was talking with Sandiford, as if the detective were just another loved one, which the director no doubt assumed he was. "Grief is a terrible thing," Caputo was saying. "After I lost my dad, I stopped eating, didn't shower for weeks. . . ."

Simone walked up to the men and Sandiford nodded politely. "Hi, Jason," she said.

The director winced as he recognized her. But he

didn't walk away. He turned to Sandiford. "Excuse me a sec," he said, and the detective joined another group. Caputo looked at Simone.

"You're the only one who has done that," she said.

"Done what?"

"Looked at me."

"Simone," he said, "I don't have anything against you. We all have jobs. You were just doing yours."

"I wish everybody else felt that way."

"They don't know," he said. "You grow up like I did, with a dad like mine, you see it from a whole different perspective. The compromises you have to make, just to get your paycheck. Life's full of murky gray, isn't it, Simone?"

"You would think they would get that, though. Randi, for instance . . ."

"Randi's different, Hart's different," he said. "They're the stars of their own shows. They have no objectivity. I've spent my whole life watching people like them, and that's what I still do. I . . . observe."

Simone carefully worded her next question. "This is going to sound pretty random," she said, "but . . . have you ever heard of an actress called Dolores King?"

Ever so slightly, his eyes widened. "Yeah, that was pretty random, all right."

"I'm . . . I'm working on a story," she said. "Her name came up in research."

Caputo swallowed. She could see his throat moving up and down. Then he smiled. "Never heard of her."

Caputo had said it himself. He was no actor. One look in his eyes, Simone could tell he was lying.

On the ride home, Simone checked at both hospitals again. Still no change, in either Walker's condition or Holly's. Then she called Sandiford. When he answered she said, "What do you think of Jason Caputo?"

"Nice guy. Of course, talent-wise he's not his father."

"No, I mean—"

"I know what you mean," he said. "We're looking into it."

She heard a dim beep. She'd forgotten to charge her cell the previous night, and the battery was dying. She spoke fast. "When I mentioned Dolores King to Jason he seemed—"

"Simone."

"Yeah?"

"I know, with the job you have, you tend to . . . pay a little more attention to famous people."

"Ed, I'm losing you."

"With this case, I'd like you to try and do the opposite. Pay more attention to the unknowns."

Simone said, "Why?" But she didn't hear his response. Her phone had timed out.

"Damn." She parked the car, walked up to her building. What was Sandiford talking about, anyway? There were famous people who were guilty of murder. *Just because someone has a recognizable face doesn't make him any better, any cleaner than the rest of us.*

Simone walked into her apartment. Where had she put the charger? It was usually plugged into the outlet by the door but . . .

She felt someone watching her. She looked up. Blake Moss was sitting on her red Ikea couch, his long legs propped up on her coffee table.

"Hi, angel," he said. "I thought you'd never come home."

Simone's breath went away for several seconds, then returned in one desperate, rushing gasp. She wanted to hit 911 on her phone, but the battery was dead, and now Moss was standing up, he was moving toward her.

Stay calm, she told herself, and when her voice did come, it was strong, clear. "What are you doing in my apartment?"

"Super let me in." He smiled. "You're a famous movie star, people open doors for you."

He was standing over her now. Simone backed up, but

he took another step closer and she opened her mouth to scream, but no sound came out. Just a hollow rasp. Gently, Moss placed two fingers over her lips. "I'm not going to hurt you, Simone."

She looked into his eyes, expecting that famous leer, that evil, big-screen glint . . . but she saw only sadness. "I mean it," he said. "I'm really not."

"What . . ."

"I couldn't do this at the funeral," he said. "It was too public." He took a breath. "I came by to apologize. For what I did at Randi's party."

"What?"

"I thought you liked it. I'm used to women . . . liking that."

"You mean you—"

"You know how it is . . . the whole bad-boy thing. I've been acting that way for so damn long, getting what I want that way for so long, I . . . I sometimes don't know when to stop." He gave her a small smile. "I thought you liked it. I thought we were . . . playing."

She stared at him. "You weren't really going to tell Dylan?"

"Why would I tell Dylan?" he said. "It's none of my damn business."

She shook her head, speechless.

"When you wouldn't let me give you a ride home . . . ," he said.

"Excuse me?"

"That's when I knew you weren't playing. That's when I knew no meant no."

Simone closed her eyes, pinched the bridge of her nose. She was beginning to get a terrible headache. "Apology accepted," she said.

"Thank you, Simone. I promise . . ."

"Now go away."

"Huh?"

"Go. Away. Blake."

He nodded and walked past her, then through her

door. She collapsed onto her couch, and put her face in her hands, thinking about Blake . . . that look in his eye as he opened the door. It was a look—not of someone who'd eased his conscience. It was a look of completion, as if he'd finished a project.

THIRTY

After Moss was long gone, Simone finally found her charger. Somehow it had slipped under the refrigerator. She plugged her phone into it, made herself a peanut butter and jelly sandwich, poured a glass of wine she knew she wouldn't finish.

She then switched on her laptop and tried to do some research on Dolores King. There was very little to be found on the actress—no images, and her bio had been redacted from IMDb. Simone did find one article in an old issue of *Fangoria*. A piece called "Was Reginald King's Death a Double Suicide?" She read. Known as a "vivacious but terrible actress," Dolores King was apparently married to Reginald for ten years. They had what Dolores used to call an "open marriage," meaning she slept around openly, humiliating her husband.

"Being who he was," said an unnamed "friend" of King's, "Reg was used to compromising—in his job, in his art, in his life." It was implied, but never proven, that King was latently gay. "He was plagued by guilt," the friend said. "Over something no one should feel guilty about—the way he was. So he let his wife get away with whatever she wanted." But it hurt him, deeply. The final blow came when Dolores announced she was writing a tell-all book about her affairs with famous men and about her husband's sexuality. Reginald was found dead in 1987, having slashed his own throat with a hunting knife. A month later, Dolores disappeared. As the years went by, less and less information became available on the actress and her husband, the few publications that had interviewed them folding, copies of their straight-to-video films now collectors' items. Before the Internet, it was a lot easier to fade into obscurity, especially if you were obscure to begin with. The other, very real possibility: Destroyed by her husband's death, Dolores King had followed him to the grave.

Or she was back . . . killing off women the way Reginald had killed himself.

Simone didn't want to think about it, not now. She was too tired. She e-mailed Greta back, thanked her for the funeral invite. Then she deleted the message from SwampDemon. She'd already forwarded it to the police and, for some reason, that tiny action—hitting the DELETE button—gave her a little jolt of power. "You're not going to get me," she whispered. "I'll get you first."

The next morning, Simone got no new word about Walker's or Holly's condition. She showered, threw on a pair of jeans and a T-shirt and walked out to her Jeep, carrying her laptop with her. She'd drive to Valley Memorial, she decided, hang out in the waiting room and run some more searches, see if she could learn anything else about Dolores King. She doubted it. She was amazed she could even find that *Fangoria* article on the woman. It was as if she'd made a special effort to vanish.

Simone had put the laptop in the Jeep when she realized she hadn't checked the trash today, and ran back to her apartment to get her rubber kitchen gloves. She kept the gloves under the sink, next to the wastebasket. But as she bent down to get the box, she noticed a new bag in her wastebasket . . . a plastic bag from a nearby drugstore. She plucked it out.

At first, she thought the bag was empty—it was that light, that odorless. But then she saw something inside. It was a photograph. She pulled it out and looked at it. Her whole body began to tremble and her face went numb.

Julie and Todd's prom picture.

Her cell phone chimed and she picked it up, and before she said anything she heard that voice, Dr. Marshall's voice, so sterile, so robotic.

"Simone Glass?"

She closed her eyes tight. "Yes."

"This is Dr. Marshall."

"Yes." *Please*, thought Simone. *Please, please, please.*

The doctor said, "Neil Walker has regained consciousness."

Simone didn't remember the drive to the hospital. She just knew that one minute she was in her Jeep and the next she was at Valley Memorial, rushing through the lobby, up the elevator, into ICU. She picked up the phone, and this time the nurse let her in without a fight. "He's been asking for you," she said.

When she got to the room, Walker was in his bed, the bandage still wrapped around his head. The oxygen tube had been removed and so had all but one of the IVs, and he was sitting up against propped pillows, thumbing his BlackBerry.

It was the most wonderful image Simone had seen in days.

She didn't say anything, just watched him for a few minutes. Until he looked at her, and he dropped the BlackBerry and his eyes lit up. "Took you long enough," he said.

Simone walked over to the bed and sat down next to him and hugged him, held him as tightly as she could without disturbing the IV. When she pulled away, his eyes were glistening.

"You're crying," she said.

"It's the morphine."

"Ah."

He brushed a hand against her cheek, and kissed her softly. "You know I'm a liar, right?"

Simone told Walker everything that had happened over the past two days, from the contents of the diskette to Dolores King to Chris and Maurice to Julie's funeral to Blake Moss. The one thing she didn't mention was what Nigel had told her about him. She figured, *Neil Walker is allowed secrets of his own.* Close to an hour later, the nurse ducked in, telling Walker they were going to move him out of ICU to a regular recovery room. He said, "Does it have a double bed?"

The nurse smiled. "No." She looked at Simone. "But you can squeeze in with him if you want, just as long as you don't get him too excited."

"Well, forget it then," said Walker.

The nurse ducked out, said, "Be back in a few."

And then, Simone said, "There's one thing I haven't told you about." She reached into her purse, pulled out Julie and Todd's prom picture and showed it to him. "Julie used to keep this in her bedroom mirror," she said. "I found it today. In my garbage."

Walker's face went white. "Did you call Ed?" he said.

"I will."

"You're staying here. In my room."

"I know." She looked into his eyes for a long, quiet moment. "But Neil," she said, "I can't stay here forever."

"Do you . . . do you have any idea who . . ."

Simone recalled Blake Moss in her apartment twelve hours before she found the picture in her kitchen trash. She remembered that look in his eyes . . . that look, as if he'd just completed a project. She remembered what he'd said: *You're a famous movie star, people open doors for you*, and she thought, *Nia Lawson would open the door for Blake Moss.* She thought about his relationship with Emerald, a.k.a. Desire. She remembered his name on Julie's "date" list—a list created long before they were co-stars. And then, she recalled what Charity had said, back in Pleasures. *She had some deal going on, said she was going to be famous.* Destiny would have opened the door for Blake Moss, too.

"Yes," said Simone. "I have a very good idea."

Simone spent the rest of the day in the hospital, hanging out in the waiting room when the nurses asked her to, and then she stayed the night in Walker's new room. She told him her suspicions about Moss, and learned that Walker shared them—he'd shared them for a while. "The only thing I don't get," he said, "is the Dolores King connection."

"I know," said Simone. "That's what we've got to figure out."

They phoned Sandiford and told him. And while he was still skeptical that a movie star had committed the murders, he agreed to send some undercover men to observe Blake at the Mann's Chinese *Devil's Road* premiere the following night. After they hung up, Walker said, "Wish I could go to that damn theater. I'd follow Moss home, see how he likes getting run off the road."

Simone stared at him, her eyes getting wider and wider.

"No," said Walker.

"What do you mean?"

"You're not going to the premiere," he said. "I don't want you in the same room with Moss."

"I wasn't thinking that."

"Look," he said, "I may not have known you for that long, but I know you well enough to be able to tell when you've got an idea."

"I do have an idea," she said. "But I'm not going to the premiere."

* * *

The screening was at eight o'clock Friday evening. That morning, Simone called in sick again and spent the day in Walker's hospital room. By five in the afternoon, her plans were in place.

Via Erika, Kathy and Matthew snagged catering jobs for the preparty, which would take place in the lobby of the Chinese prior to the screening. They would call her when Blake Moss arrived, keep their eyes on him throughout the evening, phoning her the minute he stepped out the door.

Elliot, meanwhile, had snuck over to Moss's house during the day and stealthily planted Kathy's amber bracelet under the front mat. Simone left her laptop in Walker's hospital room so he could spend the evening finding any and all information about Dolores King.

At seven thirty, Simone received the call. She was already parked at a gas station on Coldwater Canyon five minutes away from Moss's house. Calmly, she started up the Jeep, drove to her destination. She buzzed the gate until she heard the elderly woman's accented voice, saying, "Yes?" over the intercom.

"Hi," said Simone. "I'm a friend of Blake's? I was here last night, and I think I left my bracelet? It's amber beads with a silver clasp?"

"I didn't see anything like that."

"Please," said Simone, "my mom gave it to me. I think it dropped off when I was leaving. Can you check, like, the front doorstep?"

The woman sighed. Five minutes later, she was back. "I found it."

Yes, Elliot! "Oh, thank goodness," she said. "Listen, you don't have to come down with it. I'll just run up the driveway."

Simone closed her eyes, thought, *Come on, come on . . .*

In moments, the gate opened, and Simone tore through

it, running not up the driveway but around the back of the house, through the expansive grounds.

The sun had set, and with no tiki torches lit, no candles in the pool, no light at all except for a few artfully placed landscaping bulbs dotting the gardens, it was hard for Simone to find her way around. She kept slipping on plants, bumping into rock formations, and at the same time she heard the maid's voice calling out, "Hello!" and "Come back!" and "I'm in front!"

Simone's heart pounded. *Moss. Where do you keep your damn garage?* She ran past more rock formations, past a small bungalow and a large garden shed. And that's when she saw it—another driveway. A sort of back entrance, at the top of which stood a garage.

"Who is there?" She could barely hear the woman's voice now, the house was so big. *Don't worry,* she thought. *I'll be out of your way soon.* There was a window at the side of the garage. It was dark, but Simone had brought her flashlight. She shined it through the window, peered in.

She saw a Hummer and a Jaguar. There was another car she couldn't quite see. She found another window in the back of the garage, and when she shined her light through it, she saw the third car. A red Ferrari, next to a Ducati motorcycle.

Well, that was anticlimactic. She headed back to where she came from, past the garden shed. As she hurried by, she noticed the door of the shed was slightly open, something glinting from within.

Headlights.

She didn't hear the woman's voice anymore. Her phone wasn't ringing. She had time. She crept back to the shed, eased the doors open, shined her light inside . . . on an early-'80s green Impala.

Hello, Dolores.

Her gaze shot over to the bungalow next to it, a quiet little bungalow behind all the rock formations, in a hidden area of these expansive, surreal grounds. Was this the place where Blake Moss kept all his secrets?

Simone listened for the maid. Not a sound. Maybe she'd given up, figured Simone had left. . . .

She walked up to the bungalow and tried the door. It opened. Inside, it was warm. The windows were closed and the air was thick, holding the smell of a man's sweat. She turned on the lights. There was a couch in the room, a modern-looking coffee table, but no bookshelves—just an enormous flat-screen TV, an odd wash of beige and peach and brown filling the screen, a frozen close-up of something, Simone couldn't figure out what. At the end of the room was a closed door.

Simone tried it. The room was dark. She noticed a single bed pressed up against the wall. She flicked the light switch, expecting nothing more than the bed, a small, spartan man's bedroom. But then the room flooded with bright overhead light and she stood there, frozen.

The entire far wall was covered in yellowing newspaper articles from twenty years ago. She scanned the headlines: SLEAZY PRODUCER'S DARK DOUBLE LIFE: WIFE TELLS ALL! EXPLOSIVE TELL-ALL: MY STEAMY TRYSTS WITH HOLLYWOOD'S HOTTEST MEN! SWAMP DEMON CUTIE: "MY HUBBY IS IMPOTENT!" GAY PRODUCER SLITS THROAT: WIFE'S TELL-ALL TO BLAME! There were hundreds of them—many of them in multiple copies—all from second-rate tabloids long out of print. Simone moved closer, until she was standing inches away from the one titled SWAMP DEMON CUTIE. . . . There was a picture, a headshot of Dolores King.

Simone stared into the eyes, and her blood ran as thin as tap water. She was twenty years younger and easily a hundred pounds lighter, but there was no mistaking it. Dolores King was Randi DuMonde.

Her phone vibrated. She looked at the screen. A text message from Walker. Her eyes still on the article, she opened it up, then read: *Dol and Reg had son.*

She texted him back: *Dol is Randi*, but just as she sent it, another one came in, at the same time as she heard heavy footsteps coming toward the bungalow. She texted Walker: *Send help*. The footsteps drew nearer. She opened the new text message, again from Walker, just as she heard the voice, a man's voice . . .

"You found my pad," it said, as the words popped on the screen.

Son name Nathaniel.

The phone clattered to the floor.

"Blake's letting me stay here, rent free, till I can get out of debt. Isn't that nice of him?"

Simone stared at Nathaniel. He was wearing a Hard Rock Café T-shirt and baggy shorts, and he held a bloody knife in his hand. "I just killed the maid," he said calmly. "I didn't want to. She's not right for the Project at all, but you know . . . we couldn't have her hearing us."

Strange, he had one of those faces that seemed so pleasant when you saw it in passing. But when you examined him closely, when you stared into his eyes, something wasn't right. Something big.

He moved closer to her. "Your super is a nice guy. He let me in so I could mark you." He may as well have been schmoozing her at a cocktail party, save for the knife in his hand.

Knock the wind out of him. Simone moved forward, but he grabbed her shoulder and threw her to the ground like a rag doll, her knees crashing into the hard floor in front of the wall of articles. Then he kept talking, chatting her up, as if nothing had happened. "So I have been *in* your place, but I didn't go there last night," he said. "I couldn't figure out how to shame you."

Simone said, "Shame me?"

He nodded. "You don't seem to shame very easily." He laughed, a genial laugh. Then his smile dropped away. "But see, this is perfect. You're in my personal place, eavesdropping. That's what you do. Check it out: Your death. Here. That'll shame you good."

He yanked her to her feet. "Give me your fingers."

Simone tried to back up, but she couldn't move. She was pressed against the wall. She felt newsprint on the back of her neck, her arms. She lunged, tried to push him away, but he took her wrists fast in his hands. He was wearing latex gloves. He squeezed hard, cutting off the circulation. Simone cried out.

"Give me. Your. Fingers."

He took the knife. Jabbed her index finger. A current of pain shot up her arm. She screamed—a screech that bounced off the walls, echoed throughout the grounds. She'd never known she could scream so loud.

He clamped a hand over her mouth. His fingers were thick, and she smelled latex and blood—her blood, the maid's. *Thick fingers, like an overgrown child's.* The blood looked like finger paint. "No one's going to hear you," he said. "But you're hurting my ears."

Simone recalled the text message she'd sent Walker and thought, *Hear me, hear me, hear me. . . .* Nathaniel took his hand away from her mouth. *Hear me, please. . . .*

She breathed in and out and found her voice. "Don't do this. Randi isn't worth it."

He flinched at the name. "Randi," he said, "is not my mother. Dolores was my mother. Dolores is dead."

Simone looked deep into his eyes. She wanted to make him flinch again. Her finger throbbed, but the pain wasn't there anymore, so she could ignore it, ignore her blood dripping onto the floor. "Did Randi make you say that, Nathaniel? Randi is not your mother. Dolores was your mother. Dolores is dead."

"Stop it." He didn't move, though. He watched her, a strange smile on his face.

"Did she make you say that over and over and over, after she killed your dad?"

"No, no, no. My dad . . . he did that himself."

"Did she make you say that too, Nathaniel?" Simone's mouth was parched. She felt her heartbeat in her neck. "Because *she* did it. He might have taken the hunting knife to his throat, but it wasn't the knife that killed him, was it?"

Nathaniel shut his eyes. "I want you to write 'Scum' on the wall. On the tabloid stories. I want you to write it with that finger."

"It wasn't the knife."

"Stop saying that."

"It was shame. Shame killed your father. And Dolores was the one who shamed him, wasn't she?" She stared at him. *"Randi* was the one who shamed him."

He opened his eyes, and there were tears in them. Tears and fire. He raised the knife over his head, but Simone ducked, threw herself into his stomach. He doubled over, wheezing, as she ran out of the bedroom, into the living room with that strange, frozen image on the TV. She heard a long, sick animal shriek and then he was out of the bedroom, in the living room with her, rushing at her, the knife raised over his head. Simone tried to duck again, but there was no time, not now. The hand came down, plunged the knife into her chest. She fell to the floor, feeling not so much pain as pressure, as if someone were standing on her lungs, then a rush of fluid—a type of drowning from within. She heard sirens pulling into the driveway, doors slamming, voices shouting, *"Police!"* He dropped the knife. She looked up into Nathaniel's frightened face—his eyes a child's eyes—and she wished she could say it. *You feel shame, don't you? You feel it worse than anyone. . . .*

But Simone didn't say it. She couldn't speak, couldn't move. All she could do was watch Nathaniel's face fade to black, just like the end of a movie.

EPILOGUE

It was rainy season and as the plane landed at LAX, the view out the window was breathtaking, with LA awash in green. It looked like a different city, Simone thought. The Emerald City.

She had been living back in New York for the past three months. After spending two weeks in Cedars-Sinai recovering from a knife wound to the lungs, Simone gave an exclusive to the *Asteroid* (HERO REPORTER TELLS ALL: MY NIGHT OF TERROR WITH THE STARLET SLASHER!), packed up her bags and moved back across the country. For two months she stayed with Greta. Then they both decided it would be best if she found a place of her own, so she did—a rent-stabilized walk-up on the Lower East Side—and took a job as a copy editor at a major publishing house. As action-packed as her time at the *Asteroid* had been, Simone decided she'd rather read mysteries than star in them.

Nathaniel Cannell (né King) was found legally insane and was sent to spend the rest of his life in a Northern California psychiatric facility. According to published reports, he would never see the light of day. If he was ever deemed "cured," he would stand trial for the murders of Blake Moss's sixty-seven-year-old housekeeper and four young women.

Yes, four. Holly eventually came out of her coma, gave up being a celebrity assistant, and put her nurturing talents to use teaching third-graders in Watts. "We get no money. I have to buy the schoolbooks myself—but those kids beat out stars any day of the week," she had told Simone during her last visit to California. "This little boy, Sean? He asked if he could adopt me."

Simone thought about that now as her plane touched ground—how fulfillment always showed up where you least expected it: Working at a tabloid, spending time with your sister, hanging out with Neil Walker. . . .

Simone was flying out for Matthew and Carl's wedding. Though Provincetown had sounded fun to them, LA was warmer, so they were having the party here, then taking Elliot's advice and flying to Hawaii in the morning to make it legal. Since it was two days before Christmas, the wedding invitation said, *"Mele kaliki maka!"* (*Merry Christmas* in Hawaiian). Carl had designed it. Turned out he was a very talented graphic artist.

Neil Walker greeted Simone in baggage claim, and just like every time she saw him, she regretted her decision to move back East. Before she could say anything, he grabbed her and kissed her, the feel of it lingering on her lips. Then he started asking her about New York, about her sister, about everything she'd been doing during the month since he'd seen her, even though he knew all this stuff already. He and Simone e-mailed each other a hundred times a day. When he plucked her one small bag off the conveyer belt, he said, "You are the lightest traveler I've ever met. You need to buy some shoes, start acting more like a chick."

"I'll buy shoes if you stop it with the show tunes."

He smiled, but just for a moment. Then his face went serious. "Are you sure you want to do this?"

"She *asked* me, Neil," she said. "I want to hear what she has to say."

Walker's Volvo still had that new car smell, and as they drove to Pasadena, Simone inhaled it, listening to his *Wicked* CD, both of them saying very little. Tonight, Simone and Walker would go to Matthew and Carl's wedding party at the W Hotel in Westwood. They would dance and get drunk and talk a lot about the future. But for now, they were both lost in their own thoughts, thoughts buried in the past. They arrived at the place, a pretty but modest one-story on North Lake Street. It was a far cry from Randi DuMonde's previous house. In fact, it looked more like where Julie used to live.

As they had agreed earlier, Walker waited in the car while Simone walked up to Randi DuMonde's front door. Ringing the bell, Simone expected the Randi of old—the bright red outfit, the towering presence. But the woman who answered the door was just a large, middle-aged lady. She wore a T-shirt and jeans, and very little makeup. Her eyes were cloudy. For a second, Simone flashed on Wayne Deegan and thought, *That's the way it looks when you lose your child.*

"I'm glad you're here," Randi said. "Come on in."

Randi offered her tea or coffee or juice, but Simone knew it was just something to say. She could tell Randi was very nervous. "I don't need anything," she said.

When they sat down on her couch, Randi seemed relieved to stop standing. "I know we don't know each other," she said, "but I'm going to be leaving soon. I'm moving up north. There's been a lot of press. And . . . believe it or not, you're the only reporter I trust."

Simone said, "I'm not a reporter anymore, Randi."

"Must be why I trust you." She smiled a little.

Simone smiled back

Then Randi's smile fell away. When she looked into Simone's eyes, Simone saw nothing there but sorrow. Randi said, "I killed those girls."

"What . . . what do you mean?"

"I let it happen."

Simone's gaze sharpened. "You knew?"

"I didn't want to believe it," she said, "but yes."

"How?"

"Nathaniel was always a sensitive boy. He had no idea what was going on between his father and me, how cold Reg could be. I was young and insecure. . . . I'm not making excuses for myself. I turned into a castrating bitch." She looked at Simone. "I just wanted him to find me attractive. . . ."

"That's your own business, Randi," said Simone. "Who am I to judge?"

Randi took a deep breath. Her voice quavered. "Nathaniel loved his father. But he loved me more," she said. "I was never around, always with other men. And he blamed his father for that. He would say, 'It's Dad's fault. Not yours.' Even when kids in his class would tell him I was a slut."

"Randi," she said, "you don't need to tell me . . ."

"I do," she said. "It's important."

"Okay."

"After . . . it happened," she said, "I took Nathaniel to Paris. We traveled around the world, we got whole new identities. Every night, I would tell him, 'I am not Dolores. I am Randi. You are not my son. You are Nathaniel Cannell.'"

Simone frowned. She didn't get that part. She never had. "I can see why you wanted to change your identity," she said. "And I can see why you wanted to change Nathaniel's. But why did you want him to act as if he wasn't your son, Randi? Why did you want to change both of your identities to that degree?"

Randi leaned forward. "Most scandals are no big deal," she said. "You reinvent yourself. Look at Blake. People do it all the time." She looked into Simone's eyes. "But some things, you can't reinvent. A little boy . . . a ten-year-old boy. . . ."

Simone held Randi's gaze and took it in—the shock, the sadness, the deep, unstoppable pain. "I understand," she said. Because she did. She finally did.

"Good. Then we don't need to say any more."

Nothing more *was* said, other than good-bye, but as she left the house Simone knew the truth. Reginald King had not cut his own throat with the hunting knife. Nathaniel had murdered his father. Dolores had changed her identity, changed Nathaniel's—all to protect her son. But this was what destroyed Randi, this was what she needed to confess: If she had turned Nathaniel in to the police, if she had gotten him the help he needed, then all five of those women would still be alive.

Randi *had* killed those girls. And she would always carry the weight of that shame.

She walked out to the car, and got in the front seat. "How did it go?" said Walker.

"It went," said Simone. "It went."

If you enjoyed *Trashed*,
you won't want to miss **Alison Gaylin's**
next outstanding novel of suspense

HEARTLESS

Coming in September 2008.

A sneak peek follows. . . .

"You want to?" Jordan asked.

Jordan had this sultry, slurry way of speaking that made it sound less like a question and more like an exotic name—*Yawanna*. And that mouth . . . God. It made Naomi blush a little, watching it move around the words.

It had to be the beer and the pot, because Naomi never thought like this. Sometimes the girls at Santa Beatriz would look at pictures of Justin Timberlake or Enrique Iglesias or maybe some guy from a *telenovela*, and they'd say, *lo quiero*—I want him—and yeah, Naomi would nod and all, but she wouldn't get it. Not really.

At seventeen, she'd been with a guy just once. It was horrible. She wasn't big on dating either, and Justin, Enrique, all those two-dimensional boys in magazines, on TV screens, they did nothing for her at all. For a while now, Naomi had been secretly thinking there might be something wrong with her because she couldn't even *understand* what it meant to want another person.

But now . . . now she understood.

"I promise," said Jordan. "You'll love it."

Naomi's skin heated up. Her face flushed a deep red

that she was certain he noticed, even from across the bonfire and with the desert sky darkening into that end-of-day color, that melony pink. She could blame it on the beer or the heat from the fire, but still he would know. The way he was looking at her, he just *would.* . . .

But then Corinne said, "Doesn't it make you puke?" And suddenly it was as if the other two people around the fire—Naomi's American friends, down in San Esteban for summer break—had materialized out of nowhere.

Corinne's boyfriend, Sean, handed Jordan the joint, and he took a hit. "Puking is part of the experience," Jordan said. He was half holding his breath to keep the smoke in, so the words kind of snuck out of his throat. God help Naomi, he even inhaled sexy. She flashed on the baggie he held in his other hand, at the shriveled gray disks inside, and she thought, *Right. He's talking about peyote.* That's *what he means by "the experience."*

"I'll try it," she heard herself say, shocking everyone around the fire, especially herself. Naomi was a lightweight. One beer, three hits of pot, and already she was a red-faced, trembling basket case with an embarrassing crush on Corinne's cousin. The last thing she needed was hallucinogenic cactus buttons.

"Are you sure, Naomi?" said Sean, as if he were reading her mind.

But when she looked at Jordan, when she saw the way he smiled at her, the way his eyes glittered under those half-closed lids . . . Oh, she was sure. So sure that she'd say it again, over and over, and then eat everything in the baggie without taking a breath, even if it made her puke her guts out and go completely insane. She'd do it all if she could just get Jordan alone for a few minutes, if she could get close enough to touch the side of his face, to feel those soft lips against her neck, to explore these brand-new feelings. . . .

"You won't be sorry," Jordan said. And Naomi knew he was right.

Naomi stared at the two peyote buttons in her hand. They looked like slices of two-hundred-year-old squash, with little purple hairs poking out the sides.

"I can't believe you're going to eat that," said Corinne.

Naomi ignored her, which was easy to do, seeing as less than twenty feet away Sean was making sounds like a dying yak. He'd eaten his buttons around half an hour ago, and the fact he was now violently puking—a six-foot-five-inch football player with a neck the size of a Christmas ham—was not what you'd call good advertising for the peyote experience.

"Don't worry," said Jordan.

Naomi looked at him. His face was serene. "If there's nothing to worry about," she said, "why don't you take it?"

He smiled. "Already did."

"But you're not . . ."

"Throwing up? You don't always." His mouth tilted into a half smile. "If you eat yours now, we can still peak at the same time."

That pretty much sealed the deal.

Naomi held her nose, then popped both buttons into her mouth and chewed them up as fast as she could. As it turned out, peyote tasted the way cat crap smelled, only worse. She gagged instantly. *I will not throw up in front of him.* Naomi thought of a framed concert photo in her aunt Vanessa's bedroom—Ozzy Osbourne, taken just after he'd bitten the head off a live bat.

At least peyote didn't bleed.

"There's something about you, Naomi," said Jordan.

The vaguest compliment she'd ever received, and yet at this moment the most wonderful . . . *Don't throw up, don't throw up.* She swallowed the last awful bit and took a swig from Corinne's bottle of water.

"Thanks," Naomi said, but she couldn't look at him. What if she looked at him and puked and he took it personally? What if he got so grossed out that he never spoke to her again? She closed her eyes tight, rubbed the lids with the palms of her hands. This had always calmed her down, ever since she was a little girl, and after a time (Ten minutes? Twenty? Forty-five?) the nausea passed, and she was safe.

She opened her eyes, gazed across the fire at Jordan.

"Whew. Thought I lost you there for a second." He grinned—but in his eyes, deep, mysterious sorrow. The combination was close to overwhelming. Naomi's heart swelled so big, her ribs could barely contain it. She inhaled the sweet smell of burning mesquite as the dried cactus worked into her system, and the sun melted away, the sky turning a deep soft purple, the air starting to cool and swirl. . . . *Please get up and sit next to me, please, please, please. . . .*

"I'm cold," Naomi said. But the voice she heard was not her own. It was the voice of a ghost.

"Oh man," Sean was saying. "I can see. . . . Right here, in the dirt, it's like . . . some kind of latticework structure leading down into the center of the earth, like a secret civilization or . . ."

"Hitting you yet?" His voice was warm against the side of her neck. His hand stroked her arm, and when she looked down at it, she saw thousands of shimmering fish scales.

"Uh, I think so."

Jordan said, "You are really cute."

Naomi turned to see his face much closer than she expected—about two inches away from her own, a slight smile playing at the corners of his mouth. She ignored all the scales, gazing only at the eyes, those sad golden eyes. He gave her the lightest, softest kiss imaginable, and then he leaned back and just looked at her, saying nothing, the heat of him lingering on her lips.

"Wow," she said. Like a gargantuan dork.

The scales glistened in the firelight—kind of gorgeous, really, in an exotic, god-of-the-sea way—and Naomi wanted to melt into Jordan right there. She wanted to lose her own shape and turn to liquid, soak into those scales and become a part of him forever and ever as he moved through the ocean waves and, oh, was Naomi ever glad she wasn't saying this out loud. Seriously, *wow* was bad enough, but *this* . . .

Naomi caught a sudden chill up her back, as if someone was watching her, someone in the darkness, and when she glanced around the fire, she saw that Corinne and Sean were gone. *When did they leave? A minute ago? An hour?* Time wasn't moving the way it was supposed to. It half rushed, half oozed, like those clocks in Salvador Dalí paintings.

"Are you okay?" Jordan asked.

"Yeah." She closed her eyes, started rubbing them again. "I'm . . . I'm fine, I'm just . . . I . . ." Naomi's heart was doing this weird jumping thing. It felt like a chubby little robot, hopping around inside her chest, only scary-fast. She started to think, *What if my heart exploded?* Because that really did happen to some people, didn't it? They could be doing something perfectly normal—shopping for groceries or whatever—and one of their organs would up and explode.

"Naomi?" Jordan said. "It can hit you hard the first time."

"I'm . . . I feel like . . ."

"Just try and go with it." Jordan took one of her wrists, gently moved her hands from her eyes. Her vision was blurry from all the rubbing, so she blinked a few times. Her hands and arms were glowing pink, like they were made from neon. "Take a deep breath," Jordan said, "in and out. . . ."

Naomi did. Her heart slowed a little. She looked at the fire and saw . . . just a fire. No scales or neon or tentacles.

"Better?"

"Yeah," she said. "Thanks." And for a long time, they sat there, just breathing.

"Jordan?"

"Yeah?"

"Do you . . . do you have to leave tomorrow? I mean . . . could you maybe stay a couple more—"

"Listen, Naomi," said Jordan. "I wasn't going to say anything, but . . ." His words trailed into the smoke.

"What?" *You can tell me, and whatever it is . . .*

Jordan sighed. It was a labored sigh, the way a sick person would breathe. When he finally spoke, his voice trembled. "This town. San Esteban. I know it's beautiful on the surface, but it is really fucked up. There's . . . weird stuff going on, stuff I'm guessing you don't know about."

That wasn't what she'd expected him to say at all. "What kind of stuff?" Her heart started to jump again. With each word, it wedged further into her throat.

"I never should have come back here. And you . . ." he said. "You're young. You need to be careful."

She could now feel her heartbeat in her shoulders, her ears, her mouth. She swallowed hard to tamp it down. "You're trying to mess with my head, aren't you?"

"I'm sorry. Forget I ever said anything. I'm just . . . I'm tripping is all."

She turned, looked at Jordan's face. She started to tell him it was okay, just don't do it again. But then two long white fangs emerged from his mouth, a forked snake's tongue darting out between them. "Sssssssorry," he hissed.

Without thinking, she was up on her feet, running away from the fire, away from Jordan hissing her name. Scrubby plants scratched at her legs and loose dirt flew into her face, rocks pushing through the thin soles of her sandals. It was as if the whole desert was trying to hurt her, and then there were those footsteps nearing, Jordan howling, "Come back!" Jordan the Fanged Snake.

Naomi kept running, but her heart . . . It started slamming into her ribs, slamming hard, as if it wanted out now. Naomi thought, *It's about to explode.*

It was the last thought she had, before everything went black.

Naomi dreamed of a spotlight aimed at her face. When she cracked her eyelids, she saw it was the hot sun, and she was thirstier than she'd ever been in her life. Her tongue felt like a wad of dried clay, too big for her mouth. Her eyes stung terribly, and her skin throbbed—her face, her neck, the tops of her legs. She had no idea about the time, but from where the sun was in the sky, she figured it had to be at least ten in the morning. And Naomi was lying on her back with a third-degree sunburn in the middle of an agave patch, somewhere in the desert that bordered San Esteban.

She struggled to her feet as last night flew back at her—some of it, anyway. That whole exploding-organ thing . . . What had she been thinking, doing peyote with a college student? What had made her think she could *handle* that?

"Great," Naomi said to no one. Her lips stuck to her teeth. She ran her tongue over them. They were cracked and crusty and tasted like salt. She recalled, for a moment, what Jordan had said, about weird stuff going on in San Esteban. She thought about his sad, knowing eyes, how he had called after her as she'd run away . . .

Best not to think about Jordan anymore.

She stumbled between the cactuses and through a sparse area, dusted with tumbleweed and prickle bushes, Bimbo Bread wrappers and empty Pepsi cans. She tried to remember landmarks around the bonfire. She and Corinne always made their bonfires in areas that were easy to distinguish—near something tall like a jacaranda tree or a century plant—so they'd be able to find their way back to it should they wander. But this time they'd let the boys choose the place. Dumb idea.

She kept walking, trying to ignore the vicious headache, that swimmy feeling, like she might pass out all over again.

Finally she saw something that might have been the bonfire. It was about thirty feet away, near a blooming century plant, even though she hadn't remembered one of them being there last night. But then again there was a lot about last night she didn't remember. She moved closer, hoping with her whole body for the bonfire. Before she realized it, she was in a desperate, stumbling run.

Ten feet away, though, she knew it wasn't the bonfire. *Could be a pile of old clothes*, she thought. Until the smell socked her in the face.

She heard the hum of flies first. Then she saw the splayed legs, the outstretched arms, the blood, so much of it, so dark it was close to black. . . . He was still wearing his flip-flops, but the rest of him was . . .

"Jordan!" It came out a scream—an animal scream that ripped open her raw throat and tore at her insides and used all the breath in her body. . . . A scream that made her think she might lose her mind right here in this spot—because it couldn't get worse, nothing could ever be worse than what she was looking at. . . .

And then she saw Jordan's heart.